DIAMONDS
ARE FOREVER

DIAMONDS
ARE FOREVER

By

Dennis L. Mangrum

CFI
Springville, Utah

ISBN 13: 978-1-59955-065-7

Published by CFI, an imprint of Cedar Fort, Inc., 2373 W. 700 S., Springville, UT, 84663
Distributed by Cedar Fort, Inc., www.cedarfort.com

LIBRARY OF CONGRESS CATALOGING-IN-PUBLICATION DATA

Mangrum, Dennis L.
Diamonds Are Forever / Dennis L. Mangrum.
p. cm.
ISBN 978-1-59955-065-7 (acid-free paper)
1. Memory—Fiction. 2. Mormons—Fiction. I. Title.

PS3613.A537D53 2007
813'.6—dc22

2007018859

Cover design by Nicole Williams
Cover design © 2007 by Lyle Mortimer
Edited and typeset by Annaliese B. Cox

Printed in the United States of America

10 9 8 7 6 5 4 3 2 1

Printed on acid-free paper

Also by Dennis Mangrum:

Seasons of Salvation

Acknowledgments

SEVERAL PEOPLE HAVE ENDURED MY attempts to become a writer. I dubbed them my personal readers or editors. I have asked them to read and re-read chapters and to give their thoughts and impressions, even if it wasn't the first time around. It was a thankless task, especially when they had to answer to a very demanding friend who doesn't pay them anything for their efforts. How often have they heard, "What do you mean you haven't read the chapter yet? You've had it for two days!" or "Tell me something new."

So for being there for me, for suffering my abuse, and for rendering valuable insight, I thank you; for without you I could not have crafted this story.

The first credos goes to the lady of my life, Liz Mangrum, who should have been an English teacher. I think she enjoys correcting every mistake I make in grammar or punctuation, way too much.

Second, to my best friend, Laurin Rackham, who believes that sports are the opiate of the masses, who read this story from the non-athlete point of view and claims he actually enjoyed the experience.

Third, to my daughter, Nichole Jones, who incidentally has a daughter I nicknamed Indiana because she wouldn't do it formally. Nichole is my inspiration.

And last, to Natalie Benson, a soon to be daughter-in-law (she's marrying my son the baseball player). Natalie is my red-headed cheerleader, and every author must have a cheerleader.

It's a long journey from the first time pen is put to paper to seeing your words in print, so thanks, guys. Now, when are you going to get those next chapters back to me?

Writing is the fun part, trying to get a book published . . . well, that is a walk on the dark side. Of course my first manuscript was rejected so many times I gave up trying to write. My high school English teachers would have applauded that decision. I finally did try again, and Lee Nelson and Cedar Fort accepted and published Seasons of Salvation.

So now the good folks at Cedar Fort have published this, my second novel. All I can say is that you guys at Cedar Fort are the best!

Annaliese B. Cox, my editor, now understands how my high school English teachers felt when they had to read my papers. Thanks, Annaliese, for your assistance, patience, sufferance, and doggedness. And thanks to the proofreader, who shall apparently remain nameless.

Prologue

IT WASN'T MUCH OF A diamond ring, but it was all that I could afford and just a little bit more. I had seriously considered a beautiful two-carat zircon, but everyone talked me out of that. Instead I called a friend who sold wholesale jewelry. I wanted to try to get the most for the least, not that I'd tell her that. I hadn't quite gotten around to asking her what kind of a ring she liked, probably because I wasn't sure that I could talk her into accepting my proposal. I hoped the ring would help encourage her. Me? I bought the whole package. She was the one. Come to think of it, I'd probably known it since that first day, even though I had been in denial for some time. I reflected back over the last three heart-stopping months as I pointed Betsy home.

Now all I had to do was convince her that I—that we—were a great idea.

I had been captivated with her ever since the day she ran by me on the way to the top of the mountain and Dog Lake. As I remembered, it seemed like I had been standing still as she flew by me. But I must say, it was a nice view. It just didn't last very long.

At five foot ten she fit very nicely into my arms but not into the stereotypical blonde mold. She was humble, smart—very smart, except about baseball stuff. That is, in fact, a major character flaw, almost un-American. If you can believe it, she didn't even know that you got to be the home team if you won in eagle claws, nor had she ever heard of the "Curse of the Bambino." I wondered how she could be so smart and yet not know about those things that mattered most. However, I forgave her of those shortcomings, those flaws, every time she turned those baby blues in my direction. But come to think of it, they were green.

My family loved her, probably more than they did me. That even included Shannon, my only sibling, but then she's a girl and for some reason tends to side with females even though she isn't quite a self-proclaimed feminist. Shannon even defended her in our last argument in a game of over-the-line. Of course her husband sided with me. She insisted that ties always go to the girls. I tried to convince her that ties always go to the runner and not to girls. That didn't fly either.

Did I mention how beautiful this girl is? Yeah, I was smitten from that first day. I thought I might have been hallucinating, but two hours later she looked even better, and that was after my sight and ability to breathe returned from chasing her up the mountain.

In the beginning I was concerned because sometimes beautiful blondes are like big league ball players—Barry Bonds, for example. They think they live on a different planet than the rest of humanity and should be treated accordingly. But she doesn't even realize how devastatingly beautiful she is. Instead of always looking in her mirror or taking her own temperature, she asks what she can do to help.

She has never forgotten her roots, where she came from and those who helped her along the way. They are her heroes. It is their photos that line her wall of fame. Hey, I even got a spot on the wall, but it took a long time.

I pulled into my driveway. It was only a short time later that she arrived. She got there just before the pizza. We were having a night in. I had not quite figured out how or when I was going to ask her, but I wanted her wearing my ring before she left my house that night. I was just going to wait for the right moment.

When she came in, she pulled my card table over into the middle of the room and spread a fancy white tablecloth over it. She placed two chairs close together, lit two candles she had brought with her, and placed one cheesecake on the table midway between the two chairs. And only one fork.

She walked over, turned off the lights, and motioned for me to come over to the table. I smiled and asked, "Where's my fork?"

She gave me a mischievous smile and in a low, husky voice almost whispered, "I think we can get by with one tonight. Don't you, Mr. Calloway?" She was looking better and better by the minute.

I was fingering the ring in my pocket and trying to decide how to give to her. Trying to buy some time, I asked, "What movie did you bring?"

"It's a secret. But I promise you'll like it."

"Tell me it's not *Sleepless in Seattle*," I said. She just laughed and put her arms around my waist, looking me in the eye. The candlelight flickered across her enchanting features. I think I got lost in her eyes.

"Cord." She shook me. "I think someone's knocking at the door."

I groaned and started to go answer it. "I hope it's not Bishop Swenson."

She pushed me down in the chair and said, "Don't leave. You wait right here. I'll get rid of them and be right back. Unless it's the Girl Scouts, in which case we'll have to buy some cookies." I heard the door open and then silence. It was unusual since she was normally so friendly and talkative. I turned my head and saw two women in the doorway just staring at each other. It was at that point that I thought my heart stopped.

I stood and started stammering . . . I was dead, totally dead.

Salt Lake Tribune
November 26, 2004

. . . bicyclist listed in serious condition after accident in Millcreek Canyon. Mr. Cord Calloway, age 27, was riding down the canyon in excess of 30 mph when a carload of youths, apparently out joyriding, intentionally ran Mr. Calloway off the roadway. A witness to the accident saw the carload of youths, still unidentified, swerve into the biker, causing him to crash and sustain serious injuries. Police are treating the matter as a hit and run.

One

Ninety percent of the game is half mental.

—Yogiism #1

Monitors hummed on the walls. The room pulsed with faint electronic beeps. There was no other noise. A clean antiseptic smell permeated the air. Wires and tubes seemed to bind the man to the bed, although he wasn't trying to escape. The only life signs that seemed to exist were the rhythmic beeping of the machines. It had been that way for some time.

♦ ♦ ♦

I felt tired, groggy—or was it stiff? I wasn't sure. It was probably time to get up. I opened one eye just enough to try to figure out if it was still night. Something smelled funny. I couldn't see very well. Things wouldn't come into focus. Some mornings it was like that. But I needed to know if it was time to get up. I couldn't remember what was on my schedule that day. Slowly I opened the other eye. The room gradually came into a blurred focus. I realized I wasn't in my own bed. I turned my head and saw wires and tubes draped across my body. I tried to imagine where I was. I sat up, restrained somewhat by the many lines. I looked up at the monitors. My heartbeat count, blood pressure, and who knows what else they were measuring showed up on the monitors. There was an IV hooked up to my left arm. I was glad it was my left arm. I could hear the humming and bleeping of the machines. *This is crazy*, I thought. *I must be in a hospital.* Why was I in a hospital? My mind searched frantically for an answer to this question.

I couldn't remember going to a hospital. It seemed my mind was locked into a frantic loop. The same questions kept repeating themselves. Why was I here? How long had I been here? Why did I have bandages on my head? What hospital was this? Questions, but I couldn't come up with any answers. I knew I did a lot of stupid, risky things for someone my age . . . but then . . . it was coming back . . . there was a baseball game. I tried pushing my search button . . . nothing would come up, just faint remembrances of the game. I think I was near to panic. I wanted to get up and leave, but I wasn't sure I could.

I examined my body closely, starting, of course, with my right arm. I flexed my hand and then my arm. It worked. I raised it and it felt fine. I felt some bandages on my head but no pain. I moved my legs. They worked—a little stiff but functional. I tried to lift my left arm. There was some soreness in the shoulder, although not debilitating, but not enough to put me in a hospital. That was it. No injuries, but I was lying on a bed in a hospital. Weird. Maybe it was all a practical joke, I hoped, but somehow I knew otherwise.

The clock at my bedside glowed 2:00 AM. I couldn't hear any sounds of people or see anyone walking about. I examined the wires, tubes, and the IV. There had to be a way to unhook all this stuff and go find someone, find out why I was in the hospital.

Suddenly the door swung open and a very tall, maybe five foot ten, good-looking blonde wearing hospital scrubs walked into my room, reading a book. She was so engrossed in her reading that she didn't even glance in my direction. Instead, she walked over to the chair near my bed and sat down. I continued to stare at the lady. A doctor? But why hadn't she checked me?

Why was she sitting in a chair by my bed reading a book? She was a looker, that was for sure. Over the top of the book, I could see her long blonde hair. Hazel green eyes speckled with yellow. A flawless complexion and a "body by Fisher." I had no idea who she was. I would remember a woman like that.

She continued to read. I didn't know what to say. I just stared. Finally I kind of grunted a raspy, "Umm, ahem."

She was startled. She dropped her book and almost leaped out of her seat. "Cord!" she exclaimed. Her green eyes flashed surprise and then relief. She quickly came over to the bed and grasped my right hand in both of hers. She was smiling, and it was obvious that she was excited and maybe concerned at the same time. She . . . we were apparently on a first name basis. How could that be? She put one hand on my forehead. I liked the feel of her touch.

"I have been so worried about you. How do you feel?"

"A . . . well, my head hurts a little. Nothing serious though. Are you my doctor?"

"You might say that," she said smiling. She bent down and kissed me lightly on the forehead. "I've been frantic."

"I've never been kissed by a doctor before, but don't let that stop you," I said, managing a soft laugh. I usually didn't have much luck with women, especially good-looking ones.

"Cord," she said again. She looked me in the eyes and put one hand on each side of my face. She looked at me for a long time. She was beautiful. This lady cared about me. You could see it in her eyes. Finally she bent down and softly kissed me. I mean really kissed me. I couldn't remember being kissed like that, not in a long, long time, and never by a doctor.

I was shocked! I mean, she was a doll. I wasn't going to object to the kiss, but who was she? Why was she in my hospital room? But then, why was I here? I didn't think I'd ever met her before, but anyone who kissed like that, I wanted to get to know a whole lot better.

Finally, smiling, I stammered, "Is this a new form of therapy?" I continued without pausing. I couldn't stop the questions.

"Why am I in this hospital? How long have I been here? Do I know you? Not that I don't want to. But . . ." It all came out in a stream without any conscious thought. I didn't even give her a chance to answer any of my questions.

She laughed. "Some things never change, do they?" She gave me that beautiful smile. I thought she looked great even in green medical scrubs. The room was sterile, like the scrubs, with nondescript, bland colored walls and matching floors; but even the scrubs couldn't hide . . . what was her name? I couldn't remember or didn't know. She glanced over at the monitors, walked around the bed. Her countenance had changed dramatically. Now she was worried, nervous, concerned. She looked like a doctor. "Cord, lie back down. I'm going to go get Dr. Montgomery, your neurologist. I'll be right back."

Before she left the room I said to her, "Okay, I never argue with beautiful blondes."

She laughed as she left. I wanted to get up, but I decided to wait—besides, I had promised her. I racked my brain for anything involving a beautiful blonde doctor. Nothing. Then she came back. She was hurrying and strode purposely around to the far side of the bed and took my hand. I liked that. She was still concerned, maybe even afraid—that is, if I read her right.

I looked at her, and she said, "Dr. Montgomery is on his way." Just then a middle-aged man with a ruddy face, tousled greying hair, and rather rotund shape ambled into the room. This guy could pass for a biology professor who never saw the light of day. You know, one of those guys who lives in a laboratory twenty-four seven. Nice but eccentric.

"Hello, Mr. Calloway. My name is Dr. Montgomery, and it's great to see you awake and back with us. We've been wondering when you would join us." He glanced at her and continued, "Especially Dr. Jones." His visual image did not do him justice. He was as nice and friendly as he was weird looking. I could identify with this guy, doctor or not.

"Uh, thanks," I mumbled, not knowing what else to say, except to ask why I was in this place. With a kindly manner

Dr. Montgomery pressed on. "Let me ask you a few questions, Mr. Calloway. They may sound silly, but we ask most everyone who is in the hospital some of these things. Okay?"

"Sure, Doc."

"Do you know what the date is today?"

"I'm not sure."

"Take your best guess." He turned and whispered to the blonde, whose name I now knew was Dr. Jones, loud enough for me to hear, "What is today anyway?"

I decided I couldn't go too far wrong with this guy. "Umm, probably September ninth."

"Good," Dr. Montgomery mumbled and started writing cryptically on his chart. "Now tell me the name of this hospital."

"I haven't the foggiest," I stammered, wondering where I was and how long I had been here. And why. My head continued to swim with questions. I closed my eyes and tried to think back, but couldn't remember anything connected with being injured. "But it's in Wilmington, isn't it?"

"This is the University of Utah Hospital," Dr. Montgomery responded, covering any traces of surprise in his voice with glances at his chart. "It's not in Wilmington. Now, can you spell 'world' for me?" he asked and looked up from his papers intently.

Weird or not, likable or not, I wanted to quit playing games and get some answers. "You're kidding, right?"

Dr. Jones rubbed my hand and said, "I'm sorry, Dr. Montgomery, Mr. Calloway thinks he's a comedian. We just humor him." Then she tried to scold me although she was smiling. "Cord, this is serious. Just try to answer his questions. No jokes right now." But she was smiling again.

"W. O. R. L. D." I said each letter with emphasis. I was always a good speller. "Why won't someone answer any of my questions?" I asked. "How about you ask one, I answer, and then I ask one and you answer."

"Cord," her voice was so soothing. She gripped my hand a little harder. "We are trying to determine the extent of your injuries. We will try to answer all of your questions. Just be patient."

"Now spell it backwards," he said.

"T-I," I said without hesitating at all. She didn't even smile, but there was a little crinkle around her eyes. Dr. Montgomery didn't think it was funny. I could see I wasn't getting anywhere, so I said, "Okay, you guys, have it your way. I'll play your games, but I expect some answers in return. Let's see D . . . umm . . . L-R-O-W."

Dr. Montgomery made a note and went right on, "How about counting backwards from one hundred?"

"Ninety-nine bottles of beer on the wall . . ." I started to sing.

They were getting exasperated, but I couldn't help it. This whole thing was stupid. Why not just answer my questions? I wanted to know how I got here and why. I wanted to know who she was. All they were doing was asking me simple first-grade questions. "Count backwards by sevens not by ones," he instructed.

Uh-oh, trouble. I was never very good in math. "Let's see, ninety-three . . . umm, eighty-five . . . What's this all about anyway? I've already graduated from high school."

"Mr. Calloway, you were seriously injured. This is not a bit funny. Besides, it is obvious that your injury has impacted your memory. Just play along for a while. I'm a neurologist, and I'm trying to help you. Now grab my hand and squeeze," he said, holding out his right hand again.

"How hard do you want me to squeeze?"

"I'll let you know when you squeeze too hard."

Dr. Jones was still holding my other hand and stroking my hair. I could tell it was a struggle for her not to laugh.

"Okay, that's good," he said.

"Now lift up your left leg about six inches off the bed and hold it there until I say to put it down."

I lifted my leg and held it there. I was in good shape. I looked at my quad. It looked rock hard. Buff.

He said, "That's good. You can put it down." He got out his stethoscope and checked my heart but didn't say a word. Then he got one of those one thousand candle power flashlights and shined it in my eye and told me to look in different directions. I wondered again why doctors always have to use such bright lights. I couldn't see anything for the next two minutes except a bright light that looked like a train coming at me in a dark tunnel. Nothing seemed to distract him or slow him down; he just kept on asking questions. It was really hard to look him in the eye when I couldn't see anything except one bright spot.

He was writing, so I didn't think I was interrupting anything and flippantly asked, "So, am I going to live?"

"For the day," he said.

"That's it? You're not going to tell me anything more?"

"If you're nice, I'll answer any question you have when I'm through. Now tell me the very last thing you can remember before waking up."

I tried to concentrate, to remember. "I can't be sure, but it seems like I was pitching in a ball game for the Wilmington Blue Rocks. I think I came in the game in the fifth inning with the score tied and runners on second and third."

"One more question. Do you know the name of that lovely lady holding your hand?"

I hadn't expected that question. *Stall, make her laugh,* I thought. "Sure do. She's Dr. Jones." I knew that—once he'd said her name.

"Very good. What did you say her first name was?" he asked with a smile on his face. He knew he had me.

I put my hand up to my mouth and mumbled something neither of them could hear.

"Okay, Mr. Calloway. I'll leave you with Dr. Jones. She can fill you in and maybe even answer some of your questions. I'll be back in the morning." With that he started to walk out but stopped, turned, and said, "Dr. Jones, maybe he should give up baseball and try out for *Saturday Night Live.*"

"That's good, Doc. I'll give you some points for the attempt at humor," I said.

She grimaced, squeezed my hand, and said, "Don't humor

him, doctor, or he'll go on forever." Dr. Montgomery shook his head and kept walking.

Before he left the room he muttered something like, "Or maybe you could talk him into a math refresher course just before comedian school."

She was still holding my hand. I had given up on Dr. Montgomery; maybe I could get some information from Dr. Jones. She squeezed my hand again as I turned to ask her a zillion questions. I opened my mouth but couldn't think of one of them. Maybe she had hypnotized me. I just stared at her. Then she quietly said, "Cord, no joking. Do you know who I am? Do you know my name?"

"I think I asked you that first," I replied, trying to buy some time. But time didn't help. I found myself getting lost in her gaze. Her eyes were steady, unblinking. Piercing would better describe them. It seemed like she could look right through me. She wasn't smiling any longer. It was obvious she was anxious. Something I said had disturbed her.

"Be serious. Do you know my name?"

"I really don't. Not that I don't want to. All I know is that Dr. Montgomery identified you as Dr. Jones," I answered.

"Do you have any memory of me? Any at all?"

"I don't think so because I know I would remember if I had ever met you before." She smiled. At least it seemed like a smile. But she called me by my first name, and it was obvious that I must know her, but I couldn't remember.

"At least you didn't lose your wonderful personality." I wondered if that was a good thing or if she was giving me a hard time. She was quiet for some time, thinking, before she said, "Cord, tell me what you do for a living."

She used my name so naturally . . . and, it seemed, like with much feeling. "I . . . well, I play baseball, although I don't make much of a living from it. But . . . but you already know that, don't you?"

"Yes, I know that, although I've never actually seen you play."

"Why all the questions if you already know the answers?" I

asked. Maybe something had happened that affected my memory. I was starting to get a little panicky. It seemed to me that my memory was fine, and yet I couldn't remember a thing about the lovely lady holding my hand and interrogating me.

"Humor me," she replied.

"I've been trying to do just that, but you guys haven't appreciated my sense of humor."

"You did have some pretty good comebacks. No one but you would be so flippant when a doctor is telling you that you might have a serious medical condition."

"I was just giving him a hard time, trying to get him to lighten up a little."

She sighed and threw her hands up in the air. "I give up. You win. But you're not getting off the hook that easy. Now tell me in as much detail as you can the last thing you can remember."

"Okay, well it was the last game of the playoffs against the Myrtle Beach Pelicans. I had come in relief in the fifth and pitched into the ninth. I was pitching great until the ninth. Then I threw a fastball up. It was a waste pitch. The catcher knew it was coming. He should have caught it. Instead it went clear to the backstop and the runner scored from third to win the game and knock us out of the playoffs. And you know who they gave the loss to? Me!"

She was smiling again. "So you were probably also charged with an earned run and a wild pitch as well as the loss."

"Yeah. I got the loss because of a dumb catcher."

"Who were you pitching for?"

"The Wilmington Blue Rocks, in the Carolina League. It's high A ball."

I was feeling a little frustrated, but it was difficult to get very upset with her. After all, she had picked up my hand again. "Why don't we quit playing twenty questions? It's obvious you know me and probably all of the answers to your questions. However, I don't know why I'm in the hospital, how I got to Utah from Delaware, when I got to know you, and how come I can't remember any of the foregoing when my memory seems fine."

"Okay," she said. "Patience was definitely never one of your virtues."

She came around and sat on the side of the bed and started distractedly stroking my arm. "Cord, you had a very serious accident. You were riding a bike down Millcreek Canyon when some school kids ran you off the road. That was November twenty-fifth, ten days ago. You've been unconscious since then."

I tried to remember a bike accident . . . nothing. I didn't feel like I was damaged merchandise, even though my head hurt a little. "What about you—I mean us—I mean . . . how do you know me?"

She bent down and kissed me on the forehead, ran her hand through my hair, and looked at me. She was only inches from my face. Then she sat back on the bed. "You're impossible." She was stroking my hand. "Let's put it this way. We, you and I, have become very good friends." She stopped abruptly and then continued, "Maybe *friends* isn't the right word. Let's say we have become very close." She continued to look in my eyes.

"How close?" I asked.

"I can't answer for you, Cord, but we've spent almost every day together. And me, well I've kind of taken a special interest in you." She smiled again and laughed at her comment.

"Are you really a doctor?"

"Yes, I'm a doctor. I work in the ER here at the University Hospital."

My mind was racing. We were close enough that she felt comfortable kissing me. The last person that I remembered kissing was Cate. Had I kissed Dr. Jones before today? Believe me, there was emotion and feeling in that kiss. But it didn't make any sense. Even though Caitlyn—or more precisely, her family—had ended our relationship, I still felt a hole in my heart, a piece missing without her. Dr. Jones wasn't Caitlyn. Cate was maybe five inches shorter, a brunette. A fashion statement. Cate would never be caught dead in hospital scrubs. They weren't sold at Nordstrom.

She had said it was December fifth. Let's see, my last baseball game had been on September eighth, and I was scheduled to catch the flight home to Salt Lake on the ninth. Strange, though, I couldn't remember catching that flight. Yet, apparently I was in Utah and had been for the last three months. I continued to rack my brain, again trying to remember anything at all since the ball game, but nothing came. Nothing! It was like that game was the last thing that happened in my life. Then my thoughts drifted back to Dr. Jones. What was her first name? Did she say?

A beeper went off on Dr. Jones's belt. She reached for it and read the text message. She stood and said, "Don't go anywhere. I've got a patient I have to see. I'll be right back." She hurried to leave the room.

"You mean I can leave if I can get up?"

"If you move, I'll have to send Nurse Fielding in to sit on you," she said.

Who was Nurse Fielding? Did I know her as well? I was beginning to sift though some of the information that I now knew when I noticed two envelopes on the nightstand by my bed. I reached over to retrieve them.

The first was from my sister, Shannon. I could tell by the handwriting; neat, but it always looked like it was written in a hurry. She lived in Utah County. I thought she was trying to make sure that Utah County retained the highest birthrate per family in the nation. That's why she was so busy: kids. The envelope was not stamped or addressed. Only one word was written on the envelope: Cord. It hadn't been mailed, so she must have come to see me. The card in her envelope read, "We are praying for you, Cord." She was the religious person in our family. I mean, she got all of the religious genes, probably from our mother. She was always praying for me, always trying to get me to go back to church.

Then I looked at the other envelope; it was from my mother and had been mailed. It was addressed to Cord Calloway, University of Utah Hospital, Room 610, Salt Lake City, Utah. My mind, however, wasn't focusing on the envelopes but on questions. The more questions I had, the fewer answers I could come up with. I fingered the envelope.

I set my mother's envelope down and opened the drawer to the nightstand. A hospital manila envelope was lying in the drawer with my name on it. I took the envelope out and looked inside. It contained my wallet, which had seventeen dollars in cold cash; a Utah driver's license; and a credit card. There was also a photo. It was her! The kissing doctor was in the photo, and she was wearing running clothes. She looked better in running clothes than scrubs—way better. It appeared she had just finished running. She was sweating, her face was flushed, and her hair was pulled back into a ponytail. She was gorgeous, and she looked almost dignified even in black jogging shorts. So I knew her well enough to carry her photo in my wallet.

Then my mouth fell open as I looked at a black velvet ring box in the bottom of the envelope. I opened the lid. It was an engagement ring with a small diamond. I lifted the white gold ring from the box and examined it. I couldn't remember purchasing an engagement ring. Was it mine? Where did I get the bucks to pay for it? If it wasn't mine, why was it in my envelope? I scrutinized the ring, hoping it would magically talk to me and answer some questions. Maybe if I rubbed it, a genie would appear and answer three questions. Then I saw an inscription in the ring. I turned it slowly so I could read it:

Diamonds Are Forever—Cord

Diamonds Are Forever. At least it was mine, no doubt about that. I wasn't sure if the inscription was very original, but it was definitely cool. I must have purchased the ring and had it inscribed . . . For Caitlyn? No, she had ended our relationship. She couldn't get past her parents. They couldn't get past me: a Mormon, a baseball player, and no money. Three strikes and I was outta there. I was not good enough for their daughter. I remembered explaining in detail: yes, I was a Mormon, but really in name only; I never went to church, although I believed many of their teachings. Religion just wasn't a big deal in my life. I didn't care what religion Caitlyn was or what church she went to.

But I don't think they cared; religion was just an excuse. I think it was the money thing that really bothered them, or maybe me just being a hick from Utah was enough.

However, I could remember the last time I saw her, and I hadn't purchased a ring at that time. But then I could have bought it later. Maybe I had talked to her and patched things up. But all I could remember was that she had just walked out of my life, vanished.

What if I had bought it for Dr. Jones? Did I know her that well? She said that we had become more than just friends, but there's a big gap between friends and diamond rings. If I could only remember something.

I looked inside the envelope again. The only things that remained were the keys to my truck and home. I recognized them, old and worn. I looked on the nightstand again, hoping that I would find a letter from Caitlyn or a video of the last three months of my life. But neither appeared, no matter how hard I wished. My heart ached for Caitlyn. I loved her, but she had dumped me. How could I have gotten over her so quickly? But then, what did I know? Three months were gone just like that. Blown away like autumn leaves on a blustery day.

I opened the envelope from my mother. It was postmarked December 1, 2004. It was one of those get well cards with real fancy writing squished between a bunch of flowers. It had something written in an Old English-y font about getting better. But she had written on the card, which she usually doesn't do. *"I can't be there, but I know you are in good hands. Indy will take superb care of you. Your mom."*

Indy? Who was she talking about? Well, Mom had always been a little bit weird anyway. She has never been able to understand why I don't ever pitch at the start of a game. I tried to explain that I am a reliever, not a starter. She thinks if you're a pitcher, you're a pitcher, and it's only fair to get to pitch at the start of a game, at least sometimes. She just doesn't get it.

Thoughts were flying at me from all directions and all at the same time. Indy? A ring? Diamonds Are Forever? December first, September eighth, a kissing doctor, a beautiful kissing doctor, a photo in my wallet, baseball, a baseball contract for next year, "Indy will take good care of you." The dots didn't connect. It seemed like they should, but they didn't.

My rambled, confused thoughts were instantly interrupted as Dr. Jones walked back into the room. She smiled at me and sat on the edge of my bed again. She reached over and took my hand, brushing the hair out of my eyes with her other hand.

Before I got lost in her eyes again I wanted some answers. "Okay, let's assume that I was in an accident just like you said. How serious could it have been? I don't seem to have any significant pains or injuries. So how could such a minor accident have affected my memory?"

"Have you looked in the mirror, Cord? That bandage wrapped around your head is not for decoration."

"Yeah, well my head doesn't hurt very much. It couldn't have been that bad."

"Everyone told me that you were hardheaded. It's probably a good thing because your helmet was split in half. I guess you hit your head very hard. Your helmet probably saved your life. And don't forget you've been unconscious for the last ten days."

"I just don't understand. It isn't like I know that something is missing. It honestly feels like I was in Wilmington just yesterday pitching in that ball game. If you hadn't told me that I had fast forwarded three months, I would never have realized I had a gap in my memory. It's like the last three months never happened."

I looked at her. Her face had that faraway look, pained. It appeared she was trying to make some sense of this whole mess as much as I was.

"Cord, I just had the most wonderful three months of my life with you. Do you have any idea . . ." She paused, wanting to say something, but then said, "Never mind."

"You can't just say never mind. Go ahead and say what you were thinking. Remember, we promised no secrets."

"Promised? What are you talking about?"

"Well, okay, maybe I made that up, but you still can't start to say something and then stop, leaving me hanging."

"Okay, let me try to explain it this way. You know how when you're young you believe you are invincible? You can't be hurt no matter how stupid you are or what you do?"

"Sure, didn't you see the shirt under this gown with the big *S* on it?"

She rolled her eyes and continued, "Well, just like we believe we are invincible for some reason, we also think that what we do today won't matter tomorrow. We can always fix everything, make it all better tomorrow, but we can't. Our lives, who we are, are made out of our yesterdays."

"I'm getting a little confused," I said. "What does this have to do with anything? Besides, isn't that a little metaphysical?"

"Put yourself in my position. How do you think I should feel when you tell me that these last three wonderful months never happened as far as you're concerned?"

She was struggling to control her composure. Then she squeezed my hand again and said, "But you know what? They did happen, and I can remember each and every second of every day. They are not gone to me. I can't take them back. They happened to me. The problem seems to be that they didn't happen to you, at least not that you remember. So I ask, where does that leave me?"

She was quiet. She looked vulnerable. I thought about what she had said. Maybe I had bought the ring for her. But I couldn't have. Dr. Jones was beautiful, but I was in love with Caitlyn. "I'm sorry, Dr. Jones. Sometimes I have problems because I only think of how things impact my life and my feelings." I was rambling and I knew it, not making much sense. "But do you think my memory will return? Or is it gone forever?"

"Well, we didn't know until you came out of the coma that you had a memory problem, but then it's not uncommon for people who have head injuries to have problems with their memories."

"So what do I do?" I asked. "Do you know a good hypnotist?" I teased.

"We are getting a little ahead of the game. You've only been back with us for an hour or so. Dr. Montgomery will be able to work with you to discover how much damage has been done. It will take a little time to figure out the extent of your injuries. Time. We just need to give it a little time."

"But, Dr. Jones, this doesn't make any sense to me. My memory is fine. I can remember everything. I even know I had the batter 0-2, and I threw him a high fastball that got away from the catcher. He should have caught it. He knew it was coming. My sister's name is Shannon and she has three kids: Summer, Cade, and Braden. Braden is a lefty. I'm going to teach him to pitch. My father died in my sophomore year of high school. My mother remarried and lives in Texas. I went to Brighton High School and then to BYU on a baseball scholarship. I ride my bike for fun and exercise. I have a home that was given to me by my father, and I live in the basement apartment. I own a 1989 Ford pickup truck named Betsy, with 167,000 miles on it. I am twenty-seven years old, six foot two, 185 pounds, very good looking, not yet married, and I pitch in the Kansas City Royals organization. I can even remember the grand slam home run I hit in my first at bat in Little League. I can go on."

She hadn't let go of my hand, and I knew that she was trying to work with me to comfort me and make me feel better. She said, "Sometimes head injuries are not predictable. For instance, you've told me all about yourself, but you didn't say one thing about anything that has happened to you since September 8, 2004. Do you want to try?"

"I can't. I've tried. Nothing. There's nothing. The last thing I can remember is that baseball game."

"Let me tell you what I think, Cord. I'm not a neurologist, but I'm sure that you have heard of amnesia. Well, there is a form of amnesia that is called retrograde amnesia. It's where a specific block of time, of memory, has been lost or affected. We really can't explain the phenomenon. It is very unpredictable. However, if the injury is a result of mild trauma, given time, the affected memory may return. But then there is a possibility that it will never return."

"That sounds like a definite maybe. So while I'm waiting for my memory to come dancing back to me, is there anything I can do to assist its return?" I was starting to get a little anxious. I didn't like losing three months of my life.

"Meditation helps. Exposure to people, places, and events sometimes triggers the memory. Usually though, it's just the passage of time. We need to give it some time. It may come back without you having to do anything. I'm sure after Dr. Montgomery runs some tests he will be able to give you a better diagnosis."

"When can I get out of here?"

"I think that Dr. Montgomery said we can bust you out tomorrow. I've got to check something. I'll be right back."

She hurried out of the room. I picked up the ring and looked at the inscription one more time. I tried rubbing it hard this time. I needed that genie. He didn't appear, so I slipped the ring back into the envelope and put the envelope back in the drawer. For some reason, I didn't want Dr. Jones to see the ring.

Two

It's déjà vu all over again.

—Yogiism #2

My body wasn't tired. I didn't need any more rest; but ten days in a coma had left me feeling sluggish and lethargic. I needed to move. I wanted out of bed, out of the hospital. It was time to start reclaiming my life, and that included trying to figure out about my three missing months. I had to talk to Shannon. She knew me better than anyone; and no matter what, I wanted to talk to Cate. The wires and cords were starting to bug me. I didn't need them. Where was Dr. Jones? She said she would be right back. My eyes continued to move impatiently between the clock and the door to my room, waiting for her to return. The clock wasn't in any hurry.

Retrograde amnesia, I mused. It sure didn't seem to me like I was missing the last three months. But it was December; and she . . . *they* wouldn't lie to me. I wanted to scream. I had never felt so helpless. I didn't like having to rely on anyone else. Why was Dr. Jones so reluctant to tell me about the last three months?

The door to my room swung open, and I reacted way too fast. I'm sometimes plagued with what's called hoof and mouth disease. I blurted out, sounding peeved, "I thought you forgot about me . . ." I tried to bite my tongue before the words were out. No such luck. To my astonishment, it was not Dr. Jones but the infamous Nurse Fielding, who Dr. Jones had threatened to have come and sit on me. I could read her name tag and her scowl. She didn't look like someone you wanted to pick a fight with. She weighed well over two hundred pounds and had jowls that would make a bulldog jealous and shoulders like an NFL linebacker.

She turned to face me, put her large hands on her hips, and sized me up. "Excuse me. Were you talking to me?" I could tell she didn't have a sense of humor. She was one of those basic, no nonsense people.

"I'm sorry, I thought you were Dr. Jones."

"Well, I'm not Dr. Jones, but she is one of my favorite people. Way too nice to be talked to like that. You might get away with talking to me in that tone of voice, but don't you ever let me hear you talk to Dr. Jones like that. Do you realize that sweet lady has been sitting by your bed for ten straight days? She has spent every spare minute by your side. She doesn't even take a break to eat. She brings it here. For what? Humph! I've a mind to tell you what I think of you."

She went about her business without being any too kind to me. She flashed me one of those "I dare you to say it" looks and said, "I have to finish my checklist, and then I'll get out of here before I say something that I might really be sorry about."

She was scribbling notes and taking readings. When she finished, she turned to leave. "Dr. Jones is out in the hall talking to Dr. Montgomery. I'm sure she will talk to you as soon as she finishes. Why, I don't know. You definitely have an attitude problem. And I don't care if you are a professional baseball player. Do you get my drift?"

Wow! She was tough. "I'm sorry. I didn't mean it like it sounded."

Nurse Fielding looked like she could give Battlefield Annie a run for her money, and it was apparent that she wasn't afraid to say what she thought to anyone, least of all me. I didn't understand; I usually made such good first impressions. Why was she on my case? But maybe this wasn't the first time we'd met. Maybe she knew me from the last three months. I don't think of myself as a rude person. In fact I think I'm usually very pleasant, leaning toward funny. Nurse Fielding left without saying another word. She didn't have to; her expression said it all. She didn't think I was funny, nice, or anything close thereto.

I needed to get control, calm down, and think straight. I knew how to do that. I did it every time I stepped on the mound. I let it all go, all of the pressure and the tension. It's a form of meditation. I centered and talked to myself. I found my safe zone.

I almost jumped off the bed when someone touched my arm. Dr. Jones had returned and was standing quietly next to my bed. Her touch quickly brought me out of the zone and back to my hospital room. I noticed right away that I was looking up into those enchanting green eyes. She wasn't smiling. I would say it looked like she was worried. Her eyes were a little puffy, with a touch of red. Had she been crying, or was it lack of sleep?

I wondered if it was because of me. I didn't know what to say or do. Maybe it had nothing to do with me; but if it was because of me, I wanted to make it right. But I couldn't remember her . . . or us. I am a good guy in spite of what Nurse Fielding thought. I knew I was a nice, caring person. But what could I do? What should I say?

On the other hand, she could help me, which might end up helping her. She knew answers to some of my questions, but then, she was reluctant to talk to me. She just stood there staring at me with those piercing green eyes. I sensed a loss. I didn't want to add to that loss, not tonight. Besides, I wanted to know about her almost as much as I wanted to know about me. And Caitlyn . . . I also wanted to know about her. Had I seen her since leaving Wilmington? Had she called? I was finding it difficult to stay focused. Questions just kept popping up into my head.

"Cord," Dr. Jones said very softly, sitting down on the edge of the bed. "I've talked with Dr. Montgomery, and he thinks it would be a good idea if we spent some time together. Since we have come to know each other so . . . so . . . well, he thinks that the familiarity of being together again may help trigger a return of your memory. Maybe we can revisit some of the places we have frequented. Do some of the things we've done. It might help spark the return of your memory. Something might come back. He says triggers like sight, sound, or smell sometimes promote memory recovery. He would like you to keep a notebook with you and take notes if any bit of memory returns and what you think triggered the recall. Your notes may help him treat you and maybe others."

"Now that you mention it, when you kissed me it seemed like there was something right on the edge of my memory. Do you think if we tried again it might come back?"

She laughed, "Cord, you are incorrigible." But she bent over and kissed me softly. I didn't need the pulsating beeps of the heart monitor to tell me that my heart rate was escalating. However, she was still an enigma, this beautiful doctor.

When she withdrew, she looked deep into my eyes as if she were searching for something and was unable to find it. I could tell that she wanted to say something.

"What?" I asked.

"I'm only going to say this once. It's the only way to be fair to you." She paused and then, finally making a decision, continued, "Before I met you, some things had happened to me that caused me to decide that I didn't need a man in my life—ever. Sometime I'll tell you about it, but not now. Anyway, I was firmly committed to my decision, and you knew it. Slowly over time you erased that resolve.

"Now I find myself in a very awkward position. You see, I remember the last three months; they are very real to me. My days had become filled with hope, anticipation, and expectations. I had opened myself up again. I was very vulnerable." She stopped. She wasn't looking at me any longer. I could tell this was very difficult for her.

I decided to try to help her. "Let me see if I understand what you're trying to say." I paused, trying to think how to best express my thoughts. "So, it's like you had a real bad wound that finally healed. Then I came along and broke open the wound and now you're suffering the pain all over again."

"That's a good analogy, but it's not your fault. I took the risk. It's just that I didn't remember how bad it hurt, and now there is nothing I can do to fix the problem. The only thing I can really do is to make sure it doesn't happen again. It's just too painful for me right now. I need to back off for my own self-protection."

"So you think hiding behind a fence and never letting anyone in is a solution to your problem?"

"Yes."

"Well, I don't think it's an acceptable solution. I think it's the chicken way out."

"It might be, but at least I know I can survive."

I began to plead with her. "You can help me. You can tell me things we did together. How we felt about each other. Why we felt that way. Maybe we can get back to where we were." However, I didn't want to make any promises, not until I found out about Cate.

"You don't understand. There is a difference between telling and feeling. I can't tell you how you feel or how you felt. I can tell you facts, dates, times, places; but I can't tell you about feelings. And the problem is that telling you won't change anything. You have to feel things of the heart; and without a memory, well, it's like they never happened."

I was caught in a box, a rundown between first and second. I didn't want to tell her about my strong feelings for Cate because that would seal the deal with Dr. Jones; and she would forever be locked behind that fence. And I definitely didn't want to lose something I might have had with her. I needed to buy some time. "Well, we can start all over again. I mean, we can play like we just met and I just asked you out on our first date."

"Maybe, but I'm just not sure if . . ." Then she stopped and after a minute said, "Okay, this is my proposition. I'm willing to do as Dr. Montgomery suggested, show you around, take you places we've been, and do things we've done. Then we'll see. You can decide if you want to ask me on that date and I can decide . . . whether to accept."

"Deal," I said, "but answer me one question. Was I in love with you?"

"It doesn't matter how you phrase the question. I think that's something you are going to have to figure out for yourself."

I thought about her answer. It didn't help me a lot, but it gave me some time. Of course, she could decide to hide behind her fence, but that was fair because I wouldn't try to convince her otherwise, not as long as I had questions about Cate. Maybe I should have told her about Cate. Maybe she already knew. I didn't want to chase her away; but she wouldn't go away, not if she really loved me, would she?

"Dr. Jones, I feel," and I emphasized *feel*, "like I should be on a first name basis with you; and Dr. Jones seems really formal. The only problem is that I can't remember what name I used when I didn't call you Dr. Jones."

She laughed. Maybe things weren't as bad as I feared. "I guess I haven't made much of an impression on you if you don't even know my first name." A smile formed, and then softly she said, "It's Indiana, but you can call me Indy."

"You're kidding, right?"

"Nope. My father thought it was funny. I mean, with a last name like Jones you have to have a catchy first name or no one will remember you. And Indiana has kind of grown on me."

"Indy." Then it hit me. "Wait, my mother wrote on her card, 'Indy will take good care of you.' I guess she meant you."

"I've only met your mother once, but she seemed to like me; or maybe she just thought I was good for you."

"Good for me? In what way?"

"I think you had better ask your mother that one. Listen, Cord, I'm not trying to be intentionally vague. It's just that if you remember, technically we haven't even been on a first date. So how would I know what your mother meant?"

"Fair enough. But you're not going to get off the hook that

easily. Let me ask you something a little simpler. Tell me how I met you."

"Don't you want to wait until a better time? I mean, it's just past three in the morning, and some of these answers are going to take some time to explain. I do have to be back at work at noon tomorrow. I mean today."

"I'm sorry. I didn't even think about that. I'm just not tired. Besides, from what you said, I've had enough sleep the past week to last me for a month. I don't feel a bit tired. I'm curious though. Were you working tonight?"

"No, I wasn't."

"You were here just to keep me company, even though I was unconscious?"

"You might put it that way."

"I think I'm going to like getting to know you, Indiana Jones."

She finally smiled again and said, "I would say 'remembering' would be a better choice of words."

"So, are you going to remind me how and where I met a hot blonde doctor since I don't usually hang out in hospitals?"

"Okay, I'll try to answer as many questions as I can, but only for one hour. Then I've got to go. I'll tell you what. If you want, you can pick me up at the ER tomorrow, I mean tonight, at six. We can go to dinner and talk. You can call it our first date if you want. But . . . but only if you want to and feel up to it."

"Great!"

She sat on the foot of my bed. Her blonde hair was long. It hung just past her shoulders. It was pulled back on the sides and flowed down her back. She was cute, darn cute, even beautiful. After a minute she said, "Okay, I'll tell you how we met, but first you need some background.

"You see, I love to run. It's how I escape from the world. Sometimes I do my best thinking when I'm running. I get to be by myself with no interruptions. I particularly like running the trails in Millcreek Canyon. That's where we met. I was running up the trail to Dog Lake and passed you on the way.

You mumbled something rude, but I just kept going. I don't make it a habit to stop and talk to dangerous looking men who mumble."

"So I looked dangerous?"

"I didn't get a really good look at you. I came around a corner and you were staggering back and forth across the trail looking very tired or drunk. I couldn't tell which. I hurried to pass you; and I did hear you mumbling, and it didn't sound very complimentary.

"When I got to the top of the hill, I took some time for myself and walked out along the ridge trail. It's beautiful up there. Somehow you took the same trail; looking back, I think you tracked me down. You ran, or I should say speed-hobbled, up to me, stopped, bent over, and then tried to catch your breath and talk at the same time. You didn't do either very well. I thought you were going to die. To tell you the truth, I was a little afraid you were some kind of a pervert. There weren't a lot of people on the trail that day. But I figured I could outrun you if I had to. You looked like death warmed over. We talked for some time. When I realized that you were harmless, I figured if we talked long enough, you might be able to make it back down the mountain by yourself instead of my having to carry you.

"Anyway, we walked and talked. After a while you asked me if I would come to your house for dinner. You told me you were a great cook. I accepted, but I voted for neutral grounds, preferably a restaurant with some people around. So that's how we met."

"So you were afraid to come to my house?"

"On the first date, yes."

I searched my mind. At least I was trying to run the search program. A virus must have infected the program because the results were always the same; nothing found for Dr. Jones, beautiful blonde, running Dog Lake, or dinner at my house. Finally I said, "The funny thing is that I can't remember that running was one of my hobbies, and I certainly can't remember running up to Dog Lake. I must have been inspired that day or had a death wish. I have, however, been on the trail to Dog Lake many times, but always on my mountain bike. I wonder when I took up running and why?"

"You told me that you had just started running that day."

I wanted to keep her talking. I wanted to know about her, about us, but I wasn't thinking really fast or very good. Women do that to me sometimes, particularly nice looking women. Out of desperation I said, "You kissed me earlier tonight."

She interrupted me, "I'm sorry. The first kiss was because I was so happy to have you back with us. The second was just impulsive. I shouldn't have done that. It won't happen again."

"Don't be sorry. It didn't hurt. At least I don't remember any pain or suffering. In fact, maybe it could be therapeutic."

"No. That wouldn't be appropriate now. Besides, we haven't been on our first date, and I never kiss anybody before or on the first date."

"Are you serious?"

"Like I said, I was being impulsive."

"Impulsive is good."

"Are you ever serious, Cord?"

"I'm dead serious," I said, but I had a huge grin on my face.

"Listen, this kissing thing . . . well, it's all tied to . . . the past three months. I want to help you, but there are no commitments."

"Are you trying to tell me that our relationship is going to be platonic?"

"I'm trying to tell you that I don't know, but for now, yes."

I thought for a minute and then asked, "When did you meet my mother?"

"About the middle of September. I met her at Shannon's house."

So I must have taken her to Shannon's. I wouldn't take just anyone to my sister's. I couldn't remember ever taking a date to Shannon's. "And you say that I've spent parts of every day for the last three months with you?"

"Well, parts of almost every day."

How could I forget someone I had been with every day for

the last three months? She was right, apparently my memory was malfunctioning; but if I had feelings for her, wouldn't I be able to remember or feel something? There were no specific remembrances, yet there was something. My searching routine under females kept retrieving a file labeled Caitlyn. I could see a picture of Caitlyn looking like she stepped off the set after posing for a fashion magazine. She was wearing a black satin pants suit, dangling diamond earrings, and an infectious smile. Below this mesmerizing picture was a flashing red light that cautioned, "She dumped you."

How could I have read Cate so wrong? Yet my heartbreak was still close to the surface, too new to be healed. The problem was that she didn't love me, not enough to stand up to her parents. Or was it because I was from across the tracks, or because I was a Mormon?

I continued frantically to search, but I couldn't remember talking to Cate, seeing her, or anything, not since being tossed by her father. Why, then, couldn't I shake my feelings for her? Then I wondered how I could spend parts of every day with Indy when I was in love with Caitlyn. I wouldn't do it. I couldn't do it. It didn't make sense. Dr. Jones was fidgeting, nervously glancing anywhere but in my direction. It was obvious she was anxious to leave, and I knew I couldn't keep her here much longer.

"Just a few more questions tonight," she said.

"Okay, what can you tell me about my accident?"

"You were riding your bike down Millcreek Canyon and a car came too close to you. It forced you off of the road. You must have been going about thirty-five miles an hour and took a nasty fall. The car never stopped. It was apparently driven by some high school kids out joyriding. A lady saw the accident and stopped to help. She said she thought you were dead for sure. The bike was twisted and bent, and you weren't moving. She used her cell phone and got assistance for you very quickly. The ambulance brought you here."

"And I have been in a coma for ten days."

She nodded her head.

"And during those ten days, how often were you here?"

"Almost all the time I wasn't working."

I felt like I was swimming upstream. I had only learned bits and pieces of the past three months. Finally out of frustration I asked, "Okay, tell me three things I should know about you, other than why I carry your photograph in my wallet."

Her answer didn't take long: in fact it was almost a spontaneous response. She was twirling the ends of her hair and averting my eyes. Staring at the wall, she said, "Okay, first, I believe that professional sports are the opiate of the masses. I hate baseball. I don't understand it. Football is for Neanderthals; and basketball, I can take it or leave it. Second, I've supported myself since I was seventeen years old. And, third, I have a basic distrust of all men."

"Wow, I'm a man as well as a professional baseball player. Sounds like two strikes and I haven't even stepped into the batter's box yet."

"I'm sorry. You have exceeded your question limit for tonight. I'll see you later today."

"Wait, you didn't tell me why I have your photo in my wallet."

"I don't know, unless you stole it. See you later."

"Wait! How about a good-night kiss? You know . . . one for the road."

"I don't think so. You are still under a doctor's care."

"But you can't just leave me. I . . . I don't want you to go. Besides, I probably won't be able to sleep anyway."

"I can ask Nurse Fielding to come and give you something to help you sleep, or she can sit at your bedside and read stories to you until you drift off."

"No! Not her! She may strangle me or poison me. By the way, is she your personal bodyguard?"

She laughed, "Why do you ask?"

"Well, I thought she was going to rip my ears off earlier tonight."

"Be nice to her and you won't have any problems."

"I don't think she likes me."

"How could someone not like a professional baseball player who is charming, handsome, and so fun to be around?"

"Yeah, I was thinking the same thing."

"Listen, Cord, I have to go or the people that I treat tomorrow will think I am a baseball player, not a doctor. I'm dead on my feet. I'm glad you came back. I think." Then she smiled.

I watched her leave and felt the room become painstakingly empty, almost sterile. It was like the lights went out. I felt alone and frustrated. I had trouble forming good questions. It wasn't fair. She distracted me. Maybe it was because of the accident. No, who was I kidding? I wondered why I always turned into a bowl of green Jell-O around beautiful women. Or was Dr. Jones someone special? We must have been pretty serious or she wouldn't have taken it so hard.

Random thoughts continued to bombard me. Then I got a sinking feeling. I wondered if the Royals ever sent me a contract for next year. I couldn't remember signing one, but then I couldn't remember anything that happened during the last three months. If I didn't have a contract to play ball, then I would have to find a day job. I wondered if I had tried to find a coaching job yet.

That made me remember the expression on Caitlyn's face when I told him that I wanted to coach high school baseball. It would have been funny if he hadn't been serious. Everyone in their family was a doctor or an attorney or had an MBA from Harvard. A high school baseball coach in Utah just didn't enhance the family pedigree. I wondered how Caitlyn could have sided with her parents. I thought I knew her better than that.

My mind went back to baseball. If I did have a contract to play ball, what kind of shape was my arm in? Had I been throwing? Where? With whom? Spring training would start in just a little over two months. I should have received a contract if they were going to send me one. If I had a contract, it would be at home in my file, I hoped.

I needed to talk to my sister, Shannon. I knew my mother

wouldn't know anything. Besides, the only thing my mother was ever interested in was my church attendance. Then I wondered if Dr. Jones, or perhaps Caitlyn, knew about my contract. So many things to do, and I was strapped to this bed, unable to talk to anyone or do anything but let my mind run completely out of control.

Just then the door to the room swung open and in stormed my favorite, Nurse Fielding. She didn't look any happier than when she had last stormed out. "I've got to check your vitals," she said. She looked like she didn't want to be here checking me for anything. "Although you look well enough to me."

"Hey, I'm a nice guy. Didn't Dr. Jones put in a good word for me?"

"Yeah, she told me to be nice to you. I told her all I could do was try."

"Do you know her very well?"

"She's been here about two years. Most docs think they walk on water. Not Doc Jones. She treats everyone like they matter, like they're important. I've never met anyone like her."

"Is she dating anyone?" It was a set up question.

Nurse Fielding looked at me like I had lost my mind. "Mr. Calloway, let me set the record straight. I don't like you. I don't understand what Doc Jones saw or sees in you. I'm trying to be civil with you because you're a patient under my care, but don't push your luck."

She couldn't hate me any worse, so I asked away. "Tell me the truth. Did Dr. Jones come to visit me every day that I was here?"

"You'd better believe it. She gets off work, grabs something from the cafeteria, and comes in here to sit by your side. I've tried to get her to go home; but she won't budge. She even came up here on her days off."

"Is there anyone working at the hospital who is dating her?"

"I thought I told you . . ."

I hurried to interrupt her, "Okay, okay, but you know that I have a head injury, which caused some kind of amnesia. Help me.

I don't remember a thing about Dr. Jones, but I think I should."

"Doc Jones is a great doctor. She has devoted her life to her patients. She goes above and beyond the call for each one. Up until about three months ago she practically lived at the hospital. Then all of a sudden, she was only working her regular shift. I figured she had found herself a boyfriend, but she never said. Then suddenly you show up in the hospital and she's here every day. I suspect she cares about you. And that's all I'm gonna say. One way or the other, you had better be nice to her."

With that she stalked out of the room. I was left to try to find the lost three months and maybe even myself along the way.

The quicksand seemed to be sucking me down, and then I remembered something Dr. Jones had said. It was something like: we are, after all, the sum of those things we have done. Then I understood. My memory is more than just a story—it's me! It is who I am. Without that memory, I don't even know myself. I don't know who I am. But Indy remembers. She knows who I am or who I was. I wondered then if I would become the same person she had known or someone new. That was what upset her. She doesn't know what or who I may become without the missing memory. I began to understand how she must have felt.

I realized that I was missing the last few innings of my life. The real problem was that it seemed like it was still the fifth inning, and yet the scoreboard said it was the seventh inning. I needed to know about those missing innings, even if it seemed like they never happened. It mattered even if it didn't seem like a life or death situation to me. On the other hand, it seemed infinitely important to Indy. I think I was beginning to understand what she was thinking, but it was hard to understand why she was so upset. Couldn't we just start again? Obviously, we connect. What was the big deal? She was a doctor; why didn't she understand?

My thoughts became circular and were not getting me anywhere.

Three

The future ain't what it used to be.

—YOGIISM #3

THE CLOCK AT MY BEDSIDE was on pace to be a DNF (did not finish) in a marathon. I kept wanting to scream at it to pick up the pace. I wanted out of there. I pumped the "call nurse" button again. A voice droned over the speaker, "Mr. Calloway, I told you the tests are scheduled for seven o'clock. It's only six. Do you need a Valium?"

It was a conspiracy. I knew that Nurse Fielding was at the bottom of this. It was her payback. She must have told her relief that I was the curmudgeon in 503 and not to do me any favors. I felt like I was in five o'clock traffic trying to get to a ball game; every time I tried to take a shortcut, I got behind an old man with a handicapped license plate or a woman in a Suburban, talking on a cell phone, with ten kids climbing around the car.

Suddenly, one of those random thoughts that were floating around in my mind came into sharp focus. The cost of this little venture was directly proportional to the length of my stay in the hospital; and money is one of those things that has eluded me for my entire life. Simply put, I don't have any. It was a sickening feeling. How was I going to pay for this little adventure into modern medicine? Maybe they'd let me out if they discovered I wasn't a rich, professional baseball player, just a poor minor leaguer. It must be obvious I'm a tiny bit paranoid about money. But then I thought that maybe, just maybe, my health insurance, offered through the Royals organization, would still be in effect.

It's like this: the Royals, like most baseball organizations, release everyone but their top prospects each year, which terminates health insurance benefits. The organization then re-signs them just prior to spring training. It saves them a few bucks but immensely complicates my life. I wouldn't get released each year if I were a "top prospect"; but as of this date, I've yet to be so designated. The net effect to me is that each year I lose my health insurance benefits for a few months. However, I always had the option to pay for COBRA benefits. Without insurance, I couldn't pay for ten days in the hospital, not out of my pocket. The hospital bill by itself would probably exceed ten thousand dollars.

But then maybe the Royals had decided I was an integral part of their future and had sent me a new contract. I had posted good numbers last year, some of the best in their minor league organization. However, I knew that they considered me to be one of those guys that might make AA ball if I was really lucky. My only hope was that my release letter had been sent late and the thirty-day option period for COBRA had not yet expired. Or better still, they hadn't released me. I wondered if Dr. Jones would still speak to me if I bankrupted the hospital and all of her friends. I didn't need to worry about what Cate's father would think—I knew.

For that matter, I didn't even know if they would let me out of the hospital if I couldn't pay for the services. I only had seventeen bucks in my wallet, and my standard co-pay was twenty dollars; that is, if I had insurance. But then, I had my credit card. Of course, I had no idea if it was any good. I knew it would not take a ten-thousand-dollar hit even in the best of times. However, I only use my card for emergencies and then try to pay it off each month. I hoped I had continued my old habits during the last three months. It seemed my world had become loaded with new and exciting queries. Did I still own my home? How about Betsy, my truck? I hoped my bike wasn't my only form of transportation because it sounded like it might not be usable in its present condition.

And, of course, with all the discussions I was now having with myself, eventually the issue of my income surfaced. They didn't last long because there wasn't much to talk about. My checking account rarely exceeded one thousand dollars, and that was when I was receiving a monthly paycheck during baseball season.

I wondered if I might become a legend like Charlie, to whom the Kingston Trio dedicated their ballad "The Man Who Never Returned." You see, Charlie couldn't get off the train because he didn't have a quarter. In Boston, when they opened the Mass Transit Authority (MTA), they made people pay when they got off instead of when they got on. Just think, I could be here with Nurse Fielding forever. Such a warm, fuzzy feeling. I decided memory loss was not one of my favorite things.

If I escaped from my bed of confinement, I hoped that my available cash would cover cab fare to my house—that is, if I had a house. I didn't used to think so, but life is really like a baseball game. And lately, it seemed like all I was getting was nothing but a steady diet of nasty curves, and I never could hit the bender. *Patience, Cord*, I kept reminding myself. I almost laughed. Patience was not one of my virtues, not unless I had caught it from someone during the last three months.

"It's seven o'clock," said Nurse Tippets as she sauntered into my room. She was Fielding's henchman. She asked if I could get out of bed on my own or if I needed some help. She said it more sarcastically than necessary. My comeback was a little more sarcastic than was necessary, but I wasn't in a very good mood. "I hope I don't look like an invalid, because I feel great," I said as I swung my legs over the side of the bed. Then I teasingly asked, "By the way, are you related to Nurse Fielding?"

She didn't even crack a smile. No humor! She wasn't going to help me. So I said, "I can do better if you will unhook me from all of these wires." She grumbled something and then proceeded to unplug me. Nothing stopped working, like my heart, so I assumed I was good to go. She brought a wheelchair into the room and motioned for me to sit. I graciously declined her invitation to sit in the wheelchair. "I'm completely ambulatory," I responded.

She scowled at me. She had either lost all of her patience or never had any, but then maybe it was just me she hated. "You're not going anywhere except in this chair. Now, we can do it my way or you can just climb back up there in bed and I'll leave."

"That's not bad," I said. "How long did it take you to perfect your Nurse Fielding imitation?"

She still didn't laugh.

"Come on," I said. "That was at least a little funny."

Her face looked like it had been set in a plaster cast. Not even a smile. I could see that humor wasn't going to help.

Hospital gowns are not designed to be worn in public, so I asked, "Before I get in your chair, do you have something else for me to wear? As you know, this gown has an open back and, well, I don't have anything on under it."

Her reply was immediate. "I don't think anyone will be interested enough to look." Man, she was all business. "Now if you will sit down, I'll take you to get the tests and X-ray completed. Then maybe we can get you out of here." I didn't like the second choice, so I did what she asked.

♦ ♦ ♦

It took about an hour to finish the X-rays and other tests. I was wheeled back to my room and abandoned. My clothes were in the closet, so I quickly got dressed. The money thing was still bothering me, as well as the question of viable insurance. I decided that discretion was the better part of valor and sneaked past Nurse Tippets, walking out the front door like I was a visitor. I wanted to get off the subway and I didn't have a quarter. I would settle up later when and if I figured out how.

The cabbie pulled up in front of my house. The house was in

an older neighborhood that was rapidly becoming very "yuppie." I did my best to maintain the house, although I couldn't keep up with the new neighbors who were bent on making their old houses look like new.

The cabbie startled me back to reality. "That will be eleven bucks," he said.

I gave him twelve and told him to keep the change.

He gave me the "you've got to be kidding" look and said, "Thanks, I'll try not to spend it all in one place."

I was going to quote Fred, my New Jersey teammate, but the cabbie drove away before I got the words out.

Everything looked normal from the front of the house. The white paint around the windows was peeling, and the walks needed shoveling. The shrubs were scruffy looking, and the discolored concrete below the bricks needed something to bring it back to life. I walked around back to the garage, which was red brick and in about the same shape as the house, and opened the door. Betsy sat there rarin' to go like she had just pulled off the showroom floor, even if it had been fifteen years ago. Yeah, she had a few dents and some rust spots, but she was in pretty good shape for being an old maid. At least I wasn't afraid to take her offroad and get a dent or, heaven forbid, some mud and dirt on her paint.

Betsy was the name of my 1989 forest green Ford truck. I named her after a woman because she always had to do things her way. She had let me know she was in charge more than once. Consequently, I always talked nicely around her, particularly if I needed to get somewhere.

Things were looking good so far. The key fit in the door, and I walked downstairs to my apartment. I noticed a stack of mail sitting atop an old milk box. My renters used it as my mail slot. There was also a note from my renters on top of the stack. "Cord, we'll be moving out the end of the month. We liked it here, but John got a job in Provo." It was signed "John and Deanna."

Great, now I had to find new renters, someone who didn't have kids. I had tried kids before, but I never got any sleep. Plus, new renters would have to be willing to take care of the place while I was away at baseball; that is, if I went away to baseball this year. The house was usually easy to rent, but it had just become another complication in the quagmire I called my life. Their leaving also meant I would not be receiving five hundred dollars rent for this month. New renters always pay first and last month's rent up front, and I had expended my current renters' last month long ago.

I found my cell phone, but it was useless since the battery was dead. I didn't have a land line, only my cell phone. I plugged in my cell phone and then wandered into the kitchen, sat at the table, and began to sort through my mail. The first letter was from the bank. It was dated December 1, 2004. Noises from my phone advertised that it was alive again. I ripped open my bank statement: $359 bucks and change. I wasn't loaded, but at least I could eat until the end of the month. I breathed easier. I flipped through the rest of the mail to see if there was anything from the Royals. Nothing.

I needed to know if the Royals still considered me their property or if I had to find a day job. I looked under Royals in my filing cabinet. Sure enough, I found my letter of termination dated November 13, 2004. That meant that I was a free agent and I could go to any team I wanted, if there was a team that wanted me. The problem was that no one else was knocking on my door. While my status as a pitcher was in doubt, at least I still had a chance to avoid bankruptcy if I signed up for the COBRA policy within the next few days. As costly as it would be, it beat bankruptcy by a long ways. It also meant that I would not be known as the deadbeat chasing Dr. Jones.

I must have been living right the last three months because I was catching a few breaks. I decided to risk it one more time. I picked up my credit card statement from the unopened mail stack. The unpaid balance was only $122. Hot. I was three for three. I slid the current financial resource puzzle piece into place. The amount remaining wasn't big enough, but at least it wasn't zero.

Why stop now? I thought. I was on a roll. Back to the filing cabinet. Maybe I had already looked for a coaching job. Under "Real Jobs" there was nothing current. I discovered notes that were dated January of 2003; I had sent a resume to Hunter High School. At the time they had been looking for a baseball coach. I was interested, but the dilemma that I had then as well as now was the same. Do I take the coaching job and throw away my chance for fame and glory and a boatload of money? But then there was always the chance that I wouldn't even get a contract or be invited to spring training. Baseball is like that. You never know what management is thinking or what they will do until it happens.

Spring training starts in late February. Last year the Royals had not invited me to go to spring training until mid-February. Once I got the invitation to spring training, I opted for the chance of fame and glory instead of coaching. Besides, I was still chasing my dream. The folks at Hunter hadn't been real happy with me since they had to find someone else on very short notice. I didn't want to do that to someone again. So instead of committing to a real job, I opted to sit and wait, all in hopes that I would be invited to play ball again this year.

The puzzle of my life was in total disarray, and I couldn't even find the piece labeled "what do I do when I grow up?" I had no idea if I would be invited back to the Royals this year, and they could make their decision anytime within the next ninety days. What did they care if I took a job? There were a thousand pitchers just waiting to take my spot.

I went back to the unopened mail again. Now I was looking for the Caitlyn puzzle piece, the brunette model with brown, mischievous eyes: the one who was always in the middle of a crowd with everyone listening and laughing, hoping that she would cast a smile their way.

The piece wasn't there.

I closed my eyes, shuffled the mail, said a prayer, and looked again. It still didn't appear. I didn't think to check my email or voice mail. I was focused, so focused that I forgot to think. Back

I trudged to the mail stack. It was all junk mail. And by the way, I consider bills to be junk mail. I was still waiting for a ban of all junk mail.

One of my designated pieces of junk mail had a return address of Bishop Swenson, Parleys fifth ward. That was strange: the Church quit asking me for donations years ago, and I couldn't remember having the bishop as a pen pal. It was probably a result of my mother calling the Church again. It was postmarked December 5, 2004. I ripped it open. It was a handwritten note.

> *Cord,*
> *Sorry you couldn't make our appointment tonight. I tried calling you, but I only got your message service, which said, "I'm sorry, but the subscriber you are calling is not answering his phone at the present time." I couldn't leave a message, so call me when you get a chance.*
>
> *—Bishop Swenson*

That was weird. I knew one other thing for sure, and that was that I would not have made an appointment with the bishop; and furthermore, I didn't even know a Bishop Swenson. He had made a mistake, or my mother had made an appointment without talking to me. Either way, he would have a long wait if he thought I was going to make the pilgrimage to the church to talk to him. Church just wasn't my thing, not anymore.

I realized that my phone had reminded me it was ready to go some time ago. I dialed my voice mail. The first message was from Indy: "Cord, I'll be off at six tonight. I'll see you then." I had no idea when that message was left.

The next two were hang-ups. There were several calls from my mother and two from Shannon. No calls from Caitlyn, unless she was the mystery hang-up caller. But that wasn't like her. She wasn't bashful. She would have left a message whether it was good, bad, or ugly.

The note from the bishop continued to bother me, although I didn't know why. Maybe it haunted me because of an underlying guilt complex. Maybe it was just because I was curious. Regardless, I hadn't been to church in over five years. I had no reason to talk to a bishop, and yet it seemed I had. Since I couldn't remember why I had talked to him, there was no reason to continue whatever discussions we were having. I deleted his call back number and threw away the note, deciding it was my mom's fault. Most likely she had sicced him on me. She could never leave well enough alone, no matter how many times I explained to her that I was not interested in going back to church.

I didn't need to call mom back because she was like a bloodhound set loose. She would track me down the minute she discovered I had escaped from the hospital. But I did want to talk to Shannon. I dialed her number; at least I could remember something.

"Hi, this is the Davis residence. No one is home now. If you will leave a message, we will call you . . ." I pushed the red "end" button.

Dang! She's never home when I need to talk to her.

Frustration was setting in. I was just a normal guy with normal, everyday living problems. But then maybe everyone was right and I should grow up and get a real job, quit playing a kid's game. Should I give up my lifelong dream to find the answers to these seemingly unanswerable questions? I was exasperated. I wanted someone to tell me what was going on with my life. I called my agent, like that was going to help. As usual, he didn't answer my call; he never did. I knew if I had been one of his bonus babies, he would have picked up. Just the same, I left a message. "Bill, this is Cord Calloway. Have you heard anything from the Royals? Have you called any other teams to see if there is an interest? I pitched really well against some of the teams last year. Let me know what's going on. Thanks. And just in case you have forgotten my phone number, I'll leave it for you."

Agents aren't any good unless you have a big contract. The only players they ever help are those with the big contracts, and that didn't include me. I knew Bill wouldn't take a call from me, but he would talk to a team if they called him about me. I threw my phone onto the couch out of frustration and started pacing. I heard a faint sound and started digging for my phone, which was now buried between the couch pillows. The ring of my cell phone was unmistakable: "Take Me Out to the Ball Game." Once I found it, I let it play all the way through one time, just for the heck of it. The caller ID indicated the call was from Shannon. I pushed the green button. "Shannon, is it really you?"

"Well, who did you think it would be? Where are you, Cord? I called the hospital today, and they told me you had flown the coop. The last thing I knew, you still hadn't regained consciousness. Are you okay? What's going on? Talk to me."

I sat down. Finally I had someone to talk to. If anyone could help me, it was Shannon. "I'm fine, at least I think so; but I can only answer one question at a time."

"So, start answering."

"Shannon, I've got more questions than I do answers, and I was hoping you could fill in some of the blanks."

"What are you talking about? Are you okay?"

"Shannon, I'm fine—physically that is. Mentally, well, that's another question."

"What do you mean? You don't sound any worse than normal."

"Funny, Shannon."

"You didn't laugh."

"Shannon, here's the deal. It seems that I'm not quite as hard headed as you guys always thought. When I fell off the bike, I hit my head. Don't worry, I'm okay, but I have what they are calling retrograde amnesia."

"It sounds really bad. Is it catching?"

"It's like this, Shannon. If you pick up the novel you're reading and tear out the middle third of the pages, then you as the reader will know how I feel. I can't remember one thing that happened between September 8, 2004, and December 5, 2004. My life is like your novel with the missing pages. So while I feel fine physically, I have a memory problem. That's where you come in, I hope."

"I've never heard of that before. Are you putting me on?"

"Shannon, I need you to fill in the black hole, connect a few dots. Tell me about my life and what I've been doing the last three months."

"Well, since you're so communicative, I can probably condense your last three months down into about five minutes. You know it's not like you keep me informed on your comings and goings. Getting information out of you is like trying to crack open a coconut. The person you should be talking to is Indy."

"You mean Dr. Indiana Jones and not the guy in the movie with a whip, right?"

"One and the same. You know, the tall, pretty blonde, the nicest person in the whole world."

"How do you know her?"

"Cord, you've spent almost all of your time with her over the last three months. She has actually talked to me more over that time than I have talked to you. We've become pretty good friends."

"Shannon, I just met her today for the first time. I have absolutely no memory of ever seeing Dr. Jones before today."

"Well, little brother, let me tell you that you found a winner when you hooked up with Indy. In fact, about three weeks ago you told me that you had bought a diamond for her."

So the ring was for her. What a mess. Everything seemed to be screaming at me, telling me that I had fallen for Indy. Everything except for my heart. Sometimes one plus one does not equal two.

"Shannon, believe me when I tell you that the only woman I can remember is Cate, not Dr. Jones. But I can tell you that Dr. Jones is very nice looking and not a bad kisser. She does seem very familiar in an unfamiliar sort of way."

"Men," she said, exasperated. "Is that the most important thing about a woman? How she looks?"

I didn't want her to get on the feminist kick; I would never get any information. "Before you interrupted me, I was going to add that she is a great cook and has a very strong testimony."

"You're not funny, Cord."

"Shannon, I'm desperate. I have a date with Indy tonight. I mean, she's nice, but I don't really know her. In spite of what you say and everyone else says, the last significant thing I can remember was being dumped by Caitlyn."

"You just bought a diamond for Indy. You were going to ask her to marry you. Don't you remember anything?"

I wracked my brain, but nothing had changed. My feelings didn't change just because Shannon told me facts that were contrary to what my heart was telling me. Finally, I asked Shannon, "The last time I can remember talking to Cate was at her father's house when I was told I was not good enough for her. Do you think I talked to her or saw her since that night?"

"Absolutely! About three weeks ago Caitlyn showed up at your house. Indy was with you at your place when Caitlyn came knocking at your door, completely out of the blue. She hadn't called to let you know she was coming. It was a total surprise to you and Indy—and Cate, I might add. You told me that Indy left in a huff; and Cate got in her cab and drove away without saying anything. Does any of this ring a bell with you?"

"Nothing. Dang! Caitlyn was here. I need to talk to her."

"You really haven't talked much about Caitlyn for a long time. It seemed like she had broken your heart, but then you got over her. You met Indy and it was like 'Cate who?' I really don't know much about Cate, but I do know Indiana Jones; and she is the best thing that ever happened to you."

"Shannon, I don't know what to do." I was torn.

"Maybe you just need to give it some time. Try to talk to Indy. You'll remember."

"My life is like a bowl of Jell-O. I grab a handful and it just squishes out of my hands. Mom writes me a letter that says Indy will take good care of me. You tell me she is the best thing that ever happened to me. And I don't know one thing about her. Yet, I believe you, Shannon, and that's what scares me."

"Well, let me tell you some of the things I know about Indy. Maybe it will help you remember. She comes from a dysfunctional family. Her father died of a drug overdose when she was seventeen. She was living with him at the time and taking care of him. Her mother and father were divorced. Her mother wouldn't have anything to do with her because she chose to live with her father.

"When her father died, her mother got all of the insurance money because she was the named beneficiary. It should have gone to the kids after the divorce, but he forgot to change the beneficiary statement. Indy dropped out of high school to work and take care of herself. She earned a GED and went to college. She paid for every dime of college by herself. She graduated from UCLA and got a full scholarship to the University of Utah Medical School.

"I know that she had one serious relationship that went sour a few years ago. Since then she has never trusted a man. You are the first man she has spent any time with since becoming a doctor.

"And one more thing. She joined the Church after her father died. She credits the Church and its members for everything good that has happened to her since. Apparently some members took her in and changed her life. She even got you to go to church with her."

"I knew there was a reason Mom liked her. Mom thought Indy would get me back to church, right?"

"Cord, you *have* been going to church."

Some of the dots were starting to connect. Maybe I should call Bishop . . . what was his name? Maybe he could fill in a few more gaps. But then he would probably expect me to continue coming to church, or at the least try to talk me into it. It was risky business just to get a few questions answered.

"Shannon, I had a message from the bishop of my ward telling me that I missed an appointment with him last week. Do you know anything about that?"

"I don't, but I like it."

"But you know how I feel about the Church. It's fine that you love it; I . . . well I don't feel exactly the same."

"Then why did you have an appointment with the bishop?"

"I'm not sure, but I think I'm afraid to find out."

"Chicken!"

If the truth be known, I was. One of my maxims is, "If you don't want to know the answer, don't ask the question," and I wasn't sure that I wanted to know the answer to this particular question. *Change the subject,* I thought, *before I get in any deeper.* "Do you have any idea if anything happened with the Royals in the last couple of months? I mean, I found my termination letter, but I don't know if I've talk to Rick or anyone since. Have I heard anything?"

"I remember you mentioning that Rick called and said the Royals were going to invite you to spring training. I believe he stood up for you and made them ask you back. He seems like a nice guy. It's good that you've got someone in your corner. However, I think he said they weren't going to give you a contract unless you make a team during spring training."

"If I had it to do over again, Shannon, I wouldn't do it. I mean, I thought it was a big deal to be signed as a free agent and play professional baseball; but I just have to keep putting my life on hold, waiting for some guys to decide if they think I can pitch. It doesn't matter how good I do; it only matters what they think, and no one ever knows what they think, least of all me. I really believe I could pitch in the big leagues, but I also need to get on with my life."

Shannon said, "I think you talked to your coach at the Y about being the pitching coach. He told you that they already had a full staff but asked that you let him know when you're ready to really move on. One day he might have something open up. I don't know if you've tried anywhere else. I never hear from you anymore since you're always with Indy."

"I guess I had better get my name on the substitute teacher list at all of the districts. The pay isn't very good, but it will cover my basic expenses."

"Do you need any money, Cord? We can always help."

"I'm okay for now, Shannon, but I've got to go. I'll get back with you tomorrow. I have a date with Indy tonight. She has promised to try to answer some questions, although she tends to be a little vague."

"What do you mean? She's always been straight with me. That's one of the reasons I like her so much. You always know exactly what she thinks about everything. She doesn't pull any punches. She's refreshing."

"Well, I asked her if we were more than just friends, if we had feelings for one another. All she would say was that it wasn't for her to say, that I had to figure that one out for myself, that I had to listen to my heart. Well, I listened, but I'm not hearing anything except Cate. On the other hand, everyone, including you, has told me that I am involved with Indy. I'm grasping at straws, but I can't remember anything of the last three months."

"You don't seriously expect a girl to tell you whether you like her or not, do you? I mean, that's something you have to know, not something that someone can tell you. I think I'll have to take her side on this one."

"Sure, always take the female side."

"Maybe it's because I think like one of them."

"Listen, Shannon, I'll get back to you. Thanks. I really mean it."

"I know you do, Cord. I'll be praying for you."

"Shannon, you are the best sister I've ever had; course I only have one. See you later."

During the next hour and a half, I left a message with the Royals's minor league pitching coordinator. I called and started the COBRA insurance policy using my credit card. I called an old teammate who was coaching high school in Utah Valley and told him to be on the lookout for a coaching job. I called a lady I knew to inquire about emergency teaching certification. I didn't graduate in education, so I wasn't certified to teach. But I needed to get certified, if that's what I ended up doing.

I wanted—needed—to talk to Cate. The twenty-four million dollar question was if she wanted to talk to me. Even though Shannon had given me some information, it didn't seem to ring true, even though I knew she wouldn't lie to me. Maybe she just didn't know. I wondered what had brought Cate to Salt Lake. Had I known she was coming? What happened during her visit? Had I bought the ring for her or Indy? Why had she only stayed one day? Did Caitlyn know about Indy? Did Indy know about Caitlyn? They were simple questions, but I've discovered in my limited relationships with women that forgetting little details can often prove to be like walking around holding a live grenade that doesn't have the pin. Now I couldn't even remember the big things, like Indy's first name or if I had spoken to Cate in the last six months. I also knew that if Indy had been at my house when Cate appeared that the little details wouldn't matter to either of them. I would be dead!

I felt like a kid in sixth grade trying to call a girl to see if she would "go" with me. I wanted to make the call. I needed to make the call. The longer I waited, the more scrambled my stomach became. Besides, my head pounded every time I started to dial the number. I hung up twice so that I could repeat each word of my speech.

The problem was that I didn't know where to start with Caitlyn because I didn't know what she knew. I could be entering a minefield, asking open-ended questions. I didn't even know if she knew about my injury, but I was sure she didn't know about my memory, or lack thereof. I decided that the best course was to hit her with the accident and then plead a good case for sympathy. Avoid the tough questions and for sure all of the small details.

Finally I pulled her number up on my cell phone and pushed the green "call" button. It rang four times. Someone answered. It was not Caitlyn. It was a man. Great, I didn't know what to say, so I didn't say anything for a long time. What if it was her boyfriend or even her husband? Finally out of desperation I said, "I'm sorry, I was calling Caitlyn Belford."

"You and about ten other chumps have called today. It's a little annoying. I just got this phone and the number, and it obviously belonged to Ms. Belford. I don't know what to tell you, buddy, but I'm not going to put up with this any longer. I'm not her secretary, whoever she is."

"Sorry," I sheepishly replied as I quickly pushed the red button to end the call. That really complicated things. I wasn't about to call her parents' house. I didn't want my head on a platter. That left me email or a letter, if I had a good address for either. I decided to try both. I nervously glanced at the clock, which read five o'clock. I had to be at the hospital to pick up Indy in an hour. I needed a shower and a change of clothes. I would have to try to reach Caitlyn later. Right now I had to focus on my upcoming meeting with Dr. Jones. Of course, I knew that wouldn't be a problem because I was so smooth in dealing with women. I generously gave myself a 10 percent chance of success, and that was contingent upon her voluntary assistance.

What should I wear? Caitlyn was always on my case about wearing jeans and a T-shirt. She thought I looked better in khakis and a collared shirt. Her rules were almost as stringent as those at a country club. However, right now I didn't have anything formal. Indy was a doctor. What would she expect? The only thing I'd seen her in was hospital scrubs. I looked in my closet and determined that I didn't really have a choice. Levis, very faded, and a T-shirt it would be. At least the shirt didn't have writing on it. Like it or not, world—I mean Indy—here I come.

Four

You've got to be careful if you don't know where you're going, 'cause you might not get there!

—Yogiism #4

"I know it's been some time since I've spent any time with you, and I promise I'll do better. To tell you the truth, you deserved a short vacation. You're not a spring chicken any longer, but you're still a beauty." I patted the plastic dash and continued, "I've missed you, Betsy." I turned the key and the engine started purring like a kitten. It worked every time; all I had to do was sweet-talk her.

I am never late for anything. At least in that one thing, I am predictable. However, being a predictable pitcher is bad and to be avoided at all costs; and that fact by itself almost tempts me to show up late every once in a while. Almost, I say. So I wasn't out of character when I sauntered in the front door of the emergency room at 5:55. The cute, young receptionist at the front desk motioned me over, batted her eyes, and demurely said, "Cord, it's great to see you up and at 'em. Doc Jones said for you to go to the employees' lounge and she would meet you there. But if she's not around . . . I could go on a break for a minute."

Her hospital tag identified her as Alli. She was the right person to have at the front desk if you wanted to draw customers, but then, emergency rooms didn't need to advertise. It seemed like I had gone through this little charade with Alli before, or at least she acted like it. She obviously recognized me, although I couldn't remember ever seeing her before. Losing one's memory certainly has its drawbacks.

I didn't want to sound like a blither-head, but I didn't have a clue where the employees' lounge was. "How do I get there?" I finally managed to ask. I hadn't moved, and I was still staring at her. She must have thought I was making a pass or at least encouraging her.

She flashed me one of those million-dollar smiles and said, "Wow, that little bump on your head must have really affected you." She pointed to her left. "Go down that hall, second door on the left; but if she's not there, let me know."

I finally managed a halting, "Thanks." I knew I was acting stupid and flustered. It wasn't because of her. At least I didn't think it was. I was just a . . . well, maybe . . . like I said, I'm not real smooth with women, and at that moment I was completely flustered and didn't know what else to say. So without saying anything I turned and walked away to try to find the employee lounge. I didn't look back.

Everyone I passed that was dressed in scrubs called me by name and said something about how good it was to see me up and around. It was becoming apparent, even to me, that this was not the first time I had walked these halls or seen these people. I pushed open the door that was labeled "Employee Lounge." Three strangers sitting around a table all greeted me like I was a long lost friend. "Cord, it's good to see you up and around. How's baseball?"

"Umm, thanks, I don't know about baseball right now," I said. I didn't have a clue who they were, and I was too embarrassed to ask their names. "Do you mind if I change the channel to ESPN?" I asked.

"Sure, go ahead; we were just leaving anyway."

I didn't want to get into an extended conversation with people I didn't know, even if they knew me. It just seemed too complicated.

Dick Berman of ESPN started launching into a piece on baseball free agency when the door to the lounge opened and one of the male nurses sitting at the lunch table let out a low wolf whistle. "You sure clean up nice, Dr. Jones." I turned to look, and I'm sure my jaw dropped three inches. I never knew a black sweater and matching pants could look so good. My mind went into spasms. I knew I was staring, but I couldn't help myself. Right on the spot I knew I could have purchased a ring for this vision. She was a walking dream. How . . . why me? It didn't make any sense. I mean, I wasn't in her class, not by a long shot. I tried to clear my head and act normal, whatever normal was.

She tried to fill in some of the leftover airtime for me. "Well, it's nice to see you too, Mr. Calloway." She was teasing me and laughing. She liked my apparent befuddlement.

"Sorry, I was . . . umm." I was finally able to gather my wits about me. "I'm sorry, I was looking for a Dr. Jones—Indiana Jones."

Indy gave me this "not again" look and replied, "Come on, Cord, let's get out of here, and the rest of you slackers go find someone else who actually needs your attention." She was smiling as we walked out. She whispered, "This is going to be the best blind date I have ever been on. I think I might really enjoy myself tonight."

I could sense a touch of Machiavellian humor in her laughter. "Ah, that wouldn't be because you have me at a slight disadvantage, would it?" As I thought about it, I realized she knew all about me: what I liked, my habits, how I acted. But on the other hand, I hadn't even read her book. I knew practically nothing about her, except what Shannon had told me and the fact that she was the best looking doctor I had ever seen.

"You are so right, and I intend to take full advantage of it."

"Don't stay out too late, Dr. Jones," one nurse said teasingly as we walked down the hall.

I looked up just in time to avoid a collision with a guy who was either a doctor or someone impersonating one. It was evident from his glance that I had not made the list on his hit parade. His look changed to sweetness and smiles as he turned his eyes toward Dr. Jones. I didn't know what I had done to make him dislike me.

"Cord, this is Dr. Stewart, one of my associates."

"Glad to meet you, Dr. Stewart." He didn't bother even looking in my direction. I knew right away that this chap was not going to be one of my favorite things.

"Are you sure you'll be all right tonight, Indiana?" he asked.

"Yes, John, I'll be fine. In fact I've been looking forward to this night for some time." I could tell that she didn't like Dr. Stewart's attitude or intrusion into her private life. She was trying to drag me out of the gauntlet without my having to suffer too much damage.

I had only taken a couple of hits before we escaped the hospital. I was glad to be out in the night with Indy by my side. It seemed that everyone I had met loved her except for maybe Alli. And I did take notice it wasn't "Dr. Stewart," it was "John." I wondered what that was all about.

I should make the record clear that although we were alone, Dr. Jones did not reach over to hold my hand or give me a hug or anything similar thereto. She certainly wasn't playing the part of the kissing doctor any longer. She was nice, but she kept one arm's length distance between us at all times. I asked, "Where did you serve your mission?"

"I didn't go on a mission, Cord. Why do you ask?"

"I don't know. I was just wondering." She didn't get my joke. Maybe it was too subtle. Maybe I needed to be more direct. After all, if I had bought a ring for her, we must have at least reached the handholding stage.

"So, where are we going?" I asked. She was leading and I was following.

She replied, "Do you mind if I drive? My car is right here, and I've never trusted Betsy." I was keenly aware that she hadn't answered my question, but I decided to let her make the decisions, as long as it wasn't too expensive.

"How can you talk about Betsy like that?"

"Easy, watch my lips. Last time I got in that piece of junk, you couldn't get it started. You tried to convince me she wouldn't start because she was jealous of me. Your excuses, while cute, can't cover up the fact that it's just a pile of junk, not an unstable woman. Besides, I don't want to get stuck somewhere because of a jealous female." She was teasing, at least I think she was.

"You're a Chuck-A-Rama kind of guy, but do you mind if I choose where we eat?" she asked. I wondered if she also knew I was a limited budget guy.

"Heck no, you choose; but right now I am kind of on a low budget." I hated to admit it out loud. "And as you can see, I didn't dress for the country club."

She laughed; I liked that. "Tonight's on me," she said, "as long as I get to choose." She was teasing me again. I liked that too, even if she had me at a disadvantage, a fact I might be able to turn into my advantage if I played my cards right.

I watched her wrap her arms around herself and found myself wishing I was in them. It was a little chilly.

She pushed the keyless entry button that unlocked the door of a new silver Lexus. I liked how she smoothly slipped into the car and flipped her hair over her shoulder with a slight twist of her head. She glanced over at me, and I noticed for the hundredth time how her eyes seemed to sparkle even in the moonlight. She started the engine and said, "I usually let you drive, but I'm not telling you where we're going until we get there."

"Nice wheels," I said.

"I'm glad you like it since you picked it out for me."

I didn't know whether she was kidding or not. "Dr. Jones . . ."

She interrupted me and said, "Cord, we're on a first name basis. I'm just plain Indy or Indiana, whichever. I am not Dr. Jones, except around the hospital. When I'm not at the hospital, I don't like to be introduced as or called doctor. I don't like to draw attention to the fact that I'm a doctor since it really doesn't matter unless I'm in the hospital, does it?"

"Dressed like that, I don't think anyone will ever consider you to be just plain ol' anything." She was smiling again. I liked that smile. I wondered why she wanted to go out with someone like plain old me. Maybe I really had done something good when I was a kid.

"Thanks, Cord. I'll take that as a compliment. Now, you were saying?"

I needed to get this right, and it took me a minute to work it through in my mind. Finally I said, "Okay, if I ask you a question, will you answer truthfully?"

Her face suddenly took on a somber appearance. "That depends on the question." I noticed that her countenance didn't change. "But just so you know, I don't make it a habit to tell untruths to anyone for any reason." She was apparently very sensitive about some things and didn't take kindly to my questioning her honesty. I tried to get my head back above water.

"I'm sorry, I didn't mean that like it sounded. It's just that you were so evasive the other night; and well, you might say I'm still trying to put my puzzle together. I didn't mean to suggest that you didn't tell the truth." I was trying to get my foot out of my mouth again, and I had the feeling that I was making it worse all of the time.

Her features softened. "No, it's my fault. I overreacted. Go ahead, ask away."

I was about ready to start asking questions when we pulled into the parking lot of the Joseph Smith Building. "You're not taking me on a tour of Temple Square, are you?" I wasn't sure if I wanted to do the church thing tonight, yet I didn't want to sound ungrateful either.

"I'd never take you someplace that you didn't want to go. But then, I've never seen any hot dog stands on Temple Square and I'm famished. Since it's my choice, I'm taking you to my favorite restaurant. It's a buffet and they make the absolutely best desserts on the planet. In fact, they are so good that I always make it a habit to eat my dessert first. You chastised me last time we were here for eating desserts first. You got off on some kick about practicing delayed gratification and how the dessert would be better if I waited because of the anticipation. Do you remember any of that?"

"No, but it sounds really clever, like something I would say." I liked her. Kind of feisty, not afraid to stick up for herself or be herself. Refreshing. She was definitely refreshing.

As we walked into the building, I was tempted to reach out and take her hand, but I wasn't sure of the consequences. Besides, she continued to maintain her arm's length separation, and she kept her hands in her pockets and out of easy reach. It felt comfortable to be around her. I couldn't identify why it felt so, but it did. I tried to compare the feeling I was experiencing with the way I felt when I was around Cate. They were different, but I really couldn't describe why.

I became painfully aware that every guy we walked by made sure he got a good look at Indy. I was sure they weren't looking at me. I wasn't the jealous type, so I couldn't have been jealous; but I noticed.

"Are we going to The Roof?" I asked as we got on the elevator.

"Good guess," she said. "Did you read the sign on the wall, or did your memory cells suddenly spring into action?"

"I think I remember coming here for a high school prom." *The name seems familiar*, I thought as I stood looking at a large advertisement for The Roof pasted on the wall of the elevator.

"You say we've been here before?" I couldn't pull it up on my screen. I couldn't remember being here with Indy.

"Yes."

"Yes? That's all you're going to say?"

"I told you it was my favorite restaurant." Just then the hostess sat us down at a window seat. Indiana was staring out the window at the temple framed in multicolored lights. It seemed she was hypnotized by the view. I turned to look. Everything was lit up with seemingly billions of lights. It was a spectacular view.

She didn't say anything, she didn't have to; I knew how she felt. It was written all over her face.

I finally broke the silence. "I guess desserts aren't the only reason you like to come here."

"Oh, Cord, every time I see the temple, I get this overpowering sensation. It's like a giant magnet trying to draw me to it. One day I'm going inside. It's where I intend to be married."

That answered that question. Even if I had asked her to marry me, she would have said no, because I knew that I wasn't about to be married in the temple. I didn't even go to church. But then I remembered that I had made an appointment with my bishop. Like I said, one plus one doesn't always equal two.

"Okay, Indy." It almost came comfortably off my tongue. "And remember you promised the truth." I tried to lead into my first question as seriously as possible. "Do you really hate baseball?"

She laughed. She had a nice laugh. She wasn't afraid that someone would hear her. Caitlyn always considered propriety first. Indy just reacted to life. It seemed she wasn't confined by propriety. She was natural, refreshing, simple. "Cord, I can truthfully say that I have never been to a real baseball game."

"You mean you don't even know what a 6-4-3 is? Or the difference between a slider and a curve?"

She was quick. "Well, 6-4-3 is probably the combination to your locker at the ballpark. A curve is a pitch thrown by the pitcher, and a slider is when someone slides into home base. How am I doing?"

"Well, you are one and two. Do you know what that means in baseball talk?"

"Since I answered three questions, I must have gotten two wrong and one right, or one wrong and two right."

"Heaven help us," I muttered.

"Well, tell me how I did."

I shook my head. "It's a long story, but here's the short version. Every defensive position in baseball has a number assigned to it. The pitcher is one, the catcher two, first base three, second base four, third base five, shortstop six, and so on. So a 6-4-3 describes a double play in baseball talk. The batter hit a ball to the short stop who threw to second for one out, and second threw to first for the second out. The shortstop and second baseman both got assists, and the second baseman and first baseman both got put-outs."

"My word! How was I supposed to know that?"

"If you've ever watched *SportsCenter*, you would have heard Dick Berman call a 6-4-3 double play. It's the pitcher's dream because he gets two outs on one pitch."

"Okay, so I missed that one. How did I do on the other?"

"Well, a curve is a pitch that the pitcher throws, so you got that one partially right. A correct answer would have been that a true curve breaks straight down or down and out. A slider is also a pitch. It looks like a fastball but breaks sharply away from a right-handed batter if thrown by a right-handed pitcher. If thrown by a left-handed pitcher to a right-handed batter, the ball breaks into the batter."

"Okay, I got one out of three. That's not too bad. But I still think professional sports are the opiate of the masses; you know, a waste of time for those playing, except for kids. It's even worse for those who just watch. It's just an excuse to avoid doing something productive. But if you play this year, I promise I will go see at least one whole game if you are pitching. When you're not pitching, you can sit by me and tell me what's happening, pitch by pitch."

"I think we had better get some food before you pass out from lack of nourishment. You're going to need some help if that's the best you can do answering questions. This could be a long night." I went to the steak and potatoes section, and, true to her word, Indy went for the desserts. We both got back to the table at about the same time. She could hardly wait to taste the cheesecake and had a bite in her mouth before I could say anything. I wanted to get into some of my real questions, and now was about as good a time as any, if she could stop eating cheesecake long enough to answer.

"Let me try an easier question, something not related to

baseball. We, you and me, both know that I have a hole in my memory that I'm trying to fill, bit by bit. Well, you tell me that we have been seeing each other almost every day. My mother tells me you will take care of me, and my sister says you are the best thing that ever happened to me." At this point I was having trouble finding the words that I wanted to use. It didn't come out how I wanted, but I asked, "Just how involved were we?"

"Before I answer that question, I have a question for you, actually two questions: How do you really feel about me? And I mean right now. And while we are being truthful, how do you really feel about Caitlyn?"

Now that was a low blow. I was sucking swamp gas, and I hadn't even gotten out of the batter's box. I remembered that I had tried to get her to promise to answer my questions truthfully, but she hadn't elicited the same promise from me. How could I tell her the truth about my feelings for Cate and my newly emerging feelings for her? It wasn't a fair question. I concentrated on eating, although it was an effort to continue. Neither of us said anything for what seemed like forever, and I didn't dare look into her eyes.

"That really wasn't a fair question. Let me pose a hypothetical set of facts. Suppose I tell you that it is true; we were seriously involved. And also suppose, for argument sakes, that I knew about your prior involvement with Caitlyn, which you remember. Now let's say you never get your memory back so you have to determine how you feel based upon what I told you versus what you feel. Could you abandon your feelings for her based solely upon what I told you?

"My second hypothetical is similar. Suppose you elect to pursue Caitlyn because that is all you can remember, and then, out of the blue, your memory comes back and you discover you were in love with me. What do you do then? And what do I do in the meantime?"

I thought about what she had said; it was a conundrum. Neither situation had an answer, and yet both situations could possibly happen. Of course, there were a couple other scenarios: I could forget Cate and later remember that I had in fact been in love with Indy, or I could find out I had never really loved Indy. And that brought me back to the start. I had gone full circle and was none the wiser. I was perplexed and said, "It sounds like a Catch-22, no matter what I do."

Indy replied, "That's exactly how I feel. No matter how I answer your first question, and not the one about baseball, I am in exactly the same position. And for that matter, if I refuse to answer, we are still in the same position. Neither of us knows which way to turn or, in this case, what to say or do."

"So you're telling me there isn't a satisfactory solution to my problem."

"That depends if your memory returns and when."

I took a deep breath. I wasn't going to get an answer to that question, but that didn't mean that I couldn't try to fill in some other blank spots. "Okay, Indy, for now you're off the hook on that question. I withdraw the question, but let me ask you this. My sister, Shannon, said she thinks that I had been going to church with you. Is that true?"

"Yes and no."

"Can I ever get a straight answer from you?"

"You can if you ask the right question." Then she went on, "You started going to church with me, and then you started going to your home ward, with and without me. I would say that before you landed in the hospital, you hadn't missed a meeting for almost two months."

I thought about her response. I didn't feel like eating but dabbed at my food. Indy wasn't slowing down. Maybe the impact, the reality of our situation, was sinking in. I wondered about church. Why? What happened? Indy left to get her main course. I had never seen a girl eat as much as she did. After she returned to the table, I continued.

"Why?"

"Why what?"

"Why did I start going back to church? Was it because of you?"

"I'm not sure if I can take all of the credit or the blame for that matter. But I will admit that I invited you to church on more than one occasion."

"How serious did I get with the Church—and don't tell me that it's another Catch-22 question."

"I think that would be a better question for your bishop. You became fairly close to him, but my best answer is that I believe you unburied your testimony."

I wasn't sure that I wanted to find out any more information about church; you know, commitments and that kind of stuff. "Shannon also told me that you are a convert to the Church. How did that happen?" It was time to shift the focus of this conversation away from me.

"It's kind of a long story. Do you really want to hear it?"

"I sure do."

"Okay, but only the abbreviated version. For starters, my family was a mess. We lived near the beach in Venice, California. My parents divorced when I was fourteen. I chose to live with my father for a number of reasons. The main one was that he needed someone to take care of him. My mother figured that I chose him over her, but then, she didn't much like me anyway. At that time in her life she was into her own life and new boyfriends. Even so, my choice to live with my dad did not help the relationship with my mother. In fact, she still hasn't forgiven me.

"My father was an alcoholic, and, worse, he got into drugs. He would go on binges, and I would have to help him get through them. I couldn't do very much, but at least I was there for him.

"I lived with my dad for over two years. As time went on, I was missing more days of school than I was attending. I was into myself and having fun, and I had found a part-time job. I had to lie about my age to get the job. It was about that time that my father died. That really messed me up. I stopped going to school and they got tired of having me around—the school that is—so I got the boot. I didn't even graduate from high school. I did take the GED and passed. I was always a good test taker.

"I couldn't go back to live with my mother; she wouldn't

have me. And I probably wouldn't have gone anyway, so I was on my own. Eventually I found a full-time job and some friends to live with and started supporting myself. My life was a mess. I was a mess. And, no, I won't go into any further details about that time in my life.

"My boss took a liking to me. I later found out he was the bishop of his ward in the San Fernando Valley. Anyway, he started talking to me every day about life: where we came from, why we're here, and where we're going. I had never really thought about those questions. To make a long story short, he talked me into going to church, one time. He said to try it just 'once.' "

"My first attempt wasn't very good since I only made it to the parking lot. I wanted to go in but couldn't and drove away. It didn't seem to matter to him because he invited me to his home to meet the missionaries the next week.

"I had gone to four lessons before they talked me into trying church again. This time I promised to go to my home ward. When Sunday came, I almost backed out again. I got to the parking lot, but I knew I wouldn't know a soul. Besides, I couldn't remember ever being inside a church. The missionaries walked out of the door, looking for me, I was sure. So I got out of the car. They saw me and I knew I was toast.

"I couldn't believe it, but the first person I saw inside was a girl from my high school. We weren't friends; we walked on different sides of the street in high school. When she recognized me, she got a big smile and walked over to me and said, 'Indiana, I didn't know you were a member of the LDS Church.' Looking back and remembering that she knew me while I was in high school, I couldn't imagine how she could be so friendly. Anyway, I told her that I wasn't a member of any church but that I had just begun to investigate the Mormon Church.

"She was wonderful. She treated me like I was someone special, like I was her friend. Then she took me into the chapel and introduced me to the bishop. He shook my hand and talked to me for a minute. Then she introduced me to several other people whom she called 'brother' and 'sister.' They didn't look like her brother or sister, but what did I know. Then she showed me where to sit and stayed with me during the whole meeting. The elders sat on the other side of me.

"I can't begin to explain how I felt that day, Cord. It started with the first song they sang; the song was for me. I knew it. My whole body tingled. It was wonderful. The prayers that were offered and the talks that were given all seemed to answer questions I had, as if they had been prepared specifically for me. By the time the meeting was over, I was hooked. They later called me 'golden.' When the meeting ended, I just sat there enjoying the whole experience. The next thing I knew, the bishop came up behind me and asked me to come into his office to have a little chat.

"It wasn't long before I made my second mistake," she joked. She was having fun telling her story. "The first was when I agreed to talk to him. When we got into his office, he told me that he felt it was important he should talk to me. I don't know how it happened, but I ended up telling him everything I had done wrong in my entire life. After that, he gave me a blessing, and we talked for almost an hour. When I left there, I had a recommend to be baptized. I walked out of that church that day feeling like I was important to God and that he cared about me. No . . . I knew that day that God loved me.

"Well, I was baptized one week later. I haven't missed a day of church since. Those people in my ward took me in and loved me. I found an apartment in the basement of a member's house for almost no rent. My boss encouraged me to go to college. He showed me how to get financial aid. I started at the community college. Like I said, I have always been a good test taker, and I started getting really good grades. Two years later I was admitted to UCLA on a full scholarship. I graduated in the top of my class and got a full scholarship to the University of Utah Medical School.

"It was very hard for me to leave my ward. The ward members had become almost like the family I never had. I owe my life to those people. It was because of them that I was able to crawl out of the gutter and make a good life for myself. I will never be able to repay them for what they did; but you know, they don't want to be paid back. They really love me. If I don't become the best person I can be, then I will not only be letting myself down, but them as well. I could never do that. But more important, I discovered Jesus Christ. I love him with all of my heart."

She had wiped her eyes several times during the telling of her story. She seemed to be as good a person on the inside as she looked on the outside. The light she carried radiated at that moment. I was beginning to understand why everyone loved her. They wanted what she had. I could see why Shannon loved her. Suddenly I understood why everyone at the hospital was drawn to her and thought she was their best friend. She was. Still, John, I mean Dr. Stewart, seemed a little too friendly.

"Did you ever consider going into sales?"

"What?"

I was falling under her spell and had to take a breather. "Which dessert was the best?" I asked.

"The bread pudding is out of this world, and the cheesecakes are the best I've ever had."

I had to escape her light for a minute. It was so intense, but it felt good. At times while she was talking, chills ran up and down my spine. It was a feeling I couldn't remember having before. Whatever she was, she was a survivor. She had literally walked out of hell and climbed step by step, all by herself, through college and medical school. I'll bet she could even throw a ninety-five-mile-an-hour fastball if she tried.

I didn't ask any more serious questions during dinner; I tried just to enjoy her company. Besides, I was afraid of the answers I might get. I didn't see her pay the bill. When I asked the waiter for the check, he told me it had already been taken care of. She hadn't made a big deal about the bill. She had intentionally done it quietly so as not to embarrass me.

As we left the restaurant, she said, "Will you walk with me through Temple Square?"

There was no way I could refuse her anything at that

moment. Besides, it didn't seem like such a bad idea as it had a few hours earlier. "Sure," I said, "I haven't walked through the temple grounds for years; and besides, after a meal like that, I could use a little exercise."

We walked and talked. Temple Square was enchanting. I couldn't believe that I hadn't come to see the Christmas lights before. I wasn't sure why I felt so good. Maybe that too was because of her. She was something else.

We both kept the conversation light and on the surface. I was afraid to ask any serious questions. I had already tried that once, and I didn't get out of the batter's box. As we stood in front of the Christus, I felt as if he were really looking right into my very soul. I couldn't talk. I had this huge lump in my throat. I couldn't remember ever feeling the reality of Christ as I felt at that moment. More out of reaction than anything else, I reached over and grasped Indy's hand. She didn't pull it away. After a minute she said, "Maybe we should go. I've got an early schedule tomorrow." The intimacy of just holding hands had disturbed her.

I wasn't sure that I wanted to go already, but she started walking toward the Joseph Smith Building, so I hurried to catch up. I wanted to walk by her side. I didn't want tonight to end so soon. But she had the keys to the car. Maybe I shouldn't have held her hand, because it was about that time that she had suddenly become anxious and distant. Driving back to the hospital, neither of us said anything. I could feel the tension in the air. She didn't look my way but stared straight ahead. She was beautiful but looked melancholy. I wanted to get back to where we had been before she froze over.

Finally I said, still not looking at her, "I had a call from a Bishop Swenson. He said that I missed an appointment with him a few days ago. It was while I was in the hospital. Do you have any idea what that is all about?"

"No, Cord. I never knew that you had a specific appointment with Bishop Swenson. Although you've become pretty good friends with him." It felt like she wanted to say more but didn't.

As we pulled into the hospital parking lot, I said, "Drop me off over there at the curb. I don't want Betsy to see me in a new Lexus. She does have that jealous streak, and I need her to get me home tonight." She didn't laugh, but a slight smile touched her lips.

I had coaxed her cell phone number out of her earlier in the evening. I told her that I would call her in the morning. She told me she would look forward to my call, and I think she meant it. We didnt get back to talking about the depth to which our relationship had progressed or, for that matter, my relationship with Caitlyn. There were many questions I wanted to ask but couldn't or didn't dare. She likewise let the subject die.

I felt a loss when I walked to Betsy. I was trying to sort out the rush of mixed feelings. I liked Indy, yet she unsettled me. I wanted to hold her. But what about Caitlyn? I still couldn't stop thinking about her. She dumped me, but she did come back—all the way to Salt Lake—if only for a day. I didn't know what to do or what to think; and worse, I didn't know if I could even trust my feelings.

When I got in Betsy, I found my cell phone and discovered that I had two calls from my mother and two hang up calls. The hang up calls were out of area. Maybe it was my agent or the Royals, or maybe it was Caitlyn.

Five

I really didn't say everything I said!

—Yogiism #5

I did a lot of soul searching on my drive home that night. I admit that sometimes I'm slow, but I keep gnawing on it like a dog with a good bone. Indy was something special, a real lady, yet I couldn't just dismiss my feelings about Caitlyn. I knew that.

But there was something about Indy.

It was more than her good looks, more than being nice. There was a feeling like when I know I can strike the guy out with a high fastball. With a hitter I understood why I sometimes had that feeling, but with Indy I didn't know why, I just did. Dang! If I could only remember. But what if I could? Would that mean that feelings come from memory and not the heart? Are heart feelings really nothing but memory? I decided it was the old chicken or egg riddle. Which came first? Regardless, I believed if I could remember my life for the last three months, it would make a difference.

I intentionally neglected to talk to Betsy about my problem involving Indy and Cate. Instead I told Betsy she did well, patted her dashboard, and went into the house. I went straight to my computer. I wasn't sure why I hadn't looked at my email yet. I hoped there was a message from Cate since I didn't have any other way to contact her. My computer was one of those old laptops and took forever to boot up.

Eventually I made it to my email. There were seven messages. I scanned through my in-box: four were junk that I deleted, two were from my mother. I'd look at them some other time. Bingo! The last one was from Caitlyn. It was like finally receiving my acceptance or rejection letter from Harvard. Of course, I had never been smart enough to apply to Harvard, but you get the idea. Anxiety as well as fear took control. So much rested on this message. My finger was poised on the mouse, yet I hesitated to open the email. I sat there and stared at the screen. Sometimes I fear I am not a man of action.

Finally, out of desperation and the feeling of acting like a sixth grader opening a note from a girl, I opened the email. I felt my heart beating a little harder and my hands got clammy. It took forever to pop up.

> *Cord, I'm sorry about everything that happened. I know I should have told you I was coming to visit. But I wanted my visit to be a surprise. Well, guess it did turn out to be a major surprise—to us both. I guess I shouldn't have been surprised you were dating someone. I had no reason to be. Anyway, I started a new job. I am a beat writer for the* Wilmington Star. *Attached is my first article that was printed in the paper. Believe it or not, I got the job without my family's "assistance," as you would call it. This will be the first money I have ever earned on my own. Cate*

She had apparently come clear to Salt Lake to see me. She must have wanted to try to patch things up. Then she had probably believed that I had found someone else when she saw Indy at my house and then run away, assuming facts not in evidence. She didn't sign off "Love, Cate" like she usually did. I figured the email was her way of trying to open the door again, even if just a crack. Maybe she was trying to open lines of communication. But what about her parents? Contacting me would definitely be going contrary to their wishes. Maybe she had grown a backbone. Then, as if my thoughts didn't need permission to interrupt, one with flashing lights reminded me, What about Indy?

I sank back in my seat, wondering what happened to my quiet life where all I had to worry about was how I was going to get the next batter out. Questions, unanswered questions, continued to haunt my waking hours. I looked at the date of Cate's message: December sixth, five days ago. I should have looked at my email earlier. There hadn't been a subsequent message. My lack of response surely didn't demonstrate a flaming hot level of interest. But she wouldn't have known about my accident. Maybe I could use it to help dig myself out of this black hole. And if I did get back to zero, what could I do for an encore? The return of my memory seemed to be a key factor to my life; but return or not, whatever decision I made was going to hurt someone, and I would most likely be the villain.

The fact that Cate had emailed me said a lot. Maybe her family influence was waning. She had taken a job at a paper, which I was sure was against her father's wishes. He could never see his "Princeton daughter" as a cub reporter, even if it meant she had a chance of running into Clark Kent. I was also sure that her father had threatened to cut her unlimited allowance if she continued to pursue a relationship with me. Yet, in spite of her father and his threats, she had come to see me, and now she was trying to contact me again.

Maybe she had finally decided that she wanted to chase her own star, maybe even her own baseball star if she had come clear to Salt Lake to see me. I knew she had wanted to be a reporter since her graduation from Princeton over a year ago. Her father was dead set against it. He might have consented if she worked at *The New York Times* but never for the *Wilmington Star*. I liked her spunk. If she was game to step into the batter's box again, then so was I. After all, I was a good catch—just not a rich one. I clicked on the "reply" button.

Cate,

I don't know where to start since I don't know where we ended. I miss you so much. Let me explain. I had this accident on my bike. I'm okay. Don't worry about me, but I hit my head and somehow it affected my memory. They call it retrograde amnesia. What that means is that there is a period of time of which I have no memory. I can't remember anything that happened between September and December. I can't remember you visiting Salt Lake, although I had heard you did. The last thing I can remember is the day before I left Wilmington, the day you told me it would be better if you didn't see me again.

Cate, I love you . . . I think I always will. I tried to call you the other day, but your cell phone number has been changed. I miss you. I want to see you. I want to talk to you . . . but, Cate, I can't change what I am or what I want to be, not even for your father. I don't have a contract with the Royals so far this year, but I believe they are going to invite me to spring training. I could be reassigned to the Blue Rocks in Wilmington. If I don't get invited or make the team, I think I am going to look into coaching high school baseball.

Call me sometime or let me know your new phone number.

Love, Cord

I read and reread my message. I changed it and rewrote it. I wanted her to know I cared about her; yet, I wanted her to know that I was me and not someone with a lot of money or the likelihood of ever having a lot of money. I came from the wrong side of the tracks in a far off place called Utah. And, yes, I was a Mormon by birth and a baseball player by choice. My chosen life vocation was a high school baseball coach, maybe eventually a college coach.

My thoughts turned to Coach Jones, my high school

pitching coach. I didn't have a father while I was in high school. I struggled in school and was about to drop out permanently. I was a sophomore trying out for the high school team and was not doing very well. I was dejected and ready to quit. After the second day of tryouts, he asked me to stick around for a while. After everyone had gone, he moved a screen behind the plate in the bull pen and wound a rope through the netting, forming a strike zone. He still hadn't said anything. Coach Jones had just been released from professional ball; he was a pitcher. He took a bucket of balls up to the mound and motioned for me to stand by his side.

He removed his jacket, stretched, and said, "Inside bottom corner." He wound up and let the ball fly. It smacked the screen right in the lower inside corner.

"Outside lower corner," he said. Thump! The ball hit the exact spot he had designated. He threw about ten more pitches, each time telling me where it was going to hit. I was impressed. Then he said, "Take off your jacket and throw a few."

It took me a few throws to get warm. Then he said, "Inside lower corner." Before I could start my wind-up, he talked to me in a soft, slow voice. "Concentrate on the spot where the rope makes a corner. Bore into it with your eyes. See the individual twine forming the rope. Concentrate like nothing else in the world matters except that corner, and then reach out in your delivery and try to put the fingers of your throwing hand right in that spot." I missed badly with the first two. After each throw he quietly said, "Good, now continue focusing on that spot. Do not be distracted. Blank everything else out of your mind." He was trying to build my confidence. The next ball I threw smacked right in the corner. I beamed. I felt good; maybe I could be as good as he thought.

He had me throw for another half hour. He encouraged and prompted me all the while in that same positive, low voice. I started getting the hang of it. Then he said something I'll never forget. "Calloway, I've watched you throw. By the time you're a senior—no, a junior—you could be the best pitcher on this team.

But you have to decide that in here." And he pointed to his heart. "You have to believe that no one can get a hit off of you. It's all up to you."

Coach Jones spent time with me every day after practice, talking to me as I threw. He made me a good pitcher because he cared. It was because of him that my grades improved. He wouldn't tolerate a lazy player or a worthless student. He changed my life. It was because of him that I got a scholarship to play at BYU. I wanted to be like him. I wanted to turn kids' lives around. I knew I could because I had learned you could do anything you wanted if you believed in your heart that you could.

That's why money wasn't a priority in life; people were. Particularly kids that were struggling and who needed someone. I had been there, and someone had cared enough to rescue me. I knew I could make a difference. I now knew that I had been preparing since that first day with Coach Jones to become a coach. That's why being a coach means so much to me regardless of the amount of money I earn.

There was no sense in trying to revive a relationship with Caitlyn if it was just going to die of natural causes or from social economic issues in the near future anyway. She knew that baseball mattered to me, but she also knew that my family would come before baseball. I hadn't had a father during the critical part of my life, and I knew how hard that had been on me. My family, my kids and wife, were going to take top priority. Cate knew of that commitment. I thought back and remembered how hard it had been when we broke up, and I didn't want to go there again. I wanted her to have a full disclosure, to know what she would be signing on for, before she decided.

But I wondered, there was still Indy. How did she fit into the big picture? Was I just leading Cate on? I pushed send and held by breath.

♦ ♦ ♦

I didn't wake up until noon the next day—old habits die hard I guess. I might add that I didn't wake up of my own volition; it was the ringing of the phone. I fumbled with the receiver until I finally got the mouthpiece close to my mouth and mumbled a weak "hello."

"Cord, is that you? I didn't wake you, did I?"

"No, I was just getting up, but my voice hasn't realized that yet."

"Do you want me to call back when you're fully functional?"

"No, Shannon, sleeping in is one of those old baseball habits I thought I had overcome. I guess some habits die hard."

Shannon wanted to know how I was doing, if my memory was still the same, and how my date had gone with Indy. It was obvious that she liked Indy and that she wanted me to like Indy. I tried to explain to her that Indy was great but that I still had strong feelings for Cate. She explained to me that a lot of things had changed in the last three months and that as far as she was concerned, the Cate thing was history.

I heard what she said. I understood what she had told me. It was just that my brain was sending two contrary messages—or was it my heart? Maybe I was just confused.

When I finished talking to Shannon, I sat on the edge of my bed, thinking of my life and how far it was from anything normal. I remembered my first few years of professional ball. Yeah, I had been caught up with being someone important. All I could think about was pitching in the major leagues, carrying money to the bank in wheelbarrows, and basking in fame and glory.

Being a baseball player, a pretty good one at that, had impacted me as a person. As a matter of fact, baseball, in part, had shaped a large part of my personality and my habits, like it or not. I'm not suggesting that it made me a better person by any stretch; in fact, quite the contrary is probably true. It was hard, but I broke many of those attitudes and old habits several years ago. Although I have to admit, I do like to sleep; and waking up in the morning is not one of my favorite things.

Most professional athletes are superstars from the time they are just little kids. Great athletes are usually born and seem to rise to the top early in life. That means they get a stilted view of life, always believing they are someone special. They are usually revered by all of their peers and sought after by all of the coaches. Superleague teams start courting kids at the age of seven or eight. They are always the first ones taken when a team is picked. People treat them differently, and the older they get, the greater the attention.

In high school they get help with homework, and sometimes someone else does it for them. Friends and coaches drive them places, buy them things, just so they can be around them. Association with the stars seems to elevate their status. It's pure hero worship, and it starts early in life. The reality of the situation is that it gets more ridiculous the higher up the ladder one goes. Athletes come to expect favors from those labeled as friends. Now, I'm not suggesting that I am like that now, and I hate to think I was ever that way, but I'm afraid I did posses those tendencies. It's hard to avoid believing in your own superiority when you are a talented athlete.

In many ways minor league baseball players, except the bonus babies, receive a rude awakening to the reality of life. Their elite status comes to an abrupt end as soon as they sign the contract. It didn't affect me as much because I had never been a superstar. I was always just barely good enough to make it as far as I did. I kept winning even though no one believed I could. I took the fall to earth a lot earlier in life, so it didn't affect me as much as it did others. Besides, I knew I could be replaced at the drop of a hat. It put a whole new perspective on my life. I came to learn that baseball management did not indulge themselves in the same hero worship syndrome that I had grown accustomed to.

Some guys never get over it. Some drop out of professional ball and play in semi-pro ball where they can dominate and once again find stardom and hero worship.

I thought back over my years since college. The central focus had always been baseball. From March through September as a minor league player, I lived out of my suitcase, and I didn't take a big one. I was paid on a monthly basis, nine hundred dollars a month in rookie ball. It jumped to a whopping $2,100 when I made the AA roster. And out of my earnings I had to pay for my own board and room, except while traveling, and then I was given a per diem, which was enough to get me two meals a day at the golden arches. More significantly, I was only paid during baseball season, which didn't include the month of spring training.

During the off season I had to worry about getting myself ready for the upcoming season. That meant that I had to put my personal practice time ahead of work. Of course, if I wanted to continue eating and having a roof over my head, I had to find a job; and oh, by the way, the job had to end when baseball called. So whatever job I found I had to tell the employer I would be leaving in February. Those jobs were hard to find and usually didn't pay anything but minimum wage.

I usually tried to save a few bucks during the season and then hang on during the off season. I never made it. In case you haven't figured it out, minor league baseball players are not rich, and they never will be. The only way to make money in baseball is to make it to The Show—the big leagues—or to sign on as a bonus baby. Usually minor league players are financed by parents or working wives. They cannot survive on their own. So in reality, it's either The Show or nothing at all.

I also discovered that baseball has a caste system. The elite status is reserved for the high draft picks and those who signed for big bucks. Those guys can fail a hundred times and still be treated like royalty. They have been given the title of "prospect." Those guys are going to continue to climb the minor league ladder regardless of performance because the club has invested money and pride in them. The pride I'm speaking of is the "infallible" judgment of the scouts of the organization. The key to their job is to recognize talent when they see it and to never be proven to be a bad judge of talent. So they continue to push their prospects out of pride and money because bird dog scouts don't get paid unless their prospects make it to The Show. So keeping their player around is very important for their status and pocketbook.

Now, you might ask why I am telling you this seemingly

useless information. I guess it's so you will be able to understand why I do some of the stupid things I do. It's also important to understand how players, namely me, are treated by the organization. If a scout signs you, then he is always there to push you and stick up for you. If you are a free agent, like I am, then there is no one to cover your backside, and you are an easy release unless your name is Roger Clemens.

The lower caste, of which I am a member, is made up of those who will do almost anything to continue to live the dream, including earning salaries lower than the minimum wage. We in the lower caste live in the shadow of "the prospects." I lived from game to game knowing that one bad performance could be my last. Even good outings were simply excused by the scouts as, "He's a good A-ball player, but he isn't a prospect." I had learned to live in the lower class, but I did not accept that designation.

Before I played professional baseball, I considered myself an early riser. After one year of pro baseball, I acquired the habit of sleeping late. I fell in with the crowd. But in my second year, I decided that I needed to be different. I started getting up earlier. I worked hard; I was the first person to practice and the last to leave. I started keeping a notebook filled with coaching techniques. I became an avid reader. I read everything about baseball that I could find. I loved the game and all its intricacies.

I learned to see life from the other side. I learned what it means to be "big leagued" by a superstar hero who asks you to dinner but makes sure that you pay the tab. I wondered how many times I had "big leagued" friends and family over the years. It was a hard adjustment because for most of my life I had been on the other side of the fence where people always wanted to be with me and sometimes even pay for my dinner.

In the lower minor leagues, host families enable the lower caste to survive. Host families are usually provided for rookie and A-league players. A host family is a family who volunteers to let a minor league player live in their home during the season. While we were in Wilmington, a Dr. Gromwell took in five players every year. Somehow I was included in the five when I first went to Wilmington. His family liked having ball players around and associating with their kids. They lived on a huge estate. They were unbelievable to us. They fed us and even took us on overnight outings when we had days off.

I got extremely close to them. They liked me because I took such an interest in their kids. You could always find me outside playing catch with them or engaged in a game of whiffle ball. I even played hide and seek with them. I could always count on being dragged out of bed by the kids to go play. I don't know why, but kids always love me. Maybe it's because I still act like a kid. Whatever it is, I like them and they like me.

It turned out that Caitlyn Belford's family lived next door to the Gromwells, which is how I met Cate. I'm sure that the Belfords were not really happy with the Gromwells for bringing, let's say, a non-pedigreed individual into the neighborhood. But I digress.

I had league games almost every day from March first through mid-September. My games are usually over by ten thirty in the evening. By the time I ate and got home, it was usually after midnight. Consequently, I nurtured the "baseball" habit of sleeping late. That first year of pro ball I wasted my time like the other players. I usually got in a couple of hours of X-box and lunch before I had to get ready to go back to the ballpark for practice, which started at two. Even though I was a pitcher, I had to be to practice the same as everyone else, and I had to stay at the park until the game ended at night, whether I pitched or not. The next day I had to do the same thing all over again. However, after that first year, I had decided that I was going to do things differently.

I really didn't impose on my host family very much. Their house was mostly a place to eat and sleep that first year; besides, half of the season I was on the road traveling and not at their home. My schedule didn't allow me to do much except practice or play ball, but there seemed to be a lot of dead time in which I learned to play every video game created.

Sadly to say, I learned that I couldn't market my X-box skills.

I did not use my downtime wisely during that first year. I just put my life on cruise control, believing that one day I would be playing in the Bigs and would never have to worry about money, school, and the menial life tasks that are attended to by the rest of humanity, including a day job. In short, I became a slob—but a nice one. But I figured it out after that first year, and I spent a lot of time refining my coaching books. Every time I found a new drill or idea I hadn't heard before, I made note of it. I knew that one day baseball would be over for me, at least playing, and I wanted to be ready to coach the day I couldn't play any longer. I wanted to be a good coach. I gathered ideas from every coach and player I knew. I realized that different things work for different people and that not everyone is the same in this game. I learned not only the technical side of the game but also the mental side.

I remember how in the beginning I always thought I was special because I could throw a baseball sixty feet six inches, the distance from the mound to home plate, better than most others. However, it was a rude awakening when I learned that that talent didn't matter to employers off of the ball field; they wanted me to have a college degree and to work eight hours a day.

♦ ♦ ♦

I had dreamed the dream for years. It was always the same: pitching for the Red Sox in the World Series. It was hard to put away the dream and to think about returning to reality and working eight hours a day at a job. I also realized that I would most likely never be rich and famous, but there was still that chance. I knew that decision time was rapidly approaching. If I didn't make it soon, I needed to get on with life and find a job coaching baseball. I knew the impact my high school coach had on my life and I wanted to be that person, if I didn't make it as a player. I wanted to have an impact on kids and their lives.

I knew that I had been a slacker in a lot of ways, but in other ways I had been preparing myself for life after baseball. And that brought me back to my situation today. I decided to check my email before I showered or brushed my teeth, even though I didn't think my pen pals would be able to tell. I staggered to my computer hoping there would be something from Cate. Finally the sign popped up, "No new messages." Bummer.

Next I called the Royals's minor league pitching coordinator. I have this thing about swallowing pain and misery at the same time. You never take a handful of pills one at a time. Get it over with is my motto. If it's going to hurt, get it over in one shot. Sure enough, I got to hear a rerun of the message I heard yesterday. Either he wasn't answering my calls or he had taken off until after the holidays. Then I realized that Christmas was on its way.

Next I dialed my agent. I at least wanted him to know that I was still alive. His message hadn't changed either. I was taking a lot of swings, but I wasn't getting any hits. The problem was that nobody cared about my situation; nobody, that is, but me. Indy was probably saving lives; and Cate, well, who knows.

It was time to be doing something for at least the part of the day that remained, so Shannon had said. Half an hour later I checked my email again—nothing. Since I was out of fun things to do, I decided to call Indy. I didn't mean that like it sounded; I mean, she wasn't my last choice. I just didn't want to lead her on, especially if Cate was still in the picture. But I decided I couldn't lead someone on if I couldn't get closer than arm's length.

I also knew that I had to find someone to get out and throw with, and I needed a place. Spring training was approaching, and I needed to start getting ready if and when I got the call to go. Burt, a high school teammate, had volunteered to catch for me anytime. I could call him. Maybe I could talk the coach into letting me use the gym at the community college. It had been a while since I had thrown, and my arm was itchin' to air out. I reached Burt at work, but he couldn't go until the next day. Bummer.

I was back to doing nothing. I pushed the green button on my cell phone and waited. "Hi. This is Dr. Jones. I can't get to the phone right now, but if you will leave a message, I will call you back." After the beep I said, "Indy, this is Cord. I . . . umm . . . well . . . are you doing anything this afternoon or evening? If not, give me a call. Maybe we can indulge in some more memory therapy. And we need to get past that second date, so . . . "

♦ ♦ ♦

My normally clean house was super clean since I had so much time on my hands. I decided to do my Dr. Job exercises. They were designed to strengthen the small muscles around my rotator cuff so as to avoid shoulder injury. After that I did some towel drills to hone my pitching mechanics. I try to do them every day. They help me get full extension in my delivery, which increases the velocity on my fastball, and I needed any increase in velocity I could get. To be a prospect, a pitcher had to throw at least ninety-two miles per hour or be a lefty. Mostly they clocked me in the high eighties, although I hit ninety miles an hour at least once a game.

I just physically couldn't throw the ball ninety-two miles per hour. I am not a power pitcher. I am a pitcher's pitcher. That means I can locate the ball and throw it for strikes whether it is a fastball, curve, or change. I never walk people, and batters hit a lot of ground balls off of me because my ball has a lot of natural downward movement. Downward movement means a batter sees the ball in one spot, but before he hits it, it has dropped, which causes him to hit it on the ground. Ground balls are good because they are usually outs and result in a lot of double plays. I thought of all of these things as I did my exercises. I knew I had the stuff to pitch in the Bigs. My problem was convincing management and all of the scouts who thought I would be lucky to make AA to the contrary.

I had just finished my exercises when my cell phone rang. It was Indy. I was glad she called back. It sure beat the heck out of exercising.

"I was beginning to worry about you, Cord, when you hadn't called. Are you okay?"

"Except for that memory thing, I'm fine. I had to take care of some things earlier today. Are you free later?"

"I am. What do you have in mind?"

"You just be ready at five o'clock. I'll pick you up at your house. Dress warm, like in your ski outfit."

"Do you want to tell me where we're going?"

"No, turnabout is fair play. It's a surprise, but they don't have any desserts where we're going."

"Okay! I'll bring one."

"I was just kidding."

"I'll be ready. Wait, do you remember where I live?"

"I don't have a clue." She told me her address, and I reminded her I would be there on time.

I got to Indy's at 4:55 and rang the doorbell. She was ready. Cate was never ready. I always had to wait for her. I thought it was a female thing designed to teach men patience or just to let us know they would go when they were ready and not before. It must be a control issue; women learn it from birth, if not before. Maybe Indy was different. As we walked out to the truck, I said, "Now say something nice to Betsy when you get in and we'll be okay."

"Really, Cord, it's just a truck, an old beat up piece of junk at that."

"She's more like a woman than a truck. You have to treat her right or she'll just up and quit on me. Now be nice."

"What if I tell her we're not just friends but that we're dating?"

"She could have a problem with that. Let's keep it a secret between you and me. Okay?"

Betsy started right up, and we headed up Big Cottonwood Canyon. Indy asked, "So where are we going, Cord?"

"Just wait. We're getting close." Then I started to tease her again. "The other night I tried to explain to you about delayed gratification. It's the anticipation that makes it all the better." She looked at me like I was nuts.

It was easy to talk to her. Of course, I didn't ask any serious questions, and that made it a lot easier. She was so full of life and energy that it just spilled out. She was not gushy but sincere, committed, serious; she was alive. I was beginning to understand why I had spent so much time with her. I pulled over and stopped near Tanner Flats. We bundled up and got out of the car.

It was purple time, that beautiful time in the mountains just before sunset when everything is tinged in pink and purple hues. We both looked at the creek. The water was bubbling, rather than running, between and around ice formations that were scattered along the rocks and trees in the stream bed. Snow had recently fallen and covered many of the ice formations. In part it was the random irregular location of the snowcapped rocks in the stream that made the scene so spectacular. Although the stream was not as well lit as Temple Square, it was just as beautiful, but in a different way.

I threw Indy a pair of fur-lined boots. I had snowshoes in the back, and I strapped them onto her boots. "Have you ever been snowshoeing?" I asked.

"I haven't. There wasn't a lot of snow in Southern California. But I'm game to try."

"It's easy. All you have to do is walk. But in the deep snow, walking gets a little more difficult. At times it's even real exercise. If you need to stop anytime for a rest, just let me know, okay?"

"I'll be okay. But if I need any help, the only number that I have is Ghostbusters."

"Hey, this is different than the trail up to Dog Lake. Trust me. I've been on snowshoes more times than you can count."

The temperature was in the twenties and dropping, but I knew once we started walking through the snow, we would warm up fast. Snowshoeing is hard work in deep snow. I gave her a pair of poles, put on my backpack, and off we went.

I explained where we were going. "About a mile up this path the stream falls through a hole in the rock. They call it Donut Falls. It's especially beautiful in the winter." I went on trying to be in charge and under control. "Now, I usually don't stop once I get started on the trail, but if you get tired, just let me know and we'll take a rest. I'll lead and break the path. It will be a lot easier if you follow in my tracks." I was feeling real macho. I knew I wouldn't have to watch her from the back side this time.

We started up the trail. I was surprised at how fast I got tired. In fact, I had trouble talking and breathing at the same time. She, however, was talking a mile a minute while we were walking; and I didn't hear her gasping for breath like I was. I grunted or mumbled when necessary; but other than that, I became Silent Sam. Finally she said, "Cord, let me go ahead for a while. You've been doing all the work."

I wasn't in any condition to argue because I was having trouble just breathing. I asked, "Are you sure you don't need to take a short rest?" Actually my pride had just taken another serious blow. She wasn't even breathing hard, and she was carrying on a one-sided conversation at the same time.

I think she felt sorry for me. "Let's take a short break and catch our breath. Besides, it will give us a chance to look around. I can't believe the beautiful snow formations silhouetted in purple." I knew she had suggested the rest for my benefit. She could have given me a hard time for trying to be so macho, but she didn't.

We rested for about five minutes and she continued to talk. I worked quietly on restoring my breathing to normal. Finally she said, "You ready to go? I'll take the lead. It can't be much farther, and you've done all the work so far." It was getting darker all the time.

"Okay, if you'd like to, but it's a lot harder up front."

We started walking. I noticed that she kept getting farther and farther ahead of me. When she couldn't hear me answer her questions, she would stop for a minute and wait for me to catch up and then continue on with her conversation as if nothing had happened. I wanted to ask her where she got all of her energy, but I was afraid of the answer.

Somehow this was turning out all backwards. I was supposed to be the studly professional ball player. She was just a plain old doctor, although she did say she was into running. "This was a wonderful idea, Cord. I am really enjoying myself. It's good to get a light workout and the scenery is fantastic. I didn't know that winter in the mountains was so beautiful. I could really get into this snowshoeing thing."

We finally got to the falls, although there were times I thought of turning back. But a guy's pride can only take so much damage. Besides, she was leading and breaking the path. It was easier to follow. I had told her it was easy to follow, but I was still struggling. The sun had dropped below the Oquirrhs, and the purple sky behind the waterfall was spectacular. The water, as it fell through the donut hole, had created giant, upside down stalactites and intricate lacy patterns that glowed in the setting sun.

It was a little dark, so I gave her a headlamp from my backpack. I pointed to a rock ledge that didn't have any snow on it and suggested that we sit on the rock for a minute. I was breathing normally now and feeling pretty good about myself. I took the camera out of my backpack and snapped a few photos of Indy. She, in turn, wanted to take a few of me; then we tried the timer to take one of both of us together. She didn't like to smile for photos, and it took all of my ingenuity to get her to laugh. Of course I made a fool of myself, but it was for the cause. I put the camera away and in my best manners said, "Dinner is now served."

I removed a thermos of hot chocolate and poured each of us a cup. I also had a box of assorted Krispy Kreme donuts as a surprise. I said, "I'm sure these won't match the boysenberry cheesecake you had last night, but at least it's a dessert, and I need the sugar."

"I love Krispy Kremes," she said. "But you only brought a dozen. What are you going to eat?" Then she laughed. It was infectious. She was infectious. We sat and ate Krispy Kremes, drank hot chocolate, and watched as the light faded to dark. It got dark quickly. I was amazed. It was like someone turning off the light switch. Our headlamps played off of the ice and water and made the falls even more spectacular.

"I've never seen anything like this before. It's beautiful. My only question is whether we can find our way back to the truck."

"No problem, we just follow our trail." Leadership; I was born to it.

It was easier going downhill, and I walked alongside her the whole way back to the truck. I found myself wanting to be around her. She acted like she was my best friend but not my girlfriend; that part I didn't like. She was intentionally maintaining a platonic relationship. She didn't let me get any closer than arm's length, and we weren't even missionary companions.

We got back in the truck and started down the canyon. We talked freely. Then she said, "Well, now that we finished dessert, what are we having for the main course?"

"Actually, if you like Mexican, I know this new little place just down the street, Pistol Pete's. Are you game?"

"I love Mexican."

"Is there any kind of food you don't like?"

"Yeah, I think, but I just can't remember what it would be right now."

♦ ♦ ♦

After we had placed our orders and were waiting for our food, Wally walked up, grabbed me, and gave me a big bear hug. "Cord, I haven't seen you in months. Have they sent you your contract yet? And who is this beauty?" He was looking at Indy and she was blushing.

"Indy, this is Wally Peterson. He owns this joint. I played ball with his son in high school. Wally, this is Dr.—I mean, Indiana Jones." I put my arm around her shoulder and gave her a little hug. She didn't even flinch, which was a good sign.

She reached out and shook his extended hand.

"Sure, and I'm Brigham Young," he laughed. "Glad to meet you, Indiana."

It was obvious that this wasn't the first time this had happened to her. She fired right back without even hesitating, "Do you have all of your wives working out back tonight, Brigham?"

I decided I would be better off to stay out of the debate, but I usually don't do what I'm supposed to do anyway. "Wally, you're not going to believe this, but her real name is Indiana Jones."

Wally was laughing. "I'm sorry, Ms. Jones. I didn't intend

to make fun of you, but I just couldn't pass it up." By this time all of the patrons were listening to the boisterous conversation. Wally added, "If you can last through the whole meal with Mr. Calloway, then dinner is on the house. You will have earned it for having to put up with both of us. And every time you bring this lovely young lady in here, you'll get another free meal, Cord. Course she'll probably find her sanity and I'll only be out one meal."

He left to go talk to some other customers. "He's a great guy," I said. "And, believe it or not, in his day he was one heck of a second baseman."

About halfway through our meal she asked, "Cord, I've been thinking about the bike ride we took up to Mirror Lake. Do you remember the name of that rest stop by the waterfall?"

She was testing me. She wanted to find out if I had remembered anything. I thought about her question. I definitely could not remember taking such a ride with her. "Are you sure it was with me?" I asked.

She laughed, knowing that I had caught her. "Okay, so you caught me. Have you been able to remember anything since the baseball game in September?"

"No. However, there are times certain things just feel right. Like . . . I've done this before. For example, being around you feels, well, *natural* . . . good, or maybe even right. I can't really explain the feeling. I guess it's more like a shadow of a remembrance. Something's there, but I can't identify it."

"Explain what 'feels right' means, Cord."

"I feel comfortable, familiar. For instance, when you kissed me, it felt right. It felt like I had done that a million times. You know what I mean?"

"Can you ever be serious?"

"I am being serious."

She waved off my attempts to draw her into a conversation about us. I think it was hard for her to continue to talk about us in the past tense when there wasn't a present tense us. I waved at Wally and thanked him again as we left the restaurant. He shouted back, “Indiana Jones, you can come back here anytime, with or without Mr. Calloway.”

She smiled at him and said, “Thanks, Wally, I might just take you up on that offer. The food was great.” Everyone in the restaurant was looking at Indy. They all knew Wally was flirting with her.

“Do you draw that kind of attention everywhere you go?” I asked.

“What kind of attention is that? I mean, Wally is your friend and he was giving you a hard time. He wasn’t giving me any special attention.”

“Are you for real, Indy?”

“What do you mean by that, Cord?”

“Well, for starters, every guy we pass stares at you. Everyone wants to be your friend, like John, I mean Dr. Stewart. To top it off, you are not hard to look at. Most beautiful women tend to be like baseball first-round draft picks. Everyone has catered to them their whole lives and, like professional athletes, they think they should be treated accordingly. Not you. You try to ignore the limelight and downplay the attention.”

“I’ve learned the hard way that there are men who are attracted to me just because they think I’m pretty. In some instances it’s difficult to identify such men, so I chose to avoid all relationships. I think I diagnosed it as ‘fearadocious avoidance,’ which means it’s easier to avoid relationships than to get involved.

“So while I believe I have a basic distrust of relationships, it may just be that I don’t want to risk involvement again. It hurt too much. Before I met you, I hadn’t dated anyone for well over a year. But there was something about you that intrigued me. Anyway, you were different. I knew that after our first or second date. At one point I was talking, going on and on, just talking and not getting anywhere fast. You stopped me and said, ‘Indy, will you get to the point?’ I knew you couldn’t have any ulterior motives after a comment like that.

“But to answer your question, I really don’t like attention. I don’t want to be Dr. Jones. I want to just be a regular person.”

I think she might be the most honest person I have ever known. I tired to compare the two of us. I have to admit that unlike Indy, I really like attention. I want people to like me and respect me because I am a baseball star. I like to be recognized. I like it when kids ask for my autograph. The problem is that no one ever asks for my autograph or recognizes me; maybe I just think I would like it.

♦ ♦ ♦

The next week flew by. I saw Indy every day. The more I saw her, the more I liked her. She was becoming my best friend; but at this point in my life I didn't want just a friend. She, on the other hand, made sure that we never crossed over the friendship line. Now you have to understand that I tried to jump, run, sneak across the line, and come in the back door, but she caught me every time. I knew she cared about me, but she continued to retreat whenever it came to anything about us. Don't get me wrong, she was always nice; it was that I wanted more than just a great friend.

I still had not heard anything from Caitlyn. Maybe she had forgotten about me. Maybe she had decided that the nice little Mormon boy could stay in Utah and coach his little baseball team. Maybe she had realized that she wanted more out of life than baseball, hot dogs, a Chevrolet, and apple pie. I couldn't blame her, but it still took a chunk out of my heart.

I still hadn't found the guts to talk to Indy about my feelings for Caitlyn. I just didn't know what to do or say, so I avoided the topic and we continued to be just good friends.

♦ ♦ ♦

Did you ever have a really absent-minded professor? One that looked like he belonged living in a room at the end of the hall with a single light bulb hanging from the ceiling, with books, manuscripts, and papers scattered all over everywhere, making it impossible to find a place to sit, even when he asks you to sit? If you have, then you have met Dr. Montgomery. However, for some reason he inspired confidence and radiated learning, even though he was bit eccentric. Besides, if he had read all of the books in his office, he had to be a genius.

When I had walked into his office, he was half-hidden behind a pile of books, and his glasses were down on the end of his nose. He motioned for me to sit in a chair that had books and articles haphazardly stacked on the seat. I looked at the chair and he looked at me and said, "Just set those on the floor." It took me a minute to find an empty space on the floor.

I sat and he started talking without looking at me. "I've been reading about different cases of retrograde amnesia. Very interesting. Unusual . . . it's hard to get a handle on. I mean, it doesn't seem like we know any more about it than we did twenty years ago. It creates unusual situations in a person's life when it happens."

"You're telling me," I said.

He asked me a bunch of questions and then mumbled some response. I tried to understand what he was saying but didn't follow him very well. Sometimes he would look me straight in the eyes like he was trying to learn something other than from what I was saying. Other times he would not look up from the moth-eaten yellow pad he was writing on. He took copious notes as I talked. Then he asked, "Are you keeping that diary I asked you to keep?"

I had intentions of starting that, but I had never gotten around to it. "Well, since I haven't been able to remember anything yet, I haven't had anything to write." It was the best I could come up with on the spot.

"You keep that journal. You could be famous after I write your case up in one of the medical journals. Your case is quite unique."

"Well, Doc, am I going to get my memory back? This black hole thing is sometimes very annoying, and it's not doing my love life any good either."

"Things will work out," he said.

"What does that mean?"

"Just give it some time. What's the rush?"

"How about my life?" I asked.

"Have some patience, son. You've had a serious head injury. It needs a little time to heal. I have high expectations that your memory will reappear, although I can't tell you when. However, in the meantime, try to protect your head a little. Don't do something stupid and get hit again on the head. Who knows what would happen if you got another injury to your head."

"Are you telling me not to play baseball?"

"No. I'm just telling you to wear a helmet when you do."

"But I'm a pitcher not a batter. Pitchers don't wear helmets."

"There is always a first for everything," he said. He then set up another appointment after Christmas but told me to call on his private line if anything exciting happened. I wanted to ask him what he considered exciting but decided against it. Exciting to him was probably buying a new ten-pound book.

♦ ♦ ♦

As I was dropping Indy off at her home on the fifteenth of December, I realized that I had never been inside of her home. I had never had an invitation. Every time I dropped her off, she managed to get away, leaving me alone with Betsy. Evidently Betsy also believed that we were just friends. I guess she didn't have any facts to convince her otherwise

As we sat in the truck that night, Indy said, "Cord, I haven't told you before because I was hoping that things would . . . well, tomorrow I'm going to California for the holidays. I haven't seen my friends there for some time. I need to go. Will you be okay?"

I had planned on spending the holidays with Indy, but of course I had never actually talked to her about it. I just assumed we would spend the time together. After all, she didn't have anyone around here. I wondered if "anyone" included me. I can also tell you that we had passed the second first date as well as the second second date and then some. I still hadn't gotten closer to her than arm's length; and yes, I did check my breath each night. Maybe if I could make a decision about Cate, it would help.

"It's okay. I can go to Shannon's," I said, although it didn't sound like the Christmas I had hoped to have. But then, I didn't have a claim on Indy. How could I when I still had some hope of discovering what was going on in Cate's mind? I mean, just because she didn't want to be with me right now didn't seem to extinguish my feelings for her. Why, then, did it bother me that Indy would be leaving for the holidays? After all, we were just friends.

She didn't say anything. It was not like her. It almost seemed like she didn't want to go. "I had hoped you would be here, Indy. But I understand your need to see your friends."

"Cord, let me tell you a story, and then maybe you will understand. I have to go back a few years . . . it's something I don't think about, I don't talk about. But you need to know.

"Anyway, through high school and particularly college I never had time for men. It wasn't as if I didn't have the opportunity to date; it was simply not a question that was up for debate. I carried a full load in school, I worked almost full-time, and I wouldn't let anything or anyone interfere with school. I wanted to be successful in school more than I wanted anything else. I was so driven that I wouldn't even consider a date.

"By the time I started medical school at the University of Utah, I had settled into a comfortable lifestyle in the Church and at school. I was feeling pretty good about myself and my life. Looking back, I didn't realize how very vulnerable and trusting I was. I believed the Church was true, and I believed that members of the Church tried to live the gospel."

Indy was having a hard time with her speech, although I didn't understand why. What was the big deal? She had accepted the gospel into her life and worked hard in school. A lot of people do that. She started twirling her hair, and the next words didn't come quite as easily. In fact, it appeared that they were almost painful to speak.

"I met this guy in medical school, Sid Collett. He was the show of the class. He talked too much, mostly about himself, but he seemed to be the real deal. It seemed strange, but he started appearing, by accident he claimed, many places that I frequented. Sometimes it was across the table in the library or using a treadmill at the rec center when I was working out. He was always nice, and in the beginning he would just say hello or nod. As time went on he started casual conversations. Before long it became obvious that he had an interest in me.

"When he showed up unexpectedly at my ward, I learned that he was a returned missionary. He said he was meeting a friend, but the unnamed friend never showed. Then we started dating. I felt he was rushing things a little too fast and tried to distance myself from him, but he was persistent. I believed everything he said: hook, line, and sinker. My head kept telling me to slow down, but he kept pushing. He offered me the world. Here was a good member of the Church, a returned missionary, a med student, and he was interested in me. I guess you could say that I felt flattered and wondered how anyone could like me. It wasn't long before I thought I was in love with him. He was everything I had ever wanted. He even promised me a home with green grass surrounded by a white picket fence, weekly trips to the temple, and a boatload of kids."

Her speech had become halting at times, and it had become difficult for her to even speak. I wasn't sure I wanted to hear the rest of the story.

"To make a long story short, he proposed to me after we had been dating three months. I pushed all of my fears aside and said yes. You could say I was deliriously happy.

"Two weeks later the sky fell. At first I didn't know what was happening. Sid didn't show up to any classes and he quit calling. I tried getting in touch with him and couldn't. It was like he had vanished. Then I heard a rumor that I later confirmed; he had been kicked out of school because all of his college records had been forged. I later learned that he had been on a mission, but it only lasted for two months before he was sent home. He was a lie; everything about him was a lie. I have never spoken with him since, and I hope that I never have to see him again. I had a difficult few months.

"I climbed back into my shell and committed myself to my

studies. I was devastated not only because of him and who he was, but because I had trusted him so completely. I was disillusioned. Who could I trust if I couldn't trust Church members? I never wanted to face that pain again."

She stopped speaking. She was trying to hold back the tears. Finally she looked into my eyes and spoke so softly that I could barely hear the words. "I never dated another man until you, Cord. I intended to live alone. I didn't need anyone, not at any price.

"Now maybe you understand . . . I don't know. Everything's so mixed up. I just need to go. I'll call you when I get back."

With that she jumped out of the truck and ran toward her house. I jumped out of the truck and caught up to her just as she reached the porch. "Indy!" As she stopped and turned, I pulled her into an embrace. She didn't push me away, which was a good sign. Without hesitating, I turned her head and kissed her lightly on the lips. She didn't stop me. I gazed into her eyes and thought, *If it works once, twice would be even better.*

As I bent to kiss her again, she pushed me away and started to run for her house. I grabbed her arm and she stopped. I drew her back to me and kissed her again. This time it was longer. She didn't resist and melted into my arms. As I let her go, I whispered, "Call me the minute you get to home from California."

"Merry Christmas, Cord," she said. I thought she was crying, but she didn't look back.

As I was about to hop in the truck, I heard her say, "You never answered my question."

As I started Betsy I wondered, *What question?* I didn't know what she was talking about. "Why do women have to be so complicated?" I asked Betsy.

It seemed like a long ride back to my place. I wanted to call her. I wanted to ask her what she meant . . . but I couldn't make the call. She wanted or needed to see her friends, for her. It was time that I thought about someone else's needs. But I knew it was going to be a long, lonely holiday season. But what about her? How was she feeling? I could blame the problems on her. After all, it wasn't my fault that I had amnesia—but it wasn't hers either. I understood why she wanted to get away even if I didn't like it. The biggest problem was that I didn't know what to do about it.

We made too many wrong mistakes!

—Yogiism #6

INDY WAS IN THE LAND of beaches and palm trees and Cate had evaporated. I was left alone in the snow and cold with a significant portion of my memory still missing, feeling rather like Lou Costello: picked on. But at least I didn't have Abbot around yelling at me. I decided it was time I got a grip on my life and quit feeling sorry for myself. Whether or not I got my memory back, I still had my whole life ahead of me. I figured it was a good time to do a little one-on-one self assessment. As a result I devised a battle plan.

First, I needed a serious exercise routine, something that would push my body to exhaustion, which would bring on uninterrupted sleep. Second, I needed a routine to get my arm in shape to throw. Third, I wasn't sure what was third, but I knew there was something bothering me besides my loss of memory. It was right there; I just couldn't lock onto it, drag it onto my screen. It felt like I was standing in the batter's box blindfolded with a pitcher throwing ninety-plus waiting for the next pitch, not knowing where or when it was coming but knowing nonetheless that it was coming.

That was five days ago. Since then I had lived according to my battle plan. I had rolled out of bed each day at six in the morning, which was early, real early for me; and I got up even if I was tired. First thing, I always checked my email, hoping for a note from Cate, and I was equally disappointed each day. Then I jogged to the gym and worked out on steppers and treadmills for an hour.

After working out at the gym, I drove up to the University of Utah air bubble to find someone to throw with. Since school was out, there was usually someone hanging around who wanted to play catch. There were always some ball players around, but I usually got one of several excuses: "I don't have a catcher's glove," or "I've got to run." What they were really saying was that I threw too hard and they didn't want any part of playing catch with me. One way or another, however, I usually found someone to throw with, and sometimes I even talked someone into catching while I threw off the mound. If I did get invited to spring training, I wanted to be in shape, and I wanted the cannon hanging on my right side ready to go. At least that's what I call my arm. Most baseball people wouldn't call my right arm a cannon, but what do they know?

I usually arrived back at my place by noon. I tried meditation, TV, music; and I always spent some time working on my coaching book. Sometimes I even reverted to going to Shannon's to play with her kids. By December twentieth I still had not heard from the beachcomber. Caitlyn had either broken her hand or her computer. The Royals had gone into hiding. My life was in limbo, and there was no one around to share all of the fun I was having. I quit taking care of my otherwise immaculate apartment. I wasn't eating very well, and I was rapidly running out of money. Mostly, though, I was feeling unquestionably sorry for myself.

I was sorting through the bills on my desk, putting them into delay, pay, and don't pay stacks, when I noticed a file folder that didn't look familiar. A note was scribbled on the outside: Memories.

Inside I found maybe thirty pictures—photos taken during my stay in the land of shadows. The first photo showed Indy sitting on a rock in the middle of a small stream next to me. I had my arm around her and she was looking into my eyes. I knew that friends wouldn't look at one another like that.

In the next Indy was standing in the middle of a stream with a fly rod in hand trying to imitate a real fisherman. The photo was obviously posed since the fly was hanging from a tree limb; but she did wonders for hip waders. Another showed both of us sitting on the Ferris Wheel at Liberty Park. I could remember doing that with my high school girlfriend, but not Indy.

In the next she was pointing a fully loaded, large squirt gun directly at the camera with a look on her face that said "you are so dead." She was dripping wet and obviously out for revenge. The one photo that really drew my attention and almost stopped my breathing had Indy standing in front of the Manti Temple. She was dressed in a beautiful white dress. She looked so wholesome, almost serene. I loved the photo for some reason, although I couldn't say why.

I shuffled through the rest of the photos. I particularly liked the photo of her in a swimming suit, waterskiing. In another I was standing on a pitching mound ready to throw the ball; and she had a catcher's glove and face mask, squatting behind the plate, giving me the sign for a curveball. And finally there was a shot of us standing, facing each other, gazing into each other's eyes. She had on a catcher's chest protector and a catcher's masked setting on top of her head. It looked like a conference on the mound.

Last, there was a photo of both of us, and the backdrop was again the Manti Temple. I wondered why the temple seemed to have some significance to her, because it had never had any for me.

I studied each photo. I tried to remember any of the events. I wanted to feel what I was feeling at the time each the photo was taken. Nothing stirred. No sudden flashes. No soft, warm, fuzzy, happy feelings. Nothing. Three months of life that, as far as I knew, never happened; yet here was proof that it had happened. It wasn't hard to see that we were enthralled with one another. But, it was like looking at a stranger doing things I hadn't done. I yearned to feel what I thought I saw.

Suposition: suppose that I had fallen in love with Indy. Suppose further that she had fallen in love with me. Now suppose that she had been injured instead of me and had lost her memory. How would I feel? What would I do?

I would still love her, but for her it would be like she was seeing me for the first time. I wondered how I would cope, what I would do. I realized that so much of who we are today is dependent upon what we have done and felt in the past. Without those memories, how do we know who we really are, what we felt, or how we now feel? How would I respond to the situation? Would I give her a chance to try to rediscover who she was or how she felt?

The more I thought, the more I sensed the futility of the situation.

♦ ♦ ♦

I looked through the fridge—nothing. The apartment was a mess, and there was nothing to eat. I finally found some Top Ramen. I heard knocking at the door. Shannon was pounding on my door. She looked at me and said, "We're going to go get something to eat. I think we need to talk. How about a pizza?" she asked.

Fifteen minutes later we were sitting in the corner of the neighborhood pizzeria. "Cord, what's going on in your life? I haven't heard from you in two weeks."

"Nothing's going on. That's the problem, and I don't know how to correct the situation. I don't know if I'm going to get the chance to play baseball this spring. I'm running out of money. I need to rent the upstairs apartment. Indy took off for the beaches of California, and Caitlyn, well, I just don't know. My memory still has a big hole in it. Mom calls me three times a day and wants to know if I've gone to church yet. I remind her that she asked me that yesterday and Sunday hasn't come around yet so I haven't had the chance."

"That's it? From the look of your face when I walked into your apartment, I thought something was really wrong, like someone died. Cord, how old are you?"

"You know I'm twenty-seven."

"Let's see, you don't have any debt. Your home is paid for, and you normally receive monthly rental income. You don't have three kids demanding every second of your time. You are still living your baseball dream, and you have never had a real job, unless you consider baseball a job. Your college education was paid for by baseball. Do you know how many people would die to be where you are?"

"It's a good thing you don't sugar coat anything. Why not just tell me like it is? Don't hold back any punches," I said. "I mean, can't a guy wallow in a little self-pity anymore?"

"Cord, you need to grow up."

"Shannon, I've been trying. For the last two weeks I have spent a lot of time trying to put my life puzzle together. Things just don't fit, and I can't force them together."

"But that's only part of the real problem, isn't it?"

"Yeah, you're right. I think the biggest problem is that I'm just frustrated with my life. I am getting to that point in my life that I want some stability. I would like to have someone to come home to at night, someone to share my dreams with. I hate being in limbo, and it seems like every year I go through the same thing. Sometimes I think playing professional baseball is a total and complete waste of time. You never make any money. It doesn't prepare you for providing for your family or for the rest of your life. The only reason I keep hanging on is that I believe there is still the chance that I can make it to The Show; you know, live my dream."

"Where did this brush with reality come from, Cord?"

"Maybe I'm just growing older. Maybe it's because of Cate, or maybe Indy. Maybe my dream is fading. I don't know."

"It's good to hear you finally touched earth. I've been thinking the same thing for years. However, in spite of everything, I still think you've got to go play this year, if you get the chance. You can't quit baseball believing that you might have made it. It would haunt you for the rest of your life."

"Thanks, Shannon, for your support, I think."

She laughed. "Now we can talk about the good stuff. I've been dying to find out what happened between you and Indy. You were with her almost every day, and then out of the blue she decides to go to California for the holidays. Where did that come from?"

"I wish I knew what happened. Maybe it was one of those female things."

"Whatever! Men always use that cop-out when there's an issue dealing with feelings. So what did you say or do that made her decide to go to California?"

"I don't know. I really don't have a clue. I'm innocent. I didn't do anything."

"Maybe that's your problem—you didn't do anything."

"What?"

"Since you were with her almost every day, I assumed you two were back together again."

"Why would you assume that when you know I still have feelings for Cate?"

"How can Cate be so important to you? You never see her. You never talk to her. You don't even know if she is alive. Cord, how come you won't just listen to what I'm telling you? You haven't seen or talked to Cate in months. You fell in love with Indy, and you were going to ask her to marry you. Get over it. I know you can't remember, but I'm telling you the truth. Besides, how could you go wrong with someone named Indiana Jones? Things will work out over time even if you don't remember. She is one of the best people I have ever met."

"Sure, Shannon, I mean, let's just skip over the small stuff and get right to it."

"I don't have time to pussyfoot around. I have three kids and I have to economize my time whenever possible."

"Let me put it this way. You've heard the song 'If you want to be happy for the rest of your life, marry yourself an ugly wife . . .' Indy isn't ugly so that lets her out."

"Be serious. So why don't you just cast your fate to the wind and marry her?"

"Marry her? What do I do about my feelings for Cate?"

"You're going in circles."

"Tell me about it. That's what I do every day. I think about my life: baseball, work, Cate, and Indy; and no matter which hallway I walk down, I always end up at the same point. It's like I'm caught in a maze with no path leading out."

"Okay, Cord, I realize that you lost some of your memory. Deal with it. You're making more of it than is necessary. I'm telling you that you were going to ask Indy to marry you."

"I believe you, Shannon. I found some photos taken over the last three months, and it's obvious that there was something going on between us. And when I'm around her, I just feel good. She has been friendly, like missionary companion friendly, but that's it. Well, except when I came out of the coma and she kissed me. Oh, and I did steal a kiss before she left for California, and she didn't deck me"

"So what's she supposed to do, fall all over you when you keep telling her that you're in love with Cate?"

"I've never told her that. I've never talked to her about Cate."

"There you go again. I mean, she's at your house for a romantic dinner and guess who shows up? Cate! And you've never talked to her about that? Have you ever told her that you and Cate are over and that you love her and only her?"

"Okay, Shannon, if I was as close to Indy as you believe, then why hasn't she said anything to me? Why does Indy go out of her way to make sure that our relationship is completely platonic?"

"Let me ask you a question. Let's suppose, hypothetically of course, that Indy told you that you had been in love with her and that you two had made plans to get married. Would it change how you feel about her or how you feel about Cate?"

I thought about that. "It probably wouldn't, but I think I would feel somewhat obligated."

"Obligated?"

"Yeah, because it might be true even though I couldn't remember it."

"Couldn't you just believe her? Do you think she would lie?"

"No, she doesn't lie. Although she did mention that she might be able to brainwash me in my present mental condition."

"So, what's the problem?"

"The problem is that *I* don't know now if I'm in with love her. I admit I might have been, but now I don't remember. I don't know. Maybe I should be."

"So now, let me see if I understand. You expect her to tell you how you felt about her so that you will know; but even if she does tell you, that still won't be enough because you want to know for yourself?"

"Yeah, I guess so. It doesn't make much sense though, does it?" I tried to sort things out in my head. I assumed that I had purchased the ring for Indy. Was I willing to let her go without trying to rediscover those feelings? Or should I throw it all away? I needed to know more about Indy, about us: things that only she knows, things we did, things we talked about, plans we made. Maybe Shannon knew more than she was telling.

I tried fishing. "Shannon, tell me why you like Indy so much."

"Cord, she has character. She is a survivor; she is a winner; she is nice; she is beautiful; and most of all, she loves you."

We were both quiet, thinking, when she asked, "Cord, do you know if you have ever talked to her about Cate?"

"Shannon, I don't know. I can't remember."

"If I were her, all I would care about was if you loved me. Have you ever told her you loved her?"

"Well, I don't know about the time before the accident, but since the accident I haven't because of my feelings for Cate. I want to be honest with her. She knows about Cate because she was at my house that night Cate knocked on my door."

Shannon asked, "What if you hadn't told her about Cate, I mean before Cate showed up on your doorstep. Maybe she assumed that you were seeing Cate and her at the same time. Maybe she believes that you deceived her and that you were telling her one thing but dating Cate on the side."

"She wouldn't trust me . . . wait, we were having dinner at The Roof and she asked me a question that almost floored me. She asked me how I really felt about her and how I really felt about Cate. And then later when I took her home she ran into the house before she went to California she said, 'You never answered my question.' She didn't say which question."

"Well, what did you say?"

"What did I say when?"

"When she asked you about her and Cate."

"I never answered the question."

"Sounds like you gave her your answer without ever opening your mouth. The fact that you didn't answer told her all she needed to know."

"So what do I do now?"

"Cord, if you have the feelings for Cate that you say, then you had better find out if there's a future for you in her life. Although I have never met Cate, I'm sure she is a wonderful girl; but she isn't a member of the Church, and that bothers me. However, if you love Cate, then you should not lead Indy on. She deserves to know where you stand."

"But how can I do that when I don't know what happened during the lost three months?"

"Just be honest with Indy. Tell her the truth so she can get on with her life."

"And the truth is?"

"The truth is the truth. Tell her you don't know. Tell her how you think you feel about her and Cate, but that you don't want to make any decisions until you remember or figure out your feelings, and that you need some time for that to happen. I think it is time for full disclosure to both of them, and let the cards fall where they fall. You don't want either of them to think things that aren't true.

"I need to go, Cord, but my kids wanted me to invite you to come and stay with us on Christmas Eve, and then you will be there for the mad happenings in the morning. We would love to have you."

"Let's see, I could go . . . no . . . Oh, well all right, it will sure beat an empty house."

♦ ♦ ♦

Christmas blew in and out like a cold north wind. I had a great time at my sister's, but it was like playing in a baseball game that you were losing 16-1. You just want to get it over. I wanted to get my life moving forward. Oh, don't get me wrong, I love her kids; they flock to me like I'm the pied piper. I can't get rid of them. I think it's because I'm so charming. In fact, the kids all slept on the floor in my room on Christmas Eve, and we had the hardest time getting to sleep.

Christmas Day fell on Saturday. Shannon asked me to stay over for Sunday dinner. I didn't have a hot date, so I consented. The next morning they woke me up for church. So I had to—I mean got to—go to church with the whole family. Strangely, I didn't feel the old bitterness. In fact, I quite enjoyed the Christmas talks. I even liked sitting with Shannon's kids. They reminded me of me when I was a kid: I couldn't hold still either. Later that day, I went home to a very empty, very lonely house.

Two days later I got a call from the Royals. They weren't going to send me a contract, but they invited me to spring training. That meant I could go try out and see if I could make one of their teams. They were sending me a plane ticket, and I was to report to the team for spring training in Surprise, Arizona, on February twenty-fourth. The hold button on my life had just been pushed. I wanted to share my good news—at least I thought it was good news—but there really wasn't anyone to tell. The euphoria of having another chance didn't seem to be as important or exciting when there wasn't anyone to tell, anyone to share it with. It wasn't like I had a lot of options, and I had to tell someone, so I called Shannon. Sometimes it's good to have a sister.

"Cord, we miss having you around, and you know that Summer has a crush on you."

"It's nice to know that there is at least one girl who finds me attractive and enchanting, even if she's only eight years old."

"Have you heard anything from Indy?" asked Shannon.

She was particularly partial to Indy. She wasn't going to give up on the Indy thing. I wondered how Shannon and Indy had become such good friends.

"Cord . . . Cord, are you still with me?"

"Oh, sorry. Yeah, I'm here."

"Well?"

"Well, what?"

"Have you heard anything from Indy?"

"Not a word."

"What about Caitlyn?"

"Same. Maybe women over eight can see right through me."

"So what are you going to do, just sit there and wait for one of them to call and tell you she's sorry she hasn't called? You do have that kind of history. You expect girls to call you. Maybe the ball is in your court this time."

"Shannon, someone's knocking at my door. I'll call you later."

Who would be knocking at my door this time of night? Maybe Indy was back and had come to apologize. I opened the door and found a guy dressed in a suit. "You're not from the Jehovah's Witnesses, are you?" I asked.

"No, Cord, much worse—I'm Ashland Swenson, your Mormon bishop." The he laughed. "That's a good line, but it's already been used."

"Do I know you?" I asked.

"I'm afraid so." I watched as his countenance changed. "I heard you were in an accident. Are you all right?"

"Um, well I was hit on the head, and I have this memory thing."

"I'm sorry, Cord. I've been out of town or I'd have come sooner. Is there anything I can do?" Then he rushed right on, "I live down the street. We've spoken a number of times. But you didn't show up for our last appointment, so I decided it was time for me to come to the mountain. Do you mind if I come in for a minute?" he asked.

"No . . . No . . . I guess it's okay. Come in." I took him downstairs. I sat on a chair and motioned for him to sit on the couch and then explained, "When I had my accident, it affected my memory. I can't remember one thing that happened to me during the last three months. The doctor thinks I may get my memory back, but he doesn't know when or how. Anyway, what was it you came for?"

After an incredulous look and a flustered moment, he responded, "Well, actually I came for two reasons. First, you told me that you would give me one of your baseball cards; and, if you don't mind, I also brought a couple of baseballs for you to autograph. I want to give one to each of my boys. They've followed your career for some time. Second, I'm hoping that we can get together tomorrow or the next day for you to give them pitching lessons. They have been bugging me ever since you told me you would work with them on their pitching. I think we can get in the gym at church since I just happen to know someone who has the keys."

"Just a minute, Bishop." I went in my bedroom to find some of my cards to give to him. It wasn't like there was a big demand for them. I hadn't returned his call because I thought he was calling to bug me about church, yet all he wanted was one of my cards and for me to take some time with his kids. I hadn't met too many bishops who had any interest in baseball.

When I walked back into the room, he asked me all about baseball. He wanted to know where I had played in college and high school. He said, "I played catcher in high school. Of course, in Logan it wasn't hard to make the team. Some years we were so desperate for players, we considered asking a girl." We talked baseball and laughed for almost an hour. He didn't even mention the Church. I told him I had just been invited to spring training in Arizona this year with the Royals. It would be my fifth season of professional baseball.

"You know, I've been wanting to take my boys to spring training for some years. When does it start and end? Maybe we can come down this year. I need to get out with just the boys."

"If you come down, let me know. I might be able to get some tickets or balls signed by some of the major leaguers." I didn't really expect him to go to Arizona, and maybe I had promised more than I could do, but what the heck.

Then we talked about his kids and their passion for pitching. I told him that I loved to teach kids about pitching, particularly those who wanted to learn. "I can meet you over at the church anytime tomorrow, and we can throw with your kids. How old did you say they were?"

"They are eleven-year-old twins. Rush is a lefty and Blaze is a righty. They both want to pitch, and I really don't know a thing about pitching. I was a catcher. However, I do coach their Little League team. So how about high noon at the 'OK Coral'—I mean church? I'll bring my catching gear. You coach and I'll catch."

"Noon would be great," I said. I liked this guy whether he was a bishop or not. He seemed like a good guy. "Bishop, can I ask you a question?" I waited for his affirmative nod and then continued, "My sister thinks that I have been going to church during the last three months. Do you know if that's true?"

"Well, you showed up at sacrament meeting about a month and a half ago. You came in after the meeting had started, sat in the back, and left when the closing song started. The next week you showed up with a beautiful blonde, who I later found out was Indy. You stayed for all of the meetings, although you didn't talk to anyone except to give your name, rank, and serial number. I even tried to talk to you, but you avoided me. The next week you came back again but you were by yourself. I had heard all of the stories about you. You didn't want home teachers. You didn't want anything to do with the Church. You wanted to be left alone, so I was surprised when you came week after week. You can't remember going to church?"

"Nope. I don't understand what would have motivated me to start going back to church. Did I ever say anything to you?"

"It was your girlfriend. You promised her that you would give the Church a chance again. The next thing I knew was that you called my secretary and made an appointment to come in to talk to me; but you never showed up. Now I know why you stood me up. Would you like to set up another appointment?"

♦ ♦ ♦

I'm a student of the game of baseball. I love all of its intricacies, the endless possibilities, the details. That love has carried over to teaching the game, particularly pitching. I have always thought I would end up coaching one day. So I was pretty excited to teach the bishop's kids.

I arrived at the church ten minutes early; I had jogged over. The bishop was already there with his kids. I liked him even more; he was someone who also understood time. His kids were tall for their age and skinny as rails. They had big hands, which were great for pitchers. They looked at me like I was some kind of hero. I could tell the look. I introduced myself. I talked to them about the need for preparing themselves before doing anything in baseball, about getting into a routine before each practice and game. I sat on the floor and stretched with them while I talked about pitching. The bishop got right in there with us. I mean, he was even stretching.

Bishop Swenson added, "This reminds me of high school. I can remember pre-game like it was yesterday. We would all jog out to center field and stretch, joke, and talk about girls or anything but baseball. We were clearing our heads, getting ready for the game. I love those memories: the smell of freshly cut grass, the look of red dirt all over our white uniforms. My mom always used to ask me if I rolled around in the dirt just so she would have to wash my uniform."

I spent the next hour and a half watching them throw and

teaching them simple mechanics. They were both excited to try to learn how to pitch. The bishop kept asking questions or telling me to "Say it again but in English." He wanted to understand.

"When you say a pitcher is rushing, what are you talking about?" Bishop Swenson asked.

"Rushing means that a pitcher is letting his body get ahead of his arm, which usually results in high, straight fastballs or hanging curves, both of which are bad for pitchers." I couldn't believe it. The bishop was actually interested in learning about pitching. When we finished, they thanked me a hundred times. The bishop offered to pay me for the lessons. I declined. I tried to leave, but they told me I had to come over to their house and have some cookies and homemade ice cream if they couldn't pay for the lesson. I tried to say no, but there was no way they were going to let me get away. The boys even wanted to jog over to their house with me. The bishop had to drive and complained all the way to the car that he couldn't jog with us.

It took another hour to get stuffed with cookies and ice cream. Bishop Swenson's wife, Prestin, came in to meet me with their daughter, Isabell, who explained in no uncertain terms that I could call her Bell. I couldn't believe it when Prestin and Bell sat down, ate ice cream, and talked baseball. I learned that Bell, age thirteen, listened to the Bees game every night. I really liked Mrs. Swenson. When they told me the whole family loved the Red Sox, I liked them even more. They couldn't stop talking about last year's American League Championship series between the Red Sox and the "evil empire," the hated Yankees. I could talk Red Sox for hours.

The bishop brought in my baseball cards and gave one each to the twins. Bell wanted to know what happened to hers. I had to promise to bring her one. They made me feel like I was someone special. I felt like some kind of hero. I tried to escape, to go home to my empty, lonely house, but they wouldn't let me go until I promised to come over to their house for dinner on Sunday after church. I knew it. They had an ulterior motive after all, to try to get me to come to church. But church attendance never came up. The bishop also said if I came over on Monday evening, he thought we could get into the gym to throw again and call it a family home evening activity. I liked this guy.

I jogged home and realized that this had been the first day in a long while that I felt good about life. I think it was because I forgot to take my own temperature. I was concerned with helping someone else. Did I say that I liked Bishop Swenson? He wasn't an old stuffed-shirt bishop. He wasn't like my mother, who thought I would go to church just because she nagged me. The bishop was different, more concerned about me and my teaching his kids how to pitch. I'm sure he wanted me to go to church, but he made it clear that I was his friend first, not just someone who needed to be activated.

When I got home, I was in good spirits. I checked my email—nothing. Cate hadn't responded to my last email. Maybe Shannon was right. Maybe it was over and I was just too stubborn to admit it. Maybe Cate had found someone else. But I still wanted to talk to her, to get closure, to know for sure why she had come to Utah, but I wasn't having any luck.

I also spent a lot of time thinking about what Shannon had said about Indy. Maybe I was being too impatient. Maybe I needed to spend some quality time with her and even come clean and make a full disclosure. If I couldn't remember the last three months, maybe I could start again and see where it went. But I needed to be honest with her and tell her about Cate. Regardless of everything else, I needed to resolve the pending case of Caitlyn Belford.

I dialed Indy's phone and got her voice mail. "Indy, this is Cord. I apologize; I've been a real jerk. Look, you know all about my memory problem. I guess I have always been more concerned about how it affected me, and I didn't think about how it impacted you. Anyway, I got an invitation to go to spring training with the Royals, so I'll be leaving toward the end of February. I would like to spend as much time as you have available before I go. Please call, because I don't want to have to break my arm—my left one of course—just to get to see you."

I decided to try one more email to Cate. What did I have to lose?

Cate,
You know the only thing I've ever wanted out of baseball was for someone to give me a chance, someone to let me prove that I'm good enough to pitch in the big leagues. Well, all I've ever wanted from you is the same chance. Your parents are like the coaches who think I am a good AA pitcher. They don't believe I can make it in the big league. They've judged my ability without giving me a chance. I may never get my name in "Who's Who in America," but I intend to make a difference in people's lives. I may not be rich, but I will love my family. I thought we shared the same hopes and dreams. I couldn't have been that mistaken, could I? Anyway, I just want the chance to talk to you, even if it's over between us. I will always cherish our relationship.

Cord

I pushed send.

♦ ♦ ♦

I got up Sunday morning. I had decided to go to church. I owed it to Bishop Swenson, but I also wanted to understand why I had started going back to church. When I drove into the church parking lot, I stopped. I decided to put off actually going to a church meeting until next week. Just then the Swenson twins walked in front of my truck and waved. I was had! I parked. They waited for me. They made me sit with them. Prestin welcomed me like I was an old friend and reminded me about dinner. I felt kind of awkward, like I didn't belong with them or in church. Other than on Christmas, it had been a long time since I had been inside a church building—since my father's death.

Three hours later I walked out of the priesthood meeting. I met a lot of the guys who lived in the neighborhood. I had tried to keep to myself, but that didn't happen. Mormons glom onto nonmembers or inactive members who show the least bit of interest in the Church. Rush and Blaze, the twins, met me after priesthood and told me they were riding home with me. I couldn't have escaped if I had wanted. But I didn't want to; besides, I was hungry.

The twins dragged me downstairs as soon as we got to their home. "Dinner won't be ready for half an hour," said Rush, and Blaze added, "Do you play ping-pong?"

I felt I was getting set up. I was surprised that they didn't want to put money on the game when I told them I played a little.

We played for a while. I won, but not by much. A little later Bishop Swenson walked in. I thought we were all in trouble for playing ping-pong on the Sabbath. He rolled up his sleeves, took a paddle, and asked, "Who wants to get beat?"

The bishop handed me my lunch twice before Prestin told us to come up and eat. Bishop Swenson called on Bell to pray. I remembered some of the words of her prayer from my own youth. I got a lump in my throat. The food was fantastic. Finally I said, "Mrs. Swenson . . ."

She interrupted me and said, "How about Prestin? Mrs. is a little too formal for me."

"All right, Prestin. This is the best meal I have eaten in years. Thank you for having me."

Bishop Swenson jumped in. "Hey, I taught her everything she knows; but you know, she still makes me do the dishes."

"I'm good at dishes," I said.

"You're on, Cord. I'll clean up and you wash, which today means you load the dishwasher." I liked the Swensons.

Before I left, they all made me promise that I would come back next week. I didn't want to impose; but you know, it didn't seem like imposing when they were doing the inviting.

♦ ♦ ♦

There was a message on my phone when I got home. "Cord, this is Indy. I've been struggling with the idea of spending more time with you, but at least I think we should talk and then see where to go from there. Besides, I don't want you to go to spring training with a broken arm on my account. How about meeting me at the Kyoto on Eleventh East and Thirteenth South at eight tomorrow evening?"

I called Bishop Swenson and asked him if we could meet at the church at six for family home evening. "That would be great, Cord."

"But I can't come over after, Bishop, I have a date. Okay?"

"Sure, but the boys will be disappointed that you chose a girl over them. By the way, is it Indy?"

"It is, but it's kind of touch and go with her right now.

"Would you like me to talk to her? I did speak to her once."

"Thanks, Bishop, we'll see. Anyway, I'll see you tomorrow."

Seven

When asked if I wanted my pizza cut into four or eight pieces, I replied, "Four. I don't think I can eat eight."

—Yogiism #7

After we finished our pitching lesson, Blaze and Rush both gave me a hard time about going on a date rather than finishing the Monday night ping-pong challenge. Bishop Swenson, however, was on my side on this one. I barely had time to get home, shower, change clothes, and get to the restaurant by 7:55. Indy was late. I assumed the cause for her tardiness was something serious, like treating the victims of an eight-car pileup. I got us a spot in the back corner, the most private one available. Kyoto was an authentic, Japanese-style eatery where the tables are close to the floor and you are supposed to remove your shoes. I didn't know what she liked to eat, but I wanted an appetizer served before she arrived. I ordered California Sushi Rolls and gyoza, and waters for both of us.

Indy arrived at the same time as the water and appetizers. I was excited to see her. Yes, she looked great; and no, she wasn't wearing hospital scrubs. She wore crisp, new khaki slacks and a sky blue turtleneck sweater. She could be the poster girl for

"Everybody needs milk": wholesome and beautiful, if those two things exist together in this imperfect world.

I wanted to lighten up the atmosphere, no doom and gloom tonight. "Dr. Jones, I'm not sure it's fair to come to a summit meeting looking that good, particularly when we haven't agreed on the ground rules. I must object, and I also object to a rectangular table. I want a round table so you can't claim you're sitting at the head."

She didn't laugh at my attempted humor. "Thank you, Cord, I'll take that as a compliment." An awkward silence followed. It seemed to linger interminably. She seemed to be holding back. I guessed the problem had something to do with me. I hoped, however, that I could distract her with food if I couldn't dazzle her with my wit.

"Did you hear about the two blondes sitting on a bench in Oklahoma talking, and one says to the other, 'Which do you think is farther away—Florida or the moon?' The other blonde turns and says, 'Helloooooooooo, can you see Florida?' "

She smiled a little, so I followed up with a slider on the outside black. "A blonde was playing Trivial Pursuit and it was her turn. She rolled the dice and she landed on Science & Nature. Her question was, 'If you are in a vacuum and someone calls your name, can you hear it?' She thought for a minute and then asked, 'Helloooo, is it on or off?' "

Indy smiled and said, "Okay, okay, I give up. No more dumb blonde jokes tonight. You've already reached your limit." I noticed that she had eaten all of the gyoza except one. As I looked up, she smiled and asked, "What? Did you want one?"

I started laughing. Then she started laughing and grabbed the last one before I had a chance. I pulled the sushi over to my corner of the table, picked up my chopsticks, holding them like daggers, and said, "Okay, Ms. Jones, just try it."

"Okay, I'm sorry. Can't I just have one, pretty please?" So I'm a sucker for a pretty face. I pushed the plate into the middle of the table and lowered my daggers. She immediately grabbed one with each hand before I could retrieve my chopsticks and started laughing again.

"You don't play fair, Dr. Jones."

"Now, Mr. Calloway, don't you go and throw me in the briar patch."

"Okay, I take it back." I reached across the table and took hold of her hand. She didn't withdraw it. That was a good sign.

"I've missed you, Indy."

She pointed behind me and said, "Do you know that lady?" I turned to look and knew I had been had again. She was eating another piece of sushi.

We had just finished our soup when the salad arrived. I continued to stare at her with the same awe I would have if I were sitting across the table from Nolan Ryan. She continued to avoid my eyes and concentrated on the food, but she had a sly smile on her face. I decided it was time to lay my cards on the table, and I was about to start into my speech when our waiter came to take our order.

As soon as the waiter left, I said, "I know that you don't think baseball players can be serious about anything except baseball, but I'm going to try. Don't laugh, okay? After all, this is a summit meeting."

"We're having a summit meeting right in the middle of dinner? How did you get that one past the House?"

"You have to promise to hear me out. Don't get up and leave until I finish, okay?"

"Cord, I've had a lot of time to think and I just don't know—"

I didn't want her to finish her sentence so I interrupted. "There you go. I haven't even started and you're interrupting. I have the floor and I haven't relinquished it yet. So I'm sorry, but you are just going to have to wait your turn. Parliamentary procedure, you know."

"Okay, you win." She was waving the little flag that had come as part of the appetizers.

"You know that I can't remember meeting you until the day in the hospital when I came out of the coma. I've tried to get you to talk to me about our relationship before that day, but you've sidestepped each of my questions. However, thanks to my

Sherlock sleuthing abilities, I have discovered a number of things: First, my sister, Shannon, thinks you walk on water, although she won't say how you do it. Second, my mother thinks you are good for me, and that means she thinks you'll get me back to church. Third, Bishop Swenson thinks you're a knockout, to which I have to agree. And fourth, I found an envelope full of photos of us that could be used in one of those slideshows that are used at wedding receptions. So, Dr. Watson, the inescapable conclusion is that you and I were involved. Besides, you confirmed that when you kissed me at the hospital."

She looked like she wanted to say something, but I held up my hand and said, "Let me say my piece and then you can get up and leave if you want or stay and talk; and maybe, if I'm lucky, we can get back to the kissing part again."

She smiled and seemed to relax a little. The main course had just arrived. I knew I was okay so far since she continued to eat and hadn't gotten up to leave, but then there was food on the table. I went on with my speech. "I can't recreate a memory. You know that. I can't tell you what I used to feel, only what I now feel. Since I have no control over the restoration of my memory, I propose we start again. I mean, I want to be with you and see where it goes. If it was right before, then it will be right again."

"That was never my problem. I was willing to give you all the time you needed. But by refusing to answer the only question that really mattered to me, you told me all I needed to know."

It was time to throw the high hard one. I knew I had to get into the Cate thing, but I wondered if absolute truthfulness would get me off the ground or result in a nosedive from which there could be no recovery.

"Indy, in baseball when it's the bottom of the ninth and the bases are loaded and the count is 3-2, you can't throw a curve or a change or something off-speed because you have to throw a strike. Everyone in the ballpark knows what's coming. The pitcher lets go with his best fastball right down the middle, and the batter takes his best swing. I think we're at that point: straight fastballs down the middle.

"Let me put it this way. The only person I can remember dating or having a relationship with is Caitlyn Belford. I can't remember dating you. However, the last thing I can remember about Cate was that her family didn't approve of me. They said I was all wrong for her and she went along with them. She ended our relationship. That was back in September. I haven't spoken to her since that time, at least that I can remember. I did receive one email from her right after my accident. She indicated in that email that she had come to Salt Lake in November to visit me and she was surprised by something. Shannon told me Cate came to my apartment when you and I were having dinner. Truthfully, I can't remember anything about that visit and I haven't talked to her since.

"Now, I have tried to make contact with her. Do I want to see her? Yes! Do I have feelings for her? Yes! Do I have feelings for you? Yes! Do I have any idea if she has any interest in me? No! Has she moved on to another relationship? I don't know. Did I move on to another relationship? I don't know, but there is significant evidence to support that position."

She was smiling, so I didn't think I'd blown it too bad. "Indy, the entire time I was dating you I don't think I ever talked to Cate, although I can't remember that for sure. I didn't say anything to you about her because I thought that relationship was over. I never intended to deceive you. But I have to say I really can't remember.

"I need to understand my relationship with her as much as I need to rediscover the relationship I had with you. I guess that leads me to the point we are at right now. I want to try to rediscover what you and I had. I don't want to put that quest on hold while I wait to find out where Cate and I stand. Although I'm not very good at doing two things at the same time, I am willing to try. That may not be fair to you, but I don't know what else to do. So it's up to you. But don't swing too hard, okay? Remember, I only throw an eighty-nine-mile-an-hour fastball."

She transferred her gaze from the window to me. She didn't respond for some time. I had given her my best fastball, and I didn't know what she would do with it. To make matters worse, I couldn't discover anything by looking into her eyes. She should be a riverboat gambler, I thought, with that poker face.

"Cord, I've tried. I've tried to give you some time. I would like nothing better than to be back where we were, but I know now that's not going to happen in the immediate future. I promised myself years ago I would never put myself in this position, and here I am again. Before you came along, I was prepared to devote my life to medicine. I didn't need a man. I made that clear to you the first time you asked me out. And then the first thing I knew, I started caring. You were so different, refreshing, chauvinistic, funny, painfully honest—unlike anyone I had ever met. You kind of sneaked up on me, and the first thing I knew my life seemed to start down another path. It was like a wild roller coaster ride. The only problem was that the car came off the track when Cate knocked on your door.

"I can live with your not even remembering my name; that was unintentional. But Cate, that's another problem. You knew about Cate while we were dating, yet you never said a word to me. You led me to believe there wasn't anyone else. If you would have told me about her, that would have been one thing; but to not tell me and have me find out when she came knocking at your door, well, that was too much. I trusted you implicitly, Cord."

"But I've explained. I thought the Cate thing was over before I started dating you."

"You just told me that you can't remember if you saw her while you were dating me, or if you talked to her or whatever."

She had taken her swing and hit my fastball 360 feet over the center field fence. What could I say? Beg for mercy. Seek clemency. It was the only thing I had left. "Indy, I'm sorry. You didn't do anything to deserve this, and you're right. You should probably just walk out of here and never look back, but I hope you won't do that. I still want to try."

She didn't respond for what seemed like forever. "Cord, I have been lied to before by men that I trusted, and I have been deceived. I didn't know who she was; but when I saw the way you two looked at each other, I didn't want to know. After that night at your apartment, I promised myself that I would never see you again. I never returned your calls, nor did I see you again until you ended up in the hospital. I may have been a little quick and judgmental. I'm sorry. I want to believe you, it's just that . . ."

She didn't continue her thought. I didn't want to interrupt her. Besides, the food was really good. "While you were in the hospital unconscious, I spent a lot of time visiting with your sister, Shannon. She became a good friend. She tried to explain your relationship with Caitlyn, and she told me the same story you have just told me.

"So before you regained consciousness, I decided that I needed to give you some time. I thought I had. It became very clear to me after the accident, however, that you were still in love with Caitlyn. That night at the Roof restaurant you wouldn't answer my question. I let it go, and then before Christmas it just got too difficult. I needed some time. I panicked, pulled up stakes, and ran away to find myself with trusted friends in California."

She stopped speaking, and now she was looking into my eyes. I still couldn't read what was hidden in those deep pools. Besides, she was probably holding aces over kings. I didn't know what to think or, for that matter, what to say. The waiter broke the silence by asking about dessert. We both ordered vanilla bean ice cream. I wasn't sure if it was my turn to talk or whether she still wanted to finish her story, so I slowly ate my ice cream in silence.

Finally, I couldn't take the silence any longer. I had stared at my ice cream until I thought it would melt from the heat. She was looking out the window, lost to me, at least for the minute. Humor is always helpful when you're operating in crisis mode.

"Let me try to sum up the current affairs of this summit. Whereas the party of the first part, that would be me, is, let's say, mentally impaired but is willing to allow the party of the second part, that would be you, to try to assist him in recovering from his impairment. However, the party of the second part is not sure that the party of the first part can be or is worth fixing."

I saw her smile just a little, and a twinkle appeared in her eyes. "Are baseball players always able to talk themselves out of trouble, or are you just an exception?"

Maybe she hadn't hit my pitch out of the yard after all. Maybe the wind had blown it back into the park. "So, where do we go from here?" I asked. I wanted her to be the one to set the ground rules at this point.

She didn't respond immediately. I could tell by the twinkle in her eye that she was mulling over her various options. She had been playing "Taps" on the table top with her fork so hard it was making waves in my water glass. Now she was tapping out "Walk the Line." Finally she said, "Okay, Cord, here's my offer. We can continue to do things together. Try again to discover us. I will be your best friend; but no romantic ties and no promises, no kissing doctors."

"But you told me that sometimes a person's memory comes back when he does things he's done before. Some of those things act like triggers. I have a feeling that kissing just might be one of those triggers. I told you how I felt after that last kiss."

"Cord, you are incorrigible." She laughed. She had left the door open just a little, hadn't she?

"There is one more stipulation, Mr. Calloway. Since you are going to try to see both Cate and me, you have to promise that when you make a decision, I will not be the last one to know. At that time, and if Caitlyn is not in the picture, then the party of the second part will determine if she has an interest in pursing an other-than-platonic relationship with the party of the first part. Oh, yeah, there is one other thing. Since you will most likely be dating Cate if all goes well, I have decided to do likewise and date other people. Is that agreeable?"

She had called and laid her cards on the table, and it was a full house. I couldn't beat her, so I reverted to my standard battle operation procedures. "Is there any room for negotiation in the 'not-so-romantic' area of your proposal?"

"Sorry, Cord, but I think you drew the line."

"How about holding hands?"

"Cord, I'm serious."

"Okay, okay."

"I have a question," she said. "You said your bishop thought I was a knockout. Now how would you know that?"

I knew this was one of those questions designed to elicit information about something she wanted to know but didn't want to ask. She wanted to know if I had started back to church. I decided to play along.

"Bishop Swenson told me himself. His wife, Prestin, also agreed with his assessment. Blaze and Rush, his twins, however, are not so happy with you, though."

"Why would his kids have anything against me?"

"They wanted me to come over and play ping-pong with them tonight, but I told them I had a summit conference with a beautiful lady. They tried to talk me out of it, but I wouldn't give in."

"How did you suddenly become so tight with your bishop?"

I told her about Bishop Swenson's visit and our subsequent meetings and how I was now his kids' pitching instructor. I also told her that she was invited to come to dinner with me every Sunday at the bishop's house after church but that she had to play ping-pong and the loser had to do the dishes.

"When Bishop Swenson came over," I said, "I thought he was just being nice to me to try to get me to go to church. I was wrong. He's pretty cool. Plus he has agreed to let me throw to him—I mean he will catch for me while I pitch. How many bishops do you know that will put on the catcher's equipment and let me throw to them? Of course, he wants me to continue to teach his kids. I agreed if he would get some catcher's gear that fits. The Little League gear he was using won't work.

"And, by the way, just so you know, I did go to church last week and stayed for all three meetings. And I didn't do it just because I was going to the bishop's house to eat right after church. I did it because . . ." I couldn't think of a good reason to tell her so I left it at that.

"I can't imagine three hours of pure torture just for a dinner. That's pretty tough duty."

"Do I detect just a bit of interest in the fact I went to church?"

"Don't get your hopes up, buddy. It's nothing personal. It's just that church never hurt anyone."

♦ ♦ ♦

On Sunday Indy came with me to church and then to dinner at the Swensons's. Later that night I was informed that I would be participating in a Wednesday night bowling duel. It pitted Indy and me against Prestin and Bishop Swenson. The loser had to treat to ice cream at B&R. I had reminded the good Bishop that Mormons don't bet.

He replied, "It's not gambling if you know you're going to win."

I don't like to lose in anything, except maybe in bowling. I'm just an average bowler. I wanted to make it clear that this was for ice cream not bragging rights; besides, average may be a little overstated. The real kicker is that spring training was just around the corner and I didn't dare bowl right-handed; I'd have to bowl lefty. Indy tried to explain to me that it didn't matter if we won or lost, that it was just a game.

"It always matters," I said. "However, in this case, even though it wouldn't count in my win or loss column, it could count as a debit in my checking account if we lost. However, I'm good under pressure and I am sort of ambidextrous." I could tell she was not a true believer.

The next thing I knew Bishop Swenson was trying to con us into giving them a handicap, claiming Prestin was so bad that she needed bumpers to keep the ball in the lane. Can you believe it, a bishop sandbagging? I didn't buy it, and he finally agreed to the straight up offer a little too quickly. I knew I had just been fleeced.

On Wednesday I went to the hospital to pick up Indy to go to the much anticipated bowling match. Alli, the cute receptionist, sent me back to room 110 to meet 'Doc Jones.'

I was walking down the hall, and believe it or not, coming right at me like a runaway steamroller was Nurse Fielding. She recognized me from a distance and got that look like she wanted to peel my skin off in small strips. I didn't know what I had done to her. Maybe she was just ornery to everyone, or maybe she had decided she was Indy's protector and I was the bad guy.

"That you, Mr. Calloway? I thought we got rid of you some time ago."

"Um, well yes, I was released, but I'm here to see Dr. Jones."

"That woman still seein' you? Sometimes I just don't understand Doc Jones." She continued walking straight toward me. I had to step aside to avoid a head-on, full-body impact collision. I'm not sure who would have been hurt more had there been impact. I mean, I'm pretty good sized, but she wasn't about to slow down or try to avoid me. She was solid like David Ortiz, the designated hitter from the Red Sox.

I found room 110 and walked in without knocking. Dr. Stewart was sitting in a chair behind the desk while Indy was sitting on the edge of the desk. They were laughing when I entered. Indy smiled at me and said, "You know John, don't you, Cord?"

"Yeah, I know 'Johnny Boy,' the inflated ego walking around with a stethoscope hanging around his neck." At least that's what I wanted to say, but instead I said, "Yes, I believe I met Dr. . . . Dr. Stewart isn't it?" I didn't want to hang with Johnny Boy, and I wasn't sure I wanted him monitoring our conversation, so I asked, "Are you ready to go?"

Johnny Boy popped up and said, "Indy told me you were going bowling. Sure you don't need one more player?"

Indy slugged John in the arm and said, "John, I told you that we had a full group tonight."

I wasn't sure I liked this dude. He was just a little too friendly with Indy, and besides, he acted a little effeminate. Indy said, "Cord, I'll just go in and change. You can hang out with John until I get back."

"I'll meet you out by the reception desk. I think I saw an old friend out there." There was no way I was going to sit in a room and chat with Dr. Stewart. I would rather take my chance of being blind-sided by Nurse Fielding.

Indy found me staring out the window at the mountains but not seeing anything. "Did you find your friend?"

I didn't like to lie, but I already had. "No, he must have left before I got back."

I reminded Indy before we got in my truck about speaking nicely to Betsy. She just laughed. I knew she didn't take Betsy seriously. I told her it wasn't a laughing matter. I was surprised that we got to the bowling alley without any trouble from Betsy. The Swensons were already there. "Practicing?" I inquired. Indy walked over to Prestin and gave her a hug and they laughed.

"What about me?" I asked Indy. She ignored me, but Prestin came over and gave me a big hug. "Thanks, but I think Indy's getting jealous." Indy heard my comment, shook her head, and walked away. "Maybe not," I mumbled.

All too often I continued to get the feeling I was missing something, like the guy felt who got a novel where the middle chapters had been removed. I caught up to Indy as she was sorting through the bowling shoes and said, "I didn't know you knew Prestin."

"Of course I know her. I met her several times when I went to your ward with you. I really like her." With that she went to find a bowling ball. It seems I had walked into the middle of this movie too. It was hard trying to fill in the gaps all the time, so I faked it a lot.

I'm a little embarrassed to admit that I bowled the worst series in our group. Indy held up her end with the second best score. I hate to admit that even Prestin beat me. When I threw the ball, it almost broke the pins. Prestin rolled the ball slowly. I don't think you could classify it as a "throw" since the ball rolled so slowly that it practically reversed directions halfway down the lane and then continued on its leisurely way, barely making it to the pins. When it did finally hit the pins, it hit so softly that I thought the ball would bounce off the pin instead of knocking it down. But as if on cue, one pin would fall over; it would knock down another pin, and before you knew it, almost all of the pins were lying down instead of standing. It was incredible. Oh well, bowling was never my game, but my male pride did take another small beating.

Although the Swensons were about ten years my senior, I felt right at home with them. They were good people, and if I didn't know better, I wouldn't have believed he was a bishop. The bishops I remembered could eat a raw heart out of a rattlesnake without flinching.

Indy wasn't kidding about keeping our relationship platonic. She couldn't have sat any farther away in the truck. She was nice, entirely too nice, but I got the feeling she couldn't get out of Betsy fast enough when we got to the hospital to pick up her car. I told her I would follow her home, just to make sure she was safe. She tried to tell me it wasn't necessary, but I followed her anyway. Sometimes I can be stubborn too.

♦ ♦ ♦

Several days later Cory Newell, a teammate, called. Cory was my best friend in the Royals's organization. Minor league teammates usually bond like brothers since daily we all face the grim reaper named "released." Besides, we lived together for six months. Cory needed to talk. He was a mid-infielder from Iowa and had been married four years. He married his high school sweetheart one year after graduating from high school. Cory was distraught because his wife had casually informed him that she was through, that she was leaving him and had filed for divorce. She told him she couldn't be married to a baseball player. She wanted someone who had a job, who was home for more than six months out of the year. Furthermore, she hated to go to baseball games and didn't like traveling during the summer to see him play.

He never saw it coming. He felt like she threw him a nasty knuckle curve, although I remembered that he was less than attentive to her during the season. It was a mystery to me why he had married her in the first place. I guess he called me because he needed a friend to talk to. We talked for a long while and agreed to room together if we ended up on the same team this year. Baseball is tough on marriages, and only the most committed make it. I felt sorry for Cory, but I felt their marriage was probably on the ropes last year. This recent announcement didn't surprise me as much as it did him.

Cory told me he had received a contract from the Royals, and he was surprised when I told him they weren't going to give me a contract, that I had to earn one during spring training. He told me he was going to bring his car to spring training, which was great since I never had access to one during spring training. It would be nice to be mobile.

Speaking to Cory turned my thoughts to last season. I had had a great year. My stats led the entire organization in several categories. They should have given me a contract this year based only on my stats from last year. I knew it was going to be the same thing all over again. It would always be that way for me since I had signed as a free agent.

Last year I had started the season as the eleventh pitcher on the team that only had eleven pitchers. That meant that I would be last in any rotation. I had been assigned to the Burlington Bees, a single A team playing in the Midwest League out of Burlington, Iowa. It wasn't long into the season that the manager took a liking to me because I threw strikes, never walked anyone, and got outs. Halfway through the year I led the team; in fact, I led the entire Royals's minor league organization with wins, and I had the lowest ERA. And I was just a reliever. I was 7-1 at midseason with a 1.7 ERA. It was significant that I had seven wins, since relievers hardly ever get wins. I was voted to the league all-star team, the only person on our team to be so selected. In fact, I was the only person in the Royals organization that made an all-star team.

Two days before the all-star game I was told that the manager wanted to talk to me. It's never good when the manager wants to talk to you. I went into his office and he said, "Sit down, Calloway." It's always worse when a manager asks you to sit.

"Cord, I've got some good news and some bad news." My heart stopped working. I thought I was doing great. How could they be releasing me? He went on, "Congratulations on being named to the all-star team."

My heart started working again. I couldn't imagine what the bad news was or how they could release me if I had just made the all-star team. It didn't make much sense to me.

"So what's the bad news?" I wanted to get it over with.

"You won't be playing in the all-star game." If they were going to release me, why couldn't they wait until after the all-star game? It didn't make any sense to me.

"How come?"

"It seems the organization wants you in Wilmington, Delaware tomorrow."

The Wilmington Blue Rocks team is the high A franchise for the Royals. Most of the high draft picks end up in Wilmington. I started breathing again. This was great news. I was moving up to play with the hot shots after only half a season. I felt like jumping up and down and shouting until my voice went south, but all I said was, "Thanks, coach. I owe a lot to you. You trusted me and gave me a chance to succeed. I would never have been able to do what I did without your trust and help."

I stood and shook his hand and said, "How do I do this?"

"I'll have a ticket for you first thing in the morning, and someone will drive you to the airport. Now go home and pack and get ready to go. And, Cord, go up there and show those 'prospects' how to pitch. I believe you have a chance to make it."

I was lucky to have a coach who gave me a chance, even though I had been listed as number eleven at the start of the season. Now I would have to convince a new manager I was good enough to get a chance. So much depended on the manager having some confidence in me. I also did not like leaving my friends, and particularly Cory. However, I learned that nothing was ever permanent in baseball, and you did what the organization wanted or you went home.

So at mid-season I was thrust onto a new team, a team that had been playing together for three months. Everyone knew everyone and their place. As a new face on the team, it meant that

I would cut into the playing time of guys already there. Nobody liked to lose playing time, so new guys are not always welcomed with open arms. However, it's just part of professional baseball, and I had to learn to adapt.

I had a rocky start with the Blue Rocks, but after my first two appearances, I settled down. By the end of the season I had the lowest ERA on the team and the best strikeout-to-walk ratio in the organization, 16-1. I wasn't a strikeout pitcher, but I got my share of them. I throw a hard sinker and, consequently, most batters hit ground balls. My only baseball prayer is for gifted infielders who can catch ground balls. I also throw a very good, late, sharp-breaking curve and a great change. I can throw any of them for strikes at any time in the count, and that is a real advantage for a pitcher.

I knew the pitching coach and the manager had really liked me in Wilmington, and I thought for sure they would go to bat for me and make sure I got a contract this year. Consequently, I was really surprised when I didn't get one. But baseball organizations don't rank you as a "prospect" (someone who can pitch in the major league) unless you can throw consistently over ninety miles per hour. If you hit that magic number, you don't have to be able to pitch, just throw hard. They think they can teach you how to pitch. I think it's a bad theory, and one day professional baseball will figure it out. I ended up the season with a record of 11-2, best in the organization, but I was still not considered a "prospect," just a good A ball pitcher.

♦ ♦ ♦

That afternoon I had another pitching session with the bishop and the twins. This time I threw first while they watched. I went through my mechanics very slowly. Sometimes it is easier to learn if you can watch it happen rather than simply have someone tell you. The bishop turned out to be a pretty good catcher, although he always complained after a session that his thumb was broken and his hand would be swollen for two hours. My sinking fastball is hard to catch since it looks like it's going to one spot but dives downward as it gets to the plate. Consequently, catchers usually end up catching it on the thumb instead of in the pocket. When that happens, it hurts. He didn't complain, but I saw him holding his thumb and hand a lot.

It didn't appear that Bishop Swenson had an agenda to get me back to church. In fact, he never mentioned it to me. The Swensons always made me come over after a pitching session, and I usually ended up staying for dinner. I felt comfortable in their home. If I ever had a family, I wanted it to be like the Swensons. As for church, well, I just kind of got pulled along with the current. It seemed that every Sunday Indy and I ended up going to my ward and then to the Swensons's for dinner.

On Valentines Day I took Indy back to The Roof. I had been doing some substitute teaching and had a few bucks in my wallet, so I figured I could treat her this time. Besides, I had also rented the upstairs of my house to a really nice young couple. As we left the restaurant, we walked along the plaza. It was a little chilly, and I reached over and put my arm around her and pulled her close. She didn't object. That was a good sign.

"I'm outta here in two weeks, Indy. But you know, it may be harder to leave this year than ever before. I'm going to miss you."

"I'll miss you too, Cord. It's going to be lonely, but the Swensons still want me to come over to their house for dinner, which will help fill some of the time. John offered to take me bowling. So I guess I'll find some things to do to keep busy."

I was sure that Johnny Boy would try to fill in all of her dead time if she would allow him. "Are you still going to try to come down to spring training?" I asked.

"I'll see. If you get settled in and there is a good time, I'm sure I can come down for two or three days. The Swensons are planning on going, so you should have a real fan club watching."

I was hoping that the magic of the night hadn't worn off as I drove her home. It was getting harder each night not to make a complete commitment to Indy. I really wasn't looking forward to leaving her.

♦ ♦ ♦

I was about ready to go to bed when my phone started to ring. I was excited. "Indy, is that you?" I asked.

There was a long pause and then I heard, "No, Cord, it's me."

It was Cate! I would recognize her voice anywhere. My heart started beating, and I got a lump in my throat. I creaked out, "Cate, is it really you?"

"I've been in Europe for the last two months with my family. My father had some business, so he made it a business and pleasure trip, which meant that the whole family went. I got home tonight and read your email. I've done a lot of thinking and, well, I want to see you. I want to talk to you in person. I've changed."

"Cate, I want to see you too."

"I've been worried sick since I learned about your accident. Are you okay?"

"I'm fine; well, except that I can't remember anything that happened between September and December of last year."

"So you can't remember my coming to Salt Lake?"

"I've been told that you came to Salt Lake, but I don't have any idea how long you were here or if I talked to you or anything that happened while you were here."

"That's probably good, Cord, because I said a lot of things I shouldn't have said."

"Like what?"

"If you can't remember them, I'll never be the one to tell. Some things are better not remembered. But tell me about the accident. I feel so bad that I wasn't there to help you."

I told her about the accident, the hospital, and my recovery. I left out the part of the kissing doctor. I told her about the Swensons, the twins, and that I had been giving them lessons. I also left out the part about him being my bishop, although I didn't know why.

I said, "The twins have some real potential to be ball players. It is so fun to teach them and see them finally figure out pitching.

I feel like I have made a real difference to them, and I'm anxious to see them pitch this year in Little League. Bishop Swenson promised to send me videos of their games so I can evaluate their performance while I'm away."

"Who did you say was going to send you videos?"

"Oh." I realized I had slipped again, but it was too late. "Umm, Bishop Swenson is my bishop."

"Your what?"

"Well, in the Mormon church, the leader of our local group is called a bishop." There was no time like the present to tell her about my going back to church, and it was probably better to get it out now than later. "You see, I've started to go back to church; you know, the Mormon Church."

"It seems like I've read a lot about the Mormons since you left, but then maybe it's just because I notice it a lot more. I've read a couple of stories about all the help they've given in Florida after the bad hurricanes. I've seen where they even sent supplies to Indonesia following the tsunami. I've also noticed a few Mormon churches around here. I never realized before that they were Mormon churches. I also saw the Washington DC Temple; it's beautiful. I liked it so much that one day I stopped by and walked the grounds. I tried to go inside, but they told me it was for members only. I was surprised. I thought that churches were open to everyone. But then some older gentleman with a name tag that said 'Elder Johnson' talked to me for about an hour about what Mormons believe and why not everyone gets to go into temples. Do you really believe that it's possible for people to marry for forever? I mean for couples to remain married after they die?"

I couldn't believe the questions. She almost knew as much as I did about the Church, and I had been a member my entire life. "Yes, Cate, that is what we believe. I didn't go to church for several years, but lately I have just been drawn there, mostly by circumstances."

"Well, there were a number of things that I really liked about what this 'Elder' guy told me. He was very nice. I guess I was intrigued by your belief in chastity before marriage. When the 'Elder' explained to me your church's view of chastity, I began to understand you and why you were like you were. I think it was your fresh approach to life and dating that drew me to you in the first place. Most guys want an intimate relationship the first time they meet you. It took weeks before you even kissed me. For a while I thought you might be, you know, weird."

"Cate, I've really missed you."

"There are so many things I want to tell you, but I don't want to say them over the phone. I want to be there with you. I want to see you. But you will be happy to know that I've moved out of my parents' home. And no, I didn't use their money to make the move. And no, I didn't let them pay for or pick out where I am living. And yes, they are quite upset with my new independence. I love my work at the paper, although I wasn't sure I would get my job back when I told them I had to go to Europe for two months. My editor, however, approved my trip if I would send him stories and a travel log every week. So I kept very busy while I was gone."

"Cate, I . . . I . . ." I had waited for months for this phone call. This was the woman that I loved even if I had not seen her for such a long time. "I want to see you too, Cate. I've missed you. By the way, Happy Valentines."

"Too late, Cord, Valentines is over."

"When can I see you?" I wondered what I was saying. I had just had a great few days with Indy, and all of a sudden Cate called and all of my feelings for Indy just got buried. No, that was not true. I knew there was something that was unfinished with Indiana Jones, but my feelings were so strong for Cate. I had even been mistaken about her dumping me. My life was complicated and getting worse. Maybe it was good I was going to play baseball. I could escape. Maybe I would even find my memory. And if I did, where would I be?

Cate brought me back to earth. "Cord, are you still with me?"

"Yeah, sure. When can I see you, Cate?"

"Cord, you're repeating yourself."

"I guess I didn't hear your answer."

"I don't know," she said. "Did you get a contract yet?"

"Oh yeah, I forgot. I'm going to Arizona in less than ten days."

"Maybe I can con my editor into letting me go to spring training and doing an article from a female's point of view on the life of a minor league baseball player."

We talked for another hour before she said that since she was paying for her own expenses and had to get to work in a few hours, she had to go. She said she could call me from work tomorrow. I didn't want to get off the phone, but she was right. "All right, Cate," I said. "I'll talk to you in the morning."

As I hung up I wondered if I should call Indy. I would have to tell her about Cate's call, but I wasn't sure if that was a good idea.

♦ ♦ ♦

The next morning I was lying in bed, half asleep and half awake, remembering my conversation with Cate when the phone rang. I picked it up. I was excited to talk to her again. "Cate . . ." I knew I had made a big mistake because there was a long pause on the other end of the phone. I am a slow learner. That's twice in twenty-four hours.

"No . . . it's Indy." There was a long silence where she didn't say anything. I was in deep trouble and I knew it.

Finally she said, "I was talking to a friend who is an attorney about your accident, and he thinks he may be able to help you. His name is Kurt Bryan; he's in the phone book. Call him; he's expecting your call. I have to run. I'll talk to you later. Bye, Cord."

I tried to stop her, but she was gone. I tried to call her back, but I just got her recording. How could I be so stupid? I called back and left a message. "Indy, please call me."

♦ ♦ ♦

That evening I called Bishop Swenson and asked if I could meet with him as my bishop. He told me to come over to his office at nine o'clock.

When I got there that night, I had to wait until he finished with someone else. It seemed to me like I was just warming up in the bull pen, getting ready to go into a game in the bottom of the ninth with bases loaded and one out, just waiting for the coach to wave me in. Finally he motioned for me to come in. He was still the man I'd come to be friends with, but different. He still joked and made me feel very comfortable, but there was something different about him.

"Bishop, I don't know if you know, but my father died when I was in high school. I haven't really had anyone to talk to since he died. Well, except for my sister, but she's a girl. I need a guy to talk to now. Do you understand?"

"I know exactly what you mean. Go on. I'm all ears."

"I've got myself into quite a mess, and I need some advice. But I also want to talk to you about church." Not knowing quite where to start, I stammered, "Where do you want me to begin?"

"Hey, Cord, this is just me and you. Whatever, whenever. We'll sort it out."

I started rambling. First I told him the impact that he and his family had made on my life. I told him how much I owed to Indy. I told him about how I fell away from the Church, one little step at a time, until it just didn't matter anymore. I told him about when my father died. I had prayed and watched him be blessed by priesthood holders. The blessing didn't help. I told him how I had never received one answer to any prayer. "I guess I just lost all faith and hope that God really cared about me." I told him I liked the moral values the Church taught, and I had tried to live them, but I had trouble really believing after the death of my father.

Then I told him about the phone calls, my foot-in-mouth problems, and my dilemma with Indy and Cate. Then I just sat there, drained, not knowing what else to say or do. I had talked for over an hour, and the bishop hadn't said a word. He had just listened.

He was silent for several minutes, and then he asked me if he could give me a blessing.

I replied, "I'm not sure what good it will do, but sure, go ahead if you want to."

He laid his hands on my head and began to speak. I can't remember the words he said, but I will never forget the feeling I had. It is hard to describe the feeling with words, but it was warm and enveloping, and somehow I just knew that God loved and cared about me.

After he finished, Bishop Swenson sat in his chair. He had tears in his eyes. He didn't say anything, just looked at me. Finally he said, "Cord, the Lord loves you."

I began to feel my eyes tearing and blinked several times. I didn't want him to see me cry. Then he said, "Cord, do you have your patriarchal blessing?"

"No, Bishop, I never got it."

"Maybe it's time you did. What do you think?"

"I think I'd like that very much, Bishop."

Eight

Don't get me right, I'm just asking!

—Yogiism #8

I called Kurt Bryan, Indy's attorney friend. I made an appointment with him for the next day, and he told me to bring my auto and homeowner's insurance policies. Mr. Bryan worked by himself, not in a large firm. His office was sparsely furnished, but I got the distinct impression that money in his office went to pay for work and not decorations.

Mr. Bryan was a little abrupt, a no-nonsense type of guy. He asked me to tell him what happened to me. He interrupted along the way. I told him as much as I knew about the accident, which he told me was all hearsay since I didn't have personal knowledge of the events that caused the accident. He said he needed a witness who had firsthand knowledge of the accident. I told him about the lady who saw the kids who had run me off the road.

He had already read the newspaper accounts of the accident, and I found out that he knew as much about the accident as I did. He explained that he had already requested a copy of the police report. He planned on talking to the ambulance team, contacting the park ranger on patrol in the canyon that day, and, most important, obtaining a statement of the eyewitness. Then he would get back to me and advise me if I had a case worth pursuing.

He didn't sound very encouraging, but then I never thought I had a case anyway. The only insurance I had was on Betsy, not my bicycle. Before I left he casually mentioned, "Your homeowner's policy may have general liability provisions that could cover this accident, and it's also possible that your auto insurance may have some coverage for uninsured or underinsured drivers. If we can find the driver and establish some liability, and if he has any insurance, then his policy may cover the damages. If not, then either of your policies may provide some coverage."

I didn't really understand, but I nodded my head, not wanting to appear stupid. I signed an agreement with him in which he would take 25 percent of any recovery I received. I thought that was fair. As I was about to leave, he asked, "I understand that you are a friend of Dr. Indiana Jones. If you can put in a good word for me, I'd appreciate it. I've been trying to get her to go on a date with me for the last two years."

"Sure I will. I'll put you right below Johnny Boy," I said to myself, but to him I said, "If I see her." But I knew I wouldn't pass along his message any more than I would if Johnny Boy had given me a similar message.

I climbed in Betsy and considered the state of affairs of the universe and passed on offering any solutions, seeing that my life was in such a sorry state. I couldn't get hold of Indy, even if I wanted to give her the message from Mr. Bryan. She wasn't answering her phone, at least not the calls from me. As for Cate, well, it seemed she wasn't too eater to talk to me either since I hadn't heard from her since her late-night phone call. Maybe she was coming to Arizona and maybe not. Who knows? I figured I could cross Indy off the ticket reservation list for spring training. But hey, the Swensons said they might come.

On my way home, my phone rang. This time I checked who was calling before I put my foot in my mouth again. Like I said, I'm not quick, but I am steady. It was my mother. Just what I needed; another lecture about going to church. I wasn't comfortable telling her that I had been going to church, nor did I want to say anything about Bishop Swenson, not yet. She still needed someone to nag. Besides, I gave her a cause. If she got off the church subject, she would move on to marriage and grandkids, and I couldn't do any better with those subjects.

"Hello, Mother." I listened to her questions and tried to respond to them, but she just kept asking questions without waiting for a response. The only way she knew I was still on the line was that there wasn't a dial tone. She never even took a breath or paused. I felt like a batter facing Nolan Ryan, and he was blowing one fastball after another by me. I set the phone down on the seat for a couple of blocks and then picked it up again. She had paused so I said, "Yes." Then she started rambling again. I thought, *Man, if she's still in the bull pen warming up, she won't have anything left when they put her in the game.*

Finally she asked, "Cord, have you been to church yet?" Then she paused. I figured she was ready to launch into a sermon on church again. I decided to throw her a curveball and maybe she would quit talking for a minute. I said, "Yes, Mother."

Suddenly there was silence on the other end. I wondered if she had had a stroke. "What question did you say yes to?"

I responded, "Not only did I go to church, but I haven't missed for three weeks. I have dinner at the bishop's house every Sunday night, and I'm getting my patriarchal blessing next week." It would take her a while to digest that, I thought. It sounded like she had swallowed her phone. Dead silence.

"Cord, would it be okay if I talked to your bishop?"

"No way, Mom." I had no intention of giving her Bishop Swenson's name or number.

"Can I come up for your blessing?"

"Mom, you don't have the money for that and neither do I. I'll tell you what; how about I send you a copy as soon as I get it?"

"Will Indy be there with you?"

I didn't want to get into that subject, not today. "Mom, I'll call you tomorrow. I've got to go now." I hung up, not waiting for her to come up with a new request or lecture topic.

♦ ♦ ♦

The weather was so nice that I took the twins outside for their lesson that afternoon. We started with long toss. When they got as far away as they could throw, I doubled the distance. I then threw all the way to Rush over Blaze's head. Rush would throw to Blaze and Blaze to me. They couldn't believe how far I could throw, and it was good for them to understand the need to throw long. I also wanted to teach them how to handle a relay throw from the outfield. The guy in the middle was the relay man. "Position your body so that you can take the throw on your glove side. Turn your body as you receive the throw so that you are in position to make the catch and throw in one motion." I taught them details like that every time a situation presented itself. When we were finished long tossing, the bishop arrived and we started pitching off the mound. We worked on locating the fastball. The bishop was getting pretty good at catching, and the twins only threw a few in the dirt. Thank heavens for shin guards.

As we walked back to the car, I felt pretty good about my two upcoming stars. I said loud enough for everyone to hear, "You know, Bishop, you and the twins are going to waste the other teams in your league this year. I mean, you've got the two best pitchers in the league and probably 'Coach of the Year' in Draper Little League." The boys beamed with pride. It was true; they were getting darn good. They worked hard and they were quick learners. I knew the bishop was going to have one great summer with two ace pitchers on his staff.

I intended to go straight home and sit in front of my phone since I was still hoping Cate would call. The bishop and the twins vetoed that and made me go to their house for dinner. When I walked into the living room, Indy was sitting on the love seat talking to Prestin. I went into my controlled breathing technique on the spot. I wasn't prepared to see Indy, not with everyone standing around waiting to see what would happen. Everyone, that is, except for the twins; all they wanted to do was to take me to play ping-pong. They were clearly not in the know.

Prestin stood and gave me a hug. "We invited Indy to dinner. We figured this might be the last time we all get together, at least until after you get through with baseball this year."

I was staring at Indy. She was breathtaking. She smiled and shrugged like this wasn't her idea. I said, "I'm glad you came, Indy. I've missed seeing you."

It was awkward for me. The twins were coaxing me to go downstairs to play ping-pong. I made up excuses, but it seemed they weren't very good at taking hints. I wanted to talk to Indy—alone. The twins finally left after Prestin took them out in the hall and "explained it" to them. At about the same time, Prestin and the bishop seemed to vanish, leaving us alone. I'd been set up, I thought, or maybe Indy had been set up. But at least I had a chance to talk to her. The problem was I didn't have a clue what to say.

"Indy, I can explain."

"There's no reason, Cord. Your point guy, the bishop, already convinced me that I haven't been fair; that I didn't give you a chance to explain yourself, to tell me Cate had called you the night before. I guess I jumped to conclusions again."

"I understand, Indy. Let me try to explain. When Cate dumped me, she was confused. She needed to find out who she was. She needed to find out if she could walk away from money, security, and status. She wanted to figure out what really mattered in her life. She thinks she's resolved some of those issues she's been dealing with, and she wanted to tell me about it. We ended up talking about everything that had happened."

I continued with my confession. I wanted everything out on the table. "Cate is planning to come to spring training. It will be the first time I have seen her since she dropped in on us at my apartment. After she saw you she figured it was all over between her and me, but apparently it bothered her enough to finally call. I need to resolve things with Cate. They just kind of ended without ending. But at the same time, I don't want to lose you. I care too much . . . and . . . well none of this makes any sense to me. I'm kind of new to this forgetting thing."

She smiled, although it didn't seem to be one of those happy smiles. "I appreciate your honesty and sincerity."

I couldn't ask her to wait for me, although she might have if I could have said the magic words; but I couldn't. As confused as I was, I couldn't let her continue to have hope that things would work out for us, even though I cared. It just wasn't fair. On the other hand, I couldn't remember how I had felt about her, but the photos and the ring had convinced me that there must have been something pretty wonderful between us. Besides, even without those memories I knew she was something special. I didn't want to lose her, yet I needed to figure out my feelings for Cate. Maybe I should flip a coin, but I didn't have any two-headed quarters. I didn't have a clue what to do. This would be like a design-as-you-go building; figure it out on the run. I wish I knew what to say to Indy, but I didn't; and the more I thought about it, the more confused I became.

"Indy, I can't . . . It's not fair . . . I'm sorry, Indy. It's just that you've come to mean so much to me. I don't want to make any promises. I guess I need some time. I don't want to lose you. But to be honest with you, I also have to figure out my feelings for Cate. Maybe we can just be friends for now." I knew I had used the wrong words the minute they escaped from my mouth, but I couldn't drag them back.

"Friends?!" she asked, almost in disbelief. I knew it sounded like a brush-off, but I hadn't meant it that way. "Cord, too much has happened between us. It's . . . No, it won't work. In fact, I've been thinking of moving back to California. There is a position available at a hospital very close to the ward where I was baptized. I've been offered the job. I just haven't made a decision yet."

"Indy, don't. Please stay here. One of these days my memory is going to return. I don't want you to move. I may never see you again. Can't you put off your decision for a while?"

"Why are you making this so hard? It's obvious that your

relationship with Cate means more to you than our relationship. Let me get on with my life."

I couldn't think of anything to say, but I didn't want it to end like this. "Indy, I'm having my patriarchal blessing in two days. Will you come with me?"

"Cord."

"Please come with me, Indy."

About that time we got the call to come and eat. Prestin had fixed my favorite: spaghetti, garlic bread, and a great salad. It was extremely awkward for me; but everyone sat around the table kibitzing, and it was hard not to get caught up in the light-hearted bantering being thrown around the room. It was obvious to me that Indy did not have her heart in eating, and that was a first.

I watched and listened to the freely flowing conversations. I was surprised that everyone acted as if they knew Indy so well. They wanted her to join in the activities as much as they encouraged me. We ended up playing Charades after dinner. Everyone felt the tension in the air between us, but the Swensons ignored it and made the evening enjoyable. I didn't want it like this with Indy. I wasn't sure what I wanted or expected, but it was just a mess.

Before I left, Indy went to see some of Prestin's handiwork, which gave me a chance to spend some time with Ash. It was time to get some advice since it was obvious I didn't know what to do about the entire situation. "Help," I said as we sat down in his office. "I don't know what to do. I have such strong feelings for Cate, yet I probably had those same feelings for Indy before the accident. What do I do? I've dated two of the nicest women I've ever met, and I'm about to lose both of them."

Ash looked toward the heavens and shrugged. "Cord, you might be asking the impossible. When it comes to female problems, I can't offer much help. I'm not sure any man can."

So I talked about my dilemma. I tried to explain about my feelings for Indy, which were somewhat vague, and how much I loved Cate. "If I could only remember the time I was dating Indy, it would certainly help. But the photos and the engagement ring certainly indicate that we were more that just dating. I don't know why, but I feel like there is something unfinished between myself and Indy. But you know what's funny about this? Both Indy and Cate rate at least tens; and me, well I'm maybe pushing a five. I should thank my lucky stars and take either of them who would have me.

"But let me tell you about Cate. Cate is an Ivy Leaguer: pretty, smart, witty, wonderful, and very rich, at least her family is. She is used to a lifestyle involving a lot of money. She was raised to marry someone important, someone rich and famous, not a Mormon minor league baseball player from Utah. It's funny because her family almost couldn't pronounce the word Utah. They thought it was somewhere near outer Mongolia. Her family is very high society, and Mormons do not exist in their world."

I told him that Cate did not believe in any religion; not that she was opposed to it, it was just that she had never been exposed to any organized religion. I explained how her parents had banned me and threatened to cut off her money supply. End of story. "At the time I couldn't believe that she would capitulate to her parents' demands, but she did. I was wrong because I figured she wasn't about to give up her allowance or inheritance for me. Then last night she explained how she left her family and her allowance and took the job she wanted. She is now supporting herself and feels she is finally able to deal with our relationship."

Then I explained about Indy and her well-deserved distrust of men; how Indy hadn't known about Cate until Cate showed up at my apartment last November. I had never told Indy about Cate because I believed that my relationship with Cate had ended.

Finally Ash interrupted, "Cord, you might have to assume that you're never going to get your memory back. If that's the case and you think that you're in love with Cate, why do you want to prolong the heartache for everyone?"

I thought about his question. Shannon had asked a similar one. I didn't know if I had an answer to the question. Finally I said, "I don't know. Although I have really strong feelings for Cate, I don't feel the same about Indy . . . still . . . well, there is something about Indy. Something unfinished."

"Reason and logic won't help you. I think you should rely on the Lord. I think he will help you in this one."

"I hate that response because I never get answers to my prayers, or at least I've never heard an answer. My prayers just don't make it past the ceiling."

"Well, I felt real good about you when I gave you the blessing the other day. I think things will work out for you. Maybe you should just keep plowing ahead and see which door opens."

♦ ♦ ♦

Two days later I picked up Indy. I already had Shannon with me. It was obvious that Indy liked Shannon, probably more than she liked me. I was also sure that neither Shannon nor Indy understood me; but then, how could I expect them to when I didn't understand myself? Confusion quietly ruled.

When I got in the truck, I tried to lighten up the mood. I rubbed the dash and said, "I understand, Betsy. Two women, but they are nice. You don't have anything to worry about with them." With that, the truck started up and we drove to Patriarch Brown's house.

Shannon said, "What makes you think that Betsy doesn't need to worry about us? In fact we're kind of hot. I think she needs to worry."

"Not so loud. She's very temperamental."

"Cord, are you ever going to grow up?" asked Shannon. Indy just smiled. Indy had consented to go to my blessing when I told her Shannon would be there. I'm not sure she had her heart in it, but she was too nice to say no to something that might draw me closer to the Church.

Patriarch Brown opened the door and welcomed us. He was older, with snow white hair. He had an air of humility about him. The house was cozy and inviting. The spirit of the house whispered, "Peace is found here." Then he bade us to enter in a quiet yet compelling voice.

"You must be Cord Calloway."

"Yes, sir, and these are my two wives." That went over like a lead balloon. I quickly added, "Just kidding. This is my sister, Shannon, and this is Indiana Jones, but she prefers to be called Indy."

He smiled and welcomed everyone. This was a nice man. You could tell it without him even speaking. Niceness emanated from him. He was everything a baseball manager wasn't. We all sat down, and he began to talk about patriarchal blessings as if they were the most normal yet unique gift we received from our Father. After a while he quietly asked Shannon to request the presence of the Spirit by kneeling in prayer. Then he ran an old-fashioned test, "testing one, two, three," to ensure that his tape recorder was working. He stood behind me and laid his hands on my head. I held my breath and waited. It was at least a minute before he started pronouncing my blessing, but then the words just flowed uninterrupted. I was amazed by the things he said. They were so me. And he didn't know me from Babe Ruth; well, maybe the Babe, but not Greg Maddox, the greatest pitcher of our time.

He told me that I would marry a worthy LDS woman in the temple of our God and be sealed for time and all eternity. I wondered about Cate and Indy as he spoke. I was told that I would have health and strength to do those things that my heart desired. I was told that I would be an instrument in the hand of the Lord in bringing some very dear souls into his church. Maybe that's where Cate fit in, I thought. There were many more promises made that were based upon my willingness to put the Lord first.

I was humbled by my blessing and by Patriarch Brown. When he finished, I opened my eyes. The first thing I saw was a demure blonde named Indiana Jones. A tear ran down her cheek. Without her saying a word, I could feel the strength of her character and her commitment to God. Patriarch Brown even made a comment as to the strength of the testimonies present in the room.

No matter what I felt about Cate, I wasn't sure that I could leave Miss Indiana Jones behind. The intensity of the feeling surprised me.

♦ ♦ ♦

I decided to drop Shannon off at her car before I took Indy home. I wanted to try to talk Indy into a last supper. I didn't think I would get another chance to talk to her before I left for spring training. Shannon understood and before she got out of the truck, made Indy promise to keep in contact even though I would be away playing ball. Indy scooted away from me and toward the door when Shannon left.

"Can I talk you into dinner?" I asked. "I haven't eaten since yesterday and I'm starving."

"I'm not sure that's . . . well okay, if we can go to Olive Garden," she said in a tone that surprised me because it wasn't melancholy—it was kind of teasing, a little anxious.

I drove straight to the restaurant. I almost felt like it was our first date. We were both nervous, not knowing exactly what to say. What conversation we did have was surface and not about anything serious. It was like two friends having dinner, but I wasn't sure I liked the friends part. I didn't want the night to end. When we finally got to her house, I walked her to the door, thinking she would invite me in, but I had no such luck.

"Indy, can I call?"

"Cord, I can't continue to wonder, or hope or dream. I don't know what I'm going to do about moving to California. I don't want my decision to be just a knee-jerk reaction. And there is a guy in my old ward in California who recently got divorced who wants to see me. I've known him for some time, but I don't know. I don't know, but I guess you can keep in touch. Okay?"

I pulled her into my arms, something I had been wanting to do for a long time. I held her. I felt her heart beat. I wanted to tell her the things she wanted to hear, but I couldn't. Then I kissed her for a long time. She didn't resist like I expected. Finally I whispered, "I'll keep in touch, Indy." I walked quickly away. I didn't dare look back because I felt my heart was breaking. I had a lump in my throat as I climbed into Betsy and headed home.

♦ ♦ ♦

Pitchers and catchers arrive at spring training several days before the position players. Management believes it takes pitchers longer to get ready to play than the position players. However, it turns out that spring training for a pitcher is mostly about running. I've tried to explain to our coaches that we don't run the ball over the plate, we throw it. They still make us run—forever. I think it's because they don't know what else to do with us, and old-school baseball says that pitchers need to run. So we run. The first two weeks of camp is pretty boring. I mean, it's run, PFPs (pitchers fielding practice, and it's not nearly as fun as it sounds), bunt defenses, run, pick-off plays, run, back-up plays, and more running. We hardly ever get to hit. They don't believe that pitchers can hit, but I try to jump in a cage every chance I get. Usually when I get back to my room after what they call practice and I call running drills, I just want to go to bed. Most of the younger guys want to go out and party. I decline. I know what's coming tomorrow. More running.

They make us practice our skill drills until they become reactionary, until we don't have to think about them; they are automatic. For instance, we do PFP drills every day. Our coach, the drill instructor, hits ground balls that simulate infield situations involving the pitcher. Then we shift to bunt defenses. I mean, I can do those drills in my sleep, but every day we do them again. Sometimes I wonder if baseball coaches really understand the game or if they just use the same drills they had when they were playing, whether they are right or wrong. I think I would do things a lot different; but since I am not the coach, I do things their way. When I had free time, I always made notes in my coaching book about the drills and how I would change them. They need to teach the game, not just take up time.

Pitchers' arms are their most prized possessions. We react to every little pain. We protect our arms; we baby them. They are our meal ticket. However, every day we throw long toss and do one pitching station. We rotate stations on a daily basis: from throwing in a bull pen, to throwing live to batters, to resting. Although position players can hit as much as they want every day, pitchers can only throw so much. Overuse of their arms always ends up in arm troubles, the dread of every pitcher. In fact, pitchers become so paranoid about their arms that they often overreact. It's a fear that I live with every day of my life. It's why I bowl left-handed and sleep on my left side, and why each morning before I get out of bed, I stretch and test my right arm just to see if it's still okay. When a coach asks me how it feels, I always go through a couple of dry throws and then say, "I'll let you know after I throw." However, if it's a game situation and the coach is thinking of putting me in, then my arm is always "great."

Two weeks into spring training we started playing real games against other teams. I was assigned to the AAA team for the first week of games. Triple A is the highest minor league level. I was sure that I would be reassigned to the AA team as soon as the forty-man roster of the big league team was cut to twenty-eight. The domino effect causes reassignment. For instance, some guys in the big league get moved to AAA, which means us AAA guys move to AA, and then some guys in AA get bumped to A ball or get released. The saying is true, "There's no cryin' in baseball." Management doesn't even blink when they release you, and there certainly isn't any cryin'. They call you into their office and say, "The organization has decided to go another direction, and they won't be needing your services any longer."

That's it. They don't even say thanks. You go pack your bags and you're on the next plane out of there. They don't want you hanging around doing any psychological damage to those who remain. In fact they do it during practice so that you can clean your stuff out of your room before everyone else gets back so that those remaining don't have to hear the disgruntled comments of those being released. I had experienced it all. I had been sent to the coaches' office and moved from AA to A ball. No one ever told me why; they just told me where to go. Baseball management is like that. I guess it's because they don't have to treat you nice—there are too many guys waiting in the wings to take your place.

♦ ♦ ♦

Two weeks into spring training the Swensons arrived in Surprise, Arizona, the site of our spring training complex. They were staying in a hotel close to the practice fields. The practice complex we use is composed of six full practice fields next to a full-size park where the big leaguers play their spring training exhibition games. People who go to spring training can watch any of the teams they choose, from big leaguers to A ball, as they practice or play their games from nine in the morning until late at night.

The morning after the Swensons's arrival, the boys, including Ash, decided they would spend the day at the ball fields while the girls were going shopping. We were all going to meet later that night and go to the big league exhibition game. Everyone was excited to go to the game, but the boys were more excited to watch me practice and maybe get a chance to see me pitch in a game.

Prestin and Isabell had no intention of wasting the whole day watching baseball. Instead they were going to Last Chance, an outlet store for Nordstrom in central Phoenix. I think every woman who goes to Phoenix from Utah has to visit Last Chance.

Bishop Swenson and the twins arrived at my practice diamond before we even got there. They didn't want to miss anything. The bishop wanted to watch so he could learn drills to use for his Little League team. The boys just wanted to watch the whole thing. I knew they could imagine themselves doing the same thing in a few years. That's what kids do: dream.

I saw them standing by the fence as I walked in to practice and walked over to talk to them. "Here's my schedule for the day. We practice until about eleven and then we break. We have a game today at one o'clock against the Astros right here at this field. You guys go get something to eat when we break, but save a little room because as soon as I finish my game around three we can go pig out at In-N-Out Burger." I was drooling just thinking about those hamburgers. They are the best.

"Does that sound like a plan, Bishop?"

"Cord, how about calling me Ash? Bishop just sounds a little formal around here. But yeah, it sounds like a great plan."

Ash and the boys showed up at my game right on time. The boys brought their gloves, hoping to catch a foul ball. I pitched the fourth, fifth, and sixth innings against the Astros AAA team. I only threw twenty-three pitches for three innings and had two strikeouts, no hits, no walks, and six ground balls. Anything under ten pitches an inning is considered great. Of course, the twins thought I pitched like Greg Maddox. It was nice to be a hero. I worked hard to live up to their image.

After the game, we went to In-N-Out Burger. It was everything I had dreamed of and more. The girls met us that night just before the big league game. Prestin gave me the biggest hug when they finally made it. I really liked her. She was so natural and she made me feel so important. Little did she know how much I envied her and her whole family. They were the family that I never had, one that I vowed to have someday.

Prestin pulled me over to one side while the boys took off to get autographs. Ash sat several seats away from us so he could save two seats for the boys. The minute we sat down, Prestin started talking. "So, tell me how you're doing. Tell me about your love life."

"Well, it's down to nothing, unless PFPs count."

"What?"

"PFP's. It stands for pitchers fielding practice."

"Come on, Cord; tell me about Caitlyn. We've heard so much about her."

"You might get a chance to meet her. She'll be here on Saturday, and I have the whole afternoon off. Maybe we can all do something."

"Maybe she will want to go to Last Chance," she laughed.

"No. She may like Nordstrom, but not Last Chance."

"Okay, so she's not into bargains. Tell me about her."

Prestin was like my best friend; I could talk to her about anything. I'll bet everyone thinks the same thing about her. While we were talking, the boys talked Ash into going to the left field bleachers to try to catch some homerun balls during batting practice.

"Okay, but I have to tell you the short version. I played for the Blue Rocks last year. They are a high A team with their home in Wilmington, Delaware. I got hooked up with the Gromwell family." I told her about the Gromwells and their mansion in the "old money" area.

"One day the Gromwells were having a block party, with all of the neighbors invited. The Gromwells introduced us as their house guests, treating us like we were celebrities. Believe me, I'm not much good at being a celebrity, so I sneaked away with the Gromwell kids. Anyway, the Belfords lived next door to the Gromwells—but understand that next door is ten acres away. After playing with the kids I came back to get something to eat. I had just eaten some great ribs and had stretched out on a lounge chair by the pool. I'd closed my eyes and maybe dozed off. Then I heard someone say, 'Hey, slugger!' "

My mind wandered back, and I could almost hear her voice. I remembered thinking the voice was talking to someone else, and I didn't pay any attention. Then it had come again, from closer. Suddenly I had realized the voice was directed at me, and I had sat up to see who was talking. There was this slender brunette, about twenty-four years old. She wasn't dressed for swimming; instead she was dressed in slacks and a button-down shirt and looked like she had just stepped out of a fashion magazine photo shoot.

I had been taken aback by her beauty and didn't know what to say. She stood about five foot seven with very stylish short hair. She could've stop traffic. I had looked over my shoulder to see if there was someone behind me she was talking to. When I looked back at her, she was pointing her finger at me.

I continued the story out loud, for Prestin, "I stammered something like, 'Sorry, are you speaking to me?' And that's how I met Caitlyn."

It turned out that she had never met anyone from Utah. She had seen the Olympics on TV when they were held in Salt Lake, but that was about as close as she had come to Utah. She gave me a bad time about my "Utah twang" and wanted to know if I was a Mormon and if I had more than one wife. She was spunky and very Ivy League. She had her own BMW Boxer and a monthly allowance that amounted to more than I made in a whole year.

"Well, one thing led to another. Cate started coming to my games; she turned out to be my biggest fan. We spent a lot of time together when I was in Wilmington. Sometimes she even traveled to away games. She had an incredible wardrobe. I don't think I ever saw her dressed in the same thing twice. I always wondered what she saw in me. I wore jeans, a T-shirt, and tennis shoes. I was a Mormon from Utah who didn't work for a living. I just played baseball and didn't make very much money doing it. Maybe she took to me because her family didn't. She was a little rebellious.

"By the end of summer I had fallen in love with Cate, and I thought she loved me. Then we had a summit meeting with her family, and her father explained it to me." I told her about the meeting and the events that led me to walking out of the house and out of Cate's life. I had been so shocked that it had been so easy for her to let me go, but she had. And then I told Prestin all I knew about Cate going against her parents' wishes and the events that led to her coming out to see me.

"I still have very strong feelings for her. I think she still likes me, but I haven't had time to really talk to her. She said she didn't want to talk over the phone; she wanted it to be a face to face meeting. I can't wait to see her."

"I'm anxious to meet her," said Prestin. "She sounds intriguing."

But for some reason I wanted to talk to Prestin about Indy. It was like an itch that you can't scratch. So finally I asked, "Prestin, have you spoken with Indy? I really miss her . . . and yes, I say that right after I've told you how I feel about Cate. Don't ask me, because I don't understand it either."

Prestin smiled and said, "Well, I have spoken with Indy several times, and I wondered if you would be interested. She is struggling, even though she says she isn't. She hasn't decided yet whether she is going to take the job in California. She has a number of guys who are calling her, and she has gone out a few times. The guy from California though is really pressing her. By the way, Cord, do you know that she's really only in love with you?"

"She has a funny way of showing it. I mean I couldn't get within an arm's length of her."

"Cord, you just don't understand women."

"Now that's an understatement!"

"She is one fantastic woman. I hope you know that."

"I do, Prestin. I do."

♦ ♦ ♦

Our practice/game fields are very sterile, for ballparks that is. They are functional and not designed for spectators. Those watching stand or bring their own chairs. On Saturday morning we had a game against the Angels. I sat in the bull pen with the other pitchers. You can tell those that were going to pitch that day because they were concentrating on the game and the batters while the others were playing practical jokes or watching girls. In the sixth inning the coach told me to get warmed up to throw the seventh.

I was stretching when I noticed her watching me. She must have just arrived. She looked like a million dollars, and that's probably about what her clothes cost. She was a heart stopper. I didn't need this, not right before I went on the mound. I needed to concentrate on pitching, not on a beautiful girl watching me. I waved. The other pitchers who were sitting in the bull pen turned their heads to see who I was waving at. They probably would have noticed her sooner than later on their own. Guys in the bull pen never miss a good looking girl, and they didn't miss Cate.

"Hey, Calloway, where you been hidin' her?" said Brannon.

"Do you want to introduce her to the next major league star?" asked Johnson.

"Guys, I'm getting ready to go in a ball game. Leave me alone and forget about her. She's taken. As for you, Johnson, back off. She's property of the C. Calloway Foundation."

"Come on, Calloway. How can you be so hard-hearted? At least you can introduce us."

"That's not going to happen," I said. They were giving me a hard time. They were good guys, even though they were all girl crazy. Cate wasn't too hard to look at, so of course they were looking.

About that time the twins came running up and stood behind the fence to watch me warm up. They didn't say anything to me. I had previously asked them just to watch when I was warming up and not to talk to me until I was through. They followed my instructions.

The top of the inning ended, and I had to leave the bull pen for the dugout. I was going in the game in the bottom of the inning. I said to the twins, "Do you see that lady over there?" They glanced over their shoulders and nodded. "I want you to go up to her and introduce yourselves and then tell her, 'Cord sent us and told us that we're supposed to keep you company during his game.' You can also tell her that I told you to answer any of her questions she has about baseball during the game."

"But she's a girl," said Blaze.

"Hey, you owe me," I said.

"All right, but do you know her?" asked Rush.

"She came clear from Delaware just to see me pitch today."

"But what about Indy?" replied Blaze.

"Umm . . . don't say anything to her about Indy. And don't answer any questions except about baseball. Be nice to her, okay?"

"Do we have to, Cord?"

"Yes," I answered.

As I walked out to the mound from the dugout, I noticed that Cate was sitting with one twin on either side. They were talking to her, and seated right behind her was Prestin and Bishop Swenson. Now all I had to do was focus on my job. But dang, she looked good.

I threw the seventh and eighth innings and gave up one hit in the seventh, a ground ball between short and third; but I got the next guy to hit into a double play. I only faced six batters and had one strikeout. They clocked me on the radar at ninety-one miles per hour top, although most of my fastballs were of the eighty-five and eighty-eight miles per hour caliber.

I had to run laps after the game and then shower. I saw Cate talking to the Swenson family while I was running. She looked like she was having a good time. Bell and Prestin were listening to Cate talk while she was trying to stuff cotton candy into their mouths. It was so her. She was probably telling them everything she knew about me and us. It appeared that the boys had gone off to watch another game, but Cate was talking to the girls and laughing. I also suspected that she had coerced the twins into talking and telling her all of my secrets. I could be in trouble. I wondered what she would think of Ash being my Mormon bishop.

♦ ♦ ♦

When I walked out of the clubhouse, Blaze and Rush were waiting. They were my escort service to the party. Great! Just what I needed, a full audience to witness the first time I see Cate in almost nine months. And I didn't know what to say or do. "And we didn't say anything to her about Indy," said Rush. Blaze added, "I want to know how you throw that knuckle curve. That batter didn't have a chance to hit your curveball."

"Did she ask you any questions about me?" I asked.

"Yep, but we told her we couldn't say anything. We told her you told us not to tell her anything unless it was about baseball," said Rush.

And then Blaze added, "But she said, 'Oh, he did, did he? Well, we'll see about that.' "

I showed Blaze how I hold and throw my version of the knuckle curve. He was anxious to try to throw it. "I don't want you guys throwing curveballs for a while. Once you start throwing them, chances are you'll start to rely on the curve, and I want you to believe and have command of your fastball. That needs to be your 'go to' pitch. If you start throwing the curve too soon, you'll give up on mastering a great fastball. Learn to locate it and use it. Throwing curves now will help you strike out more batters, but in the long run it will make your fastball slower, and I want you to have a great fastball."

The group was sitting on a blanket in the shade of a tree, talking. It seemed that Cate was the center of attention. Not a bit surprising. I took a knee just outside the circle. Cate looked up and said, "Well now, Mr. Calloway, I've just been talking to your fan club. If I believe everything I heard from them, I would expect to see you walking on water instead of having to slum it with us mortal beings."

She smiled at me and then asked, "How come you threw the third batter a curveball with the count 0-1 with a runner on first? I thought you were supposed to throw a fastball outside to try to get the double play." She still remembered what I taught her about pitching last fall. She had become a student of the game very fast. I wouldn't be surprised if she had talked her editor into writing about baseball in the sports section.

Blaze said, "Wow, and she know's about pitchin'."

"So, you were paying attention to the game. I thought you were just beating your gums."

"Hey, slugger! Girls can do two things at the same time. It's guys who have trouble with such simple tasks. Right, girls?" They all nodded in agreement. They were all smiling like they were saying to Cate, "Go get 'em, girl."

"Wait a minute," I said. "I think everyone's ganging up on me. Where's the bishop? I need some reinforcements."

"What's the matter, Cord? You can't handle a couple of girls?" and Cate emphasized the word *couple*. "By the way, your pitching buddies in the bull pen came over and told me to call them if you can't handle me."

Prestin was enjoying watching Cate put me through the ringer. Bell was giggling. About that time Ash walked up carrying a container of drinks and started passing them out. I asked

Cate, "I guess you met the good bishop."

"I did. He reminds me of the bishop I met in Wilmington, except he's much more handsome."

"I didn't know you knew any Mormons in Wilmington."

"I didn't until two weeks ago."

"I hate to break up this social gathering, but how about we go get something to eat? Do you know anywhere fun, Cord?" asked Ash.

"I know the perfect place. It's called Pinnacle Peak, but it will take about an hour to drive there."

Bell grabbed on to Cate's arm as we walked to the cars. I wondered how come I always got left out. I didn't remember drawing the short straw. Cate glanced back over her shoulder and winked at me. Prestin looked at me and said, "I guess you'll just have to wait your turn, Mr. Calloway." Then they all laughed. It was a female conspiracy. I knew it.

Prestin saved the day when she told Bell that I got to ride with Cate to the restaurant in her car. Bell acted like she had just lost her best friend. Cate offered to let Bell ride in the back seat. I gave her the "You've got to be kidding" look. But Ash said, "I think we could all ride in the same car." I gave him the same look that I had just given to Cate, and he started laughing. Then he said, "I think Cord would like to talk," and he emphasized *talk*, "to Cate by himself. I guess I don't blame him. He hasn't seen her for a long time." Bell gave an "okay for now" sigh but added, "Well then, I get to sit next to her at dinner." I wasn't surprised that Cate had won Bell and Prestin over so quickly. She was a charmer.

Cate threw me the keys, which I caught backhanded, and she added, teasing, "You drive, slugger."

"How come she calls you slugger, Cord? I thought you were a pitcher," said Blaze.

"She's just trying to be funny," I said.

Cate teased, "But you've been telling me what a great hitter you are, slugger."

Cate got in the car and turned in the seat so she was facing me. "What?" I asked. She sat there watching me drive, not saying a word. "What?" I said again.

"Just lookin'. You know I'm here to write a story about life in the minor leagues and I need to get some story material. Besides, you're not bad looking, for a baseball player, that is."

She slid over on the seat sitting so close I was sure she could hear my heart thumping. "I've missed you, Cord," she said. "But wait." She slid back across the seat to her original position. I didn't want her to move away. I liked her close. But what about Indy? I remembered that I had decided to roll the dice and see what door opened. However, even though I was rolling the dice, and I really liked Cate, something was bothering me; I just wasn't sure what. I decided the problem was related to the lost memory and there wasn't anything I could do about that now.

"Wait? What? How come you moved clear over there?"

"Remember the 'elder' I talked to at the temple? He gave me the name and address of the local bishop. After thinking about what the 'elder' told me, I had some questions, so I decided to ask someone who might know the answers. I spent about two hours with Bishop Jackson just the other day. He seems like a nice guy, and he answered a lot of my questions." I knew she would have interviewed him just as though she were writing a story. I wondered what kind of questions she had about the Mormon Church.

"So what?"

"Just a minute there, Mr. Calloway, I need to finish. I always thought there was something unusual about you. You see, you were always a gentleman. You never tried to take advantage of me. Most guys only have one thing on their mind. Then I learned after talking to Bishop Jackson about the moral code that Mormons live. So I don't think I should be the one to lead you astray. I'd better sit right where I am."

I reached over and pulled her back and said, "There are no rules about me putting my arm around you, Miss Belford." She leaned her head on my shoulder and seemed peaceful and contented. Then she slid back across the seat. "We need to talk," she said.

"Do we have to talk now? Couldn't that talk wait? Besides, I have a sinking feeling I'm not going to like this talk." From the way she looked at me I knew I was in trouble.

"Cord, do you want to tell me about Indy now or later?" I swallowed hard. I had just taken a major hit. Maybe she had just knocked the ball out of the park. I didn't want to have this conversation, not right now.

Nine

We're lost, but we're making good time!

—Yogiism #9

THAT WAS A LOW BLOW, maybe even part of a conspiracy. I didn't want to talk about Indy right then, and particularly not to Cate. I wondered what she knew about Indy. She had seen her at my house, and I had mistakenly called her Indy on the phone, but that was it, at least as far as I knew. I didn't need this. I suspected, however, that Cate would not just let me change the subject. She did not believe in the mercy rule, but it was worth a try.

I ignored her question. "I think I can help you with that article you are writing about minor leaguers. For instance, the Royals haven't given me a contract for this year, and there are over sixty pitchers in camp. They need to cut it to forty by the time they break camp. That is enough to make everyone worry; however, I thought I was in the clear because I have been pitching so well. Then I got a call from Rick."

She understood the problem and was concerned. Maybe she was letting me off the hook. "What did he say?"

"It's complicated, but let me tell you that baseball management never tells me anything unless they're ready to tell me to pack my bags for home or a new team. I never know where I stand. They could love me or hate me and I would never know the difference. For the most part I feel that everyone likes the way I pitch—at least that's what they say to my face. I assumed that they would give me a contract any day. While Rick was at an evaluation meeting two days ago, he discovered that they had put me on the cut list. Rick was so mad that he went directly to the minor league player coordinator after the meeting. That's the top guy for the Royals's minor league organization. He got in the guy's face, 'How can you release the only minor leaguer in the entire organization who made an all-star team last year? Besides that, Calloway led the entire organization with wins, and he wasn't even a starter. And he topped that off with the lowest ERA in the entire Royals minor league organization!'

"The coordinator came back with his standard reply. 'Yeah, I know. He's a good A pitcher, but he's not a prospect.'

"Then Rick said, 'Have you looked at the stats for this year's spring training? If you have, then you would see that Calloway hasn't given up one run and he hasn't walked a single batter, and he's been pitching in AAA ball; so maybe he's better than just an A ball pitcher.'

"He finally gave in and told Rick that he would make sure all of the important people were watching me during my next two outings. If I did well, they might keep me, but they had so many pitchers that it would be difficult.

"Rick called and told me about his meeting and how important my next two outings would be. Then he added, 'It's not like I'm putting any pressure on you or anything, but then you always seem to do the best when the pressure is the greatest. I know it's not fair, Cord. You've done so well, even better than all of our so-called superstars, the high draft picks.' "

Cate interrupted, "Why don't they release one of those guys who aren't doing so well?"

"It doesn't work that way, Cate. It's all related to how much money they have invested in you and the influence the scout that signed you has with the organization. The organization doesn't like to admit that they made a mistake and signed someone to a contract who can't cut it. They would lose face and a lot of money. Instead they keep him around until he quits. For instance, that Johnson kid you met the other day. He signed for $2.2 million out of high school. He has the worst stats on the team, but he's labeled a 'prospect' and so, no matter how bad he does, he will still be pitching every fourth day. If I go out and have a single bad day, I will be on the next bus going home.

"The other problem I have is that I signed as a free agent. There isn't a scout in any meeting to stand up for me. You see, bird dog scouts only get paid if someone they sign makes it to the big leagues. It is in their best interest to keep their guys around for as long as possible. The more guys they have that stick with the organization, the more influence they have. Besides, if someone they sign turns out to be a bust, they lose credibility. Without credibility the scouts have a hard time getting anyone they like signed to a contract. I'm lucky that Rick sticks up for me or I would be long gone."

"Cord, my first article is going to be on the caste system in baseball. Before I came here I did some preliminary research including reading Michael Lewis's book titled *Moneyball.* I learned a lot about some of the radical ideas that new young management is bringing to baseball. They have used computers to try to isolate the factors they believe make players important to a team instead of relying on the 'good ol' boy' scouting recommendations. Baseball has been ruled by the 'old school' thinking for a long time. My first article is going to be an attempt to evaluate the Royals's organization using the new school and old school philosophy. I want to do a follow up article as the season goes along. It could be a very good piece. I've even tried to get an interview with Billy Bean, the Oakland A's brainchild, who is the driving force behind the new thinking."

"That brings me back to the fact that if I don't pitch well in my next two outings, I will be going home, maybe even before you finish your visit." I hoped that she had forgotten her first question. "So, Cate, tell me how you came to move out of your parents' home."

"Whoa! I let you slide that ol' change the subject by me once; do you think I'm that slow?" Cate is smart, but worse, she's like a bulldog, a pit bull. Once she takes a bite, she doesn't let go. I knew I didn't have a chance to avoid the subject for long.

"Later," I said.

"What do you mean 'later'?"

"You asked me if I wanted to talk about her now or later. I choose later."

She looked at me like I was trying to fool her with a curveball. "Do you mean later like when we get to dinner with the Swensons? I assume they know Dr. Jones since Isabell, or Bell, looked at me when I met her and asked, 'But I thought Indy was Cord's girlfriend?' Prestin was embarrassed; she looked like she wanted to strangle Bell."

They should put muzzles on kids, I thought, but I didn't say anything, choosing to play like I was thinking. Cate finally said, "This could be serious if you can't even talk to me about her."

I didn't say anything because I didn't know what to say.

"Are you in love with her, Cord?" This was don't-beat-around-the-bush Cate.

I knew I had to tell her the truth. It wouldn't be fair for her not to know the whole story. "Okay, here's the story, or at least as much as I can remember. After you dumped me in September"—and I emphasized *dumped*—"I went home. One day while I was running, I met Ms. Indiana Jones. I apparently spent a significant amount of time with her between September and December, but that's the time period of which I have no memory. We apparently hit it off, but again I can't remember anything about that relationship; and I might add, it was during the same time that you had gone into hiding. I don't know if I tried to talk to you or not. Anyway she hasn't told me much about our relationship during the twilight time. But to be totally honest with you, I believe we got very close.

"On the other hand, Cate, my feelings for you never

changed, not even after you told me to hit the road. Therein lies the problem. I know what I feel for you, and I don't know or can't remember anything about how I felt about Indiana, even though I believe we did have a serious relationship."

"So where does that leave us, Cord?"

I didn't know how to explain this; I had tried it before without success with Indy.

"Let's put it this way, Cate. I just don't know how to answer your question any more than I know what to do about the problem. So I've kind of decided to go with the flow and see what happens. Thinking about it doesn't help. I'm sorry that I can't be more specific. What I can say is that I know that I like you very much."

"So where do we go from here?"

"What I would like to do is to forget the past and just date like it was just you and me, and see what happens. No promises, no commitments on either side."

She was silent for a long time. I could see the wheels turning. Finally, she sighed and said, "Okay, we'll do it your way, at least for now." I knew she wasn't satisfied with my proposal, and I knew the subject was not dead. But at least I had been awarded a reprieve.

I figured a good offense was better than being on the defense, especially now. "So, tell me what happened between you and your father. Why did you go into hiding?"

She sighed again. "You remember when my parents told me I could not see you again and you crawled away like a wounded puppy?"

"I'm not sure that statement accurately reflects the record, but yeah, I remember. I don't think I will ever forget that night."

"After you left that night, I got into it with my parents. They tried to explain why I had no future with you. My life would be dead-ended. First, you were a Mormon, although not practicing. Second, you were a hick from Utah. Third, you didn't have any money, and you played baseball for a living—minor league baseball at that. And last, all you wanted out of life was to coach high school baseball, which was about in the same league as a minor league baseball player. Then they pointed out a number of guys who wanted to date me who came from families with money, who were going to do something with their lives, and who would be important so I would never want for money or anything.

"Let's just say I was vitriolic in my response: 'You forgot to mention character, family, honesty, or the fact that I just might love the high school baseball coach.' "

That's my Cate. She's always ready for a fight. I can just see her in her father's face. I had never seen her back down.

"I told them that you lived a moral life, that you had never tried to take advantage of me, that you were polite, that you love kids, that I knew I would always be able to trust you, that you would be a good father—not a Disneyland dad—and that I knew you loved me, not for my money but for who I was. They wouldn't listen. Finally they threatened to take my car away and terminate my allowance. I, of course, responded in my normal conciliatory manner: 'I don't need your money or your car. I don't need you to direct my life or to tell me who to like and who not to like.' They looked at me like I had lost my mind.

"Well, you know me and ultimatums. I threw my keys at them and told them I might see them later. I left and went to stay with a friend at Princeton. I stayed at her home for almost three months while I tried to figure things out. I did not call home or talk to my parents once. I spent a lot of time trying to decide what I wanted out of life, what things really mattered to me. You're not going to believe this, but I didn't go shopping for clothes once in those three months. I realized that what I wanted was a family, not a profession. I didn't want a husband who was married to his money or job rather than to me. I didn't want to sign a prenuptial agreement before I married someone. I wanted a partnership, and I didn't care if he wasn't listed in the 'fifty wealthiest bachelors in the world' or not.

"Cord, you had something that no one else I ever dated had. I wasn't able to figure it out for a long time—that's why I didn't call you. But I did figure it out. People like you because they know you will always be there for them. If they need something fixed, if they need someone to talk to, or if they just need help, all they have to do is ask. You care about people. You put yourself last. People matter more than money, power, prestige, or personal possessions.

"I know whoever marries you will get a real father for her kids and a devoted husband. You are different. You aren't like the people I knew at Princeton. Your ambitions lie in different directions, even though you will be as poor as a church mouse and only own Levis, a T-shirt, and maybe a good pair of cleats. You have a quiet, humble spirit about you.

"Anyway, my parents tried to reach me many times during those three months. I wasn't ready to speak to them. Finally, my brother, who knew where I was, came and begged me to go back and talk to my parents. My mother had called him and asked him to intervene. I went home to talk because my brother asked, not because I was ready to reestablish a relationship with my parents. I was angry at them for trying to control my life. I was angry because they chased you away.

"Well, surprise, they apologized! My dad, who has never said he was sorry for anything, admitted he was wrong. I guess they didn't want to lose their only daughter. They promised they wouldn't try to tell me who to date, where to work, or how to spend my time. I didn't believe them, but I agreed to try. Then they told me about the trip to Europe and talked me into going. I wanted to spend some time with them to see if they would really let me grow up and make my own decisions. I was still afraid to deal with my feelings for you, and I hoped time and distance would allow me to be rational and figure it out. Just before we went to Europe, I flew to Salt Lake to see you, not knowing what would happen. I couldn't believe, or maybe I just couldn't understand, why you were with someone else. I thought you loved me. I guess I thought you still cared about me. I left Salt Lake the next day. I was upset, and I tried to forget you while I was in Europe.

"I decided when I got home from Europe that I would not

return to my parents' home. I needed to live on my own. I needed to get a job that I wanted. I wanted to pay my own way. My parents were not very happy about my decision, but they were afraid to object. They did ask if I would come home and have dinner with them on Sundays. They wanted to be involved in my life; they wanted to know what I was doing without prying. They didn't say one word when I told them I was coming out to Arizona to see you. I'm sure they were not happy, but they didn't say anything."

She paused, as if inviting me to say something. "I'm not one of them, Cate. I don't run in their social circles. They will never accept me. I will never be good enough for you. Not in their eyes."

"It doesn't matter, Cord. I don't run in their circles either. You aren't going to believe this, but I haven't taken one dime from my parents since I moved out in September. I am supporting myself with my own income."

"The next thing you're going to tell me is that you haven't gone shopping for clothes since you moved out."

She punched me in the arm and said, "You don't believe me, do you?"

"To tell you the truth, you had me going until you threw in the line about not going shopping or purchasing new clothes in over five months. Now I don't know if I believe any of it."

She punched me in the arm again. "What kind of a person do you think I am, slugger?"

"I don't know, but I've never seen you in the same clothes twice."

She laughed and then added, "I doubt you could tell me what I wore yesterday. The reason you think I have so many clothes is because you simply don't notice what I am wearing and they all look new to you."

We were pulling up to the restaurant parking lot when Cate said, "Cord, before we go into the restaurant, tell me about the Swensons in twenty-five words or less."

"What do you think about them?" I asked.

"I think Prestin is someone I could really like. However, she doesn't seem like one of those Mormon women I've read about. I recall reading something Mark Twain wrote about Mormon women. He said something like, 'My heart warmed toward those poor, ungainly, and pathetically homely creatures.'

"Prestin doesn't fit that mold; she's darling. I can hardly believe she has three kids. She looks so good, and her kids are so cute."

"Cate," I said. "Bishop Swenson—Ash, I mean—has turned out to be a real friend. He came to talk to me because he wanted some help teaching his kids how to pitch. I thought he was coming to try to get me to go to church. So I started teaching his kids about pitching, and then they made me come over for snacks and then for dinner. Now I feel like one of the family. Anyway, it's because of them that I started going back to church. Can you believe that the whole family came down to spring training just to see me? No one has ever come to see me in spring training."

"Thanks, Cord, but I believe I just made the trip out here to see you."

"I know, but I meant before now."

"From the little I have seen of them, I can tell they all like you, Cord. And all the boys talk about is Cord Calloway. Did you know that even Bell has a crush on you? But I'm not jealous. Not that she's not cute, but she's a little young for you."

The Swensons were waiting in the entry when we got there. Bell immediately latched onto Cate. Prestin just smiled and said, "I can only save you for a short while, Cord. Bell seems to have found a new best friend."

Pinnacle Peak is a huge cowboy steak house that can accommodate up to two thousand patrons, western style. We all sat around a big patio table that looked like it had been stored in a barn for a hundred years. Rush and Blaze sat on both sides of me, while Cate had Bell sat on the other side of the table. Prestin and Ash sat at the ends. Prestin looked at me and just shrugged her shoulders. I laughed. Ash said, "Maybe we can use this method to help our young men and women maintain their standards."

Blaze looked at his dad and said, "What are you talking about?"

Cate told everyone about places where she had gone to eat with her parents in Europe and at home in the East. "Most of the time you have to really dress up. The waiters usually wear tuxedos, and it's all very formal. You have to use good manners and talk and act like you were in an etiquette school. Out here in the West people come in jeans, kick back and put their feet on the table, sing, have fun, and say 'dang'! In fact it looks like if you wear a tie in here, they'll cut it off and hang it on the wall." She pointed to the half-ties hanging on the wall. "My father would be appalled."

Bell said, "We're not allowed to put our feet on the table." Everyone laughed. Bell blushed and Cate quickly explained, "I didn't mean you really put your feet on the table. It was a way to explain how informal it is here. You guys have much more fun eating out than I had while I was growing up. I always had to act like a grown-up while here the grown-ups can act like kids. The problem I always had was that I couldn't make it through dinner without getting sent out in the hall to wait until everyone else was finished. But you know, sometimes I did it on purpose. My mother couldn't understand why I never wanted to go to dinner with them."

The boys couldn't care less about restaurants and etiquette. They wanted to talk baseball. "Why did you throw a high fastball with the count 0-2?" asked Rush.

"Almost all batters will swing at a fastball up in their eyes, but it is almost impossible to hit. If he takes it, then your next pitch is your kill pitch. After a batter has seen three fastballs, he won't be ready for an off-speed curveball, even if he knows it's coming. It's hard for him to adjust from fast to slow. It's your kill pitch, and you've got to get it around the plate."

While we were talking baseball, Prestin and Bell were talking to Cate about Last Chance. They didn't even hear my lecture about high fastballs. They were more interested in shopping. Girls! I'll never understand them.

After dinner we drove back to the hotel. It turned out that Cate was staying in the same hotel as the Swensons. The Swensons invited us up to have family prayer with them. Bell was already dragging Cate up the stairs. She couldn't say no, although I was sure she had never been to a family prayer in her life. I trailed behind with Ash. When I got into their room, the girls, including Prestin, were showing Cate the bargains they had found at Last Chance. It sounded like they had talked her into going with them back to Last Chance in the morning.

I said, "Cate never could pass up a shopping trip."

"I haven't been shopping for nearly five months and I think I'm due. What do you think, girls?"

"You owe it to yourself for being so good for so long," replied Prestin.

"Besides," said Cate. "The price they paid for these clothes is amazing." I wanted to ask her when price started to matter, but then maybe she really had changed.

After show-and-tell was over, Cate sat on the couch with Bell. *Enough is enough*, I thought, but how could I get jealous over Bell hanging out with Cate, except that I wanted to do it. Bishop Swenson took a minute to explain that family prayer is something they tried to do at least once a day as a family. It was a time when they all got together and remembered the Lord. We all knelt. Each member of the family said a short prayer. Bell thanked the Lord for her new friend and asked him to bless her life with his presence. Prestin asked that I would be blessed with health and strength and the wisdom to use both in my baseball career. She thanked the Lord for blessing her life with three wonderful children and a husband who served the Lord and his family.

I could tell that Cate had been touched by the simple prayers. I was glad they hadn't asked me to pray. It had been a long time since I had done that. Cate thanked the Swensons for the wonderful day. I wondered if I was included in her "wonderful day." I told the boys I would see them at the field in the morning. I wanted to spend some time with Cate, so we went out and sat by the pool. We sat facing each other on a chaise lounge, holding hands.

She always approached everything like she was a reporter, and it didn't help the romantic mood that I was trying to foster. She wanted facts, information. She asked questions like she was a practicing lawyer. I had always told her she should go to law school. She would be a great attorney.

"You know, Cord, I haven't spent very much of my life thinking about God. Those kids up there were talking to him like he was right there listening to them. In fact, I opened my eyes to see if he was standing there. There was nothing pretentious. They acted like they were having a conversation with their own father, but it was God they were talking to. I've never heard anything like that before. I felt like . . . well, I'm not sure how to describe it . . . but it was a feeling I have never before experienced."

"It was probably indigestion," I said.

"Cord, I'm being serious."

"Cate, did I ever tell you that you are beautiful?"

"Here I am trying to have a serious conversation with you, and all you can think of is how I look."

"Who me?"

She laughed and I looked at her. This was the Cate that I had fallen in love with.

"Cate, I haven't seen you in months, and when I get a chance to be with you, I've got to fight a thirteen-year-old girl for your attention."

"Cord! I will never figure you out."

"That's my line," I said. I reached over and pulled her to me and held her in my arms for a very long time. I didn't want to let go. Then she kind of gasped and said, "Cord, I can't breathe."

"I'm sorry, Cate," I said as I let her go. We stood and I pulled her back in my arms. She felt good there. Before I knew it, I was kissing her, or was she kissing me? I didn't know which and I didn't care. I finally let her go. "I need to get back to my room. I've got an early day at practice tomorrow, but I will be off around two." I squeezed her hand as I turned to leave.

"I'll try to be back from shopping by then, but if I'm not, then just hang out with the boys for a while. I'll find you."

"Gee, that just gives me the warm fuzzies," I said.

♦ ♦ ♦

Two days later the Swensons were getting ready to go back to Utah. I was sorry to see them leave but decided I just might be able to get some one-on-one time with Cate if Bell went with them. After practice I met them at their hotel. I had been able to get a couple of balls signed by the big leaguers for the boys and one for Ash. Everyone was sitting around the pool, and Cate as usual was entertaining Bell, this time in the pool. What else did I expect? Prestin was drinking lemonade in the chair next to me. "I'm sorry that Bell has monopolized Cate's time. She is so much fun to have around. Bell loves her. What about you, Cord?"

"You mean, how do I feel about Cate?"

Then she smiled and said, "I'm sorry, I shouldn't have pried. It's none of my business."

"Nonsense, Prestin. If I can't talk to you, who can I talk to? If I talk to Ash, it's like talking to my bishop." We both laughed. "You know, when I first met Cate, she swept me off my feet. I was enchanted with her. It took all of two hours and she had me wrapped around her little finger. The problem is, she comes from a world that is so different from the one in which I grew up. She's used to nice things and a lot of money. She ran with the high society crowd; that is, until she met me. But you know, she never made me feel like I wasn't her equal. I've always wondered if she started dating me just to spite her family. She is a little rebellious. She thinks for herself and doesn't like to be told what to do. She never seemed to fit with the rich and famous, at least that's what she says. Yet it's hard for me to imagine that I can ever be in her league. It's like she's a big leaguer and I'll forever be in A ball."

"You mean, you don't see what she found enticing about a big, handsome, professional baseball player?"

"Yeah, the one that drives a 1989 Ford pickup truck and who barely earns enough money to live from day to day; the man who still thinks he's a kid and is still chasing his dream instead of getting a day job."

"That's the one I have come to love," said Prestin, "the big, lovable kid who still dares to dream dreams. The one who will take time to teach a couple of boys all he knows about throwing a silly baseball, and do it with such passion that even my husband is fascinated."

"You're too nice to me, Prestin."

"You deserve it; well, most of the time anyway. I do have a question, Cord. Do you have a different girl in every city you visit?"

"Ow," I said. "I didn't think you would notice."

"Well, if they are all as nice as Indy and Cate, you are one lucky young man."

"Prestin, I promise it's not what it looks like. I don't know how this happened. I thought I was in love with Cate, and then I got dumped. Then I found Indy, but . . . I don't remember. Now I've found Cate again; and Indy, well, I may have already lost her. I've created a mess and I don't know what to do."

"Cord, trust in the Lord. He's got a plan for you."

Just then Cate came and sat down in my lap and put her arm around me, smiling at Prestin. "But you're all wet," I sputtered, "and I think you're getting me wet."

"I'm worth it," she said.

Bell ran up and said to Prestin, "Can we take Cate home with us?"

I decided this little affair had gone far enough and said, "Wait a minute now. I get to spend some time with Cate. You can't take her home with you."

Cate punched me in the arm. "Come on, slugger, you're no fun. I can see you anytime."

I wrapped a towel around her shoulders and gave her a hug. I looked at Bell. "Why would you want to take Cate home with you anyway? She's old, boring, and spoiled."

"No, she's way cool. Besides, she wants me to take her to see the Salt Lake Temple."

I turned Cate so I could look into her eyes. She was smiling that little impish smile and looking back at me. She said, "What?" and then laughed again.

She looked at Bell and Prestin, and they laughed like they had a secret. "Okay," she said, "I simply asked them if they would take me to the temple if I came to their house to visit. They said they would, so I'm going to fly to Salt Lake on my way home, that is if it's okay with you, Mr. Calloway."

Prestin said, "Who cares what he thinks? He's going to be playing baseball anyway. We would love to have you, and I won't make you sleep in Bell's room. We have a spare guest room."

"Oh, I can stay in a hotel. I don't want to put you out."

"No, you won't. Besides, if you're a friend of Cord's, well, we have to look out for you. We know he can't. All he does is play baseball."

♦ ♦ ♦

The Swensons had gone home. I was sad to see them go; but on the other hand, it meant I had Cate all to myself. We were sitting by the pool enjoying the sunset. It was one of those Arizona sunsets that turned the entire sky shades of purples, pinks, and reds. We had eaten dinner at a Mexican restaurant. I couldn't talk her into another trip to In-N-Out Burger. I heard some voices behind us and muttered, "Oh no! Quiet, they may not notice us and pass us by."

It was too late. "Cord, we've been looking all over for you. We all wanted to come over and meet your woman and, you know, kind of hang out with ya."

It was Johnson, Cory, Smith, and Holsten: friends from the team. I groaned and said, "Listen, guys, how about tomorrow?"

"No way, Cord. We are entitled to a formal introduction to this beautiful lady," said Johnson.

"Okay, this is Caitlyn Belford. She is a writer for the *Wilmington Star*, and she's out here to do a story on life in the minor leagues. She's not available, Johnson, already spoken for. Caitlyn, these guys play baseball with me. Now, it was nice of you all to drop over; I'll see you in the morning."

"I don't see a ring on her finger," said Johnson.

Cate spoke up. "Wait, I didn't catch your names."

"I'm Nate Johnson, the next big league phenom. I'm from Texas. Where did you say you were from?" He directed his comments to Cate, intentionally ignoring me and my suggestion that they make like a tree and leave.

Cate responded, "Just outside Wilmington, Delaware. Do you know where Delaware is?"

"That hurt," said Johnson.

"And I'm Cory, Cord's best friend."

"Used to be," I said. "Can't you take these meatheads somewhere else, Cory?"

"I'm Brian Holsten. I pitch with Cord."

Johnson piped up, "Hey, we were just on our way to go bowling. Do you two want to go with us?"

"Sure," said Cate. I groaned again. "Do you know what you're getting us into?" I asked.

"Cord, is that any way to treat your friends?" said Johnson.

"Friends," I said, "would just go away."

Another night down the drain. What had she been thinking? Bowling with those lugs when she could have spent the evening with just me. I was going to have to talk to her. Of course she was the center of attention as the guys all tried to put on a show for her all night. At the end of a very long night, she dropped me off at my hotel. I couldn't sit out in the car with her; I had a very early bull pen to throw in the morning. Cate promised she would be at the complex in the morning and watch me throw my bull pen. That way she could get some information for her story; and then we, meaning Cate and I, could hang out. I made her promise no more bowling, and she had to show me her fingers so I could make sure they weren't crossed.

♦ ♦ ♦

I was pitching against the AAA Diamondbacks. It seemed like just another ball game. But it wasn't! I had talked to Rick.

Every coach in the organization would be at the game to watch me pitch. I had been here before. My whole future in baseball depended on how well I pitched. My career was on the line. It wasn't just a game. Baseball is like that. You've got to learn to deal with pressure and failure. The best hitters in baseball fail two out of three times. It's how you deal with the failure and the pressure that determines if you get to continue playing the game. The only problem I had was it seemed like I had to go through that ritual every time I pitched. However, the more the pressure, the better I usually did. Bring it on. But I still had the little nagging feeling that this could be the day when the wheels could come off the wagon. Life on the edge was always precarious.

Cate was at the game, looking her stunning self. I tried to put her out of my mind even though she would be leaving the next day. She was a major distraction. My arm felt good in the bull pen, and I got the call in the fifth inning to go into the game with one out and the bases full. The score was tied.

I threw the first batter an inside sinking fastball that he hit about five hundred feet, but it was foul. He was cheating, swinging early. I threw him a great change. The bottom dropped out, just as he swung. The catcher blocked the bouncing ball and it was 0-2. I threw him a high fastball that he wouldn't chase, and I came back with a great curveball. He swung and got nothing but air. Two outs. I started the next batter with a curve, which he hit off the end of the bat right back to me. I threw to first to end the inning. I pitched the next two innings, getting two strikeouts and four ground ball outs. I was hitting the spots, and the batters were having trouble making any adjustments. I topped out at eighty-nine miles per hour. Johnson, the bonus baby, came in after me and gave up three runs and six hits in two innings. But he was one of the flame-throwing "prospects"; three runs didn't bother him or management.

"Hey, did you see that?" the coach for the AAA team said. "He topped out at ninety-five." I wondered if these guys watched the game or just their radar gun. They didn't know anything about pitching.

We spent Cate's last night alone, without any chaperones. We went to California Pizza and then back to her hotel. We had spent a lot of time talking about baseball players and spring training: how each organization invited about eighty pitchers and then made cuts to get it to forty-eight by the end of spring training. It was material for her story. These minor league players put their lives on hold, hoping for one more chance to make it to the big leagues.

"Tell me about your temple. I've been intrigued by temples since they wouldn't let me go inside the Washington DC Temple."

"You're probably asking the wrong person since I've never been in a temple."

"You've really never been in the temple?"

"No, I haven't. I know that people get married in the temple for time and all eternity. I know that families get sealed together in temples. I went there once to do baptisms for the dead when I was a kid. But other than that, you'll have to ask Bishop Swenson."

"It's an interesting concept, I mean forever marriage. And baptisms for the dead. What's that all about?"

"Cate, this is our last night together. Can't we sit and watch the sunset and hold hands and, you know? We can have this deep, religious, philosophical discussion some other time." I took her hand and drew her toward me. She pushed me away and withdrew her hand.

"Cord, this is important to me. I'm figuring out my life, and all you want to do is get mushy. What is baptism for the dead?"

I wanted to get off of this religious discussion, so I thought a quick answer would allow us to move on. "I'm not sure, but since Christ said we had to be baptized to enter his kingdom, we baptize by proxy all of those who died and didn't have the chance to be baptized while they were alive. They can either accept it or reject it."

"Why would they reject it?"

"I don't know. I really think you should ask Ash these questions. Besides, what's all of the sudden interest in the Mormon Church?"

"You know me, Cord. I'm not one for organized religion, but I am curious. I've heard some things about the Mormons that are both unique and intriguing. You might say it has caught my interest. No thanks to you."

She went quiet, introspective, and then kind of chuckled when she said, "Can you imagine what my parents would do if I joined the Mormon Church?"

"Yeah, they would probably hire a hit man to come and find me."

"They would disown me forever, favorite daughter or not. It would be the family scandal of all time." She was quiet for a minute, thinking, and then she said, "I have another question, Cord."

"Shoot." I wanted it to have an easy, quick answer.

"What if I have a sit-down with Dr. Jones while I am in Salt Lake?"

Why does it always happen to me? I thought. I felt like I was stuck in the mud, sucking swamp gas. I wasn't sure I could breathe. I had been sucker punched again. I swallowed hard.

"Cat got your tongue again, huh, Cord? Of course I wouldn't go talk to her, not that I wouldn't want to; but I'm not sure I'm ready to hear what she would have to say, not just yet. Besides, I really wanted to see what you would say when I asked the question. I guess I got my answer."

I tried to explain, but nothing came out. She didn't seem to understand or remember that she was leaving in the morning. It seemed she was more anxious to find out about the Mormons than she was in kissing me. Sometimes she asked too many questions.

We sat on the couch and neither of us said much. Neither wanted the night to end. I took her in my arms and kissed her. I liked that part, but I knew I had to leave. We promised to email or call every day. I told her nights would be better since it's cheaper. Besides, I knew if she was talking to me, she wouldn't be out dating someone else.

♦ ♦ ♦

Several weeks passed and spring training was breaking up at the end of the week. I was still around and playing with the Blue Rocks. Cory was splitting his time between the Blue Rocks and Burlington, but we still managed to spend time together every night. Neither of us wanted to go out and party like most of the younger guys. He told me how he hated everything about his divorce. He still loved his wife, but he and his wife had nothing in common. And she wasn't willing to try to fix the marriage. She hated baseball. She wanted him to get a real job and grow up. They didn't go to the same church. They didn't have any kids. Her parents hadn't liked him since the first time they met him, and they had never changed their minds since. She wanted someone she loved, and she didn't love him anymore.

I told him about Cate and Indy and my accident and loss of memory. He could hardly wait for me to finish before he threw in his two cents' worth. "I've never met Indy, but I did meet Cate, and she is one pretty special lady. She's a package deal: looks, money, personality, and fun. Besides, she likes baseball. If you decide to dump her, make sure I get her phone number."

"It wouldn't do you any good. She'd never go out with a hick like you," I said.

"Look who's talkin'—a hayseed from Utah."

♦ ♦ ♦

At the end of spring training I was notified to pack my bags and catch the next flight to Wilmington, Delaware. I had another shot at my dream. I hadn't made the AA team, but at least I was still in the game. I sent an email announcing my status to the Swensons, Cate, Indy, and my sister, Shannon. My mother had to have help just sending emails, so I figured she would get word from Shannon.

I was shocked to see an email from Indy in my in-box. I opened it. It was short and unemotional:

Cord,

I've been thinking about you. I hope that you are happy and that baseball is all that you hoped. I've decided to stay in Salt Lake. There would have been too much pressure had I gone back to California. It was easier to stay in Utah. I talked to Prestin after her visit to Arizona. She said you looked great and that her boys have placed you on a ten-foot pedestal. She seemed a little distant, but then maybe it was just me.

Indy

It seemed to me that Indy was opening the door again. I needed to respond to her, but I had to be honest. I really didn't know what to say to her. I remembered how I felt when I was around her, but . . . Cate, well . . . she was great. I had been mistaken about her reactions to her parents' ultimatum. She had turned her back on her family's money and was now self-supporting. She was everything I thought she had been and more, and did I say that she was beautiful? I thought that Cate was in love with me, but the thing that surprised me the most was her interest in the Church. Life continued to take strange little twists.

However, somewhere deep inside I wasn't sure I was doing the right thing. The name Indiana Jones just kept popping up. I thought of the engagement ring and pondered the inscription again: *Diamonds Are Forever.* It was clever, but on whose finger had I intended to place it? Cate, probably not, because I hadn't been seeing her, and that left me with Indy. I was confused. Just saying the name Indy caused warm feelings, but things had been so good with Cate.

Still, I didn't want to terminate my relationship with Indy; on the other hand, I didn't want to give her false hope. I wanted to be fair to her. Maybe out of frustration, indecision, and a need to be fair to Indy, I composed an email to her. I knew how she would take it. Maybe it was for the best.

Indy,
I can't tell you what it has been like to have known someone as wonderful as you. I want you to have the best that life has to offer. I don't want you to put your life on hold for me.
Cord

I didn't want to send it after I read it again. I stared at my computer screen for ten minutes before I pushed send, and then I regretted it. I knew that Dr. Indiana Jones was now out of my life. For some reason, I didn't feel relieved that I had finally resolved my quandary. Instead I felt a deep loss. Sometimes I wonder about myself. It seems as if I question every decision I make. I thought women anguished over decisions, not men; not real men.

I wish I had an answer to that,
because I'm tired of answering that question.
—Yogiism #10

I flew into the Philly International Airport, a short drive from Wilmington. There wasn't a welcoming committee to greet me, at least that I recognized. In fact, Cate wasn't there, nor was her father. I kind of expected him to be there with a shotgun just waiting for me to step off the plane. I hadn't told Cate I was coming, but I didn't think that was a very good excuse for her not showing. I hadn't talked to her since she left Phoenix, not that I hadn't tried. It seemed that she had been extremely busy during her stay in Salt Lake with the Swensons. She had left several messages on my phone while in Salt Lake. "I'm having a very interesting time here. The Swensons are the best. I hardly have a minute that I'm not doing something. Miss you, Cord. I'm having a difficult time catching you. I'm not ignoring you; it's just that I'm spending a lot of time . . . I'll talk to you about it later. Talk to you soon."

I wondered what she was doing that was "interesting" that had her so involved. I was glad she wanted to talk to me, but her definition of "soon" and my own definition were obviously different. I hadn't told her that I had been assigned to the Blue Rocks. I wanted to surprise her; so I guess I really shouldn't have expected a welcoming party.

Neither had I spoken to the Gromwells about housing, and now was as good a time as any to find out if there was any room at the inn. Esther Gromwell answered. "Cord, we've been expecting your call since we saw your name on the roster. All of my kids made me save the best room for you. Can I pick you up?" She knew I didn't have a car. I explained to her that I had to go to the field—we had a team meeting and practice—but if it was okay, I would come to their house in the late afternoon.

The cabbie dropped me off at Frawley Stadium. It was like coming home. Mike Myers was the manager of the Blue Rocks, and he loved me last year. When I walked in, he yelled at me, "Kid Calloway, I hope you brought your gun with you this year." He thought I was a cowboy since I grew up in the West, and he always teased me about having a gun on the mound.

I knew I would get into games and in a lot of key situations that would help my stats if I pitched well. Frawley Stadium, home of the Blue Rocks, seated 6,532, and the Blue Rocks drew over 5,000 a game. It was a fun place to play baseball, and the fans were great.

After practice, I got a ride to the Gromwells's with one of my teammates. As I was walking up the mile-long drive-way to their house—well it seemed like it was a mile anyway—Jason, their thirteen-year-old, ran down to meet me. He grabbed my suitcase and walked beside me, talking all the time. Before we went into the house, he said, "Let's play catch. I've got two mitts right over here."

"Gloves," I said. "They're gloves, not mitts."

He dropped the suitcase and I set my backpack down, and I walked and he ran to the side of the house. He told me there was a glove right in front of that small grove of oaks. He threw pretty well, but his third throw was way over my head and went into the oaks. I turned to retrieve the ball and there, sitting on a bench watching, was Ms. Caitlyn Belford. The Gromwells were all sitting on the back porch, and Esther said, "Cord, it's nice to see you, but we'll talk in a few minutes, okay? I think Cate would like to have a word with you."

I knew I had been set up—but I love these kinds of set ups.

"But I promised to play catch with Jason," I teased, as I smiled at Cate.

Cate responded with a sly smile and said just loud enough for me to hear, "You can't. I paid him off. He's outta here. I guess you'll have to settle for me."

"But, Cate, I have to throw," I weakly protested.

"Sorry, you'll have to throw on your own time, not mine, slugger." She walked over and embraced me. I held her. It felt good to hold her. Just then I heard the dinner bell ringing and Esther shouting, "Okay, Cord, that's enough time. Bring that pretty lady up here so we can feed you two."

"But I'm not hungry," I yelled back.

"Cord Calloway, we have been saving dinner for you for two hours. Now get up here."

"Did you plan this, Cate, or are you just part of the conspiracy?"

"Me?" Then she laughed, grabbed my hand, and pulled me along with her to the patio.

The Gromwells always made me feel like I was someone special. It was easy to like them. They were very rich; but, unlike Cate's family, money wasn't as important as people. They were always going out of their way to help others, never asking for anything in return. They treated me like I was part of the family, and I didn't even have a degree from an Ivy League school.

All of the Gromwells were home. It was good to see them again; and, as usual, the meal was great. It was a beautiful night, and we all exchanged tales for several hours. I watched Cate the entire hour. She had everyone at the dinner table wrapped around her little finger. Her laugh was infectious. She was witty and smart. She would tease and then turn on the charm. Everyone seemed to vie for her attention. And did I say she was a knockout?

Finally, I thought, as everyone drifted off, leaving me with Cate. She didn't have anyone else around to flirt with, so she walked over, sat in my lap, and put her arms around my neck. Maybe I hadn't drawn the short straw after all.

Then I heard someone say, "None of that! There are kids that live here."

I replied, "Then tell them to go to bed."

We sat there just enjoying each other. "Cate, what did you do in Salt Lake that was so secret?" I was anxious to hear about what she hadn't said as well as her stay at the Swensons and her visit to Temple Square.

"Do you want the short version or the long version? If you want the unabridged version, we will need more time than we have tonight."

"Okay, hit the highlights, and I'll hit the stop button if I want more detail."

"I spent a lot of time on Temple Square. I talked to some lady missionaries who were about my age. I went on every tour they offered. I heard the Mormon choir. I didn't miss anything. I guess I've never really thought much about God or Christ or that religious stuff. I've never gone to any church except for an occasional midnight Mass. I've never had a need for religion.

"On my way to Salt Lake, I decided I was going to treat my visit like I was a reporter doing a story. I intended to ask questions, make notes, and listen. At least that was what I planned. I was blown away the first day by the lady missionaries when they asked me three simple questions. Now, understand that these girls hadn't graduated from college. They were just younger than me, and I have graduated from an Ivy League school. I'm smart; I'm educated; yet their simple questions were not so easy to answer. 'Who are you? Where did you come from? and Where are you going?'

"At first I responded in my typical smart aleck attitude, 'I'm Caitlyn Belford from Wilmington, Delaware, and I can go anywhere I want.' They laughed, but they were serious, and they didn't give up easily. I guess I just never thought that I might have existed before I was born in this world. I've heard people talk about living after death but never about living before we were born. The thought never crossed my mind. I've never wondered if there was a purpose for life. Anyway, I listened to everything they said, and I couldn't think of one smart aleck response. I liked those girls: they were different. They were good people. You could see it just by looking at them. And don't ask me to explain that one; that's just how it was."

"Tell me they baptized you," I teased.

"No. But I listened to everything they had to say, and they gave me a copy of the Book of Mormon. I had to promise them that I would read it. Sister Kay—that was one of the girls—put it this way: 'The book has a promise in it. It says if you read it and ask God if it is true, he will let you know. So, if you read it and then pray, one of two things can happen: God will tell you it is true. On the other hand, if it's not true, then nothing will happen and you can throw the book away. However, if you get the answer that it is true, then you have a problem.' "

"Did she say what the problem was?"

"Cord, it's obvious. First and foremost there would have to be a God, and that's a pretty big one. Second, God answers individual prayers, which means he cares about us as individuals. And third, everything in the book is true. And you know, Cord, I'm almost afraid to read it because I don't know if I'm ready for either answer."

We sat in silence for a minute. I didn't want to intrude, but it became obvious that she wasn't going to say anything else on that subject. I put my arm around her and drew her close. She rested her head on my shoulder and sighed. I didn't want to disturb the moment and almost forgot to breathe. Finally I asked, "Tell me about your visit with the Swensons." I was hoping to bring up something less serious.

A grin appeared on her face as she appeared to think about my question. "I guess I thought that Prestin and Ash would really push religion on me, his being a bishop and all, but they didn't. They answered every question I asked, but they never brought up religion without my making an inquiry first. On Sunday I had to ask them if I could go to church with them. I wanted to see what it was like. When I heard it was for three hours, I thought twice about going. I mean, I'd barely ever been in church for one hour let alone three, but it didn't seem that long once I was there. The church meetings were different from what I expected. During the middle session, I went to a class that Prestin taught. She had thirteen-year-old boys and girls. They all wanted to know who I was and why I was in their class. Prestin told them I was a newspaper reporter visiting from back East and that I was doing a story on the Church. Then she told them she was just kidding and that I was her good friend visiting from Delaware.

"Prestin's lesson was about serving others. She told all kinds of stories about LDS people rendering assistance to people around the world, whether they were Mormons or not. I was quite impressed. I looked up the subject on the Internet after her lesson. I had no idea of the magnitude of service that is given by members of your church to the world at large.

"However, the most profound experience I had on the trip was to be a guest in their home. They treated me like I was a family member. I was included in everything. I guess I've never been part of a family who, well, acts like . . . I guess like a family. I've thought a lot about the Swensons. I felt so comfortable in their home. I could have even put my feet on the coffee table. I don't think I've ever felt like that in my own home. It was like a safe haven from the world. Can you imagine coming home to that every day? When I have a family, I want it to be like theirs. I want my home to be a haven—"

I interrupted, "Maybe it's catching, because I've felt the same thing. I love being around them, even their kids."

"Me too, and do you know, I now have a secret sister? Isabell writes me every day, email that is. She is darling and quite smart. She wants to go to Princeton when she graduates from high school, and her mother is in her corner."

"She's cute," I said.

"Yeah, I know what you mean," replied Cate. "Besides, she

really has a crush on you. But there was something else I learned, Cord. I learned how to pray. You know, this may seem strange, but I've never prayed. I didn't know how. I listened to their prayers every day. They weren't anything fancy, but they always seemed to come from the heart. It was like they were talking to God. It was like they had a relationship with him, that they knew him. I never thought of God as so personal, someone I could have a relationship with.

"Then one night we were having family prayer, and out of the blue Ash said, 'Cate, will you pray?' They all bowed their heads waiting for me to pray. I was flabbergasted. I was afraid and embarrassed. Well, I kind of stammered my way through a simple prayer, feeling like I was standing on a stage in the spotlight. Their children prayed better than I did, and I knew it.

"Later that evening, I explained my feelings to Prestin. She quieted my anxiety and calmed my soul. It was amazing how simple she makes things. She said, 'Your prayer was perfect, because it came from your heart. Eloquence doesn't make a good prayer. A prayer that comes from the heart is a good prayer, no matter what words are spoken. If we approach prayer worrying about the words we use, or we are more concerned with how others perceive us than what it is we are trying to say to God, we are making a mistake.' She was always able to make seemingly complicated things simple. But most amazing was how she was always able to make me feel good about myself."

Again she was silent, so I asked another question. "And Salt Lake, did you like the city?"

"I love the mountains and the snow. It's quite different from what I'm used to, although we did get a lot of snow at Princeton. I'm not sure that I could live in Salt Lake, though. It's not what I'd call a real city. But the Swensons did make me promise to come out for another visit. They said they wanted to take me to Lake Powell and Canyonlands."

"You mean they invited you and not me?"

"You're always playing baseball. You don't have time for vacations." She was teasing. At least I thought she was teasing.

"Hey, I found the Swensons first. I think I should have first dibbs on vacations and things like that."

"Sorry, slugger! Maybe one day I'll teach you how to charm your way into people's hearts; but sometimes you're such a slow learner."

I held both of her hands behind her back and started to tickle her. "Take it back and I'll stop, and I might even let you go."

"Okay, okay, I take it back, you big lummox." I let her arms go and hugged her. I liked her. She was a charmer. She was so perceptive, precocious. She put me to shame in so many ways. I had lived my whole life around the Church and God; well, most of it anyway. Yet I had not put the puzzle together like she had in just a few short days. Maybe she was right, I was just slow.

A thought suddenly struck me and I blurted out, "What happened to your story about minor league baseball players?"

"Well, I've submitted it to my editor. He really liked it. He is going to run it next week in three parts, three days in a row. He thinks it might even get picked up and syndicated nationally. I titled it, 'Management of Minor League Baseball, a View from the Dark Ages.' "

"Oh, great! Am I going to get blacklisted by management because I know you?"

"Don't worry, Cord, I didn't quote you or use your name as a source more than once." She paused and then softly added, "Except on every other page," and she laughed.

♦ ♦ ♦

Cate decided to stay at her parents' for the night and then come and get me for a short run in the morning. I wanted to know what she meant when she said "morning." She said, "I'll be here at six bells sharp. Do I need to call your cell phone to wake you up?"

"I'll be ready. Just make sure you're on time," I said.

♦ ♦ ♦

The first three weeks of the season with the Blue Rocks had

come and gone. I had my first win of the season, and I had been in seven games. I had a team-leading ERA, and I still had not walked a batter. The coach had confidence in me. Sometimes I closed, and sometimes I was long relief. Baseball was fun.

Cate came to every home game and drove me home afterward. I hadn't had a day off, so we really hadn't had much of a chance to do anything: like go dancing or do dumb things that girls like. She worked during the days and I worked at night. Sometimes during the games when I was not pitching, she would sneak out to the bull pen to talk to me. She also got to know all of the pitchers on a first name basis. She had become a celebrity after her article had been published. I tried to keep her away from the coaches.

As we were driving home, she said, "My parents have requested your presence at dinner on Sunday evening at five o'clock. You have a noon game that day, so you should be available."

I wondered what Ash might say about going out to dinner on Sunday, but then, I didn't want to offend the Belfords either. I decided Sunday religious ethics was probably not a good topic of discussion today.

"You mean I have to go face the firing squad by myself?" I asked

"No, I'll be there too. But it's not a 'have to,' it's a 'get to.' I think."

"What's their sudden interest in me? I thought they never wanted to see me again."

"Well, they still want to have a daughter, and I believe they understand it might be a package deal. If they don't accept you, they have a problem with me. So I think they want to try to, you know, mend some fences. By the way, it's at the club, and you can't get in there without a coat and tie. Did you bring one with you?"

"Very funny. But you do remember that I'm going to talk at a fireside in the local Mormon ward on Sunday at eight, don't you?"

"Yes, I remember, slugger. Need I remind you that I am

going as your date? I'm not going to let you go alone and have some nice little Mormon girl glom on to you."

I let that one pass. "I don't know how I let Bishop Madison talk me into doing this. I'm sure Bishop Swenson called Bishop Madison and set me up. I feel like you felt when Prestin asked you to pray. I've never given a talk at a fireside. Besides, there will be returned missionaries there and people who know the gospel. What do I know, except how to throw a baseball sixty feet six inches?"

Cate tried to look like she felt really sorry for me. "Now I understand what Yogi Berra meant when he said, 'All pitchers are liars or crybabies.' "

"What?"

"Suck it up, Cord. No one's going to ask you to quote the Bible. All you have to do is remember what Prestin told me: Don't let pride and embarrassment get in the way of saying what you want to say. They didn't ask you to give a discourse on some gospel subject; they asked you to talk about your life as a professional baseball player and how you manage to live your religion."

"You do remember that I have only been back to church for a short time."

"If you're looking for sympathy, you're going to have to look elsewhere. But be honest with them. Tell them you have been inactive. But I also think you should tell them that the things you learned when you went to church as a kid stuck and helped you make many good choices. Remember, it was your basic morality that first attracted me to you."

"How do you know so much about all of this stuff?"

"I don't. But I do know the kinds of things that would be of interest to me if I were going to listen to you speak. Tell them that I knew there was something different about you the first time I met you. I didn't know what it was, but you were different. I've since figured out it was your Church and your upbringing."

"Well, don't be surprised if I ask you to say a few words at the fireside."

"You wouldn't dare."

"We'll see. But don't say I didn't warn you. Besides, if I have to show up at 'high noon' at the 'OK Corral' and face your family, I think it's only fair that you should have to suffer along with me."

♦ ♦ ♦

I was on my way to the ballpark when I received a call. I didn't recognize the number. It was "out of area." I answered it with a hello and was surprised by the deep voice that responded.

"Hello, this is Kurt Bryan."

I didn't recognize the name and said, "Who?"

"This is Kurt Bryan, your attorney. I'm glad I really made an impression on you, Mr. Calloway."

"Sorry, I didn't hear what you said the first time. It's good to hear from you. Can I help you?" I had to improvise. His name simply hadn't registered.

"Well, Mr. Calloway, we have a decision to make. Your homeowner's and auto policies are with the same company. I have negotiated a settlement. They got serious when they learned that you had head injuries and amnesia. They've come up to two hundred thousand dollars to resolve this action. Now we may be able to get a little more with some more arm twisting, but I think it's a pretty good offer."

"You're kidding, right?"

"No, I'm serious. But understand that there is a subrogation claim that your health insurance may exert, which could reduce the total settlement that goes to you. What do you think?"

"Where do I sign?" I figured if he takes 25 percent off of the top, that leaves a hundred and fifty grand for me; and if I have to pay the medicals, or a portion of them, I could come out with close to a hundred thousand dollars. I had never seen that much money at one time—ever.

"If you accept their offer, I can have a check to you within the next ten days."

"Great, let's go for it." Maybe my luck was changing. Then

I remembered tithing. I wondered if I should pay tithing on the settlement. I had started paying tithing. It hurt to write that first check. I think Bishop Swenson said that tithing had to be paid on your increase. I figured I would have to talk to Ash about this one.

♦ ♦ ♦

Sunday afternoon arrived on schedule but before I was ready for it. Meeting with the Belfords would be like pitching to the 1927 Yankees—not good for your ERA. I couldn't imagine sitting at a formal dinner with them for over an hour, knowing how they really felt about me while they were trying to be nice. I knew I would run out of things to say in the first two minutes. Cate said they wanted to talk, and I knew it wouldn't be about baseball. That left as topics for discussion: their daughter, my religion, my social standing in the world, my resume, my future employment. See what I mean? The 1927 Yankees. Since Cate would be there, I thought she would cover my backside. It's nice to have someone in your corner when you're going to war. *Breathe,* I thought. *If you get in a tight spot, breathe, and leave the defense to Cate.* Although it always seemed she took the offense. Relying on her was the chicken way out, but what was my second option? Besides, she can be pretty tough when you get her going. I was glad she was on my side.

Cate came to my game. She always managed to sit close to the bull pen. She was a distraction and she knew it. I didn't get in the game, so I had to run poles. That's running along the outfield fence from foul line to foul line. By the time I got through and cleaned up, it was four o'clock, and we had to hurry to make it to the "OK Corral" on time. When I walked out of the locker room, she was talking to all the guys. I should have known I had to hurry. Was I jealous? Who me? I ushered Cate away from the crowd amongst a chorus of boos. I asked Cate to drive since she knew the way and drove faster than I would have dared. I didn't want to be late even if it might be for my own funeral. Over the soft music on the radio, I asked, trying to sound cool, calm, and collected, "Do you think your parents are going to vote me off the show tonight?"

"Not unless they want me to leave with you."

"Okay, I give. Do you have any idea why the summit conference?"

"Relax, Cord, I'll take care of you."

"That's what I'm worried about. Just remember, you're going with me to the fireside after dinner."

"Are you threatening me, Calloway?"

"Heck no! In fact we could just skip dinner and go park somewhere to watch the sunset."

"Is that all you think about, Cord?"

"No, sometimes I think about baseball."

"Men. I'll never understand them."

"Hey, you can't use my line. You have to at least think of something creative, something new." I wondered how I could be so lucky. I had it all. I was rich, well, richer than I had ever been before. I had a gorgeous girl driving me to a fancy dinner. I played baseball for a day job. It didn't get any better, though I wasn't sure I would feel the same way in a couple of hours. I decided to wait and tell her I was rich until a more appropriate time.

We pulled into the parking lot of the club, and I knew I was in trouble. Even Betsy would have been embarrassed to have to park next to the exotic cars filling this lot. We couldn't even park our own car; we had to leave it for an attendant. I felt as out of place as a soccer player on a baseball field. And that's bad. I fumbled though my pocket, trying to find some money to give to the attendant. I whispered in Cate's ear, "How much do we tip him?"

"Don't worry about it. It's taken care of by the dues my father pays the club." I was glad because I never carry more than ten bucks around with me, whether I needed it or not.

We were shown to a table where Mr. and Mrs. Belford were already seated. Cate gave them both a stiff, formal hug. I wasn't into hugging; besides, I was sure they didn't want to hug me, so I offered my hand. When we sat down, Cate reached over and held my hand. She made sure that our hands were on top of the table for her parents to see, and they knew she was the one who reached for my hand. Cate proceeded to tell them about my game that afternoon. They were about as interested as if they had been watching cement dry.

I guess Cate decided to take the offense. I wasn't sure it was a good idea; but at that point, I felt like an innocent bystander—well, a bystander anyway. She said, "I didn't tell you that on my way home from Arizona, I took a detour to Salt Lake. I wanted to visit the temple there and find out what the Mormons were all about. I stayed with the Swensons, a family who are close friends of Cord's. In fact, I have been adopted by their thirteen-year-old daughter as her sister. Ash Swenson is the bishop at Cord's church, and he was nice enough to invite me to a Mormon church meeting while I was there."

I knew I was in trouble now. It was like coming in the game in the ninth with bases loaded, no outs, with a tied ball game. I didn't think throwing fastballs down the middle to the number four batter was such a great idea. Her mother's jaw dropped about three inches when she heard the news. Her father was obviously a card player; that must be where Cate got the skill. His expression didn't change, even the slightest. But maybe he expected this tactic from his daughter. Maybe he was looking dead red; that's a fastball down the middle.

Her mother was so shocked that she couldn't even formulate a word, and she chose instead to take a bite of her food. Me? I didn't want any part of this conversation. I wanted to kick Cate under the table.

Mr. Belford, in a card player's voice, said, "Lately, Mr. Calloway, my daughter has taken the 'shock and awe' approach at our meetings. I know if I wait her out, she will eventually turn to negotiation." Then he asked me straight out, "I thought from our prior conversations that you were not a practicing Mormon."

I was about to respond, but Cate didn't give me a chance. "He was, Father, but things changed and he has returned to his religion. Me? I wanted to understand more about the Mormons so I went to see it firsthand. I found out it's the same there as it is here."

Her father bit. "What do you mean 'here'?"

"Well, before I went to Arizona, I met with the local bishop to find out about the Mormons."

He was fairly indignant and responded, "Cate, everyone knows the Mormons are a cult. I don't even think they are Christian."

"Oh, you're wrong, Father. Did you know that the real name of their church is The Church of Jesus Christ of Latter-day Saints? They are Christians all right. However, I will have to admit they have been labeled a cult. But did you know that *cult* is defined by Webster as a system of religious worship? They do worship God and more than once a week. It is part of their everyday life. They don't forget about God Monday through Saturday."

If Cate kept this up much longer, I didn't think we would ever get to the main course before we got booted out of here, and I was still hungry.

Her mother decided to try to salvage the dinner and turned the conversation. "Mr. Calloway, have you thought any more about what you are going to do for employment after you finish baseball?" I wondered if Cate intended to answer for me, but she slid her chair closer to mine and put both arms around my arm and looked at me. I guessed that was my clue to start throwing. I could see that impish grin on her face, like she knew I was going to dig the hole a lot deeper.

I responded, "I almost didn't get a contract this year to play baseball, so I had started to look seriously into the opportunities available for coaching high school baseball." I could tell that announcement went over like a lead balloon.

Mr. Belford responded, "If it's not too personal, what kind of an income can you earn teaching and coaching at a high school?"

"I would probably start at around thirty thousand a year. But I could work during the summer doing something else and supplement that income by as much as five thousand."

I thought both of them were going to swallow their forks. Mr. Belford said, "What if I told you that I know of a job where you could start at three or four times more than that amount?"

"I'm not into robbing banks."

He didn't smile. "Well, I have a company that deals with investment banking. I need someone to work in the business and keep an eye on the store for me. I'm not sure if I trust all of my employees."

"But I don't know anything about that kind of work. How would I know if anyone was 'taking things from the store'?"

"I can teach you."

"Why me?"

He wasn't into beating around the bush. "Well, from what Cate said, it seems we might have to learn to live with you."

Ouch. And I thought my charming personality was finally winning them over.

Cate must have decided that I wasn't throwing hard enough because she pushed me off the mound. "Dad, there you go again, trying to control people's lives. You still don't approve of my job, and now you want to buy Cord so you can control him."

"No, dear. I am not trying to control anyone's life. I simply want to provide a way that Mr. Calloway can earn enough to support a family. Nobody can live on thirty-five thousand a year. Why, I have house help who earn more than that."

I felt that Cate was trying to make sure that this meeting was a failure. She wasn't going to let her parents control her for one second, and the same went for controlling me. She was also making it apparent that "we" were involved. I was anxious to ask Cate what her parents meant when they said they might have to learn to live with me. On the brighter side, I liked her overt show of affection. She hardly ever let me get this close to her, even when we were alone. Sadly, I suspected all of this affection stuff was just an act for her parents. I believed Cate intended to control this meeting from the minute we sat down. She had no intention of letting her parents dazzle me with their money. She intended to dictate the terms. She was good, I have to admit. I would have to remember her tactics for defensive posture when needed. But then she knew that I would do anything she asked anyway. That was the problem. I knew how her father felt. I wanted to say, "Why don't you just let her tell you how it's going to be? We can save a lot of time and I might get to eat my meal."

Her mother wanted to calm the waters and again changed the subject. "Cate, we've seen your apartment. It's horribly small and you hardly have any furnishings. Why don't you come back home? It is much nicer there."

"Right! And then I would be under your thumb again. I don't think I'm up for that right now. Besides, I like my apartment, and I think it is furnished rather smartly considering the funds I have available for decorating."

"Let me come over and help you, Cate."

"No, Mom. I don't want your help, at least your financial help. I want to see if I am capable of taking care of myself without counting on you for handouts."

Mr. Belford handed me one of his cards and said, "That card has my private cell phone number on it. Please feel free to call me if you ever want to talk about the things we have discussed tonight, anytime."

To tell you the truth, I was offended by Mr. Belford's offer. I wanted to coach, and I thought that was more important than taking a wheelbarrow full of money home every month. I couldn't be bought now that I was independently wealthy. I should have said something, but then, Cate had handled it for me. Anything I said would have just caused more trouble.

We had just finished dessert, and I must say that the meal was fabulous. I pulled out my abused credit card, but Mr. Belford said, "Put that away, Mr. Calloway. It's on us," as he signed his name to the check.

We talked about little things for the next thirty minutes until Cate said, "We have to leave now. Cord is speaking to a group of youth at the local Mormon church in a half hour. Thanks for dinner." She got up and stiffly hugged both of her parents again and whisked me out the door before I could say anything else.

As we walked out, I said, "I thought that went well; that is, if you're prepared for an all-out nuclear attack in retaliation." Then I added, "Cate, you didn't orchestrate this whole dinner just to make up for the way your parents treated me at our last meeting, did you?"

"Me? You say the darndest things sometimes."

♦ ♦ ♦

There were about twenty kids at the fireside between the ages of fourteen and eighteen. The bishop introduced me and then Cate. He told them a little about each of us. He had a lot of information about Cate. I wondered where he got all the background information. He told them that she had graduated from Princeton and now wrote for the *Star* and lived in Wilmington. He explained that she wasn't LDS but had become interested in our teachings through her relationship with me. The more he talked, the more nervous I became. Getting a call from the manager while in the bull pen would have been a lot easier.

Breathe, I told myself. It ended up something like pitching. Once I threw the first pitch it got a lot easier. I told them about growing up in the Church and then how I became inactive. I explained how it was a step-by-step process, that it wasn't like falling off a cliff; it kind of sneaked up on you one tiny step at a time. "It started when I was attending BYU. First it was just little things like skipping Sunday School, not paying tithing, stuff like that. Then it turned into bigger things, and before I knew it, I was almost totally inactive. The final straw came when my father died. I had to deal with my father's bishop, and let's just say it didn't work out well, and I blamed the Church."

Then I talked about baseball. I explained that I wasn't even the best pitcher on my high school team and that no one thought I would ever play in college. But Coach Noel at BYU gave me a chance, and I became their number one pitcher by the time I was a junior. Then everyone thought even if I was a good college pitcher I would never play professionally. Then I signed as a free agent because one guy believed in me. Year after year the coaches applauded how hard I worked and how well I did, but still no one thought I could step up to the next level. Every time I did I was successful, not because I could throw a ninety-five-mile-an-hour fastball but because I worked hard and never caused any trouble. I was the first guy to practice and the last one to leave. I pitched long relief, short relief or closed, whatever they asked. All I wanted was a chance.

Then I told them about the temptations that follow baseball players. I explained that although I hadn't been active in the Church, the standards that I'd learned in my youth were still a part of me. I was surprised how different I was from other ballplayers. Then I said, "I didn't realize that I was so different until just recently. Cate told me that the one thing she noticed about me was that I was different from other people she knew. I've asked her to tell you what she said to me. And surprisingly, she consented." I knew I was in for it; but what the heck, turnabout is fair play.

Cate smiled, but I knew she would have kicked me under the table, except there wasn't a table. Then she started speaking. She was a natural speaker, and she had those kids eating out of her hands. "The first time I met Cord, it was at a barbecue. There was something different about him. He wasn't a fancy dresser. He's a Levis and T-shirt guy. And as you can see, he isn't really that good looking." The kids thought she was funny and laughed. "Well, maybe he'd be passable if someone helped him wash behind his ears and told him which shirt matched. But he was different. Maybe it was because he was a hick from Utah and spoke with a western twang." The kids laughed again and she smiled. She was loving this.

"He was definitely different. But the more I got to know him, the more impressed I became. He never tried to take advantage of me. He was polite; well, for a boy he was polite. He was humble and not caught up with himself. But there was something that I just couldn't put my finger on. I thought about it a lot.

"Then I took a trip to Salt Lake, and I stayed with a family there who had the same effect on me. They were different like

Cord was different. It was something intangible. What I did know was that I liked being around them. I felt, well, safe.

"I've never been involved in any church before, and I've never said a prayer, not until I visited Salt Lake. There I witnessed a thirteen-year-old girl pray—no, I mean *talk* to God: talk to him like he was her father, like he was right there. She has a personal relationship with her God. The whole family believes that life has a purpose. It was like they have a rope tied around a pole that they hold onto. And it doesn't matter how hard the wind blows; they are always safe because they have hold of that rope.

"Looking back, Cord wasn't any different from the people I met in Salt Lake. He was just different from the people I had grown up with and gone to school with. I've decided that he was so different because of his church, because of his upbringing, because of his relationship with his God. Now I know he wasn't active in his church when I met him, but he still had that aura about him."

After Cate finished, the bishop thanked us for speaking, and he especially thanked Cate for expressing her outsider's view of Mormons. He then told the kids that we would be happy to answer any questions from the audience. Both Cate and I answered questions for the next half hour. I think everyone was enchanted with Cate. Of course, that wasn't anything new.

♦ ♦ ♦

When I got home that night, I had a letter on my desk. It was from Patriarch Brown. It was my blessing. I got it out and read it again very carefully. As I read it, I pictured Indy sitting on the couch in Patriarch Brown's home. I couldn't shake her image. I knew she was good through and through. I pulled my ring out of the drawer and read the words again: *Diamonds Are Forever.* I saw Indy's, not Cate's, image. *That's weird*, I thought.

Eleven

Don' t always follow the crowd,
because nobody goes there anymore. It's too crowded.
—YOGIISM #11

WE WON THE FIRST HALF of the season in the Northern Division of the Carolina League. That ensured us a spot in the playoffs that started in September. For the last game of the first half, our manager had nine different pitchers each throw an inning. I pitched the fifth inning and only faced three batters. Cate didn't see the final game of the first half because she had to go to New York on business. As if work mattered more than my game, I thought. After the game I decided to skip the celebration and the champaign and get some sleep. There were a few fans standing around the players' entrance as I left the ballpark. I tried to slip past them unnoticed, my eyes on the ground. I thought I had escaped when some guy said, "Can I get this ball signed? I think this is the one that you hit out of the park tonight."

"I'm sorry, you've got the wrong guy; I'm a pitcher not a hitter." I handed the ball back and looked into the guy's face for the first time. He drew me into a hug. "Bishop Swenson, what are you doing here?"

"I told you to call me Ash. And it's nice to see you, too, Cord."

"I'm sorry, you caught me off guard." He gave me another hug. I wasn't into hugging, but I made an exception for him.

"Can you hang out for awhile? Maybe we could go get something to eat," he asked.

"You better believe it. Do you have a car?" I said.

"Does a sporty, silver Honda Civic count?" he asked.

It was good to see Ash. He explained to me that he had a business trip that took him to New York, and he had skipped a big banquet to come down just to see one of my games. "I came all the way from Utah to see you pitch, and you only threw five pitches and one inning. I hardly got my money's worth."

"That's how it is when you're throwing gas," I quipped.

I was anxious to hear how my proteges were pitching. As we climbed into his rental car, I said, "Okay, Coach Swenson, tell me how your season is going, and I'm dying to hear about my two star pupils." I wanted to know how his Little League team was doing and particularly how the twins were pitching.

"We only have two more weeks left in our season, and we're in first place. If we stay on top, then I will be the coach of the all-star team. Even though Blaze and Rush are only eleven-year-olds, they're the best pitchers in the league. It's not even close. Of course, I am their father and probably a little biased. Even if I'm not the coach, the twins will make the team. All of the other coaches know they're the best pitchers in the league. Each of the boys has five wins so far this season, and Blaze has one no-hitter. They owe it all to you, Cord, and I can't tell you how much of a hero you are to them. As a matter of fact, the first thing they do when they get home after practice is get on the Internet to see if you're pitching; they don't even want to talk to me about their game."

"I knew they were going to be good. Can you imagine how good they will be when they learn a curveball? Maybe next year we'll let them throw it, if they promise to use it only in certain situations."

"They will do anything you say, Cord."

I was proud of those kids. I told Ash I was going to call them the first chance I got.

"You just don't know how much it will mean to them. I can't get them to do anything unless I tell them that you told me to have them do it. Of course, like I said, I'm just their father," he said jokingly.

I really had made a difference. I could just see them out there on the mound, completely controlling the game. I think it made me feel better than when I got seven strikeouts in three innings. I wondered why.

We got to the seafood restaurant and were seated. I asked Ash to tell me about Prestin and Bell. "Prestin thinks you are one of her kids. In fact, she asked me the other day if I thought you would object to us adopting you. It's 'Cord this and Cord that.' Sometimes she even beats the twins to the Internet to listen to your games. How do you do it, Cord? She doesn't give me that much attention."

"It's easy. All you have to do to get a mother to like you is to be nice to her kids."

"That may be true, but I think there might be more to it in this case."

"Well, I do have a natural charm that attracts all the good-looking women."

"I should have known that after meeting Indy and Cate," said Ash. He continued, "What really surprises me is the interest Prestin has taken in baseball. She's a regular baseball junky. In fact she hung this quote on the fridge the other day so that everyone could see it: 'Kids are always chasing rainbows, but baseball is a world where you catch them.' And she accuses me of being the biggest kid of all.

"It seems we do baseball every day except Sunday. We have two or three games a week and practices two other nights. Plus, we listen to your games and watch the Red Sox whenever they're on TV. Prestin says I have spent more time with the family this summer than at any time since they called me to be bishop. She's right.

"For the first time, I found ways to delegate a little more. I try to be more efficient with my time. I've decided that I'm not going to miss this time with my boys. However, that does mean I miss your games sometimes, and I even schedule my interviews later in the evening. Not Prestin though; she doesn't miss a game, yours or the twins'. She's become a real student of the game. Just the other night she was downright hostile about my assistant coach and said she could do a better job."

I could see their little family at the game. I was sure that Prestin would be the type that would let the umpire know every time he missed a call. I asked Ash, "Was Prestin a cheerleader in high school?"

"She was; how did you know?"

"I don't know; she just seems the type. Does she yell at the umps and tell the boys what to do from the stands?"

"Yes again. Some of the mothers won't even sit close to her. I tried to tell her that she had to be nice; after all, she is the bishop's wife. She told me that she added some balance to the family: one nice and one feisty. She says things that I would never dare say. Just the other night after the game, Indy asked, 'Is she always like that?' I told Indy that Prestin makes her money ragging on the umpires."

Indy. The name brought back a whole flood of feelings along with the image of a beautiful blonde doctor: a fighter like Prestin but in a different way. I could imagine Indy as a mother: teaching, protecting, and being willing to fight anyone or anything that threatened her kids.

I didn't want to ask Ash, but I couldn't help myself. "So, how is Indy, Ash?"

"Any particular reason you ask, Cord?"

"Bishop, I don't know. Even though I decided I would pursue Cate, I can't get away from images of a blonde doctor. I find myself thinking about her all the time. Every time I see a tall blonde, my heart starts racing. On the other hand, I think I really like Cate. And yet, more often than not, I wake up in the middle of the night dreaming about Indy. I really can't explain what's going on."

Ash didn't say anything. It was like he was going to let me try to sort this one out for myself, and I wasn't doing very well. I wanted some input, some help or advice. I tried again to invite him to join in the conversation. "Yet, as much time as I spend with Cate, and as good as I feel around her, I keep finding myself thinking about Indy."

He didn't take the bait and stared at me. Maybe he didn't want to play psychologist today. But I continued hoping that he would give me a complete diagnosis. "Bishop, I did something really stupid the other day. I emailed Indy and told her not to wait for me. I didn't mean it like that, and I wish I could take it back. I thought it would be in her best interest. I'm an idiot."

"I know, she told me. Your email devastated her, even though she knew it was coming. I felt sorry for her, Cord."

"Tell me, Bishop, why can't I shake my thoughts about Indy when I think I am ready to make a commitment to Cate?"

"It seems that you are trying to convince yourself that you are in love with Cate in spite of your feelings for Indy. Maybe you're just afraid to make a commitment to anyone, and playing one against the other always gives you an easy out." I wondered if that was what I was doing, but there was probably a much simpler answer. Like a split personality disorder or something.

Then he stuck the needle in a little deeper. "But you don't need to worry about Indy; I think she's dealing with it. She's had some time to prepare, so maybe she will be able to move on with her life."

That didn't give me the warm fuzzies, but I didn't know what to say or do; so I let it drop. I decided to talk to him about Cate. "Did you know that Cate is really intrigued with the Church? I think she might join someday."

"Cate is a wonderful girl. We love her, and I think you're right. She'll make a great member. In fact, she talks to Prestin quite often and always seems to have a question of the day. Will it make a difference to you, Cord, if she joins the Church?"

"I think I'm in love with her. I want to be with her every

minute. I can't get enough of her. She's wonderful, everything I could want and more. But if that's the case, tell me why I keep thinking about Indy. I barely know her—or should I say, remember her."

"Cord, we've talked about this before. I don't know what to tell you except that when I gave you that blessing, I had the distinct impression that things will work out for you. The Lord has a plan for you, so I'm not sure there's much I can say or do. Besides, you know I like both of them. Bell has adopted Cate as her sister. She wants to be like Cate. And Prestin sounds just like you. She tells me how much she likes Cate and how good she has been for Bell, and yet she tells me how much she loves to be around Indy. She wants to know what you're going to do. I don't know what she expects me to say."

"It would be a lot easier if you just told me what to do, Ash." Our little talk hadn't done anything for me but help to confuse the issue.

Ash wondered if I had been able to remember anything or if there had been any more complications because of my missing memory. "It's still a blank. Here in Wilmington it doesn't matter much, because no one knows I have a hole in my memory. I appear to be the same as always. But when I was home, situations kept occurring that made it seem as if I was walking in on a movie that was half over; and everyone knew what was happening except for me."

Then I brought him up to date on recent events: how Cate's father called a meeting to try to mend some fences with me. I remembered that I needed to thank Ash for setting me up with my local bishop and speaking at the fireside. He denied everything, at least I think he did, but he was laughing the whole time. I joined him laughing as I told him how Cate stole the show. "That's so Cate. She will make a great member."

"Ash, my blessing said I would marry someone in the temple and be sealed forever. Do you think that could be Cate?"

He dodged my question again. I guessed he wasn't going to tell me what to do. After dinner he drove me to the Gromwells. I made him come in so I could introduce him as my adoptive dad. It was a good night. I loved talking to Ash, even if I didn't get a lot of answers. Needless to say, my dilemma remained. I thought I needed some of his insight, but maybe I just need to talk.

"Baseball is such a simple game," said Paul Richards, the manager of the Baltimore Orioles. "It's just throwing and catching and hitting and running. What's simpler than that?"

I wondered why women and relationships weren't that simple.

♦ ♦ ♦

"Hi Prestin, it's Cord. I called to talk to Blaze and Rush." I wanted and needed to talk to the twins.

"What about me? Don't I count?" She made me talk to her before she would get them. Finally she made me promise to call her in the day to talk about my female quandary. Maybe she would give me some advice, unlike her husband. She also needed to talk to me because she wasn't sure that Ash was calling the right pitches. And then she laughed.

The twins weren't awake, but Prestin said they would get up for this call. She went and woke them. They jumped out of bed the minute she told them I was on the line.

Rush finally found the downstairs phone. "Hey, I heard that you guys are both undefeated. That's great! And don't worry about Blaze getting a no-hitter, Rush. It was probably against the worst team in the league; and besides, lefties always have an advantage." They both tried to talk at the same time, and each wanted to tell about his game and how he struck out guys on the high hard one. They told me they were throwing long toss every day and doing the Dr. Job exercises, and that their arms felt great. They wanted to know how I was doing and I started to tell them, but they interrupted and quoted all of my stats. They knew them better than I did. They wanted to know when I would be moving up to AA. They wanted to know how good the other pitchers on the team were and who was my best friend. They wanted to know which guys I liked and which ones got the big signing bonuses.

They told me that their mom had put together a video of some of their games, and that they were going to send it so I could watch them pitching.

I thought back to that first day I watched them throw and remembered how eager they were to learn techniques. With just a little help, they were now the stars of their league. I knew it was not all my teaching. They had some talent to start with, but I had helped them. I had made a difference in their lives. No one could ever take that away from me. I liked that feeling. That's why I want to coach. I want to make a difference in kids' lives.

But on the other hand, I knew there wasn't a lot of money in teaching or coaching. I wanted to be able to support my family, if I ever had one. Mr. Belford's offer would allow me to make a good income. How could I pass up such an offer? And I could always coach Little League after work and get the same satisfaction. Couldn't I?

I promised the twins to call them again and closed. "Make sure your mom films the all-star games; I want to see you guys rule." My fan club went back to bed, but I'm not sure they were able to sleep. They were high on baseball and their own success.

♦ ♦ ♦

I hadn't seen or heard from Cate for two days. The last I knew, she had gone to the Big Apple on business. Two days and no word. It was looking like another night with the Gromwell kids. Our game ended at nine thirty. I cleaned up things around my locker and just hung out. I didn't have any reason to get out of the park. In fact I was the last person to leave the clubhouse. The ballpark was dark, and I was feeling lonely as I walked toward the front gate. "Hey, slugger, do you always make your women wait so long?"

"Cate!" It was good to hear her voice again, but she wasn't about to get off the hook that easily. "I wish you had told me you were coming tonight. Then I wouldn't have let them line me up with Belinda."

"Well, I guess you'd better call Belinda and tell her you won't be there. I've got other plans."

I walked over to where she was leaning against a streetlight. She had that impish smile that turned me three ways sideways. I leaned close to her without touching her. I was only inches from her face. "Give me one good reason."

She put her arms around my neck and kissed me very tenderly. I gathered her in my arms and kissed her back. I pulled back enough to look her straight in the eye; and, trying to keep a straight face, said, "That's not good enough." She punched me in the stomach, grabbed my arm, and led me back into the stadium. She didn't say anything but led me past the third base dugout and onto the field. There, behind the mound on the infield, was a table set with real silver and fancy plates, lit by candlelight. She motioned me to sit in one of the chairs. She sat in the other and picked up a little bell and rang it. A waiter appeared, dressed in a tux, and delivered a salad for each of us.

"You think you can get out of the doghouse that easily?" I asked.

"Mr. Calloway, you should watch your tongue and speak with a little more respect. You are now addressing a special piece writer for *The New York Times*."

"Well, Ms. Belford. I think congratulations are in order."

I got up to congratulate her properly, but she said very formally, "Cord Calloway, will you please control yourself and sit down? We are having dinner."

"Forget that, Ms. Belford," I went over and lifted her off the ground with both my arms around her. Then I set her down and assumed the dance position and started moving to the beat of the music coming from a stereo by the table. The song was an old favorite of mine, "Unchained Melody." She didn't say anything, but she rested her head on my shoulder.

"You don't mind very well, slugger," she said.

"Everything I know, I learned from you."

Finally she made me sit at the table. We had a great dinner. She told me how she had arranged to use the infield and have the dinner catered. She told me how she had been offered the job at the *Times.* They had loved her piece on baseball and wanted her to continue to do some investigative reporting on sports from the female perspective. "I tripled my salary, got a huge expense account, and I can live and work from any location I want."

After dinner, we danced some more. In a very soft whisper she invited me to a formal ball that would be held in five days at the downtown Hilton. It was a very exclusive affair, which meant you had to have a lot of money to be invited. We would be going with her parents; and yes, I would have to wear a tux. I tried to give her some excuses, but she raised her hand and told me that the Blue Rocks didn't have a game that day, she had already ordered the tux, and that I didn't get a vote on this one. She explained that this was a very important function for her father, and this was just another one of his efforts to try to mend fences. After the ball we would all be driving up to their beach house and staying for a day. She promised to have me back in time for practice. "And you can bring your mitt and we can play catch," she said.

"It's a glove, not a mitt," I said.

"Whatever," she said.

It was a night to remember. Cate was like that: completely unpredictable and yet so enchanting; so feisty, yet someone I just wanted to hold; so independent, but someone I wanted to protect. She pushed me to be a better person. She made me look inside myself to discover who I really was. She was never at a loss for words and drew everyone around her into her special enchanted world. I often wondered why she had chosen me.

♦ ♦ ♦

Saturday morning, the day of the ball, I was called into the coach's office. Like I said before, you only get summoned into the inner sanctum to be released or moved up in the organization. I was not really happy about the invitation. I couldn't decide if it was good or bad news when I walked into his office. He asked me to sit. He was very formal, and all I could think was that the ax was about to fall. "Cord, I'm sorry to see you leave, but you have to report to the Wichita Wranglers tonight. Your flight leaves in two hours. You'll be going with Obrey. Maybe you can catch a ride to the airport together. I've appreciated your efforts here, Cord. You have done everything I've asked. I hope that I get to see your name in lights one of these days."

I was going to the AA team! People are often taken from AA to the big leagues, although some go to AAA first. It was a big accomplishment. From Little League to AA baseball; about the same chance as getting hit by lighting. I wished I could call my father. He would have been as excited as I was.

I was elated as I left to start packing. When you play minor league baseball, you are never so unpacked that you can't assemble your belongings inside two suitcases within twenty minutes. As I threw the suitcase together, I remembered I had to thank the Gromwells, and Cate . . . Oh no! That night was the ball. I fumbled through my pockets for my cell phone. I pushed green for go. She answered. "I'm glad you called, Cord. I will be over to pick you up at six sharp. Now don't be late, and don't forget the tux."

This was not going to be easy. "Cate, I've got some great news and some not so good news. Where shall I start?"

"I don't want to hear either if it affects your appearance tonight at the ball."

I decided I might be able to soften the blow if I told her the good news first. "I just got promoted to the Wichita Wranglers. They're the AA team for the Royals."

"I'm so happy for you, Cord." Then there was a pause as the reality of the situation set in. "Well, happy and sad because Wichita is a long way away."

Then almost as if she was afraid of the answer she asked, "So, do I want to hear the bad news?"

"I catch a plane in two hours."

I heard a long sigh on the other end of the phone. "You're kidding, right? Are you trying to tell me in a roundabout way that you can't come to the ball tonight? My dad is going to kill you. He'll never understand how baseball can come ahead of his daughter."

"I'm sorry" was all I could say. "I might be pitching tonight in Wichita. Do you want to meet me at the airport? I don't know if I'll see you again until the end of the season."

"You're not getting rid of me that easily. I'll be there." She got my flight information and promised to be there as soon as possible.

She came running in through the doors of the airport and almost collided with me. I could tell she had been crying, and that wasn't like her. "I just didn't expect this, slugger. I'm so mad at you and yet so happy for you, I don't know what to do with you."

I drew her into a hug and said, "Hey, we've only got a month and a half of baseball left this season. It's not like forever. Besides, you can come and visit me anytime you want."

Just then Obrey and his wife walked up. I could tell she had been crying too. Being my normal sensitive self, I asked, "Is she happy or sad?"

He replied, "I don't know. You can never tell with women."

She said, "We just rented an apartment. I have to resolve that lease, I have to pack all of our belongings, and I have to drive our car out to Wichita. I'm not sure how I'm going to do it."

Cate said, "Hey, I'll help you pack and I might even be able to help you drive. I've never been to Wichita, and they tell me it's a beautiful city in the middle of nowhere, where the wind blows out to left field all the time. It's a pitcher's worst nightmare."

That's how Cate is, always willing to help anyone. It wasn't long before we had to get on the plane. I promised to keep in contact and added, "Maybe I'll see you in Wichita in a few days."

She smiled and said, "You should be so lucky, slugger."

♦ ♦ ♦

I arrived in Wichita in the afternoon and I pitched that night. I pitched two innings and gave up three runs and five hits. It was one of those nights where I was throwing good pitches and they were hitting ground balls, but they had seein' eyes on them and they kept finding holes through the infield. It didn't help that the infield made two errors and booted a double play. I hate starting in the hole, and my ERA in AA ball started at a lofty 13.5. Anything under a 2.0 ERA is good. A lofty 13.5 is bad: the kind of ERA that gets you a meeting with the coach and a plane ticket home.

I got some good news though. Cate was driving to Wichita with Obrey's wife. They expected the drive would take about twenty hours, and they intended to stop and sleep along the way. I tried to call her cell, but my call kept getting routed directly to her voice mail. I assumed she wasn't receiving a signal or had turned her phone off.

It wasn't much later that my phone started ringing. I thought it was Cate, but the caller ID said "out of area." I knew better than to assume who it was and put my foot back in my mouth. It turned out to be Prestin. She said she had been listening to the pregame for the Blue Rocks and heard that I had been sent to Wichita. She was happy for me. We talked small talk for a few minutes and then she said, "I asked Ash what you were doing about Cate and/or Indy. He said that you were as torn as I am and let it go like it didn't really matter. Lately, if it's not about baseball, he doesn't have any interest. So, I want to get it straight from the horse's mouth."

I knew she was good friends with both Cate and Indy, and I knew I could trust her to keep a confidence, but I didn't know if I could answer her question. "Well, Prestin, if I have to be completely honest, I believe I'm in love with Cate, and I think she is in love with me. She has looked into the Church and is intrigued by the whole gospel philosophy. I don't know if she has heard voices or seen a vision, but she is definitely interested. Regardless, I would be surprised if she didn't join the Church soon. I could marry her now, but it wouldn't be in the temple. My blessing says I will marry in the temple, and that could happen in a year if she joins the Church. I can't imagine living without Cate."

"Have you popped the question yet?"

"Do you mean am I engaged?"

"Well, yes. What do you think I meant?"

"Prestin, every time I get out my engagement ring with the intention of asking Cate, I see this image of Indy standing in front of the Manti Temple. I guess it's because I have a photo of her in front of the temple. I don't even know if I was there or if I took the photo. I just can't remember. I don't understand and it's driving me crazy. I can't make a commitment to Cate when I keep thinking of Indy."

She seemed as perplexed as I felt. "I'm not making any sense am I?" I asked.

She laughed. "I always thought it was women who were supposed to be irrational, illogical, and unable to make decisions."

"You're not helping me any more than Ash. Don't you have some advice? If not, tell me what you would do, and don't tell me to go pray like Ash did, because that didn't help."

"Cord, let me ask you a few questions. When you're standing out there on the mound looking at the batter, who decides what pitch you are going to throw next?"

"I do, of course."

"Why not the catcher? Why not the umpire? Why not let the computer tell you what you should throw next?"

"I'm the one who saw his last swing. I'm the one who knows how my stuff is working. I'm the one who's looking in the batter's eyes. I'm the one who is going to get a W or L beside my name. I don't want someone else deciding if I win or lose."

"Well, Cord, I think you just answered your own question."

"But I can't tell Indy to wait for me when I think I'm in love with Cate. It just wouldn't be fair to her. I don't understand the feelings I have that surround the image of Indy. I think Cate is the person for me, but then why do I keep thinking about Indy? If I could only remember those lost three months, it might help. But then again, how could it help when I think Cate is the one?"

She kind of laughed. "And I thought that women were hard to understand. You take the cake, Cord."

"So, tell me. What would you do?"

"Oh, no. The ball's in your court. I'm not about to put myself in between you and two of my best friends."

"You're not any better than your husband. I need some help, some advice, Prestin. Come on, tell me what you think."

"I can't make this call for you any more than I would try to call your pitches in a big game. However, I will feel very sorry for the girl who gets left out in the bull pen and never got in the game. They are two of my favorite people for entirely different reasons. I want to continue to be their friend regardless of your choice."

Prestin sighed and then added, "If I had to describe Indy in a single phrase, it would be 'gold-medal winner.' You put her in the deepest hole and she will find a way out. She was left alone with no one to help her, and yet she found the Lord. She was a high school dropout and became a doctor. She is humble about her accomplishments to a fault. She's a superstar, yet she treats us commoners as if we are doing her the favor being her friend. She is Dr. Jones when at work but would rather be known as just plain old Indiana. She has been deeply hurt by the men in her life and figures that it is probably not her calling to be a mother or a wife. But she always manages to find positives in her life. Every mother would be proud to call her daughter.

"Cate, on the other hand, is as refreshing as a beautiful spring morning and just about as unpredictable. She is vivacious and able to capture the hearts of everyone she comes in contact with. She is a breath of fresh air. She is very smart. No matter what question she is faced with, she seems to be able to winnow the wheat from the chaff. She is breathtaking; a head turner, a hero to all but herself. Everyone stands in line just to listen to her talk, hoping for her to smile at them."

Prestin was quiet for a minute and then sighed. "I don't know. Your choice isn't going to be easy, but I think you should always make God a part of any permanent relationship; and sealing in the temple will help to cement that relationship."

"So, you don't think I should marry Cate unless she joins the Church?"

"I have no doubt that Cate will join the Church one day. You can see that she is a daughter of the light."

"So, what are you saying?"

"Cord, I saw you when you were dating Indy. There was something special: a synergy, a combination that produced an unexpected result. Besides, how could you go wrong with someone named Indiana Jones? Yet I too have been captured in Cate's spell, and I don't think I want to escape that either."

"You're not helping to resolve my dilemma, Prestin."

"You're right, and that's why I have been so anxious to hear what you think. Because if it were up to me, I would probably drop back ten and punt."

"Tell me about Indy."

"Do you want the truth?"

"Do you think I can handle it?"

"Indy has buried herself in her work. She hasn't said, but she was pretty well devastated when you left. You see, during those three months you can't remember, she got swept up in the whirlwind called Cord Calloway. You broke down all of her defenses. She never told you about your relationship and her feelings because she knew that telling you wouldn't recreate the feelings you once shared. She knew you either had to remember or rediscover for yourself; and since you haven't done either, she has tried to bury her feelings. Now I'm not sure if she would get out the shovel if you came back. She's buried her feelings pretty deep. She doesn't blame you: she's beyond that. She knows that some things just happen."

"So, what are you saying?"

"Maybe you should forget about Indy and pursue Cate; and while you are doing so, you should see what Cate's intentions are about the Church."

"You're probably right, Prestin."

I mused, "You know, sometime during my lost three months, I purchased an engagement ring. It is inscribed *Diamonds Are Forever*, but I'm not sure who I was going to give it to."

"Oh, Cord, it's so you. How could she not love it? And if you have the ring you must have decided . . ."

She stopped right in mid-sentence. I told her to finish what she was going to say.

She mumbled some words that I didn't hear and then added, "I think I understand your dilemma." I could tell she was unsure what to say. Then she gave a feeble excuse. "I've got to run, but know we'll be listening to your games every night on the Internet. We love you, Cord. And call me when you figure out the identity of the soon-to-be Mrs. Cord Calloway. I can hardly wait; I'm dying to read the last chapter of your book."

As she hung up the phone I muttered to myself, "Yeah, so am I; it's the in-between stuff that has me worried."

♦ ♦ ♦

I had a message on my cell phone from Cate. I discovered it after batting practice but before the game started. "Cord, Tianna and I got here this morning. I talked to my office and I was informed that I have to be back in New York tomorrow. I have an early plane in the morning. I will meet you after the game tonight. Oh, and I really like Tianna. She was nice and thanked me a million times for helping her. So far, from what I've seen, Wichita isn't exactly what the chamber advertised, except for the wind, that is."

I was sitting in the bull pen when she walked down the aisle carrying a hot dog, a bag of popcorn, and a drink. The closest seats to the bull pen were right above where we were sitting. She yelled loud enough for everyone to hear, "Hey, slugger, how come you're not in the game?"

I tried to play like I didn't know who she was talking to. She started dropping popcorn on me and saying with a Texas drawl, "Ya'll want some popcorn?" She knew she was embarrassing me and was enjoying herself immensely.

Two guys sitting with me in the bull pen did not know Cate. "Hey, Cord, who's the chick who's trying to hustle you? She's pretty good looking. If you want us to take her off your hands, we can do that."

"That's okay. She's with me. Just my little sister trying to be funny."

"I ain't his sis, at least last night I wasn't his sis," said Cate, egging everyone on.

"Just ignore her. She'll go away," I said.

♦ ♦ ♦

After the game I met her out front, and we went to a nice restaurant that advertised really good, old-fashioned home cookin'. I wondered why it was that everyone who ate out wanted home cooking, while those who had to stay home wanted to eat at a restaurant. Halfway through the meal I asked, "Cate, did you ever start the Book of Mormon?"

"No, not yet. I've been thinking about it, but I don't know if I'm ready."

"You've been avoiding that book since the start of summer. You've studied about Mormons. You've talked to Mormons and non-Mormons. You've visited the temples. You've stayed with the Swensons. You've been converted socially and maybe intellectually to the Church, but you've never tried to find out if the book is true or if God really exists."

She started playing with her hair. She did that when she was nervous. "You're right, Cord. I don't know why it's so hard for me to take that first step. Besides, it's your fault. You take up all of my reading time. Maybe when I get home and you're still out here watching the wind blow out to left field, I'll have time."

"Cate, what are we going to do when baseball is over?"

"What do you mean 'we'?"

"Well, I'll be going home to Salt Lake, and you will still be in Wilmington, and that makes you a GU."

"A what?"

"A GU—a 'geographically undesirable.' I mean, that's a pretty long commute. Do you think you would like to move to Salt Lake to work?"

"As you know I can have my base of operations anywhere I want. But I'm not sure if moving to Salt Lake right now is the best thing. I mean, under the present circumstances. It's just, well, I just don't know."

"So what do you think?"

"I think it's up to you."

I was pretty sure I knew what she was saying, and I wasn't sure that I was ready to ask just yet. Cowardice, I think you call it. I knew that my ambivalent response was not what she was expecting. Maybe I had the same dilemma as Cate was having when it came to reading the Book of Mormon.

We walked over to her hotel, neither of us saying much. I knew we had come to that point in our relationship where we needed to move forward or we would be falling backwards quickly; but I couldn't pull the trigger. Her flight was leaving at six in the morning, so she had an early day. A shuttle would take her to the airport, and since I didn't have a car, this was it. I didn't know when I would see her again. I still had another month and a half of baseball. I held her in my arms for a long time, not wanting to let her go and not knowing what to say.

"Okay, slugger, don't go getting soft and emotional on me. I'll be back soon."

Somehow she knew how to make things seem right. I sure didn't. "Okay, I'll see you when I see you," I said after giving her a long kiss, one to remember. With that I turned and walked away, not wanting her to know how I felt about her leaving. At least I would be able to focus on baseball since I wouldn't be doing anything else.

♦ ♦ ♦

In the Carolina League I thought a long bus trip was three hours. In Wichita you are just getting started in three hours. Travel by bus is just part of the daily routine of minor league ball players. After Cate left, I got into the baseball routine: sleep, eat, play baseball, think, and then do it all over again. You can throw in sightseeing trips to places like Round Rock, Texas, and even Rider, Texas: home of the Rough Riders. We even went to Springfield: Springfield, Missouri, that is. Riding buses is cheap for the team but hated by the players.

My tour of the cities consisted of seeing whatever existed between the ballpark and the hotel, which was not usually very exciting. Most players kill time by hanging out at the bars where they meet the camp followers. Me, I bypassed those excursions and went straight to bed after eating, or sometimes I worked on my coaching book. I tried to make it a habit to ask my friends and roommates how they would handle different situations or how they would run practices to make them more efficient and worthwhile. I tried to add all worthwhile comments to my book for future evaluation. Since I had nagged Cate about reading the Book of Mormon, I decided that the least I could do was to read it myself. In order to avoid appearing to be a religious fanatic, I cut a fake cover for my Book of Mormon and started taking it everywhere with me and reading it every day.

♦ ♦ ♦

I had successfully avoided my mother's phone calls, but one night I inadvertently answered my cell without looking at the caller ID.

"Cord, you haven't returned my calls."

"I'm sorry, Mom, I just . . ." but then she cut me off and started with her questions. At least I didn't have to make up an excuse. The first thing she wanted to know was if I had found the Church in Wichita. She just didn't understand. In minor league baseball the Sunday games usually start around noon. That means we have to be at the field by nine, and we don't leave until three or later. Since most wards meet during that time frame, it is almost impossible to find a church to go to; and besides, I don't have a car and it's not like Salt Lake City where there is a chapel on every corner. I never explained it to her, I just told her I was trying. It saved a lot of wasted words.

♦ ♦ ♦

Saturday night games were always crowded. Since I wasn't

pitching, all I had to do was hang out in the bull pen, watch the game, and of course listen to the chatter as the rest of the pitchers tried to pick out the best looking girl sitting within VR (visual range). Sometimes it gets really boring in the pen, so guys watch the girls or invent games to play, that is, except for those that might have to pitch. Those guys are busy studying the hitters and going over pitching charts. I wasn't interested in participating in any games; I had too many things on my mind. I tilted my chair back against the fence, and soon I was in a stupor, caught somewhere between dozing and pondering, hovering more toward Never Never Land than conscious thought. The fence I was leaning against was chain link and gave a little bit so I could almost rock myself to sleep.

"Are you Cord Calloway?"

My dream ended abruptly with those words. I wasn't sure they came from dreamland or from the land of the living. I looked around for the likely suspect. Standing behind me was a nice looking gentleman with a kid who was a dead ringer for the Little Leaguer of the year. He had his glove on his left hand, a good sign if he was a pitcher, and wore a wrangler baseball cap. I smiled and said, "Yes, sir, that's me."

"My son, Brett, has been watching you since you came to play for the Wranglers. You've become his hero. He wants to be a pitcher."

"Mr. Calloway, would you mind signing my glove?" Brett offered his glove over the fence with a permanent marker. He looked like a pretty good left-handed pitcher, and I hadn't even seen him pitch. He just handled himself like a pitcher. It's hard to describe unless you've been there. I wondered why anyone would choose me to be their hero. There were much better candidates on the team than me. I'm just a reliever.

"Sure, Brett. What would you like me to write?"

"I've been thinking about that, Mr. Calloway. How about, 'Cord Calloway, the Mormon Hurler'?"

"So you're LDS," I said. That must have been why he had picked me, a Mormon.

"Yes, sir. My dad's the Young Men president of the ward not far from here."

I looked them over. They sure looked like Mormons. I swear I could pick out a Mormon on a busy street every time. There is just something about them. "Well, it's nice to meet you, Brett. I've been thinking of trying to get to a church meeting, but our schedule is so busy I haven't had much time, and, well, I don't have a car or know where or when to go."

I was trying to make an excuse as to why I hadn't gone to church. I'm not sure why I felt the need to make excuses. Maybe it was because they knew I was LDS and I didn't want to disappoint Brett. I wondered how they knew that; it wasn't like I had LDS stenciled on my forehead.

"Well, my dad has a car, and we can pick you up if you want to come to our ward," said Brett. His eyes had that puppy dog look that said "Just pet me." How could I turn the kid down? I felt a little guilty.

"I'm sorry, Brother Calloway," said the man. "Brett's sometimes a little presumptuous. Oh, and my name's Robert Barrett."

I continued to wonder how they knew I was LDS. Brett's straightforwardness hit me between the eyes like a fastball down the middle, so, being unable to think, I said, "Brett, I would love to come to your ward one of these days." But I knew it would be unlikely that I would ever actually end up going to their ward.

His face lit up and he said, "Great. Maybe you could come to my deacons quorum and talk to us about playing baseball . . . and, well, tomorrow would be a great day since you don't have a game."

I had forgotten I didn't have a game the next day; and, actually, I decided I really would like to go to church. Before I could say anything, Brother Barrett said, "I can't pick you up in the morning because I have a meeting, but I could send Brett and my wife, that is, if you would like."

"That would be great, and if you like I could say something to the deacons quorum."

"I would appreciate that, Mr. Calloway, and I'm sure that the boys will love it."

♦ ♦ ♦

Church started at nine o'clock. I was on the curb waiting at eight thirty. The Barretts were right on time. Sister Barrett was as nice as she looked. By the time we walked in the chapel I felt like we were old friends. Of course I was introduced to at least a hundred different people. I didn't remember one name, which wasn't unusual. Brett continued to tell everyone that I pitched for the Wranglers, which drew a variety of responses and looks.

Sacrament meeting was actually enjoyable. I thought back over the road that had brought me back to church. It was because of the Swensons, or had it been Indy? Whichever, it was not an overnight hike; it had been a long trek, one step at a time. I had come to know that I wanted the Church in my life. Even if I didn't know for sure that it was true, it was the best thing that had happened to me. And I wanted a family like the Swensons. As I thought about it, I guess the only real question that bothered me was if there was really a God and Christ. If they actually lived. I understand that it's a pretty big issue for Christians, but I just didn't know. I felt like I could buy the Joseph Smith story; my problem was that I just didn't know about God or Christ. Oh, I felt it was right, but I didn't really know.

At the end of sacrament meeting Joyce, Sister Barrett, took me to the Gospel Doctrine class, introduced me to the teacher, and left. She had to go teach Primary. I sat down by myself on the back row and waited for the lesson to begin.

The teacher started by asking in his prayer that his students might have some understanding of the things he was about to speak of. It wasn't a typical prayer, and it made me think. Then he started his lesson. I wasn't really listening to his words. I guess you would say I was listening without listening, more thinking or feeling than listening. About halfway though his lesson he held up a picture of Christ.

My eyes locked on to the picture.

I don't know how to describe in words what happened next, but let me explain it as best I can. I had this feeling that started at the top of my head and spread to the bottom of my toes. It was definitely a feeling. It didn't burn and it wasn't cold. I don't know exactly what it was, but it was all-encompassing. I knew something was happening to me and I had never felt it before. Once engulfed or surrounded by this feeling, my mind became clear, free of all thoughts except one: *I am Jesus Christ, your older brother.* I didn't hear a voice and I didn't see a vision, but I knew in my heart that Christ existed.

I have no idea what the teacher said that day or what his lesson was about, but the feeling stayed with me for some time, at least it felt like a long time. I wondered how I could have ever questioned the fact that Christ lived. I knew he was as real and as alive as was I. It was so simple.

I was in kind of a fog the rest of the day, yet I was alive with feeling. Things were important; life was important. My life was important. I knew that I had some catching up to do for my years of downtime, and I had a few things that required some repentance. But I knew that the Lord cared about me. That realization hadn't happened from nothing. It had been a result of a series of small steps, all going in the right direction, and most were the results of the Swensons and perhaps Indy being a part of my life. I needed to talk to Ash and Prestin and the twins . . . and maybe even Indy. I wanted to thank them; no, I needed to tell them how much they mattered to me. I needed them to know what they had given me.

The Barretts had invited me to dinner. I apologized but told them I had some things I needed to do and asked for a rain check. I tracked down Brother Barrett and told him that I would like to speak with him one day in the near future. I told him I couldn't thank him enough for bringing me to church and promised to call. I had talked to the deacons and loved it. Brett was beaming. I liked the fact that he looked up to me, and now I knew that I had some shoes to fill to be worthy of that kind of respect.

♦ ♦ ♦

About a week later I received the videotapes of Blaze and Rush. They were doing just a few things wrong. I called and told them drills to do to help correct their mechanics. They had both made the all-star team and Ash was named the coach. They had won their district and had moved on to area. Ash was having the time of his life. He tried to explain how he felt watching his kids have success in baseball. I completely understood because I felt the same way about them. I took the opportunity to talk to Ash about my experience with Christ and its carryover effect. It was nice having a father figure again, someone I could talk to who understood me, who cared about me.

After my disastrous first game in Wichita, I had eight appearances without allowing a run and lowered my ERA to 3.2. Not great, but it was getting better. In twenty-two innings I only had one walk and it was an intentional walk. I still don't think it's fair to count an intentional walk in pitcher's stats, since it's the coach who makes you walk the batter. Anyway, I had one win and no losses. I had been used as a closer and a long reliever. The coach was starting to believe in me.

I talked to Cate every day. Her work had become a lot more involved and intense than she expected, and she couldn't get away as easily as she had thought. I looked forward to our conversations. One night, out of the blue, she said, "Cord, you are not going to believe this, but I started reading the Book of Mormon."

"That's great," I said. "I started reading it when you left, and I'm about halfway through. But what got you off your dime?"

"Well, I decided I would start going to church. I met with the bishop, and he suggested that I meet with the stake missionaries. I agreed and they started coming over once or twice a week. They talked me into starting to read one page at a time. One of the missionaries is from Salt Lake and has been out for over a year. He's really nice. The other is a local guy who's an attorney. His name is William James Winthrop. He's a returned missionary himself and has been going on splits with the full-time missionaries every now and then. He's been really helpful. He's even invited me out to dinner twice to talk about the Church and answer any of my questions."

"Is he short, fat, and balding?" I asked.

"No, as a matter of fact, he is quite good looking. He's a soccer player, and still gets in a few games a week."

"Did he tell you about playing soccer in response to a gospel question?"

"Cord, really."

"Is he married?" I asked, knowing what the answer would be.

"No, I don't believe so, but he is very nice and completely harmless. You're not jealous, are you?"

"Me? I don't have any reason to be jealous, do I?"

"Really, slugger, do you think I would dump you that fast? Besides, he doesn't play baseball. But I'll tell him to hit the road if you want."

"No. But you can tell him that missionaries always go two by two, and none of this dating stuff in the name of teaching the gospel."

"My, my. I've never seen you this riled before. But you don't have to worry. You stole my heart a long, long time ago."

I wasn't sure I was satisfied with her response, but since I wasn't prepared to ask her to wear my ring, I couldn't very well forbid her from dating some stupid soccer player, could I?

"Oh, I almost forgot. I've arranged to go to Salt Lake on September fifteenth. The Swensons are going to take me on a trip to the Canyonlands and Lake Powell, and they might just let you come along if you ask really nicely. You will be home by then, won't you?"

"I think the last day of the championship series is September twelfth. So even if we make it to the finals, I should be home." I wanted to ask her if she planned to bring Perry Mason along to answer her questions but decided against it. William James Winthrop sounded like some wimpy Ivy League guy who was rolling in dough that was earned by his father. *The Belfords are probably in love with the guy*, I thought.

Twelve

Never give up, because it ain't over 'til it's over.
—Yogiism #12

The Wranglers had ten games left in the season, and we were on track to win the second-half championship. That meant both teams I played with made it to the playoffs; and if either team won the playoffs, I would get a championship ring. I didn't even know my ring size, probably because I had never been on a championship team.

The problem with making the playoffs was that it extended the season. I didn't want our season extended past September fifteenth. I was anxious to get back to Salt Lake since I knew Cate was going to be there to go to Lake Powell with the Swensons. Indy, well, I hadn't heard from her; not that I expected to, but I wished that she would call. I don't know why all of a sudden I thought about Indy. Random thoughts are sometimes hard to explain.

♦ ♦ ♦

On August twenty-second we were home at Lawrence-Dumont Stadium playing the Round Rocks. I got the call from the dugout to go into the game in the sixth inning. The score was tied 3-3, so all I had to do was to hang a couple of zeros; and if we could score a run, I would get another win. Opportunities for wins don't come around very often for relievers.

As I stepped onto the mound, there were guys on first and second with no outs. I threw a great sinker on the inside black to a big righty who was hitting third in the order, and he hit it foul about six hundred feet, or something like that. I mean he hit it a mile. I knew they didn't have a tape measure long enough to measure the distance, but you know foul balls only count as a strike. *If that's all he's got, I don't have to fear this guy*, I thought. He reminded me of a kid in Little League who hit every pitch foul between the third base line and the house across the street. All I had to do was pitch him inside. I came back with another fastball inside, and he hit it foul again, but not quite as far this time. My next pitch was a set-up pitch, and I winged a high fastball up right in his eyes, but he wouldn't chase it. Normally my next pitch would be a curve since the batter had seen three fastballs in a row. However, instead of throwing a curveball for my kill pitch, I opted for a fastball away, hoping to get a hard ground ball up the middle for a double play. The batter, however, pulled off the ball and swung so hard he almost broke his back but got nothing but air. He walked back to the dugout muttering something about me being lucky.

I threw a fastball down and away to start the clean-up batter. He hit it hard to second base for an easy 4-6-3 double play to end the inning. It was a textbook inning for me and I was feeling pretty good. We scored three in the top of the inning, so all I had to do was to hold the lead for two more innings and I would get my fourth win against one loss for the season at Wichita.

A lefty led off the next inning. I threw him a good outside sinking fastball. He stayed inside the ball and hit a rocket shot right back up the middle, right at me. I tried to get my head out of the way of the ball.

♦ ♦ ♦

I sat up in a bed. As my vision slowly cleared, it seemed I was in a hospital. I saw Cate sitting next to my bed, working on her laptop. I was surprised to see her. I hadn't seen her since the meeting with her father. I wondered why she was here, and, for that matter, I wondered why I was here. She was as beautiful as ever and totally absorbed in whatever it was she was typing. I decided that my first guess had been right. It was a hospital. The bed and monitors gave me my first clue. Besides, I don't have a bed that folds in the middle nor heart monitors mounted near my headboard. I reached up to feel the left side of my head. It was bandaged and my head hurt when I touched it. In fact, I realized that it hurt even if I didn't touch it. I couldn't remember injuring my head. I imagined that this was what a hangover felt like. If that was the case then I wondered why anyone would ever drink.

Maybe I was dreaming or caught in a time warp. I stumbled out of my stupor and my attention returned to Cate. I hadn't seen her since last September, other than the time she just showed up at my apartment when Indy was there.

I logged onto my memory scanning program. I could remember meeting with Cate and her parents the day they told me I just wasn't going to cut it with the Belfords any longer. My name had definitely become a hiss and a byword around their house. Not only had I not seen her, I couldn't find any reference in my memory banks to any conversation with her since that night. I remembered leaving Wilmington several days after the "Battle at Belfords" for Salt Lake. The baseball season had ended. That last week I think I was in shock, but I remembered flying home to Salt Lake. I couldn't believe that Cate had sided with her parents or that she could just drop me. Maybe I had misjudged her.

I did, however, remember meeting Indy.

I had dated Indy for three months. In fact, I couldn't remember going a day without seeing her. It was around Thanksgiving that Cate showed up at my place, unannounced. But she had left the next day and I hadn't talked to her.

My attention came back to the moment. How did I get injured? I felt the bandage on my head again. It still hurt. Where was Indy? Was I at the University Hospital? I couldn't imagine why Cate was here and not Indy. What if Indy walked in while Cate was sitting in my room? Maybe she already had. But then, maybe something had happened to Indy. Maybe that's why she wasn't here. Nothing made any sense.

Then my memory scan brought up an image of myself riding my bike down Emigration Canyon. That was the last thing I could remember. It seemed like yesterday. Maybe I had been injured riding my bike. I tried to clear my head by shaking it, which caused more pain. That was stupid. I decided not to do that again. Thinking wasn't getting me anywhere; maybe I should just ask Cate.

"Cate, is that you?" I managed to croak.

"Cord, you're awake. How do you feel? You really had us worried."

"Well, I've got a sore head, but my arm feels okay." I raised my right arm to check it out for injuries. "How come I'm in a hospital and where did you come from?"

"You don't remember?"

"Remember what? The last time I saw you, you didn't care if I lived or died. Your parents made it clear that my name had been permanently deleted from their welcomed guest list and instead identified as public enemy number one."

She ignored my comment and asked, "Don't you remember getting hit in the head by a line drive while playing baseball the other night?"

"What? It's November. You don't play baseball in Utah in November."

"Great! Here we go again," she said.

"What are you talking about?"

"Let me ask you this: can you remember your biking accident and your stay in the University of Utah Hospital?"

"Is that how I hurt my head? While riding my bike down the canyon?" In that case I was right. This was the University Hospital.

"Sorry, Cord, it's the Mercy Hospital in Wichita."

"Wichita? What am I doing in Wichita? And how did you end up here?"

"Cord, you're a head case. Let me go find your doctor. He wanted to see you as soon as you regained consciousness."

"Wait. How long have I been unconscious?"

"Three days. The doctor has been very concerned with your injury because of your prior head trauma."

"What prior head trauma? I can't remember you throwing anything at me. I just left when I was asked to go. What are you talking about?"

"Let me get the doctor first. I need some help on this one."

She left the room and left me with a lot of unanswered questions. I tried to get up, but I had wires strung like a web across my body. "What's going on here?" I exclaimed, but nobody answered. A line drive, Wichita, baseball, three days, a head injury and a previous head injury; what was that all about?

It was only a minute until Cate came back with a doctor trailing behind. He walked straight over to my bed, smiled at me, and said, "Mr. Calloway, I'm glad to finally meet you. I'm Dr. Hagen. I've been treating you for the last three days. You took a nasty hit on the noggin."

"That may explain why my head hurts, but . . . what was it that hit me? Wasn't I riding my bike?"

"No, you weren't riding a bike, you were playing baseball. But let me ask you a few questions." He was busy looking at the monitors and had his stethoscope on my chest. He was probing around my head asking me if it hurt when he applied any pressure. I responded when it hurt, and it hurt more often than it didn't.

"Do you know where you are?" he asked.

"Cate said we are in Wichita. But I've never been there in my life. If I'm in Wichita, I don't have any idea how I got here."

"Do you know what today is?"

"I'm not sure, but probably around November twenty-fifth."

"Can you spell *world*?"

"Sure. W-O-R-L-D."

"Can you spell it backwards?"

"Why are you asking me these silly questions? Sure, I can spell it backwards, D-L-R-O-W."

He responded, "I'm simply running you through a few simple neurological tests to try to understand the seriousness of your injuries. If you cooperate, it will make this a lot easier."

"Okay, but I'm telling you I'm fine, well, except for a sore head."

He asked me to count backwards from one hundred. I started and got to eighty before he stopped me. Then he asked me to count backwards by seven. I had to do the subtraction in my head and got through about four series before I gave up. He then asked me to grab his hand and squeeze. I did as directed. Then he said, "Raise your left leg six inches off the bed and hold it there." It wasn't very hard, but I was starting to get annoyed. Next he got out one of those very bright flashlights and looked in my eyes. Of course I was blinded for the next two minutes.

"Well, you look pretty good considering how hard you were hit."

"I told you I was okay. Now will you tell me how I ended up in a hospital in Wichita?"

"To start with, it is not November twenty-fifth—it's not even November. Tell me the last thing you can remember."

"The last thing I can remember is riding my bike down the canyon. I think it was just yesterday." I was racking my brain to see if anything else would pop up, but nothing showed on the screen.

"Can you remember pitching for the Wichita Wranglers?"

"Well, I know they are the AA team for the Royals organization. I pitched in Wilmington last year—that's the Royals's high A team—but that's as far as I got. And no, I've never pitched for the Wranglers."

He pulled out a file and started leafing through some pages. Then he said, "I received your medical records from the University of Utah today. Do you remember being in that hospital for a head injury?"

"Nope, never happened."

"Mr. Calloway, let me explain a few facts to you. Maybe it will help. You were involved in a bicycle accident. You were treated at the University of Utah Hospital and were diagnosed as having retrograde amnesia. Do you know what that means?"

"I've heard of amnesia." I noticed Cate trying to stay out of the way and out of the conversation. Quite unlike her.

"Well, retrograde amnesia sometimes happens when you sustain a head injury, although it's a unique and rather rare form of amnesia. When it does occur, it can mean that you lose a portion of your memory. Your records indicate that you lost your memory of everything that happened between September and December of 2004. Is that still the case?"

"Are you asking me if I can remember anything that happened since September?"

"Well, yes, but it's August 26, 2005, right now. So I guess what I mean is, can you remember anything that happened since September of last year, of 2004?"

"What do you mean it's August?"

"It appears, Mr. Calloway, that your recent head injury has again caused amnesia."

"I don't understand." I was frantic. My mind was racing. I was trying to grab hold of what he was telling me. How could it be August? That would mean that I had lost a good portion of a whole year of my life. I couldn't remember anything since riding my bike down that canyon, and that was in November. Had I really played in AA baseball? That was great, except I couldn't remember it. I could remember being worried about even getting a contract to play ball and yet they're telling me I got clear to AA. Wow! I was impressed.

"Well, sure I can remember a lot of things that happened since September." But I had a major problem because I was in the hot box. Just about everything I could remember involved my relationship with Indy. In fact, I could remember buying an engagement ring for her. I wasn't sure that I wanted to disclose all of those details, not with Cate standing right next to Dr. Hagen.

It probably wouldn't be prudent. That left me in a quandary because I didn't know how to answer his question without talking about Indy.

Then the doctor asked, "Can you remember going to spring training with the Royals in March of 2005, and then to Wilmington for the first half of the season, before getting reassigned to the Wranglers here in Wichita this June?"

"No, but keep talking. It sounds great. I always dreamed of playing AA baseball."

"You don't remember being hit by a baseball, a line drive, three days ago?"

"No, I don't. Is that what Cate was talking about?"

"Yes, Mr. Calloway. You were hit three days ago, and it appears that you have again suffered retrograde amnesia. I am concerned because this is your second head injury in less than a year. As I said, this kind of amnesia doesn't happen very often, and it is even more remarkable that it happened to you twice in one year. However, since you can now remember the time period that you couldn't remember after the first injury, there is a good chance you might eventually regain the memory that is now missing. By the way, this is 2005."

He shuffled through the rest of the papers, looked carefully at all of the monitors, and then at me and said, "I don't think there is a good reason to keep you in the hospital, but you need to continue to be seen by a neurologist because of the severity of the recent accident and your recurring retrograde amnesia. I think I can release you tomorrow, but I want you to go back to Utah and be examined and treated by Dr. Montgomery. He's a well known neurosurgeon; and, since he treated you for the first head trauma, it would be best that he continue. Besides, you're through playing baseball for this year. We are not going to risk any further injury right now."

Dr. Hagen had promised to come back and see me that evening and again in the morning. He wanted to make sure I was okay before he released me to go back to Utah. When he left that afternoon, I was confused. I mean, I believed him, but the entire tale sounded like it was straight out of *The Twilight Zone.* If what he said was true, last year would have been my year to remember. I had made it all the way to AA ball, but then . . . what had happened to Indy? Did I ask her to marry me? Did she turn me down or did she accept? In either case, Cate's presence was still a mystery because I couldn't have it both ways.

I needed some questions answered and Cate was my only option; but I needed to be careful because I was very good at putting my foot in my mouth. My conversation with Cate was going to be like trying to figure out what pitch to throw to the next batter. I needed to guess what the batter thought I would be throwing so I could throw something else. But then the batter, or Cate in this case, was much smarter than me. I wouldn't get anything past her, not even a nasty slider. That thought brought me back to reality. How did Cate find me in Wichita? Was she here before I got hit, or did she come after I ended up in the hospital? How come Indy wasn't here? That was what I really wanted to know.

I watched Cate finish speaking to the doctor. She turned slowly. She looked like she was deep in thought. Although she was looking straight at me, she didn't notice that I was staring at her. She to was trying to figure out this mess. She always looked so good, like she had just stepped out of a fashion magazine, and she always had this spunky chip on her shoulder like she could take on the world. But right now she looked a little disheveled.

"Cate, how did you come to be in Wichita?" It was a harmless question, one that she wouldn't be expecting.

She shook the question off without really thinking about it, preferring to remain in her world of thoughts. "Tianna Obrey called me when you got hit and I caught the first flight headed this way." The answer surprised me.

"How do you know Tianna?"

"I helped her drive out here after you and her husband, Ken, got sent to Wichita. Don't you remember you had to leave the day of the charity ball? I had already rented your tux. It was a major event. So instead of going to the glamour ball of the year,

I helped Tianna load up her things in her car and drive to beautiful downtown Wichita. It was a long drive, and we got to be pretty good friends."

"But I thought your parents put me on the 'do not contact' list and voted me off the show."

"Well, Cord, I don't know how to break this to you, but I left my parents' home last September. We, me and you, got back together again this last February, and I went to spring training in Arizona to see you. We had a great time in Arizona. It was there that I met and got to be very close to your good friends the Swensons."

"You mean Bishop Swenson came all the way to Arizona to see spring training?"

"Yes, and he brought all of his family. I guess you don't remember teaching the twins either."

"The who?"

"Bishop Swenson has twin boys, Rush and Blaze. They are eleven years old, and you spent a lot of time teaching them how to pitch. They have become the stars of their league and you are their hero. They will be crushed if you don't remember them."

"I don't have a clue what you're talking about."

"That's too bad because those kids idolize you." She was responding, but she still seemed lost in her own little world.

Neither of us said anything for what seemed like forever. Finally Cate asked, "By the way, do you remember that you started going back to church?"

"Yeah, I think I went a time or two." I remembered going with Indy and we had talked to Bishop Swenson, but I didn't want to get into that conversation. *Shift gears*, I thought.

"Was I winning when I got hit with the line drive? I guess I didn't catch the ball."

"Somehow I knew that question would come up," replied Cate. "No, you didn't catch the ball; but you managed to get your head in front of the ball and kept it in the infield, so no one scored. However, they say everyone thought you were dead. Don't you know you're supposed to use your mitt to stop the ball and not your head?

"Glove," I reminded her.

She didn't even heed my correction. "They stopped the game for at least a half hour until they got you off the field and into an ambulance."

"Did I get the win or the loss?"

"I believe you got the win and they even saved the game ball for you. Men. I'll never understand them."

She shook her head and looked completely dismayed. "By the way, I have talked to and explained your condition to your mother and your sister, who were very concerned about you. However, it wouldn't hurt for you to call them when you get time."

She sighed; she was still in her own world. "And I thought my mother was out of touch. How do you deal with yours?"

I laughed and said, "I know what you mean. Sometimes when I'm talking to her, I can put the phone down and come back ten minutes later and she won't even know I was gone."

Although I was trying to keep the conversation going with Cate, I was thinking of the time I had spent with Indy. I had intended to marry Indy. But Indy wasn't here and Cate was. Why? I started processing the information I had. Wilmington was Cate's hometown as well as the home of the Blue Rocks, so I could have seen a lot of Cate while I was there. Besides, she said she had come to spring training. Maybe Indy had turned me down. Maybe I had fallen in love with Cate again.

After coming out of my stupor of thought, I decided to try to get some more information. "Cate, let me try and get this straight, because I'm not very smart and I hope that you can help me. You're telling me it's August 2005, that I played with the Wranglers since June of this year, and that prior to coming to Wichita, I was in Wilmington, and that I saw you nearly every day." I didn't know quite how to ask the questions that I wanted to ask, but I tried.

"So tell me, Cate, about our relationship during the last six months. Just where are we?"

"You mean other than that you asked me to marry you?" She smiled and appeared to be returning to the world that I inhabited.

My mouth must have dropped open, or I looked like I was in shock, because she turned up her smile. Was she teasing? I kind of stammered, "I did? What did you answer? I don't see a ring on your finger."

"No, slugger, I was just kidding. You didn't ask me to marry you."

She appeared to be thinking. "Well, I'm not sure where to start. A lot of things have happened since February that have changed my life and, for that matter, your life too. But now . . . I'm just not sure . . . Maybe we'll just have to wait and see."

She stopped almost in mid-sentence like she was trying to decide how or what to say. Then she continued, "However, before you got promoted to Wichita, we spent a lot of time together. I explained to my parents that you would not be swept under the carpet and that you were a permanent part of my life. In fact, my father offered you a very good job that I declined on your behalf, for obvious reasons. As for me, I now work as a writer for *The New York Times*. Other than that, my only earth-shattering news is that I have been seriously investigating the Mormon Church. I have also made some very close friends in my ward in Wilmington. By the way, can you remember Isabell?"

"No. Who is she?"

"Bell is Bishop Swenson's thirteen-year-old daughter and she is now my sister. She's adopted me. I try to talk to Prestin, your bishop's wife, maybe once a week. We have become very good friends. In fact, I am scheduled to go to Salt Lake in mid-September to go to Lake Powell and the Canyonlands with them. You were also invited. Oh, yeah, I almost forgot the most important thing. You led the team with a 1.8 ERA and ended up with five wins and one loss while in Wichita. That's pretty good for a reliever. The coaches loved you. Then again the only black mark you got this summer was for not making the charity ball with me in Wilmington. My parents were not very happy with you for missing the big dance."

I was confused to say the least, because if I hadn't yet proposed to Indy, I had intended to. And yet, I was apparently seeing

Cate a lot. Cate should have been out of the picture. I never dated two girls at the same time. It just wasn't me. I was a one-woman guy. What had happened to Indy? I didn't know or I couldn't remember when I last talked to Indy. Maybe I had talked to her a lot too.

I didn't want to ask Cate about Indy. That was dangerous ground. I wondered if Cate knew about Indy; but again, that wasn't a good question. Oh, it was a good question, but not to ask Cate.

So I took the offense. "I'm not sure that you answered my question, Cate."

"And that question would be?"

"Us. What about us?"

"First, I want you to tell me what you think or remember about us."

"That's not fair, Cate, because I don't have any idea what has gone on since last November."

She thought for a minute and then said, "Do you want me to tell you straight out?"

"Sure. Go for it."

"What if I make something up? How would you know if I was telling you the truth?"

"I guess I'll just have to believe what you tell me."

"That's my point, Cord. Since you can't remember anything, you won't be able to verify anything I say. You may hear what I tell you, but it won't make any difference since it will be just a story to you."

"I like stories."

"But don't you understand? That's all it will be: a story. That's why I can't tell you about us. All I can tell you is about me; what I think, what I feel. 'Us' means two. 'Me' is only one. I'm not sure if I want to tell you what I think or what I feel. I want to know what you feel, what you think. Whatever I think or feel isn't really going to matter to you unless your feelings match mine, right?"

"But it might help me to understand what I was thinking or feeling."

"Let's give it some time. The doctor is hopeful that you might get your memory back any day, and so we just might be spinning our wheels for nothing. Besides, it's not like you won't see me since I will be in Salt Lake on the fifteenth of next month."

That would be a problem. Cate in Salt Lake just when I needed to find out about Indy. I was in the hot box again, and I wasn't a good base runner. I didn't know what to tell Cate. Maybe if I talked to Indy—that is, if she was talking to me. How could I explain the situation to either of them when I couldn't explain the situation to myself? I was sure that spending time with Cate right after getting back to Salt Lake would be a bad idea, like giving up a lead-off home run. I didn't know what to do. But maybe I was worrying about nothing. Maybe I was on Indy's "do not contact" list.

♦ ♦ ♦

Cate left later that day since she had to get back to work in New York. We had talked a lot and I had gotten tidbits of information about the last nine months. But none of it rang any bells. As the day progressed, it was apparent that Cate was upset; maybe distant is a better word. She seemed, well, sad. It was hard to see her go. I knew I had strong feelings for her; and when she left, it felt so final even though I knew I would see her in just a few days. I didn't want it to end even though I was in love with Indy. I knew I could have fixed the problem; but I couldn't, not until I had a chance to see and talk to Indy. Cate had sensed my hesitancy. She was a very special person. I wondered what I was doing, if I was doing anything right. I knew I was letting my feelings control my actions. I just hoped that I wasn't making a worse mess of my life than it already was, because it was entirely possible that Indy could have already sent me to the showers.

After Cate left I decided to call Shannon; maybe she could help. "Cord, it's nice of you to call. I mean we have gone almost the whole summer without hearing from you because you said you were tied up with Cate and baseball, in that order. Then out of the blue Cate calls to tell me that you are in the hospital with a serious head injury. She said you got your head in the way of a line drive. We have been worried sick."

"I'm okay. They said that I have what they call retrograde amnesia. They told me this is the second time that it has happened this year. I guess I believe them but they could tell me anything. It seems that I can't remember anything that has happened since last November."

"Cord, are you putting me on?"

"What do you mean? Why would I put you on?"

"Well, you have been known to try to slip one past me at times, and I heard almost the same story last December."

"That's what they say. I didn't believe them at first. I mean, I thought it was November not August when I woke up in the hospital. I don't know how I could forget practically a year of my life and not even realize that much time had passed. But, they told me I got all the way to AA ball and that I spent the whole summer with Cate. None of that rings true. The last thing in my memory is spending every day with Indy while falling helplessly in love with her. Help!"

"Are you sure you're okay?"

"My arm's fine, although my head hurts if I shake it; but they're going to let me come home tomorrow."

"Great. That's good news. Will Cate be coming with you?"

"Why would you ask if Cate's coming?"

"Well, I thought you were almost engaged to her."

"Umm . . . I don't know about that, but, no, she has to get back to her job in New York. Shannon, this whole thing is really weird. Cate has told me a lot of things that happened this summer. She said she told her family that I was a permanent part of her life. How can that be when I was ready to ask Indy to marry me? It sounds like maybe I made a real mess of things."

"Cord, this is incredible. When you had your bicycle accident, your couldn't even remember dating Indy and you believed you were still in love with Cate. Now you can remember dating Indy but you can't remember anything that happened for most of this year, including seeing a lot of Cate."

"Shannon, when I regained consciousness, Cate was sitting in my room. I didn't know what to do. I couldn't imagine why she was there instead of Indy. On the other hand, I don't know if I've spoken to Indy since last November. I don't know if I asked her to marry me or not. I don't know if she turned me down. I don't know what to do since I'm hopelessly in love with Indy. And to top everything off, Cate told me she is investigating the Church and that I have been attending church on a regular basis. What's that all about?"

She sighed and then she laughed and said, "I'd really laugh if I didn't know this was for real. I had never heard about retrograde amnesia until last December; and now all of a sudden, it happens to you not once, but twice. I think you had better start wearing a helmet everywhere you go. You are either accident prone or you don't have that hard head that Mom always said you had."

"Shannon, they said that the first time I had this amnesia that was a result of a bicycle accident. I can't remember a bicycle accident. Give me some information. Was I weird or what?"

"Cord, you were a mess. You couldn't remember anything from the time you were playing ball in Wilmington in September 2004 through December 5, 2004, when you woke up from the accident."

"So that means that I couldn't remember meeting or dating Indy?"

"That's right, buster, and that's about how you treated her. You told me time and time again that you still believed you were in love with Cate and that Indy was, well, just nice. I always told you that I thought you belonged with Indy but you weren't buying it."

"So what do you mean? How did I treat Indy?"

"Like she was nice, or a friend, but that you were in love with Cate. I think you sent her an email soon after you got to Wilmington in early April that basically said, 'Thanks for the good times but I've found someone else, so hit the road, Jack.' "

"That bad?"

"Yep. Oh, I tried to tell you. I tried to warn you that you had some pretty deep feelings for Indy; but, no, you were dazzled by your memories of Cate. You wouldn't listen to me."

"What a mess. Everyone is telling me I'm in love with Cate, and yet I'm in love with Indy and want to be with her forever? Don't get me wrong. I *was* in love with Cate, but that ended."

"Well, as I see it, Cord, you have a problem. You've got Cate in your pocket but you don't love her; and now that you remember that you love Indy, she's gone because you told her you were in love with Cate. Maybe you should just stick to baseball."

I meekly, very meekly and humbly, asked, "So, what if I call Indy? Will she talk to me?"

"I think she'll hang up if she knows it's you calling. Besides, the last thing I heard, she was dating some doctor guy. But I don't know that for sure. I would say that you probably hurt her as bad as she could be hurt. She was fairly devastated, and I don't think she will be very anxious to let you waltz back into her life again."

"But she's a doctor. She has to understand that it wasn't my fault; I had amnesia."

"Nice try, Cord" she replied, but it was obvious that even Shannon wasn't buying into that excuse and she was on my side.

"You're right. She is a doctor, but she is a female doctor. And remember the first rule, women aren't always analytical and logical; and besides, Indy is in the lockdown mode. She's trying to protect herself. You just sealed the deal when you told her to hit the road."

I went back to my humble and meek voice. "I've got to talk to her, Shannon. Maybe if you called her and explained what happened . . ."

"Oh, I've already told her about your getting hit by the line drive. She said that she hoped you would be okay, and then she quickly changed the subject. Too quickly, I thought. But she didn't want to hear anything else about you, that's for sure."

"Pleeeease, Shannon, try to explain to her how I feel."

"I don't know, Cord, I'll think about it."

"I'll be home tomorrow. If you call her today, maybe you can soften her up. Maybe I'll bump into her at the hospital since I have to go see Dr. Montgomery. That's the doctor who, I'm told, previously treated me. Anyway, it would be nice if you could explain to her how humble I am and that I want to beg for her forgiveness. That I'm sorry. That I love her."

"I can't promise anything."

"Can you do me one more favor?"

"You already owe me."

I cut her off before she could continue. "Will you call Mom and tell her I'm okay? I don't think I'm up to having a conversation with her today."

"Sure! Why don't you just ask me to do all of your dirty work?"

"Hey, what are sisters for anyway?"

♦ ♦ ♦

On the flight to Salt Lake I tried to put a few pieces of my life puzzle together. I wanted to know what everyone else knew, the things I couldn't remember. I wanted to know if I still had a chance with Indy. I wanted to know how I had done pitching for the Wranglers. I wanted to know how to get my memory back. I wanted to know all about the relationship I had with Cate. I wanted to know what motivated me to start going to church again, and I ruled out my mother. The problem was that I didn't have all of the pieces. I knew I had fallen for Indiana Jones and had purchased a ring for her. I wanted her to be my wife. I remembered that. I couldn't remember if I popped the question, or, if I did, what she had answered.

But Indy had told Shannon that I had said that I was no longer interested in her, thanks but no thanks. Such a comment seemed absurd considering the fact that I loved her. I wondered if she was dating anyone from the hospital. In light of everything that had happened, I was sure that Indy didn't want anything to do with yours truly. One way or the other, I intended to talk to her. I wasn't going to let her just waltz out of my life.

Then my thoughts turned to Cate, beautiful Cate. I had fallen for Cate, no question. But since her family gave me the heave ho, I . . . I what? I still felt like I liked Cate a lot, but my heart was committed to Indy. I just couldn't explain why I would have spent everyday with her this summer. I couldn't remember, but it must be true.

I could remember going to church once or twice, but no more, and yet everyone told me that the Church had become more important to me than baseball. I doubted that, but everyone talked like it did.

Then there was baseball. I had made it to the Wichita Wranglers, AA baseball, and nobody had ever thought or given me a chance to get that far. Yet I had not only made it, I had apparently pitched like I deserved to be there. It would be the pits if I played AA baseball and couldn't remember one pitch. My record at Wichita was impressive, but then that had never mattered to the organization in the past. Maybe, just maybe, I would get a contract next spring.

My mind was spinning through "what if" situations but it froze when it landed on Cate again. What if my memory came back and I remembered that I was in love with Cate and not Indy? My puzzle was completely scrambled, but I couldn't think about that. I was on my way to try to patch things up with Indy. Losing your memory was like having your hard drive crash. All of the files, all of the memories . . . gone! And no one could fix it.

I guess I had never thought about it, but my past really defined who and what I was today. Without that memory it was hard to really know who I was and for that matter whether I was in love with Cate or Indy. I couldn't even say what happened yesterday because half of my yesterdays didn't exist. Maybe that was what Cate and Indy were feeling: hopelessness. There was no way to fix it. The feelings couldn't be restored because they didn't exist. Maybe I should start all over; but I wasn't sure I could talk either of them into that proposal. And suppose my lost memory returned. Where would I be then? So much for that brilliant idea.

Basics, I had to get back to basics. I had to get Indy to listen to me. I was sure if she heard me out, I could convince her that I was worth salvaging. It would be a tough sell; but being a doctor, maybe she would give me a break, be more understanding, have some sympathy. I just hoped that Shannon had been able to talk to her. It would be just my luck to find Indy with someone else's ring on her finger.

Everything seemed so circular. I wasn't getting anywhere. I didn't even have a plan of attack. What would I say to her? "Oh, Indy. I'm sorry I didn't call for the last nine months, but it seems I just forgot about you, I mean us. But it wasn't my fault." That didn't sound very good, even to me. It was up to Shannon. She was the answer. She had to come through. Maybe she could soften up Indy.

But what about Cate? Should I give it some time, see if my memory returned rather than jumping without knowing? But what if my memory never came back? And so it went. I found myself in a spiraling, circular nosedive with the ground rapidly approaching. Maybe I should take the approach a batter takes to the plate, just see the ball and hit it, don't stop to think about it. If you think about it, you'll never hit it.

♦ ♦ ♦

As soon as I got off the plane, I went straight to the University of Utah Hospital to see Dr. Montgomery. Standard medical office procedures require that they put me in a waiting room all by myself for ten to fifteen minutes. They did . . . all doctors do it. They must learn it in medical school. Twenty minutes later the door opened and a fairly stout nurse stalked in. You know her type, capable of eating small children in a single bite. Her name tag read, "Fielding" and I remembered seeing her when I picked Indy up at the hospital. She looked at me like, "Look what the cat dragged in." I thought, *She's certainly not very hospitable, and I thought nurses were supposed to be nice.*

Then in a no-nonsense, biting voice she said, "You've got a lot of nerve, Mr. Calloway."

"What?" I asked. I wondered what had happened to my captivating personality. What had I done to her? Wow!

"You heard me, and I don't need to say it again, especially to the likes of you."

"Have I done something to offend you?"

"Yeah," she said, "you're still breathing." She checked my blood pressure and checked a few vital signs. She didn't say another word. I wasn't sure I wanted her touching me; but if I said or did the wrong thing, I was sure she would really touch me.

I couldn't believe anybody could be so rude. I always thought I was a pretty likable guy, but then maybe she treated everyone like they were someone special.

She wanted to take a sample of my blood, and I was sure that she used an oversized needle and jabbed it extra hard when she put it in my arm. I made sure it was my left arm. She slammed the door when she left and said, "The doctor will be along in a minute."

What a delightful person, I thought.

It wasn't long before some weird looking guy came in to talk to me. His hair was sticking out in all directions, the buttons on his coat were mismatched, and he must not have shaved for three days. This guy could pass for Columbo. His name tag read Dr. Montgomery. *Well, it takes all kinds*, I thought. He had a stack of papers; some, he said, were reports from Wichita. He asked me the standard questions that I could rattle off by heart. He seemed nice, way better than the bulldog nurse. He didn't volunteer any information but continued asking questions and making notes on his weatherbeaten rumpled note pad. Then he started to poke around my head, which I thought was getting better. There was hardly any swelling and no real visible marks. Besides, the injury was mostly covered by my Wichita Wranglers baseball cap, which he made me take off during the examination.

"You are a very unusual case, Mr. Calloway. I will have to write up your case for one of the medical journals. I've never heard of anyone having an occurrence of retrograde amnesia twice in the same year. Of course, most people don't sustain two head injuries in such a short period of time. Yes, very unusual," he said as he fumbled through his beaten up notepad.

"Did you keep that notebook I asked you to keep when you were here before?"

"I don't know, Doctor. That's in the time period I can't remember."

"You're right, my boy, you're right," he said to someone other than me. At least he wasn't looking at me. He was fumbling through his reports.

"And you can now remember everything that was blocked after your bicycle accident. But now you can't remember anything since that accident. Is that right?"

"That's right, I think."

"Head injuries are all so different. We really don't know how or why only certain blocks of memory are affected, but they are. Usually they don't last a long time, but then sometimes they are permanent. I'd like to write your case up and submit it to our neuropsychological medical journal because it is so unique."

"Is there anything I can do to help restore my memory?"

"Not really, and I wouldn't recommend another blow to the head. Who knows what effect it could have on you? The main thing I want you to do is to keep in touch with me if you have any signs of pain or of memory restoration. Why don't we set you up with an appointment two weeks from today and then play it by ear."

As I left the room, I saw Nurse Fielding coming my way. I turned and went the other direction. Once a day was enough for me. I decided to leave via the emergency room with the chance I might run into Indy. It must have been my lucky day because she was just coming out of an office as I turned down one hall. She turned my way and saw me. She looked like a deer caught in my headlights. She wanted to run, but before she could turn, I said, "Indy."

"Hello . . . um, Cord. I guess you are here to see Dr. Montgomery."

"Yeah, but I was really hoping to see you."

"Well, a lot has happened since I last saw you." It appeared that she was having a hard time talking to me, but she was too polite to just walk away.

Apparently Shannon hadn't softened her up very much, but I wasn't going to walk away without throwing my best pitch. "I really want to talk to you. I need to talk to you. I am so sorry about everything and I need to explain. Is there a time we can get together, like tonight over dinner?"

"No, Cord, I'm just not up for that."

"But you must understand. I couldn't remember us. But now I can. I need to talk to you, Indy." I was pleading. I gave her that look that I reserve for umpires who clearly blew a call.

I could tell that she wasn't enjoying this conversation. It was hard on her to talk to me. She wouldn't look me in the eye but stared at the floor or anywhere except at me.

Just then the office door opened and Dr. John Stewart walked out. He looked at Indy and said, "I didn't think you were going to wait for me, Dr. Jones. I thought I was going to meet you in the cafeteria." He turned to look at me down his nose and asked, "Don't I know you?"

I responded, "Maybe I've seen you around the hospital."

He then shook my hand. Indy said, "John, you met Mr. Calloway last December."

He stroked the back of his head and neck and turned toward Indy. "Oh, yeah. He was the minor league baseball player, right?"

He seemed to emphasize the word *was*, and it seemed that he knew a lot more about me than I knew about him. He grabbed Indy's arm and said, "It was nice to meet you again, Mr. Calloway," and led Indy down the hall.

He was obviously trying to brush me off, and it looked like he had succeeded. But I wasn't giving up that easy. I said, "I'll call you, Indy."

She responded without turning, "I'm glad that you're okay." My chances of having her accept my offer of mediation weren't looking very good. It was like facing a batter with a full count who is looking dead red. And Dr. John Stewart, for some reason I didn't like him. He could take a flying leap as far as I was concerned.

As I was leaving, I passed the receptionist. In fact, I looked twice. On my second look she seemed to recognize me and said, "Is that you, Cord Calloway?" Maybe I was famous around here. Maybe they got the cable TV feed from Wichita.

I stopped and looked at her badge. It read *Alli*. I replied, "Yes, I am Cord Calloway. Do I know you?"

"You've already forgotten me?" she asked as she smiled. It was a smile that was inviting.

"I'm sorry. I got hit on the head and it's affected my memory."

"No need to apologize. I remember you when you were dating Dr. Jones, but I guess that's over now. She and Dr. Stewart seem to hang out now. Hey, but I always told you to give me a call if you wanted to do anything." She was scribbling a note on one of her business cards. "That's my cell number. Call me anytime."

"Thanks, I might just do that, Alli," I said.

Since Indy hadn't offered to give me a ride home, I had to take a cab. I wasn't used to taking cabs. I thought maybe I could ask Alli . . . no, I didn't want to go there.

♦ ♦ ♦

The house looked good. The tenants had been doing a good job taking care of it. I went downstairs, retrieved my mail, and went into my apartment. It needed some airing out. I shuffled through my mail and found one from an attorney. I don't like attorneys, and I don't like them sending me letters. Probably bad news, and I didn't need any more bad news right now; but I opened it anyway. A check fell out, made out to me for one hundred fifty thousand dollars. I thought maybe I had won the lottery. Then I read the letter. Apparently Mr. Bryan was my attorney, and he had settled my accident case and was forwarding me my share of the settlement. *Wow, I'm rich!* I thought. Maybe attorneys aren't bad guys after all.

I had a message on my phone from Cate asking me to call. I called back, and she was excited to hear my voice. She wanted to know how I was feeling and how my visit went with the doctor. She wanted me to know that she would be here in a week and that she was excited to see me and the Swensons. She reminded me that we were all going to Lake Powell. I couldn't turn her down, and it didn't look like I would be busy with Indy anytime in the near future, not with the good Dr. Stewart hanging around.

Then she said, "You've got to call the twins and Prestin. I explained to them about your head injury and that you don't remember the last nine months or teaching them pitching. They care a lot about you and want to see you. Oh, and since your memory is so bad, I think I should give you a heads up. You developed a very personal relationship with Prestin. She became almost like a mother to you. She wants to talk to you too."

"Thanks, Cate, what would I do without you?"

"Well, when we were at the hospital, I had the distinct feeling that your heart was somewhere else and that you just wanted to get rid of me. But then maybe it was just indigestion."

I didn't know what to say. Finally she said, "I guess nothing has changed with you."

"No, Cate. That's not how it is. I really am looking forward to spending some time with you. Everything's so mixed up. Keep in touch and thanks for the information. I'll get hold of the Swensons."

"Love you, Cord."

I responded, "I can't wait for you to get here, Cate." I don't think that was exactly the response she wanted; but hey, I was trying to be nice. But then, nice guys never get the girl in the end.

Thirteen

We have a good time together,
even when we're not together.

—Yogiism #13

"Okay, bottom line, did she agree to talk to me?" I asked. Shannon had talked to Indy but she wasn't exactly spilling the beans; and yes, I had already tried bribery. She seemed to be enjoying my suffering just a little too much. Maybe she was just getting even with me since I had been known to tease her occasionally when she had been dating. But then again maybe she was just trying to protect me from the inevitable.

After beating around the bush, Shannon finally said, "Indy didn't say yes but she didn't say no either. Cord, this is how I see it. She is very fragile right now. You really hurt her, even though it may not have been intentional. As a result I think she has turned inward for self-protection, hiding behind her wall. I'm not sure she's willing to return to the scene of the accident yet."

"Did you tell her that it wasn't my fault? I just forgot . . . forgot that I love her but that now I remember in technicolor."

"I think she understands intellectually what happened, but emotionally is another thing. I think she could have lived with the fact that you couldn't remember anything about her if you had been willing to try to work through it, to try to rediscover that which was lost. But you couldn't be bothered because the only thing you cared about was Cate. It was like one day you were madly in love with Indy and the next day it was Cate. You didn't forget about Cate; and to make matters worse, you just moved on without seeming to miss a beat."

"But I forgot because of the amnesia."

"Yeah, you forgot about Indy but you didn't forget about Cate."

She was right. That was how it appeared but that wasn't how it was. I could explain what happened and I think everyone could understand it intellectually, but that wasn't the problem. I just hoped that Shannon had convinced her she should give me another chance.

"Did she say anything about her relationship with the vaunted Dr. Ego?"

"Who's that?"

"It's that jerk Dr. John Stewart. He acts like we should all bow down to him. I met him at the hospital the other day. He made sure I couldn't talk to Indy."

"She did say that she was dating someone, but she didn't say it with much feeling. I got the impression that she's just treading water, passing time. I don't think she is looking for a relationship right now. I think she gave up on that."

"That's good news."

"I don't think you understand. The 'no serious relationship' part also includes you."

"Yeah, but I haven't struck out yet. I've only got two strikes on me, and I'm a good two-strike hitter. So how do I get her to talk to me?"

"Well, I think if you pester her enough, she might just give in to social pressure. You know the old saying 'the squeaky wheel gets the oil.' But she has to believe that you are sincere; really sorry. Beg for mercy. Don't stop calling her. Make her believe she is the only person in your life who really matters, next to me of course. If none of that works, you could fake an injury while she's on duty in the ER." By this time Shannon was practically laughing.

"Okay, I can try that, but there's this one little complication."

"Cord, how do you always manage to get yourself in trouble?"

I ignored her comment and tried to act like it was no big deal. "Well you see, Cate's coming to town in five days to go on a trip with the Swensons to Lake Powell, and I'm sorta invited to go. If I don't go, then it will be over with Cate for sure. Besides, I promised I would go."

"You've got to be kidding me. Just a little complication. You sit there and profess your enduring love for Indy and that you will do anything to get her back; and in the same breath you tell me that you've got to go to Lake Powell with Cate. Cord, one of these things doesn't belong. Don't you get it?"

"But Cate says I promised her."

"Could you please change your last name and not tell anyone that I'm your sister? And by the way, don't ever ask me to call Indy again if that's all it matters to you. Here I was trying to convince Indy to talk to you, but I'm on Indy's side if you go to Lake Powell with Cate."

"But I promised."

"I can tell you if Indy knows that you're going to Lake Powell with Cate next week, you have absolutely no chance of ever talking to her, even if you got injured and had to go to the ER. It'll be strike three, and I would completely agree with her. Cord, how do you always get yourself into these situations? I swear you must go around looking for them."

"I don't try, Shannon. It's just . . . well . . . I don't know."

"It would help a lot if you could make up your mind. I mean, you can't keep two women on the string very long without losing one or both of them. You're playing with fire."

"Yeah, but I didn't mean for it to happen. It's not my fault."

"Oh, like that one's really gonna fly. How many times do you think you can use that line?"

"But I'm pretty sure I have chosen. I'm in love with Indy; I bought a ring for her. Now she won't even talk to me. Suppose that no matter what I do, she won't talk to me. That she really has written me off. Now if I tell Cate to hit the road, she will. Then what happens if I can't convince Indy that I'm her knight in shining armor?"

"Okay then, why not just choose Cate, go with the flow? Besides, everyone tells me that Cate is one in a million and very rich. How can you go wrong?"

"Because I believe that Indy is the one."

"Then it sounds like you have chosen. All you have to do is to tell Cate you're not going to Lake Powell. Problem over."

"How can I do that?"

"Are you serious?"

"So what do you think I should do?"

"I'm not going to choose your wife for you. I'm not going there. You'd blame me for the rest of your life. I'd rather have you roll the dice. But maybe you just have to be willing to make a decision and stick with it. Or better still, you could always try prayer."

♦ ♦ ♦

I left messages on Indy's cell phone and at the hospital with Alli. Indy didn't return any of them. Maybe she would turn me in to the police as a stalker if I continued to harass her. Messages didn't work, and I was tired of talking to her voice mail. I called to see if she was at work and was told she wouldn't be in until later that night, so I knew she would be home. "Okay, Betsy, you know the way. Let's go, gal." If Indy wouldn't come to me, I was going to go to her. She needed to tell me face to face to hit the road.

I knocked on her front door and waited. I didn't really have a plan, I just needed to talk to her. Keep it light. Don't be melodramatic. Use sympathy. Beg. Whatever worked. The door finally opened. She just stared at me. And let's just say, it was not a I'm-glad-to-see-you stare. Before she could slam the door, I said, "Indy, just give me ten minutes."

"Why?"

"Because I let you beat me to the top of Dog Lake. Because I'm handsome. Because I'm a professional baseball player. Because I love you. Because I'm cool. Because I don't know why. I just need to talk to you."

She softened and I could see the beginning of a smile. "You didn't let me beat you to the top of Dog Lake. You barely staggered to the top."

"Okay, so I exaggerated a little. How about it? Ten minutes for old times' sake then."

I started to go in the house, but she put up her hand and said, "Not in here. We can sit on the front porch. You now have nine minutes and fifty seconds."

She was tough. She didn't even smile when she said it. She did, however, look at her watch. It was now or never. I pulled a little black velvet box out of my pocket. "Last November I bought this for you. But before I could give it to you, I got konked on the head and forgot why I bought it."

"You mean you forgot whom you bought it for." And she emphasized the significant part of the sentence: *whom*.

I couldn't slide anything by her. I couldn't lie to her. Suck it up and tell her the truth. "Okay, you're right. I always believed I bought it for you, but now I *know*. I remember."

"You've got seven minutes left, Cord."

Man, she was tough. Even my wit wasn't cracking the wall. I thought the ring would at least buy me some time. She hadn't even looked at the ring. It just sat there on the table. "Open the box, Ca . . ." It was out before I could swallow it. How could I? I was so dead. Maybe she hadn't heard.

"No, Cord! I'm sorry. I'm Indy. Cate is the other one." She let that sink in, relishing every minute of my pain. Then she said, "Now let me get this straight. You say you bought this for me or did you mean Cate?"

"That's not fair. I didn't mean . . . I just slipped."

"No kidding! You should practice your lines a little better." But she was smiling a little and that was a good sign, I thought.

"Look, I'm not very good at this kind of stuff."

"You have three and a half minutes left."

I had given her my best shot. The problem was that I blew the punch line. I didn't know where to go from here. I felt sweat running down my back. For some reason I just blurted out, "Is Nurse Fielding the one behind all of this? For some reason she hates me."

She laughed. Maybe I was making some headway. So I added, "Go ahead and open it. If you look at it, you will know it was for you."

"Cord, I've moved on. I went through some pretty hard days and nights before I was able to put you behind me. It wasn't easy, and I don't want to ever go through that again. I guess you could say that I'm not willing to take the risk."

"But, Indy, every day is a risk. Everything we do is a risk. All you can do is to try to put the odds in your favor. That's what pitching is all about, trying to put the odds in your favor. You can throw a perfect pitch, low and away on the outside black, which should cause the batter to hit into a double play; but the batter can still hit it out of the park. But knowing that, you still want to put the odds in your favor. Trust me. I will never hurt you again."

"Let me ask you a couple of questions, Cord."

"Okay, shoot."

"Tell me how much time you spent with Cate since February and what promises you made to her."

I was in trouble again. "Are you sure you didn't go to law school?"

"That's not an answer to the question."

"I know, but I don't know the answer to that question. I honestly don't remember anything since last November."

"At least you're being honest. Let me ask you another question. What happens if you wake up and, suddenly, all your memory is restored and you not only remember that you saw Cate frequently but that you had also asked her to marry you?"

I think she enjoyed seeing me squirm. "Indy, I love you."

"Cord, I really believe you believe you love me today, but what about tomorrow? Trusting you doesn't seem to put the odds in my favor."

There, she did it again. She should have been a lawyer. "But you're a doctor. You've got to understand none of this has been on purpose. I didn't intend any of this to happen."

"I understand and I'm not blaming you. We, you and I, well, maybe we're just victims of circumstances like the double play ball that got hit for the home run. We tried; we just didn't make it."

She was talking baseball, and that shifted the advantage to me. "Well, after you give up a home run, you still have to throw a pitch to the next batter. Try again. You can't do anything about the last pitch." That was good. I had her there.

"But what if it was the bottom of the ninth and it was a walk-off home run?"

Dang! Where did she learn so much about baseball? "But in our case it wasn't. We still have two more innings to play, and the score is tied."

"I have another question."

I knew I was in trouble. I hadn't done very well on any of the questions yet, so I decided to take the offense. "I'm sorry, but you just used up your full quota of questions with the last one." She ignored me, although she did smile again. My wit was making a difference. I knew the serious approach wouldn't work.

"Okay, here are my last two questions. I understand that Cate is coming to town to go to Lake Powell with the Swensons. And I heard that Cate is a wonderful person, but understand this: that doesn't mean I have to like her. So here are my questions. First, are you going to tag along on the Lake Powell excursion? And second, if you go are you ready to tell her that you have proposed to me? I take it that you have an engagement ring in that black box."

It was a gut punch. I could feel myself staggering. I suddenly had a jolt of inspiration. I needed to buy some time. I couldn't answer her questions. Maybe my memory would return, maybe she would come to understand that she couldn't live without me.

I needed some time to resolve the Cate issue, even though I had a gut feeling that Indy was the one. Then I remembered some chick flick that Indy had made me watch. It was about a couple who agreed to meet on the top of the Empire State building two months later if they were still in love. That might work, and it was the romantic kind of thing that just might appeal to her. I really didn't want to stop seeing her just after I had found her again. The question was if I was willing to sacrifice the short-term needs for the long-term goal. It's like walking Manny Ramirez so you can pitch to Jason Varitec.

"Okay, here's the deal. I love you, Indy. You are the one that I want to spend the rest of my life with, but I need some time to tie up a few loose ends. On the other hand, you're not sure about anything, especially me. I propose that we take some time and seriously consider if we are meant to be together. I won't bug you. I'll give you some time, even though that's not my preference. So here's what we'll do. We'll take some time to resolve our problems. So let's say we pick a time to meet up again. The Roof restaurant, on the first Friday in December at eight in the evening. If you want to try again, then meet me there for dinner. If only one of us shows up, then we will both know it's over."

"I didn't know you were such a romantic. But you're not very original, and all this time I thought you were asleep while watching my chick flicks. You must have been paying attention some of the time while playing like you weren't interested."

"What are you talking about?"

"Remember the old movie *An Affair to Remember*, the story line of which was later used in *Sleepless in Seattle*? But it was a nice try anyway."

"Really?"

"You don't really expect me to believe that you thought this one up all by yourself, do you?"

I was scrambling, something I don't do very well on my feet. I went on in spite of her mocking my every suggestion. "Listen, it will give our relationship the test of time. Maybe I will find the rest of my memory. Maybe you will remember that you can't live without my charming personality. What do you have to lose?"

"But I've already made my decision. I don't need to rethink it."

"But what if I *am* the one? What if we *are* meant to be together?"

"What if I've already found someone else?"

Now she was hitting below the belt. Just keep her talking, since she had forgotten about the time limit. "If you have, he isn't the right one, and you will regret your decision not only for the rest of your life but for all eternity. Do you know how hard it would be to live without me forever? You could never watch a baseball game again without thinking about me."

"Okay, okay, it's a deal. But no promises and no contact until then. I don't want you to bug me between now and then. One other thing: if I don't show, it won't be because I was in an auto accident; it will be because I have moved on for good. So don't come looking for me."

I said, "Let's shake on it. First Friday in December at eight at The Roof."

She reached out her hand to shake. I took her hand and held it with both of mine. "Indy, I love you. I'll be there."

"There you go again, making promises. It's like someone telling me to trust him."

I pulled her toward me and kissed her ever so lightly. She didn't resist. That was a good sign. I got up to leave.

She said, "Cord." I turned, and she held out the little black velvet box. "You can take this with you. You may need it before December."

Another sucker punch. She didn't fight fair. I took the ring and started to walk away when she whispered, "Cord." I stopped and turned. "You didn't answer either of my questions. Nice try, though."

♦ ♦ ♦

I drove out to the airport to pick up Cate on Friday night. I parked and walked to the security checkpoint to wait. My heart was racing. I was confused. I had spent days trying to figure out how to tell Cate that I was in love with Indy. So far I hadn't come up with any great ideas. The last thing I wanted to do was to hurt Cate, and I didn't want to ruin her whole trip to Lake Powell. The only person I really had to talk to about my predicament was Shannon, and it was obvious that she was not going to help me make any decisions. The more I thought about it, the more confused I became. I was sure that Indy was the one, but it wasn't easy to shut the door on Cate. I still had a lot of feelings for her, and something had happened this summer if I spent a lot of time with her. In the end I decided not to decide anything but to just roll with the punches and see what happened. Something would come up, at least I hoped it would.

I could see her coming; everybody could see her coming. Most men followed her with their eyes, and I guess I was just as guilty as they were. Stunning described her best. She put her arms out as she approached, and what was I supposed to do? I hugged her and, well, I kissed her or she kissed me. *I handled that really well*, I thought. She put her arm through mine, and we headed downstairs to get her luggage. She was excited to be back in Salt Lake. It was hard to dampen her enthusiasm; it was infectious. By the time we were in Betsy, we were laughing about her experiences of the past few weeks.

Then she asked out of the blue, "Cord, do you remember where we went to dinner with the Swensons during spring training?"

I thought about it. No, I couldn't ever remember going to dinner with the Swensons. In fact I couldn't remember meeting anyone in the family except for Bishop Swenson. Cate's enthusiasm seemed to lose a little steam, but she asked, dreading my answer. "Have you been able to remember anything that happened since last November?"

I had to admit to her that I was still missing the most part of a year of my life. It seemed for a moment that she was fighting an impulse to say something because her countenance changed for a brief minute. Then the light came back on and she said, "That's too bad, Cord. We made a lot of memories during that time that I will never forget."

She became almost melancholy. Maybe she would talk to me about my lost year. "Maybe you can share them with me during the next couple of weeks," I said.

"I'd like that."

We fell into an almost painful silence. It was Cate who spoke first. She wanted to try to soften the blow that my missing memory was about to have on our friends. She was always thinking of others. "Have you talked to the twins since you've been home?" she asked.

I had to admit that I hadn't, although I didn't explain to her why I had purposely stayed away from the Swensons. She told me that they would be crushed if I couldn't remember them, so she explained as much as she could about my relationship with them. She knew that they listened to my games every night on the Internet, that they had won their league championship, that both had played on the all-star team, and that Ash had been their coach. Then she told me about Prestin and how much time I had spent with her and that Prestin wanted to adopt me as her son. "She was like your second mother."

"Are you serious? Isn't one mother enough for anyone?"

She laughed. See, I was funny. "No, I mean you talked to Prestin about things you wouldn't even talk to me about. I sometimes wondered whom you liked the most. This is going to seem strange, introducing you to her, to them. You knew them before I did. But I've already explained to Prestin about your injury, and she promised to explain it to the kids. The twins, well, you won't be able to get rid of them. They live and breathe Cord Calloway. I told Prestin that I want to spend some time with you without the boys or their sister, Bell, and she promised to help."

"This is going to be weird, Cate. I mean, I should know them, but I don't know them at all."

"Yeah, that's hard."

"Yeah," I said. "It's just that this memory trouble sometimes creates some difficult situations. Like with you. There are things I know I should know and feelings I should feel. I wish I could remember. I wish I could feel. I'm sorry."

"I'm sorry too, but maybe we can fix some of the problems. Things will work out. We have too much going for us for to fail."

I didn't mean to get so serious so soon, but she had the answers I needed. "Cate, I still really need to know about us. Tell me what we did. Tell me our promises. Tell my why your father would offer me a job paying more than I will ever earn anywhere when your parents don't even like me. And why did you turn the job down for me? Tell me about our dreams."

She thought for a minute and said, "Okay, I'll try to help fill in some of your blind spots. But first, I need you to help me because since the day you got hurt I've felt like I've been on the outside looking in."

Great, here we go again. My favorite game. And I used to be able to hold my own in Twenty Questions. But then women weren't usually involved in my games and they never play fair. Besides, our games only involved baseball questions. I wondered why it felt like I was being set up again. But I couldn't refuse. "Sounds fair to me," I said, knowing that nothing about this conversation was going to be fair.

"It seems that I've become one side of a triangle. I'm sure that you never meant it to become that way, but it has. The problem is that whatever happens to the other two sides affects me; and right now I seem to be the only one left out in the cold. I don't know what's happening. So before I make a complete fool of myself, I want to know where we, all three of us, are heading. For starters, you need to come clean and tell me about you and Indiana Jones. What promises have you made to her? What dreams do you have with her? What do you remember of your time with her? And most important, where does that leave us?"

I didn't know what to say, but I knew whatever I said would prove to be a disaster. She broke the silence. "You're not very good at hiding your feelings. You wear them on your shirt sleeve. I could tell the minute you woke up in the hospital that you had changed the channel. I presumed after talking with you that your recent bash on the head had done something to your memory. Is that true?"

She was like an attack dog. How could I answer any of those questions? I wanted to avoid these questions, at least for now. I had to try to dodge, to hedge and avoid direct answers and to be funny at the same time. I needed to change the mood. "Objection, compound question. Which one do you want me to try to answer first?"

"How about the last question?"

"Yes. My memory has returned. I can now remember things that happened before the bicycle accident."

"In that case, I assume since you didn't answer my first question, that you now remember all of the time you spent with Indiana. After we broke up but before you were in the bicycle accident. Is that right?"

"Yes, that's true."

"And you can't remember one thing since your bicycle accident."

"Correct."

"Okay, that brings us to today. You've been in Salt Lake for a couple of weeks, and I'm sure that you have spoken with Indiana about your relationship with her. She probably wonders about me and you, correct?"

See, I knew I was in trouble. I didn't want to have this conversation today. This was supposed to happen later. "Yes." I decided one syllable responses posed the least threat.

"So where do I stand? Where do we stand? Do we still have a triangle?"

Humor. Maybe I could try humor again. "Are you sure that you didn't go to law school?" Man, I had just endured the toughest cross-examination from Indy; and now Cate was taking her best shot. It wasn't fair. I didn't stand a chance. Maybe I should fake another injury; or better, fake sudden amnesia.

I had to think about her question. I was slow in my response, so she answered for me. "You haven't answered my questions. I hope that it doesn't mean what I think it means. Talk to me, Cord."

I blew my breath out and sighed. "Let me try to explain this whole mess, Cate. But to do that I need to start at the beginning."

I didn't know where I was going, but it was better than stammering and letting her continue her cross examination. I breathed deeply, looked her in the eyes, and said, "Okay, I can remember leaving your parents' home after being told that I was not good enough for you. I can remember that you disappeared after that night, and I didn't hear from you or see you again until you came unannounced to my apartment in Salt Lake and surprised Indy and me together. The next time I remember seeing you was when I awoke in the hospital in Wichita.

"I can remember leaving Wilmington after baseball ended last year and returning to Salt Lake. After I got home I met Indiana Jones. I can remember dating her a lot, and she came to mean very much to me. I can't remember being with you in spring training or in Wilmington this summer. I can't remember meeting with your father for dinner. But worse, I can't remember anything about us since I was in your home for the 'Battle at the Belfords.' I don't know what we did, how we felt, what we promised. That's why I need your help. I need to understand. I need to know about us." I felt good about my response and it was right off the top. Chalk one up for me. And all along I didn't think I was good on my feet.

She just stared at me. I could see the wheels turning. I knew she was trying to evaluate me, to decide if it was worth it—if I was worth it, if we were worth it.

"Fair enough," she said. I reached over and held her hand. She squeezed my hand and smiled. I was in trouble and I knew it.

♦ ♦ ♦

We pulled up in front of the Swensons. Their Suburban was

already fully loaded and looked like it was going on a safari. Two boys were tying things to the luggage rack on top of the car, and a young girl was apparently waiting for Cate's arrival since she was sitting on the grass watching every car. Cate pointed out Bell to me and Blaze and Rush, the twins. As soon as we stopped, Bell ran up to the car and hugged Cate. I mean, you could tell that she was devoted to Cate. There was no doubt that Cate was her hero. The boys hopped down from the car and meandered over. I could tell they were a little hesitant to do or say anything. Cate jumped in and tried to put everyone at ease. "Cord, this is Rush and Blaze, or is it Blaze and Rush?" They were nodding their heads and then shaking them. I couldn't tell which motion went with what declaration. They were good-looking kids; tall for their age with long fingers. They had perfect bodies for pitchers; that is, once they filled out their skeleton frames with a little muscle.

"I'm Rush, and this is Blaze. Are you okay? We were listening to your game the night you got hit with the line drive. The announcer said that it looked serious. As soon as it happened, we had a family prayer for you. Then we started calling the hospital to find out how you were. It wasn't until the next day we found out you were going to be okay. You had us pretty worried."

I couldn't believe it. A family prayer for me. No wonder I must like these people so much. "Thanks, guys. I'm sure it helped. But next time can you remember to add something about my memory being okay?" Bell had her arm around Cate, and they were both watching the exchange. Cate looked like the perfect mom. Kids seemed to like her as much as men did. I looked at the twins and said, "I understand that you guys are my star pupils. Are you bringing your gloves to the lake?"

"We wouldn't go without them," said Blaze. "Dad's going to bring his catcher stuff so we can throw."

"That's good. I can hardly wait to see how you guys throw. Cate told me you were great."

Just then a nice looking lady came out of the house. When she saw me, she exclaimed, "Cord!" She broke into a run and threw her arms around me.

Cate said, "See what I told you, Cord? I think you like Prestin more than me. I didn't get a hug like that."

Prestin smiled at Cate and said, "Yeah, but you're just the girlfriend." Then she hugged me again and said, "I'm so happy to see you, Cord. You look great. How do you feel?"

"Like I've just been mauled by a she bear."

Everyone laughed and Prestin said, "Well, you had better get used to it around here. I'm a hugger. By the way, I'm Prestin, your second mom, since you have obviously forgotten. I have that effect on most men, and umpires wish they could forget me."

Bishop Swenson was trailing Prestin and was watching the whole scene with a smile. I recognized him and waved with my one free hand. No wonder I liked this family so much. Cate was radiant, and she was enjoying this reunion. She was different from when I first met her. I'm not sure what it was, but I guess she just seemed more content with life.

Bishop Swenson came over and gave me a hug. "I'm so glad you're home, Cord. We've missed you at our Sunday dinners. Besides, the twins have been practicing, and they both think they can beat you in ping-pong now."

We all sat down on the front lawn and talked and laughed and enjoyed each other. This was how I wanted my family to be, I thought. I looked at Cate, who was enjoying every minute. She had never known another family like this. Her family would have been sitting in suits and formal wear at a fancy table set for a seven course meal, saying things like "May I?" "please," and "If you don't mind, could you . . . ," and not much else. Her family would never be caught sitting on the lawn in a front yard displaying emotions in front of all the neighbors. But Cate was thriving in this environment, and Bell was sitting by her side holding her hand. I had to smile. Cate caught me looking at her and winked. How could you not love Cate?

♦ ♦ ♦

We were about to leave when Ash called everyone together in the house for a family prayer. We were driving two cars. Prestin had talked Bell into riding with them for half of the trip to allow Cate and me to have some alone time, which for once I was not sure was a great idea, but didn't dare say so. It had been a hard sell, but Cate promised when we stopped in Nephi for dinner that Bell could switch cars and ride the rest of the way with us. At least I knew that I would only be on the witness stand for the next two hours.

After family prayer, Cate said, "Before we leave, I would like to tell you all a story. Okay?"

Everyone sat back down and looked at Cate. She started, "There was this young lady who thought she had the world by the tail. Very sophisticated, worldly, and yet she knew nothing about God. She had everything she wanted that money could buy, and she thought she could buy happiness. Then she met this hick from Nowhere, Utah. His sophistication was limited to throwing a baseball sixty feet six inches and eating at McDonald's for lunch. At least that's what she thought. But he was kinda cute. Then one day he introduced her to a real family. She got to spend some time with this family. One night they had a family prayer, just like we had today. In those simple prayers she heard the children talking to God like they knew him, like he was their friend. The family . . . well, she decided she wanted a family like that. Then these nice missionaries told her, 'Hey, this book is magic. God has promised if you read it and pray about it, He will answer your prayers.' So this big lunk says, 'All you have to do is read it. If God doesn't answer your prayers, then the book is a hoax and you can throw it away. But if he does answer, well then, you have a problem.'

"Well, this girl carried that book around, wanting to read it and yet afraid of what might happen if she did. Then one day, she bit the bullet and started reading. She read it from cover to cover in two days. By the time she was through, she didn't have to ask God if it was true because he had already told her before she had even finished it.

"What was she to do? Her parents would disown her and cut her out of their will if she joined the Mormon Church. She only knew a few people who belonged to the Church. She would have to change her life entirely if she joined. She spent many days and nights wrestling with the knowledge that God had given her and its impact on her life. It seemed whenever things got dark, she saw this image of a beautiful thirteen-year-old girl telling her she could do it, that she would always be there for her and with her.

"Well, if you haven't figured it out by now, the worldly girl in the story was me. The hick from Utah is none other than Cord Calloway, and the little girl who was willing to always be there for me is Bell, my sister. The book's true. I know. So what do I do now?"

She shrugged her shoulders, wiped a tear from her eye, and threw up her hands in a surrendering gesture. "But I want all of you to remember that I'm going to hold each of you responsible for what happens to me because it's your fault."

I felt something tugging at my heart, or maybe it was my whole soul. Cate knew the book was true. I had always wanted to have that knowledge, to feel what she was feeling. Even as I said those words to myself it was as though I was repeating from memory old hopes and wishes . . . and for some reason they didn't seem as important as they once had been. In fact now that I thought about it, I really didn't have any doubts as to the truthfulness of the book. When had that happened? I wondered why. How?

Bell grabbed Cate in a bear hug. Prestin had tears running down her cheeks. Ash turned away for a minute before turning back with glistening eyes. "Cate, we love you."

Me? All I could do was stare in shock. Cate wanted to be a Mormon! And I didn't remember any of the story. Was I now an active Mormon? I remembered going to church with Indy last fall, but what had happened over the last few months? Would I ever remember?

The boys all slapped her on the back and congratulated her while I sat with my mouth open. Ash told her he would talk to her more about the technicalities of joining the Church when we got to Lake Powell.

♦ ♦ ♦

"Tell me about it, Cate."

"About what?"

"About what happened while you were reading the Book of Mormon."

I could tell she was trying to control her emotions. She took a full minute and then in a halting voice, choked with emotion, she said, "It was strange. I didn't see an angel. I didn't hear a voice. Yet there was something there every time I picked up the book. The more I read, the more I felt this strong feeling in my heart. At times I almost couldn't contain the feelings. At times I just cried it felt so wonderful. It just happened. It wasn't earth shaking except to me. When you gave me the book I wasn't ready. I was afraid. But after being around the Swensons and seeing what a real family is like and the personal relationship they have with God, I decided I wanted to know if it was all a bunch of hooey. If it was true, then there couldn't be anything more important. And I have to tell you, little Bell was there with me all the way."

I wondered why she hadn't considered me to be the one there with her every step of the way. I had given her the book, and it was me that had continued to pester her. But then I didn't even know for myself, did I? But there was this nagging feeling or voice, I couldn't tell which, that seemed to repeat, "You know."

She was crying, and I had a lump in my throat. Then she started laughing. Finally between breaths she gasped, "Can you imagine me trying to explain this to my folks? I mean, I don't have any facts, any evidence. All I have is this feeling. They aren't going to buy that, but guess who they're going to blame." Then she started laughing again.

"That wouldn't be me, would it?" I asked. By now she was laughing hard enough to start crying again. I said, "I'm not so sure it's really funny, but you'd better make sure you tell them when I'm not anywhere close to Wilmington."

Then she got serious again. "Cord, this thing with the Church . . . I want you to know I'm not joining because of you . . . I mean, you introduced me to it, but I'm not going to join because of you, because of us. I'm going to join because it's right for me, no matter what happens to us. Do you understand?"

What she was saying had affected me. "Cate, I think I'm about as new to this church thing as you. I mean, I did grow up in the Church, but I fell away and now I've only recently rediscovered it. For some reason it seems that it has come to matter to me."

Then the smile left her face and she got serious again. She told me all about how confused she'd been after her parents had ended our relationship, about her need to know whether she could really live the kind of life I would have given her, and about how she'd finally gotten everything figured out and decided to give us another chance. She continued, "That's about the time that I came to Salt Lake to try to make amends. I went back without even getting to talk to you, thinking it was all over. Eventually my brother called. He knew where I was, and he talked me into calling Dad just to talk. The short version is that we met and came to a mutual understanding that I would not shut them out of my life, and they wouldn't try to force me to live my life under their direction. I went to Europe with them, and when I got home, I read your emails and eventually came out to Arizona for spring training."

Cate then went on to tell me about our week in Arizona with the Swensons. She told me of the things we talked about and the time we spent together. She told me about her falling in love with the Swensons and their family, of visiting Salt Lake and meeting the sister missionaries, and of going to church in Wilmington. She told me about Will: William James Winthrop, an attorney who had volunteered to help teach her the lessons. He was single.

I interrupted her, feeling a little bit jealous, although I wasn't sure why. "Tell me, you aren't dating Will, are you?"

"He has taken me out a number of times. My parents like him. He fits into their mold, coming from a rich, well-established family; and he is an Ivy Leaguer, graduating from Yale

Law School. The only drawback they see is that he is a Mormon and a returned missionary."

"And . . . ?"

"And what? Do I like him? Well, yes. He's turned out to be a good friend, but am I in love with him? No! I lost my heart to a baseball player from Utah the first day I met him. The feeling's never gone away."

I couldn't look at her. My heart was pounding. I wondered how to deal with this. Cate was going to join the Church. She was confessing her love for me; and Indy . . . what was I going to do?

Cate went on to tell me about her new job and how well she was doing. She talked about our conversations of the last six months. Living in Salt Lake would not to be the problem for her that she had once thought it would be. She believed that I would make a great high school coach, and she didn't object to the fact that I wouldn't make a lot of money.

Listening to her talk made it clear that we had made a lot of plans for our tomorrows. It sounded like I was in love with Cate. I asked her if I ever mentioned Indy and she told me no, that it was a closed door as far as she had been concerned; closed, that is, until the last injury.

I was nervous and not very sure about any of my feelings, but I finally asked, "Cate, did I ever tell you how my relationship with Indy ended?"

"No! Like I said, you just never talked about her. I asked you some questions about her, and you told me that you couldn't remember anything about dating her. You told me she was very nice and that's all. I never doubted you. Now I think it's time for your 'true confessions,' since I've spilled my guts."

I guess honesty is the best policy. I hadn't really planned what I was going to say, so I just jumped right in. "Well, when I woke up in the hospital in Wichita, I was shocked to see you there. I thought our relationship was over. I remembered leaving Wilmington believing that you had sided with your parents. I was mad, or I guess looking back I was more hurt that you would base your decision about us on social status, financial status, and my being a Mormon. I tried to forget you because I was mad or hurt. It didn't work. Then I met Indiana. I fell in love with her, Cate. I was going to ask her to marry me, and then I got in the bike accident. After the accident I couldn't remember even meeting her, let alone dating her. But when I woke up in the hospital in Wichita everything had switched. I could remember everything about dating Indy, but I couldn't remember anything that happened since.

"Now that I've been back in Salt Lake, I've tried to contact her many times. She won't have anything to do with me. Finally I went to her house and tried to get her to out with me. She told me that she wasn't ready to do that and didn't know if she would ever be ready. She said she had moved on and couldn't go back because it was too painful. She wouldn't even talk to me." Yeah, so I left out some details, but they wouldn't help anything or anyone at this point.

"So how do you feel now? I mean, I don't want to know what you *think*, I want to know how you *feel*. And I want an honest answer."

"Cate, I feel like I'm in love with Indy."

She wouldn't look at me. She just stared out the window. She didn't say anything, and we just rode in silence for what seemed like forever. Finally she spoke softly, almost whispering. "Then what are you doing here? Are you here just to ensure that you have a fall-back position if you can't make things work out with her?"

She was hurting and it was my fault again. "I'm sorry. If I could only remember." I was quiet for several minutes. I tried to make things better. "Honestly, I guess I'm trying to buy some time, hoping that the rest of my memory returns so I can put the whole puzzle together. If only I hadn't been hit by that baseball. It may sound selfish. I know I have some pretty deep feelings for you. I always have and always will."

"And if your memory doesn't return?"

"Then I don't know."

She was again silent for a long time. She rubbed her cheek. I thought she was crying softly, but she wouldn't look at me. I felt like a jerk. How could I be putting her through this? She didn't deserve it.

♦ ♦ ♦

We had eaten in Nephi, and Cate had decided to ride with the Swensons and let the twins ride the rest of the way with me. They were excited to be able to ride with me, and Bell just wanted to be with Cate. It was only fair. I felt like a clod, but at least I would get to talk baseball for the rest of the way, and I knew something about baseball. I loved to talk baseball. I didn't know or understand women and relationships; they had always been a mystery to me.

Fourteen

You can't think and hit at the same time .

—Yogiism #14

"And stepping into the batter's box, swinging from the right side, is Albert Pujols, maybe one of the best hitters of all time. He's facing the rookie, Blaze Swenson, a hard-throwing lefty. The first pitch is on its way: a nasty, sinking fastball, down and away from Albert, catching the black for a strike. Albert turns to look at the ump, a nasty stare. Blaze comes back with another sizzling, outside fastball. Albert takes a mighty swing and drives a ball deep to right, but it might be going foul, well beyond the right field bleachers. The Fenway crowd is on its feet, mourning because the Cardinals have just won the game. A mighty cheer fills the stands as the ball slices foul at the last minute.

"Breathing deeply, Blaze rears back and wings a high fastball that is cookin'. 'Ball one,' cries the Blue. He winds and delivers a hard breakin' curveball. The crowd moans as the ump signals ball. Blaze lets his next pitch fly, his signature fastball, down and away on the outside black. Pujols swings, catching nothing but air . . . it's by him for strike three, and the Red Sox win! The Sox win! The Sox win! . . . A great performance by this young rookie pitcher from Draper, Utah, the hometown of the famous Cord Calloway."

Cate was announcing as Blaze was throwing a make-believe game. I exclaimed, "At least you could pit teams against each other that are in the same league. I mean, the Card's are in the National League and the Red Sox are in the American."

"Haven't you heard of the crossover games, Mr. Calloway?" See what I mean? You never argue with a woman or a reporter.

Ash was catching, and I was standing behind the mound on a beach on the shores of Lake Powell. I coached the twins as they threw each pitch to the make-believe batters. And Cate continued announcing the make-believe game. These kids were pretty good; way better than I was at their age. We talked strategy for each pitch and then evaluated the pitch, its location, and movement after it was thrown. I told them how they could improve their pitching mechanics. I yelled out to Ash, "Hey, man, you've got a couple of prospects here: first round picks in the 2012 draft."

"They had a good teacher," responded Ash as he stood. You could see the sweat soaking through his clothes. Wearing catcher's gear in this heat was hard work, but he didn't complain. In fact, I thought he really liked being part of their training.

Cate gave up calling the game and started heckling the players. "Well, you can certainly tell that they got all of their talent from their mother. I can throw the ball back to the pitcher better than you, Ash. That's the third one you've thrown over Rush's head."

"Will the fans and announcer kindly refrain from taunting the opposing players or I'll throw you out of the ballpark," I responded.

"You'd better get some help, slugger." Then Cate started screaming and running. I was in hot pursuit. I closed in on her, snatched her off the ground, and stalked over to the lake. I was standing knee deep in water. She was fighting me all the way. The boys were cheering. Blaze screamed, "Throw the announcer in the lake."

She yelled back, "But I gave you that last outside fastball, and it was off the plate!"

I lifted Cate as high as I could and dropped her into the lake. She came out of the water and took a step toward me. Then she stopped. "You, you Neanderthal . . ." then she started to smile. I let my guard down and relaxed. At that instant I got hit from the back and fell face first into the lake. As I climbed back to my feet, Bell was standing over me, pointing. "You pick on Cate and you have to deal with me, slugger."

"Yeah," replied Cate. "Thanks for your help, Bell. The big lunk always tries to throw his macho, big man stuff around . . ." I picked her up one more time and jumped back into the water, holding her as we went under the surface.

She came out sputtering, "See what I told you? When you aren't very smart, you have to impress everyone with . . . ," but her words were cut off as she went back under the water.

She scrambled back to her feet and threw her arms around me pleading, "Please, I've learned my lesson. I was wrong. I will never . . ." She hugged me and I relaxed, figuring the game was over. But suddenly she pushed me in the chest, and I fell backwards over Bell, who had sneaked up and kneeled behind me. I sputtered as Cate put her arm around Bell and they swaggered back to the beach. "That's not fair," I cried. "You took advantage of me."

Then she said to Bell, loud enough for everyone to hear, "Remember, men only have one thing on their mind. That's why they're so easy to distract." They strutted across the beach.

Ash, trying not to laugh, said, "Cord, haven't you learned that you can't ever win an argument with a woman?"

That's how the week had gone. Baseball, waterskiing, boating, hiking; we did it all and we did it as a family. Cate was right: I did like the Swensons. Cate was in love with them. It was obvious that the twins idolized me, and Cate couldn't shake Bell. Consequently, there was very little time when Cate and I were alone. That was good and it was bad. Unfortunately, I knew what the conversation would be if I ever got her alone.

At family prayer that night Cate shocked everyone when she asked, "Do you mind if I say prayer tonight?" She was amazing. She poured out her heart to the Lord, thanking him for leading her to people that knew him. She thanked him for the Swensons, who did not just preach a good sermon but were a living sermon. They taught her about true happiness and families. They introduced her to her God. She thanked him for me and for what I had meant in her life. She asked that Bell be blessed, the sister that she never had. It was a simple and humble prayer, and we all felt choked up with emotion by the time she finished. She looked around, her eyes glistening. "What?" she asked, but she was smiling that teasing smile.

Ash replied, "Cate, we love you."

♦ ♦ ♦

Cate talked about her newfound infatuation with the West. I could tell she was transfixed with the beauty of the lake, the canyon, and the setting sun. The two of us were sitting on the deck of the houseboat, alone for once after a day of exploring some of the fabulous arches around the lake. Cate had never seen anything like Glen Canyon, except in pictures. The West was taking on a new, beautiful wild vista that Cate had never imagined. She was intrigued by the large open spaces, the alluring magnificence of the sculptured arches and mountains. She found the wild, wild West to her liking.

She interrupted the silver silence, speaking without looking at me. "It seems like you've avoided being alone with me all week, and we've never talked. I'm sure this is as hard for you as it is for me; and, well, I just want you to know that I will never forget you and what you done for me. I love you."

I didn't say anything, and the silence was so thick it could almost be cut with a knife. I reached over and held her hand and let the silence continue to roll. I didn't want to hurt her. Cate was incredible. How could I not love this beautiful woman sitting beside me, offering me her complete love and devotion? She was lovely, inside and out. She was spectacular. Me? Well, I was just a minor league baseball player. She wasn't a minor leaguer in any category! No way—Caitlyn Belford was a big leaguer!

I knew she wanted me to respond, but I couldn't say it. Yet I knew that because I didn't, she would understand the answer I wasn't verbalizing. And I didn't want that.

"Cate, I've never known anyone like you."

♦ ♦ ♦

Cate and I had left the lake in Betsy. It was a long quiet drive to the airport in Salt Lake. She was leaving, flying home to Wilmington. I had the distinct impression she was also flying out of my life. I loved this lady. She was enchanting, fun; everyone loved Cate. Letting her go was one of the hardest things I had ever done. I knew that. Yet all I had to do was tell her I loved her and that I wanted her to be my wife; that's all and she would have stayed.

"Cord, I'm afraid."

I knew what she was talking about. I just didn't know how to solve the problem. I had made a commitment to Indy, and I needed to let Cate go. But I didn't know if Indy would even have me. I was about to try to muddle through an "I'm sorry" speech when she interrupted me before I could start.

"Don't say it. I don't want to hear some noble speech about fairness. Besides, I also saw the movie *Love Story.* I remember only too well when Alli McGraw said, 'Love is never having to say you're sorry.' Maybe if you don't say anything, it won't seem so final."

I walked her to the security gate and held her for a long, long time. I was anxious. I didn't want to let her go. I kissed her softly and held on to her fiercely. She said, "I will always love you."

I almost lost it, but regained my composure. "Cate, I'm not sure exactly what love is, but if it is to cherish, to adore, to respect, to want to be with, to thank God for creating you, then I do truly love you. I've never met a better person in my life, whom I respect as much as I do you."

"Thanks for the lift. Bye."

With that she turned and went through the security gate. I stood there watching. She never turned around. She never looked back. I had a huge lump in my throat. I wanted to run after her. I wanted the pain to stop, for me and for her. I was the cause of all this turmoil—me and my memory. I didn't intend for any of this to happen. Cate was wonderful; she deserved better. I had a huge hole in my heart. I left, not wanting to go. I left, not caring where I went. I wasn't even sure I wanted to talk to Indy. "Why do things always have to be so hard?" I screamed at myself as I drove down the road, not really caring where I was going.

♦ ♦ ♦

The score was tied 1-1 in the top of the seventh, the last inning, with one out and guys on second and third. Blaze was pitching a great game. It was the annual Halloween tournament held in St. George, Utah. I was helping coach at a weekend tournament for a twelve-year-old superleague team on which Blaze and Rush played. I called time out and walked out to the mound. I gathered the infielders, catcher, and Blaze together and said, "We're going to put this guy on to load the bases. If Blaze can throw it on the outside and keep it down, we have a good chance of turning two. We'll play the corners in so if the corners get a ground ball, it goes home to first. Same for you, Blaze. But watch for a suicide squeeze. Blaze, if the batter squares to bunt and you see the runner break, throw the ball right at the batter. He'll bail out to avoid being hit, and maybe we can get the runner coming home. Watch a decoy, like slide wide, a trick play or fake bunt and slap. Any questions?"

It looked like they all understood what I said, so I finished, "Good. Let's shut them down right now so we can get to hittin' and win this thing."

They were just twelve-year-olds, but we had gone over these things in practice. I just wanted to remind them so they would be prepared for everything. The intentional walk was issued. The next batter was swinging for the fence and pulling off the ball. He barely fouled off two good outside fastballs before hitting a one-hopper back to Blaze. He fielded it and threw home for the force, and the catcher relayed it to first for the inning-ending double play. Just like we had planned.

In the bottom of the inning Rush led off with a triple down the right field line and came home to win the game when Josh hit a clean single up the middle. We went to the championship game. Neither Rush nor Blaze could pitch, having used up their allotted innings. We lost the championship game 5-2 to a good team from Las Vegas. It was a great tournament and the twins were definitely at the top of their class. You could hear the kids on the other teams talking about the twins. They didn't want to face them. And Prestin and Ash were very proud of their kids. Me? I loved it. I loved coaching every minute of every game.

Later I sat by the pool talking to Prestin. She said, "Cord, I know that you haven't spoken to Cate since she left. I know it has been hard for both of you. But I want you to know that she got baptized last week. Ash flew back to baptize her. William, you know the guy that is dying to go out with her, wanted to baptize her, but she wouldn't agree to it. She was prepared to come back to Salt Lake if Ash hadn't been able to fly out there. Ash is really proud of her. She has come to mean a lot to us; but you know that."

"How is she?"

"Doing okay, that is if you can be okay with a broken heart. I don't know if she will ever get over you. However, you know Cate. She is something special She'll put the pieces back together even if it takes her some time. And you're not going to believe this, but both of her parents were present at her baptism."

"Prestin, I just didn't want . . . she didn't deserve . . . she is an incredible lady." Imagine! Cate had joined the Church. She was everything I could ever want and more than I would ever deserve. I wondered when and if the ache would ever go away.

"So, where do you go from here, Cord?"

"I wish I knew, Prestin. The other night I ran across this envelope of photos that Indy and I had taken."

I showed her the photos. "This one is of Indy standing in

front of the Manti Temple in a beautiful white dress. She had taken the dress with us to Manti so that I could take that one picture. She never said why she wanted that photo. And you should have seen her try to explain to the guy at the Top Stop why she was using his restroom to change into a white gown. There wasn't anywhere else to change in the whole town. It didn't take her long to wrap him around her finger."

I figured if I talked to Prestin it would help. I was feeling pretty low. I continued on with my story. "Earlier that day we had gone fishing up Manti Canyon. She's a 'go for it' girl. She put on the hip waders and walked right out in the middle of the stream. Before we went up the canyon we had gone to the park and I showed her how to cast a fly. Of course there is a difference between the park and the stream; there weren't any trees or bushes in the park. But there are trees everywhere along the stream, and Indy caught more trees than she did fish. I was constantly untangling her line from the trees. She did catch one nice little Brookie, but she wouldn't take it off the hook. She made me do it for her. She yelled so loud when she hooked the little guy that I was sure she scared the fish into hiding halfway up the canyon. That's when I took this photo of her standing in the creek.

"You could see the excitement on Indy's face, and she looked downright cute standing in the middle of the stream in waders trying to cast a fly. It wasn't long after I took this picture that she slipped on some moss and fell into the cold water. I tried not to laugh but couldn't stop. She was covered with ice cold water but got right back up and started casting again; of course, all she caught was more bushes. Never frustrated, she just kept telling me to hurry and get the fly unstuck from the tree. 'I can't catch fish with my fly in the bushes.' I finally taught her to drop the fly over the bank and let it drift with the current. She wasn't having any luck with the fly, so I tried to get her to try worms. No way that was going to happen. Besides, she said she had read *A River Runs Through It* and knew that the ultimate insult to a fisherman was to be called a bait fisher from California. Since she was from

California she wasn't going to complete the couplet.

"We finally stopped fishing, although it really turned out to just be casting practice. When she stripped off the waders, she was soaked. I told her, 'Hey, the purpose of waders is to keep the water out, not in.'

"She wasn't about to let me off the hook and said, 'Well, if you would have explained to me about the moss, I wouldn't have fallen. So it's your fault.' The fall didn't phase her. In fact she looked great in jeans and a T-shirt, even if she was wet.

"When we returned to Betsy, we retrieved our lunch and found a large rock that was flat enough for both of us to sit on. She picked up her guitar and started to play and sing. She tried to shame me into singing along with her. But that wasn't going to happen. Besides, I like to watch her sing. She sounded great to me, but then what do I know. I thought everything she did was great, even casting flies into the bushes.

"Once back in Manti, she had to get cleaned up—I mean makeup and all, so that we could take the photo. I don't know why the Manti Temple or why the photo, but I gave up trying to figure out women a long time ago. The picture had to have just the right lighting. We shot photos for over an hour until she got the one she wanted. Then we had to hang out in Manti until dark so she could see the temple all lit up. Now let me tell you, there's not a lot happening in Manti. I mean there's not even a stoplight. You can drive through Manti and not even know you were there. But she was right. The temple was spectacular at night, all lighted. As we drove away, she continued to watch the temple fade into the distance. Her last comment was, 'You can almost see the temple from Ephraim. It's beautiful. I'm going to be married in that temple.' Although I don't think she was saying it to me as much as she was saying it to herself."

I had become a little melancholy during the telling of the story and Prestin could tell. I couldn't help it, but I continued in spite of my feelings that were about to bubble to the surface. "I don't know, Prestin. I honestly believe that I was meant to be with Indy, but after everything that has happened, I don't know if she will have me. I've thought a lot about my memory and my feelings. I wonder, if I suddenly got all of my memory back, if it would change how I feel, not what I think but what I feel, about Indy or for that matter Cate."

"Cord, I can't remember being in a situation where I've felt so bad and yet so happy at the same time. I wish I had a magic wand to wave and make everything better, but I don't. But no matter what happens, know that I will be here for you."

I knew that Prestin would do anything for me. I knew she would be there for me, and just knowing that helped me. After a minute I asked, "Do you think that feelings really come from the heart and not your head? Are they a basic sense like taste, something over which you have no control? Something that just is? Or do they come from your head, your brain, your memory as a compilation of past experiences?"

"I think you're tying to force things. Give it a little time. Things will work themselves out."

"But I don't have time. First I told Indy it's over because I couldn't remember anything about her. Then I had to call time out because I could remember everything, including the fact that she was the one. Then I apparently fell in love with Cate but had to tell her I had to take it all back because I just remembered that I was in love with Indy. Both of them understood the problem, but it felt like I was playing a game of tennis with their lives."

"You know that we think the world of Indy and we love Cate." Prestin said. "As hard as this is for you and them, I know that things will work out the best for everyone. Doesn't your blessing tell you that you will marry the girl of your dreams?" She poked me in the ribs and laughed. "I guess the only problem you have is, which dream."

♦ ♦ ♦

"I really can't tell you anything, Cord."

"Why not, Shannon? Aren't you my sister?"

I was pleading. I needed some help. "Blood's thicker than water, you know. Now come on, talk."

"I know, but she's my friend. It's not fair to ask me about things that were told to me in confidence. It's like the runner's code; anything you say to your running partner is privileged. Indy only talks to me because she knows she can trust me. I can't break that trust."

There must be another way, I thought. "Okay. I can respect that. Let's see if you can help me without breaking a confidence. Do you know if she is serious with that jerk doctor?"

"You don't think that question is covered by the confidence privilege?"

"Probably. I guess I could always go ask Nurse Fielding since she likes me so much."

"Let me just say this: I don't think that Dr. Stewart is the problem."

"If he isn't the problem, that only leaves me."

"Not necessarily. There's Indy. You know that she has a problem believing that relationships last. She broke her own rules when she fell for you. Then you up and found someone else. And that's the problem. Trust, hope, faith, and belief are all tied together."

"She's got to know that it wasn't my fault. I just didn't remember."

"How do you sell that one?"

"Well, it's like an intentional walk. The manager makes you walk a batter to set up a defensive situation in your favor. A pitcher doesn't want to walk the batter because it goes against his stats. Everyone understands that the walk shouldn't be counted against him, but it is; and it's not his fault. Likewise, having retrograde amnesia wasn't my choice, and it shouldn't be held against me."

"Nice try, but you have to remember that females are creatures of emotions. Logic and reason don't always carry the day. They tend to rely on feelings and the heart."

"Oh well, is she dating anyone else?"

"Privileged information."

"What kind of a chance do I have of her meeting me in December?"

"What do you think, Cord?"

"I think she should meet me, and then we could live happily ever after."

"Let me ask you this question. What if she says, 'Okay, Cord, all is forgiven,' and then the next day you get your memory back and you decide that you are in love with Cate. What do you do then? And what does she do?"

"Just because I can remember doesn't change how I feel." But even as I said it, I knew that memory did impact feelings. I needed some help from my sister so I tried to explain.

"I mean, feelings are more than just memories, aren't they? And I really do believe that I love both of them; but with Indy it feels like I've come home. So even if I remembered everything about my relationship with Cate, I would still feel like I should be with Indy."

"It sounds to me like you've got it completely worked out. I mean, there's no doubt in your mind. It's clear as mud. Maybe we should rename you 'fear, doubt, and indecision.' "

"Indy has to understand. You need to convince her that I'm the one."

"I'm sure she does understand. But if you remember, after she fell in love with you, you forgot all about her, remembering only Cate. So much for your memory philosophy, because it wasn't too long ago that nothing would change your mind. You only cared about Cate, and you left Indy with nothing but a note. 'It's been nice knowing you.' So is she now supposed to say, 'Okay all's forgiven,' wondering if it will happen again?"

"Yeah, but things are different now."

"Well, just how different are they? Let's see. You're going to promise her that nothing will change your feelings even if you do remember your time with Cate, because now you 'know' you love Indy, because you 'feel' like you love her right now. Do I understand your theory?"

"Yeah, that's more or less what I'm trying to say."

"Sorry, I don't think that one's gonna fly. But I'm curious as to why you think things are different now."

I wasn't getting anywhere. Shannon was as hard to convince as both Cate and Indy. It was probably a conspiracy. I gave up and resorted to bottom line stuff. "Okay, Shannon, I give. Will you do me one favor? Will you tell Indy that I love her and that nothing will stop me from being at The Roof on December second?"

"If it comes up, I might. But I'm trying to stay out of the middle of your love life, because nothing that happens to you is conventional or rational, and all I can do is get in trouble."

♦ ♦ ♦

"Now tell me again why you quit going to church," Indy probed.

"Let's see . . . I guess . . . well, I guess . . . I guess I don't really have one specific reason. I think it started right after my father died. I had some problems with the bishop at the time of the funeral. Then I started missing meetings here and there. Pretty soon one thing led to another and I just stopped going. The more I stayed away, the easier it was not to go. Maybe I started feeling guilty, like I wasn't good enough to go. It wasn't long before I got really tired of do-gooders trying to get me back to church again. I resented it. And then my mother jumped on the bandwagon. I've never liked to be told what to do. At some point I began to believe that I didn't need church to worship God. I knew I was basically a good person. After that, I started resenting everyone that tried to get me to go to church, and it became a battle of the wills."

"So you quit going because you were showing them they couldn't control your life. Is that right?"

"You make it sound like it was my fault."

"No kidding."

I was sitting in the back of the chapel during sacrament meeting remembering the first conversation I had with Indy about why I didn't go to church. After that I had a standing invitation to go to church with her every Sunday. It was strange that I didn't get annoyed with her persistence like I had with my mother and the other do-gooders. She was persistent, I'll give her that, as persistent as Tom Glavine is at throwing his fastball low and away on the outside black. Most weeks I told her that I was going to go to my own ward, and I had good intentions; but then when it came time to pull the trigger, I found some reason not to go. Finally, one Sunday morning Indy just showed up and told me to go put on some nice clothes because we were going to church. I couldn't think of a reason not to go when she put it like that. After that first step, the first time, it became easier to go again. She was like that. Full steam ahead. I almost laughed out loud remembering how she, let's say, *encouraged* me to go back to church.

While sitting there a faint fragrance caught my attention, so I breathed deeply and memories suddenly flooded back. The scent was Obsession, Cate's favorite perfume. The smell briefly disoriented me, and my thoughts went adrift but in a different direction. Somehow, I was with Cate at the Pinnacle Peak Restaurant in Arizona!

For a minute I remembered sitting on the bench at the western-styled restaurant. The sensation was almost overpowering. I struggled to fill in the gaps in the memory of that day, but just as quickly as the vision came, it left, leaving only an unconnected memory of the moment.

It was frustrating to live life knowing there were parts of it hidden in the shadows. This was the second time in the last two days that I had had a memory flash jump out of the shadows. I tried to grab it each time it happened, but the connectors eluded me. Other memories were there. I could sense them, almost touch them, but they were just out of reach. Dr. Montgomery had told me that things such as smell, touch, or sight could trigger the return of my memory. He had warned me that my memory could return like a flood that I couldn't hold back or just seep back one drop at a time. It was so frustrating. Yet, I could still remember the warm feelings I had at the restaurant with Cate. They had been real. I tried to understand how those feelings for Cate could co-exist with the feelings I had for Indy.

That night I went to speak at a fireside for the youth in my ward. Bishop Swenson had asked me to speak to the kids about maintaining their values while living in the world. He wanted me to talk about my experiences while playing professional baseball. I was about halfway through my talk when I stopped in mid-sentence. In my mind I saw Cate with me in that fireside in Wilmington, Delaware. Cate was answering questions. I could see her; I could hear her. She handled the questions better than I did. She had become the center of attention, the leader, and she wasn't even a member of the Church.

My reverie was interrupted when I realized the noise I heard was Bishop Swenson clearing his throat. Apparently I had spaced out when the wave of memories hit me. But Bishop Swenson brought me back to the present even though I wanted to continue to explore those memories. I stumbled through the balance of my speech without making too much of an idiot of myself, and then I answered a lot of questions from the kids.

After finishing I sat down in a chair waiting for the meeting to close when my mind immediately reverted back to the fireside with Cate. I wondered where Cate had acquired her knowledge of the gospel and how easy it had been for her to talk about it. She blew me away. The more glimpses I had of my time with Cate, the more I understood why I loved her. I wondered if I had jumped the gun, if Indy was really the one. Every new memory brought new feelings. I was under attack. I couldn't trust my feelings or my memory. My clever theory about memory and feelings seemed to be justification or maybe even rationalization. Maybe feelings were really tied to memory, which would mean that there really wasn't such a thing as feelings of the heart.

I glanced around the room, and there, hanging above the fireplace, was a picture of Christ. I had seen that picture before. Suddenly my body was flooded with a feeling; it was more like a remembrance of . . . "I am Jesus Christ, your elder brother." I knew this had happened before. It was in Wichita. Then I remembered a Sunday School class and the same picture. It was not just a remembrance . . . it was much more. I wondered how I could have ever forgotten that feeling, that experience. It was so all encompassing.

I was still sitting in my chair while everyone else was eating cookies and drinking punch. Ash surprised me when he asked, "What happened to you? All of a sudden it was like you went into a trance."

"That's exactly what happened. I was caught up in a flashback of a fireside in Wilmington where I was supposed to be the speaker but Cate became the center of attention. It was one of those memories that I had forgotten. I didn't want to leave it. I tried to connect it to other memories because I couldn't remember how I got to the fireside or what happened after the fireside." I explained to Ash and Prestin, who had just walked over, about the memory jolts from the missing time period that had started yesterday and had increased in frequency since. Ash asked me several questions to see if my memory had returned. He questioned me about spring training: I couldn't remember. He asked questions about ping-pong games and teaching the twins: it wasn't there. Prestin reminded me of her Herculean efforts to give me some time alone with Cate because Bell wasn't about to let Cate out of her sight: It wouldn't come up on my screen. It was frustrating. I couldn't force it. The memories came when they came. However, I began to wonder if recovering those memories would be in my best interest.

I had discovered that I had some pretty deep feelings for Cate, and yet at the same time I still felt that I loved Indy. Maybe Shannon had been right. I didn't know myself as well as I thought; and if I didn't know my own feelings, how could I expect either Indy or Cate to understand?

♦ ♦ ♦

Every night I went home to be by myself. Something wasn't right with this picture. I wanted a wife. I wanted some kids—boys to teach baseball to. Maybe a girl, but just one. I wondered how Indy would be as a mother. Committed, I knew that. Her kids wouldn't be slackers. She would be right there with them every minute. She wouldn't be a part-time mother, even if she was a doctor. She seemed to be able to separate and prioritize things and put those that matter most first. All except for me: I didn't even make her list. I also knew that once you made her black list you didn't get off. I was probably on that list. In the same moment I wondered what she might be doing tonight. Was she hanging out with the dumb doctor? Was she wondering what I was thinking about? Was she lonely?

And what about Caitlyn? Was she lonely? Whatever she was doing right now, she would have people around her. She would be the center of attention. She would be entertaining them, and they would love every minute of it. I knew I liked her and wanted to be around her. Who didn't? And what about her kids? She would be like the Piped Piper. Kids would follow her everywhere she went. They would love her. She would have them eating out of her hand. She was so sophisticated, so smart; and yet everyone always felt comfortable around her. I could see her in a nice house, the decorations simple yet classy. But I didn't know if I could see her in my house. She was used to nice things, and my place wouldn't rise to the status of nice on any scale. How would she do in my house? Probably better than I do, I decided. She just seemed to improve things wherever she went; and she would make me a better person, I knew that.

The absolute commitment I had to Indy wasn't quite as absolute as it had been before the memory flashbacks started to invade my mind. Those memory sparks made Cate come to life. They made me remember why I liked her, and it was more than just like. I had some pretty deep feelings for Cate. I decided that I could probably live happily ever after with either of them. However, at that moment I was almost certain that neither of them would even want to set out on that voyage with me.

One thing I did know was that I didn't want to hurt either of them, and yet I knew that I had done exactly that to both of them. But I also knew I hadn't done it on purpose, and I assumed that they knew it even if they didn't understand. If I hadn't had the accidents and memory loss, things would be different. Wouldn't they?

I wanted to pick up the phone and talk to Indy; or to Cate?

To both? I needed to talk to someone about my memory. I decided I would try Dr. Montgomery. Maybe he could give me some information; but I needed a father to talk to. It wasn't easy not having a father. Ash? I could talk to him. Yeah, maybe sometime, maybe Thanksgiving. (Since Shannon had invited Indy for Thanksgiving, who had no real family, the Swensons had invited me to theirs.) Shannon? I used to be able to talk to her, but she was so tight with Indy that I didn't know whose side she was on. Right now I decided to try Dr. Montgomery. Of course I would have preferred Indy or Cate. They were the ones I needed to talk to. The problem was that they didn't want to talk to me.

♦ ♦ ♦

"But Dr. Montgomery, these memory sparks bring back all kinds of feelings I don't remember and feelings I didn't know I had. How can a memory change feelings of the heart? For example, I am in love with Dr. Jones with all of my heart. Totally committed! But then all of a sudden I remember . . . I am in a room with Cate and . . . well . . . I have deep feelings for Cate, but just different. How can I feel like that about two people?"

"Don't you understand, Cord? Your mind is like a chalkboard. It was full of memories of Cate and Indy. When that portion of your life with Cate was erased, all you knew was your time with Dr. Jones. The problem is that it wasn't erased, it was just misplaced. Now you have found the lost chalkboard, or at least portions of it. So when your memory returns, it doesn't just come back with a series of hard facts. It comes back with all of the feelings associated with the event such as hope, despair, or happiness."

"I think I understand; but, well, how do you explain this? Inside I have a soul, me. It is who I am. What I am. How can my soul scream at me that Dr. Jones is my soul mate; and yet, on the other hand, make me question those feelings every time I have a return of memory involving Cate? If that is the case, can I ever trust what my heart or my soul is saying?"

I paused for a minute and then continued. "But I guess the

real problem I have is, let's assume I believe that right now I am totally committed to Dr. Jones with all of my heart, with all of my feelings. What is going to happen if more of my memory comes back and I discover I am in love with Cate? Will that change how I feel about Dr. Jones?"

"Cord, the mind is very complex. Amnesia, particularly retrograde amnesia, is a mystery to us. We have no idea why you lost just a segment of your memory. It doesn't make any logical sense, but it happens. Most of the time people recover the lost memory; sometimes they don't. There are other cases where people have absolutely no short-term memory and it's tragic. They can't remember what they did ten seconds ago. We don't know why or how it happens. Can you imagine being one of those people, never knowing what you feel or felt, or what you did just minutes ago? But I digress. Let's get back to you. During the past year you have been traveling along two parallel roads. If you fully recover your memory, then we could say that the two roads merged. In that case you will have the two sets of memories that will be real and in some instances competing. For instance it is entirely possible that you might be equally in love with both women."

"That helps a lot, Doc. I'm not sure if I want my memory to come rushing back. It would be like getting caught in a hot box between first and second base."

"You're probably right, Mr. Calloway, but I don't think you get a vote. You cannot control the return of your memory. However, I suspect from the frequency of the episodes you are having that the rest of your memory is going to come rushing back to you, like waves at the beach, one right after another."

♦ ♦ ♦

The day before Thanksgiving I went to Shannon's unannounced. The weather was unusually warm for this time of year, and she was having a picnic in her backyard with her kids. Her husband would not be coming home until later that night. Needless to say, I got an invite to share the picnic if I agreed to cook the burgers.

As I sat on the blanket, I was attacked by three of the kids. I called for help, and Shannon came out and scolded all of us. She reminded the girls that this was going to be an elegant picnic as she set out some very fancy dishes and glasses. "The girls decided that we have boring meals, so they voted to have a fancy picnic."

That was all I heard . . . my mind flashed back to Frawley Stadium in Wilmington. A table on the infield. Fancy glasses and china. A beautiful woman. Dancing on the infield. Feelings of love on a special evening. Cate did it all for me. She had been waiting for me as I left the clubhouse after a night game. "Hey, slugger, do you always make your woman wait so long?" Then she had led me back to the infield and the dinner. How could I have forgotten?

"Are you going to flip the burgers, or are you going to let them burn?" Shannon had been talking to me. I had not heard her. I had been away, again. "I'm sorry, Shannon. Another chalkboard just popped up."

I walked to the front of the yard thinking. I said, "Go ahead and get started." I was trying to recapture the memory, to live it again. I wanted to tie it to something, a time. But I was unable to drag any more associated pieces of the puzzle back to the present.

Shannon knew what was going on. I had informed her of the flash backs that occurred when parts of my memory returned. They were unpredictable, always popping up at weird times and places. Triggers seemed to be the moving force. As I sat down with my burger, Shannon asked, "Was it good or bad?"

"That all depends on how you look at it. But suddenly, I was back at a special dinner Cate had arranged for me after a ball game. It was on the infield of Frawley Stadium. We danced and ate. Shannon, I really love her."

"Who? What are you talking about?"

"Cate." Then we talked for two hours. I say talked, but I really had a chance to bear my soul. Shannon listened but wouldn't tell me anything about Indy. I think she began to understand my feelings a little better. As I was about to leave, she said, "Indy is struggling with this too, Cord. Last week she went back to California to talk to her bishop and friend. She understands your problem and that it's not of your choosing. The problem is she just doesn't know if she's willing to risk it again; to step between the lines and play the game again."

♦ ♦ ♦

I had a hard time getting to sleep that night but when I did, I was gone. As the first ray of sunlight poked through my window, I jerked awake. It was there! It was all there. I could remember everything: Cate breaking up with me because of her parents; the accident on my bike; getting to know Cate; the Roof Restaurant; Donut Falls; spring training in Arizona with Cate and the Swensons; the Blue Rocks; Cate in Wilmington; Cate in Salt Lake; Cate in Wichita; Indy running up the mountain; Indy at Temple Square; sitting on a houseboat at Lake Powell with Cate; the twins' pitching lesson; the line drive. It was all there. The puzzle was complete, and no pieces seemed to be missing. I felt so in control. I knew me, all about me.

Then I remembered a dinner I had gone to with Cate and her parents. She was telling them that I wasn't going away and that they had better get used to me. I saw Indy kissing me at the hospital. I remembered Cate at the hospital in Wichita. I remembered the squirt gun fight with the Swensons and Cate and dining at Pistol Pete's Mexican restaurant with Indy and snowshoeing up to Donut Falls, not feeling the cold. I saw Nurse Fielding running me down in the hall; Cate walking away at the security gate at the airport, never looking back; Indy in a white dress in front of the Manti Temple; Cate calling me slugger; Cate showing up in Salt Lake unannounced when Indy was there. It was all back. Then I knew what Peter Gent, a noted sports reporter, had said was true: "Baseball players are the weirdest of all. I think it's the organ music." And me and my life fit that category without qualification. I had just never thought to blame it on the organ music.

I wanted to call Cate. I wanted to call Indy. But what would

I say? I loved them both, but at different times and in different ways. I idolized Cate. I was totally caught up in her aura. She was always the center of attention, and now she had even found the gospel. With Indy I felt at peace, complete, like I had finally come home. The problem was that the times and places had now become the same. Polygamy was out. Then I became convinced that I didn't want to call either of them. And the more I thought about it, the more I wasn't sure that I wanted either to know that I now knew everything, that I remembered; because I didn't know what to do or what to think about any of it.

Fifteen

Always go to other people's funerals,
otherwise they won't go to yours.
—Yogiism #15

The minute I walked into the Swensons's home on Thanksgiving, Blaze and Rush hauled me down into the ping-pong room. I almost didn't make it as the aroma of turkey, pumpkin pie, and other mouth-watering goodies drew me to the kitchen. Ash was waiting downstairs and we played doubles: Blaze and me against the bad guys. Of course we won; however, the scrapbook moment caught Ash diving wide for a shot, hitting it back miraculously on the table before crashing headlong into a lamp and making a whole lot of noise that attracted the attention of the house cop.

"Ash, if you're going to break things, I'm going to have to make you go outside to play," threatened Prestin.

We all threw in our two-cents' worth. "Yeah, Ash, quit breaking things."

We played for about an hour, changing teams and finally reverting to singles. The competition was intense. Then the girls came down and wanted to be included. That signaled the end of "win at all costs" because we now had to play for fun. They talked us into a game of cutthroat. Wouldn't you know it, Prestin won. Rush put me out when he made a bad paddle hand-off to me and I couldn't recover. At least that's my story and I'm sticking to it. As we left, Ash muttered loud enough for everyone to hear, "We'll never hear the end of this."

Then the boys went out back and played catch, pitching to imaginary big league batters. After that we got into a game of full-body contact whiffle ball. I was having so much fun that I forgot about my memory restoration and the impending disclosure. Finally, Prestin made Ash come in and help in the kitchen. I volunteered, but she told me to entertain the boys and keep them out of her hair and away from the food.

I hadn't eaten any breakfast and I was starving. When we finally heard the dinner bell, I was more than ready to eat. I sat down and reached for the garlic mashed potatoes before I noticed Ash and the rest of the family bow their heads. I quickly withdrew my hand and bowed my head. Ash offered a blessing. It was a simple but humble prayer of thanksgiving; and at one point he said, "Bless Cord that through prayer, he will be given insight and understanding into resolving the indecisions that trouble his life." The words hit me in the stomach like a fastball. He knew the struggles I was agonizing over. Two right choices!

The dinner was fantastic. I felt like I would have to roll away from the table rather than walk. I finally had to convince Prestin I couldn't eat another thing. She looked disappointed, but everyone else had finished long ago. Being the polite person that I am I said, "This meal is worth having to do the dishes." She tried to talk me out of it, telling me that Ash had to do them by himself.

"Me?" Ash inquired. We both got up and sent Prestin in to watch the football game on TV. I washed and Ash dried because he said he knew where the dishes were stored. Pretty soon everyone else vacated the kitchen. Finally I was able to ask Ash, "So how do I decide?"

"Decide what?"

"In your prayer you asked that I be given assistance in understanding the mess that I've made of my life."

"I said that?"

"Well, something like that anyway."

"I'm still lost."

"Ash, we need to talk. I'm sorry to have to dump my problems on you, but you're it since I don't have anyone else."

"Hey, that's why I'm here, Cord. You can talk to me anytime; but please, tell me it's not about women."

"Sorry, but it directly involves two of them."

"Great! Do you know that neither you nor I nor any man who has ever lived will ever figure out women for as long as we all live? And any man that tells you he understands women is lying."

"Well, my problem is not so much figuring them out as it is figuring me out."

"Well, this should be simple then; baseball, hot dogs, apple pie, and Chevrolet."

"Yeah . . . that was probably true two years ago. However, things are a little more complicated around here since my head injuries. Are you ready for this?"

"Fire away."

"I haven't told anyone yet except for Dr. Montgomery, but over the last week my memory has been returning bit by bit. Then this morning it was all back. I woke up staring at a completed puzzle."

"That's great, Cord. I'm sure that you're happy about finally getting your memory back."

"What makes you think that makes me happy?"

"Well, I assume that's what you wanted the whole time."

"Yeah . . . but you've heard that the worst thing the Lord could do for us would be to answer all of our prayers, right? Now I understand why. I guess you can say that I've created some pretty serious problems; inadvertently and without malice I might add. But solving those problems may be harder than slip-sliding along in the bliss I knew as retrograde amnesia."

"Are you saying that it was better living in the shadows? Wondering?"

"If you would have asked me that question yesterday, I would say, 'No, I want to know, I want to remember.' Now that I remember, I'm not so sure it was such a hot idea. While I lived in LaLa Land, I believed that I was in love with one person. However, you and I both know that the 'one person' was really two, but only one at a time. So now I've got to unscramble the mess and figure out a new batting order. So far I think I've really messed it up.

"I now remember how this all happened. It seems the retrograde amnesia affected a different part of my memory each time around.

"I know this sounds like a soap opera, but I've always been a one-girl guy. It turns out that it ain't true; and maybe I've been two timin' two lovely ladies, neither of which wants me in her life right now. However, it wasn't willful or intentional. But as it stands now, I may have blown my chances with both of them."

I thought about what I really wanted to say for several moments. "Ash, now that I look back, I've always known deep down in my heart that Indy was the one. I'm not sure if I can tell you how I know, I just do. It would be like attempting to describe the taste of chocolate or how your feel when you throw a perfect fastball low and away on the outside black and the batter hits into a double play just like you planned. It's like . . . well trying to describe how you know that Christ exists or that the gospel is true. All I can say is that she is my other half.

"However, even saying that and believing it to be true, I know that there was a time that I was in love with Cate. Right now Indy won't let me see her or even talk to her; and I think I broke Cate's heart when I took her to the airport. I didn't want it to end like that; and to tell you the truth I'm not sure that I ever wanted to end it with her. But then I didn't want to lead her on either. I don't know if I've done the right thing or if I've ruined everything. What I would like to do is to talk to both of them and explain, but I'm chicken and I don't want to make things worse. However, somehow I think it would be best for all of us to have some closure, don't you?"

"Are you ready to do that, Cord?"

"I think I've already done it. I just haven't closed the deal." I told him about my *Affair to Remember* deal with Indy but that I didn't have any idea if she would show.

"On the other hand, I more or less told Cate that it was over. The problem is that I left it hanging. I'm not sure that I can talk to her again; it's just too hard for both of us. Cate is the best and I do truly love her. I just can't talk to her, not right now. I don't know what to do."

"Maybe I can help, Cord. I can talk to Cate. I'll explain it to her. She was devastated but she is putting her life back together again. She understands what happened and doesn't blame you. But still, that hasn't made it any easier. She has even had some answers to her prayers; and although she doesn't know how she can ever fix her heart, she knows that God loves her and he will help her get through this hard time."

Cate was that kind of person, the kind that everyone loves. I knew she would be okay, but I still felt bad for her and for me. I loved her and it hurt. Leaving her at the airport was one of the most difficult things I have ever done. I still wasn't sure that I had done the right thing.

"Ash, do you think that I'm making a mistake?"

Ash reached in his pocket and pulled out a coin and said, "Heads it's Indy and tails it's Cate. Call it while it's in the air. No two out of three's either."

"Are you serious?"

"If you have a better solution, why don't you tell me about it."

Maybe he was right.

I'm not quite sure how to describe it, but I found myself loving two fantastic women, probably neither of which I deserved. I guess I felt both innocent and guilty—at the same time. Maybe the only solution would be to walk away from the two I loved most in the world. That would be the noble thing to do; but I wasn't feeling noble.

Ash interrupted my thoughts. "Cord, flipping a coin would be the easiest way, but I don't believe that it's the answer." He put the coin back in his pocket. "Have you tried prayer?"

"Bishop," I responded with a laugh. "Me and prayer; well, they just don't mix. I've tried prayer, but I don't think my words get past the ceiling. If I didn't do anything until I got an answer to my prayers, I would die an old man and still be single, still waiting for an answer."

Ash replied, "If you want me to choose, you can forget it. I don't want either of them to come lookin' for me. No, Cord, this one's up to you. However, I don't think you have to make this decision in a vacuum. The Lord will help you, just like he let you know that he existed."

"Great. I just explained to you about me and prayer. I'm not asking for you to choose for me, but which one would you choose, Cate or Indy?"

"Nice try, Cord."

"I thought you were going to be like my father or best friend and help me make decisions."

"I am. I'm trying to teach you how to make an important decision. However, if I make it for you, then you won't learn anything about decision making and you will always be able to blame me."

I decided to try another approach. "Okay, Bishop, tell me how I know I've found the 'one,' my chosen soul mate. And don't tell me that I can be happy with many different women because I don't believe that for a second. I can't believe that I lived forever before I came here and didn't find one woman that I wanted to share the rest of eternity with. I don't believe that God wouldn't give me a chance to meet that 'one' person. It wouldn't be fair. I believe that I am what I am in part because of that person, because of the time we spent together in the pre-existence. Marriage is important because it's forever. To suggest that marriage is left to chance, that I can marry a number of people, just doesn't make any sense, not if there really was such a thing as the pre-existence."

"I guess I believe, at least in theory, that there is such a thing as soul mates, but I also believe in agency. Therein lies the rub, because what you're asking is for the Lord to tell you that you've found your soul mate. If he did, wouldn't it be violating the principle of agency? On the other hand, is it fair not to let you be able to know that this is the 'one'? Maybe the Lord just puts you in a time and place position for you to be able figure it out for yourself. Maybe agency puts the ball back in your court, Cord. You still have to make the decision."

"Great, but how do you know you've made the right decision? I think that was my original question."

"You said you believe Indy is your other half, and besides you've already committed to Indy and essentially terminated your relationship with Cate. So what's the problem? What's wrong? Are you questioning your decision? Are you asking me if you made the right choice?"

I hated it when someone answered my question with another question. I felt he was making me call the next pitch. I knew how to do that; I'd done that to a thousand batters: evaluate their strengths and weaknesses. Indy would be a great mother, but then so would Cate. Indy would make me a better person, as would Cate. They were both nice, and I remembered my father telling me to make sure that the person I married was nice. My dream of becoming a high school baseball coach hardly measured up to the accomplishments of either Cate or Indy; but I thought both would support my decision. When I thought about Cate, I wanted to be around her: everyone did. When I thought about Indy, I saw determination, absolute commitment to God, to life. She would never accept anything less. When I heard the name Indy, it seemed so right. I loved Cate, and yet I loved Indy on a different level. I had this gut feeling; it was a pain and didn't help at all.

"Cord, if you earnestly pray, then you have to trust your feelings. Once you've accepted that choice, I can promise you that life will go on, for all of you. Oh, I don't mean that someone won't be hurt or even devastated, but eventually each of you will find happiness, because that is God's purpose. I don't remember who said this, but maybe it can be your measuring gauge: 'With true love, you give everything and want nothing, because you have everything.' "

"The problem is that I'm not sure Indy agrees that I am her chosen one, and I don't know what I can do to convince her."

"Maybe, but you might have a lot of fun trying to convince her."

♦ ♦ ♦

I hadn't talked to Indy, but I was getting anxious. I needed to talk to her, and I wasn't really excited to wait until December. Besides, she might not even show up. And yes, I had tried praying; and as I predicted, nothing happened except I kept getting the distinct impression, 'You already know.' I always answered myself, 'If I know, how come I'm so confused?' And no, I hadn't seen a vision. I still hadn't told anyone but Ash about the return of my memory because I knew when I made that announcement, I would no longer have any excuses.

I tore the calendar page off of the pad and threw it away. Another day gone. It was the twenty-sixth of November—a whole year since the accident—and I hadn't done anything because I didn't know what to do. I realized that I wasn't such a hot commodity. Maybe Indy had moved on. I hoped it wasn't with that beaked-nose jerk Johnny Boy. I didn't know what else to do, so I got down and prayed again.

As I got up from my knees, I had one very distinct impression. I was hungry! I decided to go to the store to get something to eat. I hadn't eaten all day. No, I wasn't fasting. I had already tried that. I just didn't have any food in the house, and I was too lazy to go to the store. I looked at the clock; it was after four o'clock. It was time to get something to eat.

When I got home from the store, I was surprised to see a note taped to the door: a note that looked hurriedly scribbled. It was folded in half and on the outside said, "Cord." I recognized the writing immediately. My stomach started doing flip-flops. Why did I have to go to the store at the wrong time? She had been here and I was gone. So much for fasting and praying. The only answer I got was to go to the store, just when she came. I knew that prayer never worked for me. All I got was the ceiling and now a note.

I hurried into the kitchen and dropped half of my groceries on the way. I held the paper up. It didn't have a lot of words, and I couldn't read them through the folded paper. Maybe she had made the decision for me, like hit the road.

So much for the idea that I ever had any control over anything, that is except which pitch to throw with no balls and two strikes.

I debated on whether I should open the note or throw it away. That was easy: I couldn't throw it away. But I didn't know if I wanted to open it. I put my ice cream in the freezer; I didn't want it to melt, and this decision might take awhile. Maybe I was just afraid. It was the same feeling I had when my school grades arrived and I was worried about being eligible to play baseball the next year.

"What the heck," I said out loud as I tore it open. I read it quickly and then went back and tried to digest it.

I came by. I wanted to talk to you, but you weren't here. I'll be at Temple Square until seven tonight if you want to talk.

I didn't think twice about my answer, but I knew that I had to shower and shave. I hadn't done that yet that day. It took me about a half hour to get out of my house. Before heading out, I tried calling Indy a few times to let her know I was on my way, but there was no answer. Maybe she'd left her phone at home. "Don't fail me now, Betsy," I said as I turned the key over. Nothing. There was nothing. I decided that the battery must be dead.

"I'll never forgive you, Betsy. First thing tomorrow you're going to the junkyard. I won't even try to sell you to some poor slob. I'll let them mangle you and recycle you, and it won't bother me in the least. This is the most important day of my life and now you pull this trick on me." I was about to get out and find someone to give me a jump, but I tried one more time and the engine roared to life.

"I take it all back. You are the best," I said as I pointed Betsy to Temple Square.

It was a warm evening for November; no snow on the ground. I found a parking space two blocks away and started running. It was just after six o'clock, and I didn't want to miss her—she still hadn't answered her phone. It was dark as I entered from the south entrance and raced by the log cabin and then the Assembly Hall. There were people walking all over. The Christmas lights were spectacular, but I didn't care. I tried to catch a glimpse of every female's face that I passed. The Tabernacle was open and I hurried inside. Two people sat in the rear; but as I approached, I knew neither was the one I was looking for. I ran outside; it was six thirty. Maybe I should pray; there wasn't a ceiling here. *Pray on the run*, I thought. Where could she be? *Inside*, I decided. She wouldn't be outside for two hours on this cold evening.

The Christus! I ran around to the north door of the Tabernacle. I looked up as I ran. Someone was sitting alone on a bench by the statue. I sprinted to the building. People were looking at me like I was weird. Once inside, I tried to calm myself. I had to try to breathe normally. It was hard since I hadn't run that much since spring training. I took off my coat; I was sweating. I walked up the spiraling ramp to the statue.

As I got close, I could tell it was her. I wanted to run up to her and put my arms around her and live happily ever after, but I decided against that approach. *Grovel*, I thought.

She appeared to be deep in thought. I passed in front of her twice and she didn't even notice me. Finally, I walked over and knelt on the floor right in front of her.

"Indy."

Her eyes came into focus, and she looked like a deer caught in a car's headlights. She was ready to bolt. I didn't say anything; I didn't want her to run. I didn't know if she wanted to try again or if she was ready to tell me it was over and that she had discovered that Johnny Boy was Mr. Right. "Indy," I said again very softly.

She smiled, "No one says my name like you. I've waited a long time to hear you say my name again."

Beg, I thought. *But be careful, she could still run*. There was so much I wanted to tell her; I just didn't know where to start. I looked up into her eyes. "It came back. Everything."

She looked puzzled, "What?"

"My memory. I can remember everything, and the most vivid thing I can remember is a beautiful doctor bending over to kiss me just after I regained consciousness."

"That's all you ever think about," she said. But she was smiling. I wanted to get up and hold her, but I was afraid to do anything.

I knew there was one thing she couldn't refuse. "It's five days early, but I'm really hungry. How about we go get something to eat?"

"I'd like that," she said. "I'm starved."

And they say food is the way to a man's heart. In this case I believe you can add Indiana Jones to that list—and not the one with the whip.

I got up. I reached for her hand and we started walking. She didn't pull it back; that was another good sign. I wasn't sure I was hungry anymore, but I knew she would be. Neither of us said anything. There was too much to say, and I didn't know where to start.

We were seated in The Roof restaurant in the same seat we had sat in before. I had to let go of her hand, but I didn't want to. I wanted to sit close to her, not across the table. I marveled at her beauty. Her cheeks were rosy, her hair so blonde, her smile so radiant. I really couldn't think about food. Finally she said, "I'm hungry. Can we go get something to eat from the buffet or are you going to just sit there with your mouth open, drooling?"

"I'm not drooling." And I motioned for her to go first.

"I'll follow but I don't want dessert first."

With that she got up and went straight to the desserts.

I should have known. I went to get some real food. When I got back, she had three kinds of dessert lined up. "I knew you were one of a kind, because no one eats desserts first but you," I said.

"I run. Or can't you remember going up to Dog Lake?" I could remember. I could remember her passing me like I was standing still.

I still didn't know if I was here to be beheaded or forgiven. I was voting on the side of forgiven, but I wasn't sure. *Grovel,* I thought. *Don't give her a chance to drop the ax.*

"Indy, I've wanted to call you. I've wanted to come to the hospital to see you, but I'm afraid of Nurse Fielding."

She laughed. "She is a little over-protective."

"I'm so sorry for all that I've put you through. I've tried to blame it on the accident, my loss of memory, but there really isn't an excuse. It's really all my fault. Maybe we can try again, I mean . . ."

"Cord, we're eating. Let's enjoy the meal. We can talk later."

Good! At least she was thinking there was going to be a later, although my stomach was tied in three knots and I wasn't sure anything I ate was going to stay down for long. We finished the meal. Small conversation was acceptable. I often caught her staring toward the temple and the lights with a faraway look in her eyes. She wasn't staring at me, although she would glance at me from time to time but look away as soon as I made eye contact. I hoped that she was dreaming of the two of us and not trying to decide how to break the bad news to me.

After she had her fill of desserts, she went to get some prime rib and scalloped potatoes. She could eat more than I could. By the time we had finished eating, it had been snowing for about a half hour. It was one of those warm evenings when the huge snowflakes gently fall but quickly melt when they hit the ground. "Do you mind if we go back over and walk around Temple Square again?"

I wouldn't let her pay this time; besides, I was rich. As we walked out the door, she reached for my hand. That was definitely a good sign. I probably wasn't going to get the ax. I knew if I fed her, she wouldn't be quite so hostile.

I didn't want to let her say whatever she had to say before I could plead my case so I jumped right in. "Indy, I've missed you. I just want to be with you. I love you—"

"Slow down. I only have a few questions. That's why I came to see you before our arranged D-Day. Do you really remember everything?"

"Yes, everything. The puzzle is finished."

"Okay, that's good. In that case please tell me how you feel about Cate."

"What if I tell you how I feel about you?" I asked.

"Oh, we'll get to that part if we get past the first question. Now tell me about Cate. And I want the truth, the whole truth, and nothing but the truth."

I took a deep breath, trying to decide what to say. I decided not to think about it but just let it roll. "Cate is fantastic. She seems to be able to cast a spell on people. I was caught in that spell, Indy. I . . . well . . . I fell in love with her. She changed her whole life. She joined the Church. She left her family. She is wonderful. I don't know a person who doesn't love Cate."

Indy wasn't looking at me. I could tell I wasn't doing very well. She said, "So does that mean that you want to marry her?"

"No, Indy. You didn't listen. I'm in love with *you*."

She still wasn't looking at me. "So let me understand what I think you've just told me. You're in love with Cate and you're in love with me. I think I have a problem with that."

"No, I didn't mean it like that." I scrambled to recover. "What I meant was that I love Cate—but I'm in love with you. Everyone loves Cate. But, Indy, I've always felt that in my heart you are the one. I want to be with you forever."

"Do your really think it's possible to love me and yet love Cate?"

"Look, I'm not sure if I understand it either."

"Does that mean that I'm number one today, but tomorrow I could be number two? But for today you chose me?"

I blew out my breath. I was making a mess of this. It was so simple and yet it was complicated. "Indy, I'm just a dumb baseball player. Ask me what pitch I threw to Tom Taver in the third game of the season during his second at bat last year, and I can tell you not only what pitch I threw but why. I'm trying to answer your question, but the problem is it isn't about baseball."

"What's so difficult? I asked you about Cate and you told me you love her but you want to be with me. Forgive me but I'm having a little trouble processing that statement. Do you want to try again?"

"Indy, I have always loved you. I just forgot for awhile. I mean not intentionally, not literally; you know, I had the head injury. Then I got my memory back. When I got my memory back, I realized what a mess I had made of everything. It was like I was two people, and neither told the other what was going on. So I had to take charge and sort it out. Indy, you are the one: the one I was meant to be with. I just forgot for awhile. You don't have to worry about me waking up one morning and remembering I am in love with someone else. All of that has been resolved."

"How can I be so lucky?" she said. "That's just what I want—to be with someone who is in love with someone else."

Things weren't going as I had planned, but then I really never had a plan anyway. So I scraped the philosophical approach and went for the physical approach. I pulled her toward me and kissed her. I didn't ever want to end that embrace. She was my split-apart, my mirror image. She was as much a part of me as I. I couldn't explain it to her, but I hoped she would try to understand. We broke the kiss but still held each other. I mean . . . I think she held me too. That meant there was still hope. I also think she kissed me too, although I wasn't exactly sure.

The snow continued falling; the flakes were gigantic. They drifted slowly downward, turning colors as they reflected the multicolored lights of Temple Square. I reached up and brushed some of the flakes off her hair. She smiled and said, "Would you like to come by my place for awhile?"

She had never invited me into her home before. This was

definitely a good sign. "I would love to."

I walked her to her car and said, "Would you mind driving me over to Betsy? She's been acting up a little lately, and this is one invitation I don't intend to miss." We got to Betsy, and she started on the first turn of the key. It was a sign. All was well in the universe—well, except for Cate.

Indy was waiting on the porch for me and invited me in. She sat in a chair and motioned for me to sit on the couch directly in front of her. I said, "Don't you think you would be more comfortable on the couch next to me?"

"Probably, but right now I want to talk; and if I sit over there we won't get any talking done."

More good signs. "That's okay with me," I said.

She smiled and leaned back in the chair, but her eyes never left mine. "Tell me one more time because I'm not sure if I understand your relationship with Cate."

The up-front approach was not working. I decided to water it down a little and maybe it would come out better. "Okay, Cate . . . " I did it again.

She was smiling this time; but nonetheless, she took her best shot. "No, Cord. We've been there before. I'm sorry you get confused with names, but I'm Indy, the blonde one. That's how you can tell the difference."

I started to apologize, but she cut me off. "No need for excuses, Cord. I understand completely how you can be confused since you claim to love both of us."

"Indy, I have always loved you, but I loved Cate in a different way."

"And you explained all of this to Cate?"

Dang! She doesn't give me an inch. Another sucker punch. "Well, sort of."

"Sort of? What does that mean?"

"Well, I more or less told her when I took her to the airport in September and I haven't talked to her since."

"You were hedging your bet, weren't you? You were not going to do anything until you knew what I decided. Right?"

"No, Indy, that's not true. I really don't know what to say to her. I talked to Ash about it and he promised he would call Cate and try to explain it to her. I never intended this mess to happen. I've always been a one-woman man."

It felt like I was on the hot seat and I wanted off.

"How much did you love her, Cord?" she said softly and with a lot of emotion.

I wasn't going to let her lead me down that path. It wouldn't help anything. "Not as much as you," I said.

"Did you kiss her?"

"Let me see . . . I don't . . . wait there may have been . . ." I stood up and walked over to Indy and pulled her onto her feet and into my arms. It was time to end the talkin'.

I dreamily said, "You know I was never a believer, at least not until now."

Indy was completely taken off guard. "What?"

I knew she wasn't following my train of thought so I had to explain. "They say a pitcher's first strikeout is like a first kiss—you never forget it. Now I believe; even though that wasn't our first kiss, it sure seemed like it."

An hour later I walked to the door, holding her hand. She had not asked one more question. That was a good thing. "I'll be by to get you after work tomorrow evening from the hospital, but you have to promise to call off Nurse Fielding. Send her to the south wing or the south pole for that matter."

Indy laughed. "She's not that bad."

"Have you ever been run over by a steamroller?"

"Is that why your nose is so flat?" she said smiling.

I kissed her one more time and started to open the door. "Don't you think you should call Cate? Don't you think you owe it to her?" she asked. "Like tomorrow?"

I groaned, caught myself, and said, "First thing."

"Good, because you can tell me how it went when you pick me up."

♦ ♦ ♦

"Cate, it's Cord." There was no response on the other end. "Cate?"

Cate finally responded, "Is this a necessary call, Cord?"

"Cate, my memory has returned; all of it. I . . ."

She interrupted me. "Cord, I'm not sure I want to hear what you have to say. I probably already know. But I've been waiting for this call. I have a few things I would like to say to you."

I got ready to be blasted.

"You opened my eyes to a whole new world. I got to know God. I found his Church. I discovered real families and learned that they can be forever. I've made new friends for life. I have an adopted little sister. I learned what pitch to throw a batter to get a double play. I wouldn't trade one minute of the life you introduced me to. I know what I want in a husband. I want someone to take me to the temple. No matter what happens from this point on in my life, it is going to be better than it ever was before, and I will never accept less. So thanks, Cord, for everything."

"Cate . . ." I didn't know what to say. I had a huge lump in my throat and it was hard to breathe.

She replied, "I've heard it told that the saddest words of all to a pitcher are three: 'take him out.' Now I understand why."

The phone went silent; she was having a hard time speaking. Then with a muffled voice choked with emotion she said very softly, "I hope you've found what you're looking for. I can't talk anymore. Thanks again. Bye."

She was gone. She had broken the connection, or had I?

I was overcome with emotion, heartsick. My head hurt. Cate was such a wonderful person. What had I done? She didn't deserve the cards I had just dealt her. It didn't seem right that I could be so happy with Indy at the expense of Cate. I wanted to fix it, but I couldn't. I didn't know if I had ever experienced such despair, felt such responsibility for another.

She was forever Cate, nice. She thanked me. She just thanked me. She could have told me that I was a jerk. But no, she just thanked me. Maybe I had hoped she would yell at me, be mad. But no, she was gracious to the end. She was pure class. And me?

I felt a huge loss, a black hole in my life, an emptiness.

I went running. I wanted it to hurt. I tried to rationalize. I tried to justify. It didn't help. I knew I had done the right thing, but it didn't make me feel any better. It was all my fault, and yet it was not me suffering. I didn't have to pay the price. Finally, I decided I was wallowing in a pit of self-pity. I ran until I couldn't run any more. It hurt, but it didn't help. Eventually I ended up back home.

I called Ash and told him what happened and how I felt, and how gracious Cate had been.

"How did you finally decide, Cord?"

"I'm not sure, Ash. I prayed. I fasted. I thought about it. I flipped coins, two out of three, three out of five. I drew straws. I couldn't make any headway. I prayed again, and nothing happened except I had this feeling. I was prompted to go to the store and while I was gone, Indy came by. So much for praying," I said. "She left me a note; and Ash, after I read the note, I knew I had made the right decision."

"Do you think you got an answer to your prayers?"

"Maybe." I knew it was, but I was not going to give him the satisfaction. "But Cate . . . I feel so bad."

"Cate will be okay."

"I know that, Ash. But I hurt for her. She was an important part of my life."

"Maybe someday you can be friends, Cord."

"It just doesn't seem fair that I can be happy and that she . . . she doesn't deserve the pain."

"Cord, I'll talk to her. She won't be alone."

"Thanks, Ash, for all you've done for me." I was rambling. Things just came out in no order. "I . . . I have a date with Indy tonight."

"Let it go, Cord. Everything will work out. Indy is good for you. But remember, Cord, Indy has feelings that are as intense as yours. If you only focus on your own feelings, you will be making a big mistake. It's time that all three of you got on with your lives."

♦ ♦ ♦

It was about six o'clock in the evening when I walked through the doors of the emergency room to find Indy. I was walking a little lighter. My feet didn't seem cast in concrete. I was, however, vigilant. I didn't want to walk into Nurse Fielding. I was nervously fingering the ring in my pocket. It wasn't much of a ring. I mean, it wasn't showy. It was simple, but to me it couldn't be replaced.

Alli waved at me as I approached. "You never called," she said.

"I lost the number. Besides, I'm kind of spoken for, I hope."

"That's too bad. We could have had a lot of fun."

"Umm, do you know where I can find Doc Jones?"

"Sure, check down in A101. Call me if things don't work out," she said.

As I walked down the hall, I saw Dr. John Stewart talking to someone. He gave me a look that was well, let's just say, less than friendly, but you know what? It made me feel warm, really good. I wanted to slap him on the back and say, "Nice try, Johnny Boy!" but I refrained and gave him a big smile. I looked around again for Nurse Fielding.

As I rounded the corner, I almost bumped into the battle-ax as she came out of a room. I said, "I'm sorry, I was looking for Dr. Jones."

She indicated with her thumb to look next door. She didn't say anything, but I still didn't like the look she gave me. Maybe Indy had asked her to stand down. I don't know.

Then I heard her voice, "Oh, Cord. I'm just about done. Why don't you go sit down in the waiting room. I'll be right out."

"Is there somewhere besides the waiting room?" I asked. I didn't want to have to sit and talk to Alli again. "But somewhere I won't be accosted by Nurse Fielding?"

"Sure. My office." At my hesitant glance in the wrong direction, she said, "It's the last door on the left, down the hall. I'll meet you there."

I walked into her world. It'd been so long, I barely remembered the place. It was clean, with diplomas and a few photos scattered around. On her desk I noticed a picture of the Manti Temple. That gave me an idea, and I dropped the ring back into my pocket.

♦ ♦ ♦

Indy did not have to work the next day. I had told her I would pick her up at nine in the morning, to wear some jeans and a casual shirt, and be sure she brought her ski jacket.

She looked radiant when I picked her up. "By the way, do you always look this good in the morning?" I asked.

She smiled, "No, sometimes I try. Today I was just going with you so it was just the basics. You know, nothing fancy."

"Do you mind if we use your car? I don't think Betsy will be up to the task. Besides, she's still jealous."

"Sure, if you tell me where we're going."

"I can't do that. It will ruin the surprise. It's a secret."

She didn't ask again until we were just entering Nephi, about ninety minutes into our little excursion. "Cord, we can't go into the temple without a recommend."

"Did I say anything about going to the temple? Patience is an important virtue, and good things happen to those who wait," I said trying to sound serious.

Half an hour later we were leaving Ephraim. It was just a minute or two later that we came around a bend in the road. There sat the Manti Temple like a sentinel on the hill. It stood out not only because it is the biggest structure around, but also because it's on top of a small hill. It was magnificent. Legend has it that the very spot on which the temple is located was dedicated by the prophet Moroni during his wanderings as a place for a temple to be built in the latter days.

Indy couldn't hold still, she was so excited. I expected she knew what today was all about, but she was willing to let it play itself out. Still, she was anxious. I pulled up in front of the temple and stopped. I turned the engine off and turned to face her. Then

I kissed her gently and asked, "Are you hungry?"

"Umm . . . hungry? Umm, what do you mean?" She was surprised by the question.

"Like food. Do you want to eat? I've never seen you pass up food."

"Yeah, I guess so. Did we come all the way down here just to eat?"

"I fixed us a picnic, and I know a very private place that has a spectacular view of the temple."

"It's a little cold for a picnic, isn't it? I mean, there is some snow on the ground."

"I didn't know you were so fussy about climatic conditions when there was food in the balance. I thought all you cared about was if there was enough to eat."

"Well, within limits, I guess that's true."

"Trust me," I said.

"Whenever anyone uses those words, I know right away to hide my wallet."

"Yeah, but I'm different." I started the car and drove to a little hill about a mile from the temple. The road, better described as a two track, was dirt and seldom used. I think Indy thought I was going to ruin her car, but she didn't say anything. The hill was very private and had a beautiful view of the temple grounds. I stopped and turned off the engine, leaving the music playing. It was a local country western station. I reached into the back seat and lifted the picnic basket into the front seat between us. Indy looked at me and rolled her eyes. "Humor me," I said.

I handed her the turkey and I took the roast beef sandwich. I had a can of pop for each of us. "Before we eat, would you say a blessing?" I asked. She bowed her head and said a short but humble prayer. I started to eat. She was still very suspicious or maybe thought I had lost my marbles. I had parked so she could see the temple while we ate. I kept the conversation rolling, continuing to talk about mundane things. I had Twinkies for dessert. I flipped her a Twinkie. She opened it and out fell a rolled up sheet of parchment. She picked it up and read:

My dream, the focus of my life, has always been
pitching in the major leagues,
standing in front of fifty thousand screaming fans,
all watching and waiting
for me to hurl the ball to their best hitter
with two outs in the bottom of the ninth,
then I would walk off the field, looking at those bewildered
fans as I registered a strikeout to win the game.
Then I found you, Indiana Jones,
not the guy with the whip but the kissing doctor.
Suddenly, holding your hand, watching you smile, listening
to you laugh mattered more to me
than pitching a baseball game in the big leagues.
I can't believe it, but it's true.

I wasn't sure if she understood my attempt to explain how I felt about her. I'll bet she felt like I do when the manager comes to the mound, gathers the infielders around, and says, "First and third, watch the leave early, or delay; we'll use bunt three, hold your position for a fake bunt steal; throw it down and away unless he squares to bunt then keep the ball up; could be a straight steal, the guy on first can run; corners in, middle double play depth; comebacker, short will cover the bag; oh, and throw from the stretch."

She continued to read,

If you are still interested and are curious,
then get the shovel out of the trunk and find
the buried treasure marked with an X.
The directions are on the reverse side.
I hope you brought your GPS.

She looked up at me, wiped the back of her hand across her eyes, and said, "So you really are a romantic at heart after all. And all of this time I just thought you were a chauvinist." She got out of the car and opened the trunk and started following the map. I exited the car, grabbed my shoulder briefcase and camera, and started following.

"Which direction is north?" she asked.

"So female," I said as in disbelief. "Turn left just past the yellow fire hydrant." Then I pointed north. She gave me one of those, that-was-real-cute looks, and she started counting off the steps.

Finally she came to a large pine that sheltered the ground from the snow. On the ground was a fire-engine red X. She started digging. It didn't take long before she struck something hard. She dug carefully and finally pulled out a steel box about twelve inches square and five inches deep. Taped to the back of the map was a key that opened the box. I continued to take photos of Indy as she worked to open the box.

Inside the box was an envelope addressed to Indy. She carefully opened the envelope and read the note:

I've had this ring since November of 2004.
You are my true love, the other half of me.
You are as much of me as I am.
Without you I could never be whole.
The smaller envelope is yours if you so choose.

She was crying, and I had to wipe my cheek at the same time. She pulled out the smaller envelope and opened it, removing the ring. Then she really started crying. She looked me in the eyes and held my gaze. I had a huge lump in my throat and couldn't say anything. Finally she looked down at the ring and slipped it on her finger. Then she got up, walked over, put her arms around me, and held me. She was shaking and crying. I hoped she was happy. You can never tell about women. Then she kissed me and I decided she was happy.

"I take it that's a yes?" She didn't say anything but kissed me again. *Oh well, so much for oral commitments,* I thought. Besides, I always liked action instead of talkin'.

I was finally able to get control of the situation, or at least I thought I had, when I said, "Okay, here is what we are going to do." She looked at me like I was losing it again.

"Trust me," I said. She laughed.

I handed her a sheet of parchment and a permanent pen. "Both of us are going to write one paragraph on each of three subjects that I have listed here. We will then put the pages in the box and re-bury the box. On our twentieth anniversary we will return with our kids and open the box."

"You surprise me every day, Cord. I didn't realize you were so sentimental. You really are a romantic. Does this mean that you really liked all of those chick flicks you have been bad mouthing?"

"Just don't tell anyone or I will deny it."

"Oh, I'm going to tell a whole lot of people about you, Mr. Calloway."

We leaned against the tree trunk and spent the next half hour filling out our sheets as well as taking time out to embrace each other and even kiss a little. She wanted to read what I had written. I told her she could, in twenty years. We placed them back in the box and I dug a hole deeper than the original and we buried our treasure. I set the camera up and took portraits of the two of us with the Manti Temple in the background.

It was a leisurely drive back to the city of salt. I don't remember a day that Indy had ever sat so close to me. Usually she was plastered to the outside door, but not today.

After several moments of silence I said, deadly serious, "Indy, you've got to promise me one thing."

"I'm all ears."

"When we die, you have to promise me we'll be buried sixty feet six inches apart."

"You're kidding, right?"

"Nope. That way I'll always know where home is."

Sixteen

We were overwhelming underdogs.
—Yogiism #16

It was close to six in the evening when we pulled up in front of Shannon's house on our way home from Manti. I told Indy it was okay to tell Shannon, but not in front of everyone. I knew Indy would end up telling her all of the gruesome details; and after all, I did have an image to maintain. "How about you just calling Shannon when you get home?" I had suggested. We were stopping; so much for my suggestions.

She was bursting at the seams to tell someone, anyone, and Shannon was the closest person. Before we got out of the car, Indy issued me strict instructions. "Now when we go in, I don't want you to say a word. I'll handle everything, okay? Do you understand?"

I looked at her sheepishly. "I thought that the priesthood held the powers of administration and the head of the household."

"You do when it comes to all major decisions."

"And what do you consider a major decision?" I asked.

"I'm not sure. I can't think of one right now, but I'll let you know when one arises."

"Okay, okay. This is one of those chick things, right?"

"That hurts. You think I would intentionally try to embarrass you?" She laughed again. "Besides, everyone in this house knows you're a big pushover."

I decided to let her think she was in charge. We walked up to the door and Indy knocked; but I opened the door and yelled, "Is everyone presentable?"

Shannon replied, "All but James, but it would take us a month to get him presentable."

The whole family was sitting around watching TV. Shannon was looking for an excuse to get away from the ball game and jumped at the chance. "And just what have you two been up to?" She looked at me and I glanced away.

"Cord? What's up?"

I sheepishly responded, "You'll have to ask Indy. I've been told to let her do the talking."

I knew I looked guilty. Shannon gave me that okay-but-you're-not-off-the-hook-yet look and turned to Indy. Indy was beaming, and she had a sly smile that said, "Go ahead and ask me, because I'm dying to tell you."

Shannon reached out both hands to Indy. Indy held her hands out to Shannon. Shannon let her gaze travel down to Indy's left hand. She excitedly exclaimed, "I knew it!" She grabbed Indy in a hug and said, "It's about time I got a sister. Now come in here and tell me every detail and don't leave anything out. Cord, go away; we have to talk. You can go watch the game. We won't need you for awhile."

"What's all the commotion?" James asked.

I replied, "I think it's one of those girl things." I sat on the couch to watch the game and asked matter-of-factly, "Who's winning, how many outs, and what's the inning?" You have to know those details in order to play the game, or watch it in this case.

One of the kids replied, "Cord, it's December. They don't play baseball in December. Besides, it's a football game. Can't you tell?"

It took at least thirty minutes before the girls came out of the kitchen. Shannon and Indy were both smiling and both had slightly red eyes. James glanced up and saw his wife and then looked back at the game. "What's the problem? Did someone die?" he asked without looking back at his wife.

Shannon looked at Indy and smiled, "I didn't think of it that way, but who can say."

James was trying to divide his attention between the ball game and his wife and wasn't doing either very well. "What do you mean? Either someone died or he didn't."

"Do you know the difference, Gube?"

James was totally perplexed. Finally I tried to help him. "They are trying to be funny. It's no big deal. Shannon's just trying to tell you that I'm—I mean, *we're*—getting married."

"Who's getting married?" asked James.

"Me!" I responded.

"To whom?" he replied teasingly.

Shannon waved her hands "See what I mean? Don't bother trying to talk to him while he's watching a ball game. I think he goes brain dead."

Indy laughed. I got up and Shannon came over and gave me a hug. "Well, you finally got something right, little brother."

James interrupted, "Shannon, there's a ball game going on."

I said to James, "No big deal. Shannon can explain it to you when the game's over. We've got to run. See you guys later."

♦ ♦ ♦

"So what did you tell Shannon?" I asked when we were in the car. I prepared for the worst.

"The whole truth and nothing but the truth," Indy responded. She had that look on her face like the cat that ate the mouse. But she was still beautiful. The light seemed to radiate from her. She was as happy as I had ever seen her. I was glad for her, but I didn't like all the attention she was bringing our way.

"No exaggerations?" I asked.

"Of course not. Why would I exaggerate?"

"Do we still have to stop at the Swensons's?"

"Of course. You need to set up a time for your interview for your recommend. Besides, I've got to tell my friends. I've been waiting a long time for this. At times I thought it would never happen, and now I want to show off my ring and tell everyone what a romantic you really are, Cord Calloway."

I just groaned. "I guess I can't talk you into minimizing the details, can I?"

"Not on your life. I want everyone to know the real Cord Calloway."

"Don't tell the twins, okay?"

It was nine when we got to the Swensons's. Blaze answered the door. He loudly announced, "Hey, Rush, Cord's here. Let's play ping-pong. Go get Dad."

Prestin came down the stairs and welcomed us warmly. "So are you two just hanging out?"

Blaze was dragging me into the game room when I heard Prestin scream. I was in trouble. Ash walked in from his office and asked, "What was that all about?"

"I think it's one of those female things," I answered.

We played ping-pong for about forty-five minutes before the girls walked in. Prestin ran over to me and gave me a hug. "Congratulations, Cord."

Ash looked puzzled. "Congratulations?"

Prestin knew I hadn't said anything to anyone in this room and wanted to make me pay. "I guess Cord didn't tell you guys."

"Tell us what?" everyone asked.

I tried to save a little face. "I was going to tell them, but you know. We got involved in a couple of heated games, and I just forgot . . . I mean I lost track of time."

"It seems like everyone knows something except me," replied Ash.

"What about us?" asked Rush and Blaze in unison.

Indy folded her arms across her chest and said, "Well, that's good, because I'm anxious to hear what Mr. Calloway has to say."

Prestin chimed in, "This could be good."

Great! Just what I needed: the spotlight and everyone staring at me. Then I couldn't help but ask, "Did you bring the microphone?"

Indy replied, "No, but we can all hear if you talk really loud."

I put both of my hands in my pockets and said, "Bishop, I guess I need to talk to you about getting a recommend."

Prestin laughed out loud. "That's the best you can do, Cord?"

Ash looked at me, and I sheepishly avoided his eyes. I stammered and kicked at the floor while everyone watched. Prestin and Indy were particularly enjoying my discomfort. "Well, I asked Indy if she would like to change her last name to Calloway."

The girls laughed. Ash had figured it out but was not about to let me off the hook either. He playfully asked, "Well, the suspense is killing me. What did she say?"

"She said yes, but it took a lot of talkin' to get her to agree."

"It did not," replied Indy.

Then Prestin decided to stick the knife in a little deeper. "Cord, aren't you going to tell Ash how you asked her?"

"Naah. You can probably do a better job than I can, but wait until after we leave."

Finally Blaze said, "Will you guys get this mush stuff over so we can finish our game of ping-pong?"

Indy walked over to Ash and held out her hand to show him the ring. He drew her into a hug and said, "I don't know whether to congratulate you or pray for you."

It was my turn. "Come on, Ash, we men have to stick together. Don't you remember? It's the boys against the girls."

He replied, "Yeah, you're right. Prestin, you can tell me later. Let's finish our game."

Prestin was enjoying the exchange but wanted to have the last word. "Come on, Indy, we'll leave these Neanderthals to their game. Let's go talk about shopping for a really nice, expensive wedding dress and some bridesmaid dresses."

Blaze looked at me and asked, "Did you ask her to marry you?"

"Yeah, and she said yes."

"Does that mean you can't teach us pitching anymore?"

I replied, "Naah, we can use her as our catcher."

Before we left, Ash said to both of us, "Now as your bishop I want to give you two some advice. I want you to follow this rule from now until the time you get married. There are three rules and you can violate any two of the rules at any time but never all three at the same time. Do you understand?"

I asked, "Aren't we a little old for this discussion?"

"Age is not the determining factor here. So here are the simple rules: one, a long time; two, stationary; and, three alone. For instance you can be alone and stationary but not for a long time, or you can be stationary for a long time but not alone. Do you understand?"

Then I asked, "Are these rules for Indy's benefit?"

Indy slugged me in the arm and said, "Cord."

As we were leaving, Prestin said, "Cord, you surprise me. I didn't know you were such a romantic. I know the social editor at *The Tribune*. I was just thinking this would be a great story."

"Thanks," I said. She just laughed.

"Just kidding. You know I would never do anything like that."

♦ ♦ ♦

I didn't stay long at Indy's house that night because she had to work the early shift in the morning. She was exhausted, but she didn't want me to leave. She said, "I probably won't get any sleep tonight anyway."

"That's okay. I don't want someone to die on you in the morning because I kept you up all night."

I turned to leave but was stopped dead in my tracks when she said, "You thought you were going to get away with it, didn't you?"

"Get away with what?" I asked. I didn't have a clue what she was talking about.

"You haven't told me about your conversation with Cate."

"Umm . . . well . . . it's a long story. I'll tell you tomorrow."

"Good, because I'm dying to hear all the details."

♦ ♦ ♦

I was worried about Betsy starting. I had talked to her all the way over to Indy's. I assured her that I wasn't dumping her, just adding a new partner, and that there was nothing to get jealous about. She must have bought into the story since she started on the first crank.

"That's my girl," I said as I patted her on the dashboard.

Early the next morning I got a call from Fred, a friend I had pitched with in A ball. He had been coaching at a local high school. But he was moving, which meant that he had to give up his coaching position. Since high school baseball started the last week of February, he said it was going to be hard for the school to find someone qualified to coach. If I wanted the job, it was mine. He said he had already talked to the principal.

"Fred, you know I've always dreamed of coaching high school baseball, but I don't know if my career is over or if I still have a chance to make it to The Show. I haven't received my contract for next year; but if I don't, then my decision will be made for me."

"That's a problem, Cord. Because of the short time fuse, they have to hire someone and have him in place before the first of the year. That means they have to know within the next two weeks."

"Okay, let me see what I can do on my end. I can do some calling and try to find out the Royals's intentions . . . it all depends . . . wait! I didn't tell you, Fred, I just got engaged last night. I guess I should discuss this with the future Mrs. Calloway."

"Congratulations, Cord, we should get together. I would like to meet the lady. How did you talk her into marrying a professional ballplayer who doesn't have any money and leaves home for six months of the year?"

"You know, Fred: charm. Women have been clamoring for

my attention for as long as I can remember."

"Yeah, I know, you're a real charmer, Cord."

"Tell your principal that I'm interested but that I have to talk to the Royals and my future wife."

"Will do, but remember he is going to interview a bunch of people just in case you don't take the job. He can't wait long."

"Thanks, Fred. I owe you one."

This was exactly the job I had always wanted; and to make it even better, it was the school that the twins would be attending in two or three years. It was perfect. But then I wondered if I was ready to quit playing, not ever knowing if I could have made it to the majors. On the other hand, minor league baseball wouldn't pay the bills, nor would it train me for a productive job in society. If I didn't have a chance to make it to the "Bigs," it was time to hang 'em up. However, I had posted some really good numbers last year in AA. They take a lot of pitchers from AA right into the majors. I just didn't know. However, all of this worrying might be for nothing since I still hadn't seen a contract and it was getting late in the year.

I wanted to call Indy. I needed to talk to her, but I needed to figure out myself what I wanted to do. Maybe, I thought, this is one of those major decisions that the priesthood holder got to decide. If I played baseball this year, Indy would have to stay here in Salt Lake. She couldn't just walk away from her job, especially since I never knew how long I would be in any one town. I wasn't sure I wanted to get married and leave the next day for points unknown. I wondered if I still had a chance to make it to the big league. Maybe I should put off the wedding until after baseball, but that didn't sound like a great idea. I could ask Bishop Swenson, but he would just tell me to pray. Maybe I could ask Indy to pray for me since I never got any answers.

I had dreamed since I was a kid of pitching for a major league team. I played baseball because I loved the game. That's why I wanted to teach kids. I wanted them to learn about this great game. There is nothing like standing out there on the mound when everyone on your team, everyone on the other team, and all of the fans, are watching every move you make. Of course, with the good comes the bad. I mean I've had coaches walk out and take me out of the game because I just gave up four runs. Then I didn't feel too great. In spite of all of the pressure on pitchers, there is nothing in the world that compares to standing out there on the bump and throwing to a batter who is trying to knock it out of the park. It's war. It's the best.

But I was going to be a married man. Did I have to dream new dreams? Should I turn in my old cleats for new ones? Was I giving up something good for something better? Or would I always wonder, *what if?* Obviously, I was nowhere close to knowing what I wanted to do when I went to pick Indy up from the hospital that evening.

As I walked into the emergency room, Alli motioned for me to come over. "I heard you got engaged. Congratulations, I guess. But remember, if it doesn't work out, I'm still waiting for your call."

"Thanks, but how did you hear?"

"Are you kidding? Everyone in the hospital knows. Dr. Jones is one of the favorites around here. Everyone is excited for her except for Dr. Stewart."

I asked, "What's his problem?"

"He's been trying to get her to marry him for two years."

"Poor guy. I really feel sorry for him. By the way, do you happen to know if Nurse Fielding is working tonight?"

"She sure is. Why do you ask?"

"She hasn't liked me since day one."

"Most of the people around here feel very protective of Dr. Jones; but Fielding, she's in a whole other category. She thinks she's Dr. Jones's mother, and she doesn't like people she doesn't think are right for Dr. Jones. She's like an old mother she-bear."

"I know that. So I need to avoid her. Where can I find Dr. Jones?"

"I believe she's in the employees' lounge waiting for you."

As I walked down the hall, I saw Nurse Fielding heading my way. I ducked into the men's room before she saw me. I needed to have a talk with Indy about that lady. As I stepped into the men's room, I ran smack into good ol' Johnny Boy. "Excuse me," I said trying to step out of his way.

He looked at me like I looked at batters who are stepping into the batter's box. "What are you doing here?" I wanted to ask. "You don't have a chance against me. You should go take a seat on the bench before you embarrass yourself." He didn't say anything, just stepped around me and walked out the door. I thought, *He's a sore loser, but then he never had a chance anyway.*

I exited the men's room, and there was Nurse Fielding waiting for me. I wasn't sure I was ready for her. She walked over to me and poked her finger in my chest each time she said something, as if she wanted to emphasize her point. "Mr. Calloway, I see you finally talked Doc Jones into marryin' you. She's a sweetheart. I only want the best for her, and maybe you can make her happy because she deserves it. As long as you do that, me and you will be okay. Do you understand? Now give me a hug." With that she put her arms around me and gave me what I imagined was as close as to a real bear hug as one could get.

Then without another word she turned and walked down the hall. I think she made her point. I needed to talk to Indy about old Mother Hubbard. I walked into the lounge where Indy was sitting with four other women. She looked me up and down with that sly smile and said, teasingly, "Cord, what are you doing here?"

"Well, Nurse Fielding just told me I had to be nice to you or she was gonna come lookin' for me. So I decided I'd better take you out to dinner."

The other women all laughed, and one said, "Congratulations, Cord. I hope you know you're getting the real deal when you get Doc Jones. We are really happy for you guys." Indy then introduced me to them as Johnny Boy walked in. Indy said politely, "Cord, you remember Dr. Stewart, don't you?"

I responded, "Umm . . . I believe so. Didn't you say he was dating Nurse Fielding?"

Everyone laughed, everyone except for ol' Johnny Boy. Indy said, "He's teasing, John." But John either didn't get the joke or just didn't like me. I didn't know which and I really didn't care. Indy got up and gave me a hug and I kissed her.

Someone asked as we were leaving the room, "So, when's the date?"

Indy replied, "We haven't decided, but you know, neither of us is getting any younger."

"Tomorrow," I said. "We're going to elope." I noticed that good ol' Johnny Boy wasn't smiling. *Strike three,* I thought, *you're outta there. You shouldn't have stepped into the batter's box in the first place.*

She punched me in the arm and said, "Cord Calloway, are you ever serious?"

We drove to Olive Garden for dinner and had just ordered our food. I was anxious to talk to Indy about baseball, coaching and/or playing. I wanted to make some decisions and I wanted to set a date; and tomorrow wouldn't be too early if I had anything to do with it.

Cord, are you sure that you've resolved the whole thing with Cate—I mean in your head and your heart? I don't want to hear you say two years down the road, 'Man, did I make the wrong choice!' "

"Indy, I have always loved you. I've loved you since the first time you ran past me up the trail to Dog Lake. 'Course the only look I got was from the back, but it looked pretty good."

"Cord."

"Well, it did. But then I got to know you, and I discovered you were actually better on the inside."

"Cord."

I was laughing, teasing, but I meant it. Then I said, "Looking back—that's a pun of course." But then I got serious. "This amnesia, this whole memory thing has made me take a new look at who I am."

"Is this another way of trying to tell me about you and baseball and our life together?"

"Actually, I do need to talk to you about that; but, no, to answer your question.

"Now listen," I continued, "because I think this is kind of original. I believe that we are now a mixture of what we have done and the things we have dared to think. Without a memory of those thoughts and actions, we exist only in the present. I lost my memory of you, of being with you, of thinking about you. It was as if it, us, never happened. That's weird to think about because I always thought love was a feeling that you have in your heart and not your head. It's like I thought if I loved you, I believed I would have known deep down that I was in love with you even though I couldn't remember that fact."

"So, what's your point?"

"Now that I'm looking back, I realize that I did have some of those feelings all along, I just didn't realize what they were. For example, when I saw the picture of you by the Manti Temple, something registered in my mind, but I couldn't identify it. Even when I fell in love with Cate, there was something deep inside that kept tugging at my heart. I just never realized what it was until I got my memory back. Then I knew it was you."

"I feel bad for Cate."

"I do too, Indy. I really do."

"Do you need to talk to her, Cord?"

"There's nothing I can say right now. Maybe later, but not right now."

"Well, maybe I need to consider putting a bike helmet on you twenty-four/seven so you don't get hit on the head and forget me again."

We had finished our salads when I finally had the opportunity to explain to Indy about Fred's call and playing baseball versus coaching. I explained to her about the short time fuse I had if I wanted to accept the coaching job. Then I said, "If I do go play again, I will have to leave in about two months. Do we have time to get married before I go, or should we wait until I get back? I guess I'm asking how you feel about my going away for six months?"

"It's not going to take me two months to get ready to be married. I guess I hadn't really thought about you leaving for baseball and being gone for six months. I don't like that idea. I guess I could come out and see you every other week, but that's not going to be really fun. Still, I want you to make the decision of when you hang up your cleats. I'm not going to let you have a chance to blame me for the rest of your life for quitting baseball. I can live with it. Can you?"

I wondered why everyone kept hitting the ball back in my court. All I wanted was a little help. "Look, Indy, I don't know. I want to play. I think I still have a chance to make it, but I've always wanted to coach. I don't want to leave the game never knowing whether I could have made it. But maybe my dreams need to change.

"Have you tried praying, Cord?"

"Somehow I knew you were going to ask that question." I tried to explain to her about me and prayers and then said, "Since I don't have a lot of luck with getting answers, maybe you could pray for me."

"I don't think it works that way."

"Well, how about you pray about us and whether I stay and coach or go and play?"

"How about we table this discussion for tonight. I've only been engaged one day and I want to enjoy it. We can make those decisions tomorrow. Let's just enjoy ourselves tonight."

"Now you're talkin'," I said. "Maybe we can find the kissin' doctor again."

With that she put her arms around my neck and kissed me for what seemed like forever.

♦ ♦ ♦

I called the minor league pitching coordinator for the Royals the next day. I told him that I hadn't received my new contract, and I wanted to know if they intended to send one. He hemmed and hawed and said he wasn't sure but added that they may bring me to spring training to see if I could make a team. I told him if I didn't have a contract that I was going to accept a coaching position at home and that I had to make a decision within a week. He promised to get back to me. It was only six days until Christmas, and it would be hard to find anyone in the organization that would make a decision prior to their administrative meeting the week after Christmas.

I had talked to Ash about the coaching versus playing opportunities, and although he offered advice, he would not tell me what I should do. The twins were torn. They wanted me to coach their high school team, but they wanted me to try to make the big leagues. I echoed their feelings. I guess by the new year the decision would need to be made one way or the other—I just wondered what it would be.

♦ ♦ ♦

I love this game, everything about it from the red dirt and the freshly cut grass to the burly umpire behind the plate and watching the batter dig into the batter's box. I stood on the mound looking at all of the screaming fans. This was where I wanted to be. I knew that! Indy was watching, she would always be there, and I knew that. I wasn't through with baseball, and I knew that for sure. I also knew that no matter where I am, as long as I'm standing on the pitching rubber I'm only sixty feet six inches from home.

Epilogue

I don't want to play golf.
When I hit a ball I want someone else to go chase it.
—Rogers Hornsby

THE HOOPING AND HOLLERING OF the fans and student body had not yet subsided. The Draper Ducks had just won their second round playoff game in the 5A State Tournament, and Blaze Swenson had pitched a complete game, winning 5-3. His brother, Rush, had singled up the middle to drive in the two go-ahead runs in the third inning. Rush and Blaze were freshmen and had led the Ducks to their first state tournament in five years. Prestin had heckled the home plate umpire from the first pitch and had almost been tossed out of the world. Ash refused to sit by her. Besides, he couldn't sit; he had to pace. He loved to know that one of the twins would be the starting pitcher, and from that second on he couldn't wait until it was over. He had to pace.

A *Tribune* sports reporter spoke to me after the game. "I think we have a first here: two brothers, freshmen pitchers, winning the first two games of the state tournament. These two kids look pretty good. They were throwing like seasoned veterans, not freshmen. Do you think you have a shot at winning the tournament with these two kids on the mound?"

"Blaze and Rush are pretty talented pitchers, but they are just two players on our team. I'm sure if you asked them, they would tell you they won because of defense. We're young, but 'we,' the team, are going to give it a run. As long as our pitchers throw strikes, we should be in every game."

I looked down the left field line and saw Indy. She was trying to hold back our two-year-old twin boys. They wanted to get on the field. After every game they ran to home plate, took an imaginary swing at a ball, and then they started running around the bases. It was a race. It took them a long time to get around the bases; their legs weren't very long. Their Draper Duck baseball hats tipped crookedly as they ran. When they finally got back to home plate, they would attempt to slide in the red dirt, coming up colored brick red; and then they'd jump up and raise both hands above their heads in triumph. Then they would do it all over again. I waved at her, "Let 'em go."

With that they were off. She walked up and stood by me as I finished the interview. I put my arm around her. Just then Prestin came running up and grabbed me in a bear hug. "Thanks, Cord. They never could have done it without you."

I had taken this coaching job three years ago, and I had never regretted it for one second. I worked the kids hard and they learned the game; and now, all of the hard work was paying off. But as for Blaze and Rush, I can't express how I felt every time one of them stepped onto the mound. In some small way I knew I had helped them become the pitchers they were. But that was only half of the story because they had also grown up to be outstanding young men.

Sometimes I still wonder if I could have made it to the big leagues, but there's something to be said for working, teaching, and watching kids turn into men. I wouldn't trade those feelings for anything. I put my other arm around Indy and she kissed me. She whispered in my ear, "Well, Coach, what are you going to do for an encore?"

Just then the twins slid into home, laughing together after their race around the bases. A photographer snapped a picture as they got up covered in dirt.

I thought it just didn't get any better than this.

Indy and I had married in the Manti Temple three years before on January tenth. Ash had acted as my escort during the sealing session and Shannon had been Indy's. I realized I was lucky to be in the house of the Lord with Indiana Jones Calloway. Many things had happened to turn my life around, including some lady sprinting past me on the way up to Dog Lake. Some of those events I didn't recognize as being significant until I looked back. Then I saw some of the doors that were closed to me even as others were being opened. Maybe some of those prayers had actually made it past the ceiling and I just hadn't recognized the answers even though they had hit me with the force of a two-by-four. I know I'm a little slow.

I now recognized those people who kept dragging me back on the path. Shannon was always around, never pushy, but a constant beacon of light. It was Indy who finally got me to take that first step back. She wasn't as gentle, but I probably needed someone to explain it to me. Then there were Ash, Prestin, and the twins. They were always an example of everything that was good, and Prestin even taught me how to push the umpires to the very brink of getting tossed out of the game. I wanted what the Swensons had. It just took me awhile to figure it out.

Inside the temple walls I had looked into Prestin's and Ash's eyes, and I couldn't believe the joy that filled them because of me, because I was in the Lord's house. They were experiencing the promise of the Lord, "And if it so be that you labor all your days . . . and bring, save it be one soul unto me, how great shall be your joy."

And sitting there, I thought of Cate. I had felt that same joy as she discovered the gospel. Cate . . . I thought of Cate. I prayed that she would find someone to fill the void in her life as Indy had filled mine.

Of course my mother was there. She had worn out three sets

of ears explaining how she knew I would eventually come back to the Church. "However," she added, "if it hadn't been for Indy, he may not have made it." Of course, she only knew half of the story, but she could have heard the rest if she had listened rather than talked. I looked at Shannon as she watched Mom ramble on. We laughed quietly. Everyone wondered what was so funny.

After a short honeymoon in Hawaii, we had returned to Salt Lake, where I accepted the head baseball coaching job as well as teaching English at the new high school. One year later Indy gave birth to twin boys. I thought it was another sign; only seven more to go and we could have our own baseball team. Of course, they would all have to be boys. They had been a handful, but I loved every minute. We took them to the baseball field every day once they started walking. They were our team mascots, and they loved all of the attention they got from the players, who believed that they brought us good luck. Each player would have one of them touch his bat before every game, for good luck.

Indy still worked part-time and made more income in two work days than I made in a whole month. We had used my personal injury money and her savings to build a new home in the Draper area and moved in about the time the twins were born.

The Royals had sent me a contract for their triple A team just before I was married. But somewhere along the way, I discovered that my dreams had changed.

Indy knew what I was going to do long before I did, but she let me figure it out for myself. She said that this was one of those major decisions. After I had finally decided, she gave me a poster to hang in my office showing a Little League player with the sun to his back standing ready to pitch a baseball. His shadow was displayed prominently on the wall but not as a Little Leaguer, but as the man of his dreams as a big leaguer. My dream was to make each of my kids, as well as all of my players, into "the man." I now have poster-sized picture in my coach's office hanging next to that poster. Indy also gave me it to me. It is a picture of me trying to catch balls thrown at me by each of the twins at the same time. Each is trying to wind up like a pitcher. The caption on the top of the poster reads, "My Boys Forever," and below it was a quote from Mary Leary:

> *Baseball is where boys practice being boys,*
> *And men practice being boys,*
> *And they get real good at it.*

DENNIS L. MANGRUM GREW UP in Salt Lake City. He attended West High School in the days when if you didn't beat them during the game, you did after. His English teachers considered him a jock who dabbled in academics. He attended the University of Utah on a football and wrestling scholarship and continued to dabble in academia, graduating with a master's degree in civil engineering. He later attended law school at the University of Utah and then practiced law in California for twenty years before returning to Utah.

While practicing law in Utah, he was also the pitching coach at Brighton High School. He coached his son Micah, who pitched for BYU and went on to pitch professionally for seven years. He also coached his son Shane, who went on to play for Harvard. His youngest son is now playing for Brighton, with his dad coaching from behind the fence.

Dennis and his wife live in Sandy, Utah. A baseball junkie and a die hard Red Sox fan, the bumper sticker on his car reads, "I Don't Brake for Yankee Fans."

0 26575 70657 4